CROWN OF PREY

CALIXTO WAYNE

DARNOLDO PUBLISHING LLC

To my best friend, for always having my back.

CONTENTS

CHAPTER ONE

F otlin detested ceremony. Preening and fawning over those who had yet to accomplish anything. Why should his brother, Matlin, have a parade to send him off to war? He had not fought a battle or even killed a single foe. It was his eldest brother's own bungling of the battle of Fort Hope that led to the war. And for that failure he was pampered with ceremony and entrusted with leading Loach's forces into another war.

And what did Fotlin get to lead? The City Watch. The joys of being the third son. Matlin was entrusted with the armies, while Setlin administered the duchy's mines. When Matlin succeeded, the family and duchy bathed itself in glory. When Setlin succeeded, riches cascaded upon the duchy.

When Fotlin succeeded? Nothing. Just a bunch of ungrateful louts asking him what he wanted. Praise? You did your job, Fotlin. That should be good enough. Now go catch some more pick pockets and imprison a few more drunks.

He heard the snickers and the whispered names. Lord of the Lockup, Warden of the Streets. He heard and he remembered. Soon he would prove himself. War always granted opportunity to the cunning.

First, he needed to deal with matters in the city, before he found himself displaced from his own meager titles. Even the commoners recognized the opportunity provided by war. As a result, crime was rampant throughout the city. Thefts ranged from everyday goods such as clothes, food, and weaponry, to items used in making luxurious goods. Jewelry and rare books were burgled from the rich and the temples. Many of the Eldritch Society's artifices and devices were pilfered. And the duchy's mines had experienced an increase in stolen gemstones and diamonds.

The last at least was not his fault. The mines were technically located outside the city of Loach, even though the shafts connected at certain points within the city. Their security was the purview of the duchy and not the City Watch, therefore making those thefts fall under Setlin's responsibility.

And so Fotlin navigated a narrow edge. Appease the merchants, the temples, and the societies, and the local support for him would grow. Powerful friends coupled with his family name would lead to titles. And the instant Matlin faltered, Fotlin would fill the void. His brother could not avoid the assassins forever. Eventually one would find the mark.

Until that day came, he would bide his time. Clean up the muck from the streets. Hangings would need to increase. Fear of the law would keep the populace in line. He would have order while the war raged.

Hangings may not have the pomp of a parade and ceremony, but they certainly drew a crowd, and made a lasting impression. Fotlin smiled as he entered the city jail. He would seize the opportunity and forge his own name out of the chaos. Nothing, not even his older brothers, would prevent him from achieving that goal.

Chapter Two

R andall found shopping day beyond tedious. Food and clothing were all fine things to have, but where was the thrill? Where was the excitement? Where was the profit?

Basic survival was a dull monotonous task. It made him feel like a rat scurrying around, picking out little bits and pieces here and there. It was so much simpler to swipe a loaf of bread or a pair of gloves. Incredibly easy.

But one did not live for fourteen years on the streets of the city of Loach by doing things the easy way. Randall was not like most of the other urchins while growing up. He observed before rushing through the markets. It was amazing what one could learn by biding their time and simply using their eyes.

The boys and girls who stole from the merchants were all caught eventually. The merchants were in the markets every day. They recognized the regular faces, and were wary to protect their business interests. Merchants called the guards when their own wealth was threatened. But swipe the purse off of a passerby who was not patronizing their store or stand? Well that quite simply was not their problem.

Randall scratched out a living as a child by keeping a low profile, and being circumspect around merchants. Since then, he moved beyond simple pick pocketing. Snatching purses was only lucrative in large numbers, and that was certain to attract the wrong sort of attention. Thieving was much more difficult when the city watch was actively searching for you.

It was why Randall graduated to burglary. The city watch was not posted inside homes, stores, temples, and the like. A thief need only worry about being caught, or spotted by the denizens of those locations. And a good thief knew how to be silent and avoid detection.

Randall purchased four loaves of bread, a wheel of cheese, and a wrapped package containing an assortment of dried fruits and meats. He gently slipped the parcels into his burlap sack and continued his shopping. By his count, he needed a few bottles of wine and mead to fill out their food needs. Some of the little ones also needed new gloves and boots.

Well, new to them. Frostbite did not discriminate against urchins. Even in the early days of spring, toes and fingers could easily be lost.

The Thieves Association was unlike other societies and guilds from what Randall observed. Instead of being selected and trained in the craft of thievery, one merely participated in the activity. Thieves routinely poached territory, but when threatened by outsiders they banded together.

Randall had yet to deduce how to advance within the Association. That would come with age. Instead, he looked after himself and numerous of the other young thieves in the Northeast Markets. He taught them what he knew, and tried to provide for them as best he could. The young urchins chipped in of course, but they lacked the knack for picking the correct pockets. He discovered that he needed to subsidize their survival if they were to abide by his no thieving from merchants in the market policy.

It was a worthy investment. Already some of the other young teenagers were beginning to grasp the knack of petty burglary. If more learned, he would not have to depend on the Association for further advancement. They would be able to sustain themselves. If they were cautious.

The war made things more difficult. Every two-bit thief saw it as an opportunity to make some quick gold. There were a string of burglaries recently, causing the watchmen to be more vigilant than usual. He had to admit that some of the burglaries were rather impressive. Breaking into the temple of Vatoil and stealing old books and the ceremonial dagger? That took real skill. The Vatoilians were not exactly the warmest bunch. That was to be expected of the followers of the god of winter.

Shouting from across the market drew Randall's attention. The watchmen were pursuing a young girl of maybe eight years of age, her dark hair cut short and ragged. A red-faced merchant screamed in rage while shrieking for the watchmen to catch the girl.

Randall sighed in resignation as he watched the pursuit. It was too late for the girl. The merchants in this area already knew her face. They were sure to remember it now. She was reckless, and if she survived this long, she had most likely stolen from more than one merchant's stall.

The chase was short-lived. Watchmen were positioned all around the market. They closed their net in on the girl and tackled her. Randall winced as a crunching sound split through the normal market noise. The girl howled in pain, sobbing as the watchmen dragged her off to jail.

The little urchin's sobs faded into the distance, and a sense of normalcy quickly returned to the market. Randall made eye contact with Tigun, and shook his head ever so slightly at the thirteen year old boy. Tigun would pass the word and see to it that the pickpockets abandoned the market for the morning.

Randall went about his shopping, keeping an alert eye out as he walked. Security increased in the past few days, ever since Prince Matlin departed the city to lead the army. Randall could have easily sent some of the younger urchins out to purchase their supplies, but then they would have missed out on so much information. By walking the streets, he could hide in plain sight and observe the watchmen.

He made mental notes of where they were stationed, what streets they patrolled, and the numbers and weaponry at each location. The difficulty was not in counting or observing, but deducing which watchmen were actual threats. Who had good hearing? Who was smart? Who could run fast? Who was lazy? All important questions that could result in life or death.

The main change that Randall noticed was the new posts for the watchmen. They were now located outside of the temples, society buildings, and merchant consortiums. That would certainly make things more difficult. Assuming one was inclined to enter those buildings through the front door. He would be concerned when they started posting watchmen along the rooftops.

Randall ducked through the streets passing through the normal human bustle of the city. He walked past a red caped bravo, unshaven mercenaries, teamsters on their wagons, wives going about their household shopping, merchants in their thick wool cloaks, and tired miners staggering home from their shifts. Randall easily blended into their ranks and let himself be swept up in their current.

He was cautious in returning home. Each day he made certain to take different routes so that his face did not become familiar to any watchmen or merchants. Just another face in the crowd, that was his goal. Never part of someone else's routine.

The wind remained brisk and cold, making his circuitous route miserable. It was all that he could do to resist sprinting back to the hideout and the sweet warmth of home. But if he did not respect his own rules, the other children certainly would not follow them.

Randall made his way into the warehouse district near the northeastern gates. Blending into a crowd was not an option in these parts of town. However, the merchants did not bother to keep the area well lit. The alleys were cloaked in shadows even during the day. Randall clung to them as he scuttled about.

Home was an old gemstone warehouse. Small, compact, and most importantly, abandoned for years after the owner went out of business when one of the ruby mines was finally exhausted. The warehouse was the smallest on the block, and was offset from the main road, with its only access point being a dark alley.

Due to the warehouse's small height, it was easy to scale and reach the roof. From there it was a simple matter to mantle over to the rooftops of other warehouses. Once he was on the rooftops, he was in his element, and the thieving game began.

Randall climbed up the wall and slipped in through one of the warehouse's upper windows. The warehouse was not of an open design, like the warehouses designed to hold iron and other cargo. Rubies were small, and easy to lose. The owner had installed walls into what was now Randall's home. The rubies were stored in those rooms behind lock and key, presumably to make it more difficult for the workers to steal the cargo. The locks had not proven difficult for a den of thieves. Now those rooms served as bedrooms for his crew.

He slipped through the warehouse floor and into his bedroom upon the back wall. He stored his burlap sack beneath his hammock. Every street urchin that called the warehouse home had a hammock. Randall had spun the silk threads himself, and woven them together to form the hammocks. It was not much, but at least he could keep everyone off of the cold floor.

Randall had tried to fashion clothing from his silk webs, but the results were less than pleasant. The clothing had to be woven too thick and bulky to actually provide protection from the cold. It was sticky, itchy, restricted the wearer's movement, and drew unwanted gazes from the city crowds. Instead, he limited his weaving to more mundane items that provided utility to their little group. Hammocks, blankets, ropes, and the like.

His silk items were meant to be supplements for their counterparts found throughout the city. A silk blanket worked, but he preferred a nice warm woolen blanket. And woolen blankets they had aplenty. Stacks of blankets and cloaks lined the corners of the main warehouse floor. Most of the money they stole was spent on such basic necessities. Building a fire during the winter would be easier and more cost efficient, but they lacked a hearth, and lighting a fire in the middle of a warehouse seemed a poor idea.

Tigun was waiting for him on the main warehouse floor. The boy was sitting on a wooden crate, his feet dangling idly above the ground. The sandy blonde haired boy breathed a sigh of relief. "I was worried the Watch got you, man. What took so long?" he asked.

Randall scrambled onto a crate opposite Tigun and stretched his legs with a sigh. "Nah," he said dismissively as he shook his straight brown hair out of his eyes. "I had to finish some shopping. Mindy needed some new winter boots."

Tigun laughed. "Street urchins with shoes and clothes. Man, what sort of thieves are we?"

"You're right," said Randall as he frowned. "Only during the winter then. We'll go barefoot during the rest of the year so as not to draw attention to ourselves. And not during burglaries. Too noisy."

Tigun slumped backwards letting his head dangle off of the far side of the crate. "Me and my stupid mouth," he groaned, his voice echoing off the far wall. "At least tell me that you have some targets for us."

"Yeah. Five blocks northeast from the North Market there is a trading consortium," said Randall. "They have grown sloppy and overconfident with the extra watchmen on the streets. The building should be accessible from any of the buildings next to it. Your choice on how to enter. Just be careful when inside. I can't tell who or what is inside."

"Sounds like fun," said Tigun. "I'll take Blake and Johnny with me. They sneak well. And they need the experience."

Randall grimaced. Blake and Johnny were only twelve. "You're right," he said in resignation. "Just be careful."

"Steady and cautious gets us home safe," recited Tigun. "Where will you be?"

"Did you go to the ceremony and parade for Prince Matlin?" Randall asked.

"Nope. I was acquiring a few items and coins from a blacksmith who was enjoying the revelry." Tigun danced a slender dagger between his fingers. "Just like yours."

Randall smiled. Tigun knew their business well. He would have been careful in acquiring the dagger. "Very nice," he said in congratulation. "But back to the ceremony. There was a priest of Pojomi presiding over the event. Real fancy shindig. And the High Priest of Pojomi wore this lovely amulet. It was shaped like some sort of cat, you know, the type Pojomi worshippers go crazy over. Anyway, it looked like it was made of ebony, and had these large square emeralds for eyes. Should fetch a pretty price from any caravans from Talendor."

"Stealing from the High Priest of Pojomi? Are you insane?" hissed Tigun, as if saying the words any louder than a whisper would cause the god of the hunt to materialize within the warehouse.

"These large scores are what will get us out of this warehouse," insisted Randall.

"If you say so," said Tigun in frustration. "But I think you just enjoy it."

"Of course," said Randall as he bounced off of the crate, flipping between the palettes of crates left behind on the warehouse floor. "Why do it if it isn't fun?

Chapter Three

R andall waited until dusk, and then he waited some more. The darkness was a thief's friend. It sheltered the thief as he moved throughout the night.

The real trick was learning how to move about in the darkness. People relied on their sense of sight, and for good reason. Vision let one see guards, footholds, hiding places, and precious valuables.

Randall made it a habit to go out at night and acclimate himself to the black of night. The goal was not so much as to improve his night vision, but his night hearing. He learned to listen, to try letting his ears to pick up even the faintest of noises. A creaking sign in the night could easily be a thief's escape route if one was merely aware of its presence.

The city of Loach had always been a military fortress first and foremost. There was order to its construction, each section of the city having its own layout and defenses. Walls were built in rings leading ever outward. They made foot traffic tedious, as it tended to clog up along choke points. However, the walls were phenomenal for thievery. They provided easy access to the rooftops, and were very helpful at throwing off pursuit. Guards were not a common presence upon rooftops, nor did they have that much experience in rooftop pursuits.

Randall leaped easily between fortification and rooftop, steadily making his way to the Temple District. It was less of a proper district, and more of a series of winding streets lined with temple after temple. There was no rhyme or reason as to where the temples were set up. As evidenced by Bollian, the god of diplomacy, somehow having his temple located next to the temple to Ormun, the god of war.

The temple of Pojomi was an impressive structure that resembled a tower more than a temple. The god of the hunt was one of the more popular deities in Loach. His predatory nature and praise of strength worshipped amongst the populace. The growth of the congregation naturally led to the growth of the temple. But due to the constraints of real estate in the temple district, the Pojomites only had one direction in which they could build: up.

The temple had a pointed roof with and a balcony that stretched around the entire top floor. The balcony was secured by a railing. That would be Randall's entry point. People loved to store their valuables in high places. Unless the Pojomites possessed some sort of religious bias against human instinct, he was most likely to find the amulet near the top of the tower.

Gargoyles dotted the outside of the tower. Large monstrosities of stone appearing every few floors. It was strange that an order dedicated to the hunt would hide in a structure guarded by sentries.

The gargoyles would be his route to the top floor. Randall removed a silk rope slung about his shoulders and tied the end into a loop. It took three attempts before he managed to snare a gargoyle around the head.

He tugged twice on the rope before trusting the gargoyle to hold his weight. Randall carefully climbed down from the roof of the temple he was standing on, and let himself fall slowly in the direction of the Pojomi temple. The soles of his feet connected softly with the wall. Hand by hand he climbed up the rope shrouded in darkness. As long as the Pojomites did not stick their heads out of the windows, he would remain unseen.

Randall reached the first gargoyle with relative ease. He removed the rope from its head and craned his neck up. The climb would be tricky from here on out. He would need to throw his rope across the building, multiple floors above his head, and climb the gargoyles in a zig-zag pattern until he reached the top.

He reached a hand underneath his shirt and spun a clump of silk webbing out of one of the glands on his abdomen. He needed to weigh the rope down, so that it would be easier to aim, and actually reach the gargoyles. Otherwise, he would spend most of the night tossing the rope up at gargoyles and praying.

He looped the next gargoyle and continued his climb. Fifteen minutes later, and he had scaled the tower, swinging himself up onto the balcony. The balcony was clear of snow and other signs of the elements. Someone at least frequented the area to clean it. Randall eased himself up against the doorway into the tower and paused to listen. He did not plan on being caught at all, much less before laying eyes upon the amulet.

After five minutes he determined that the temple was not going to become more silent. Risk was part of thieving after all. What would a good burglary be without that rush of adrenaline?

Randall tried the handle of the door, it was unlocked. He smiled to himself. The Pojomites must not have expected anyone to try and break into the temple from this altitude.

The interior of the temple was what Randall expected from the ostentatious tower. Marble tile covered the floor, kept to a fine polish. Statues of various predators lined the walls, from large cats, to bears, to birds, and to some sort of sharp toothed fish creature with which Randal was unfamiliar. Randall paused before an ebony statue of a spider. Rubies were inset into its eyes. A pity it was so large.

Everything in this room was of the highest craftsmanship and material. It must have some sort of relevance to the Pojomite order. Maybe a shrine for the highest members of the order?

Regardless, it appeared that Randall was hunting in the correct area. He poked his head out of the exit to the shrine and peered every which way. He scuttled down the hallway, careful not to let his calloused heels slap too loudly against the tile floor.

He poked his head into each room as he went by. He found libraries, conference rooms, and shrines. Everything was well kept, and well crafted. The upper echelon of the clergy definitely resided in this area.

He found what he was looking for in a sort of trophy room. There was one entrance, and on the far wall, a rich assortment of trophies were stored behind glass cases. All the relics were connected in some manner to hunting. There were ancient spears and arrowheads. A suit of carefully sculpted armor, colored orange with black stripes, that would be too heavy for him to remove. Jewelry and sculptures of animals and animal heads made up the vast majority of the room.

Randall found the ebony amulet sitting in a simple glass case. A small metal plaque was attached to the marble pillar holding the case. It read "Spirit of the Jaguar". Randall assumed that the jaguar was the animal whose features adorned the amulet. It was not as if jaguars prowled within the city of Loach.

One other item attracted his notice. A dagger whose blade gleamed and shined, nearly translucent. The hilt was made of gold scales and the plaque read "The Diamond Talon".

Randall promised himself that he would only steal the amulet. The more he stole from the Pojomites, the more they would search for him. It would be hard enough to fence one item. Each additional item stolen increased the risk that someone would talk, and lead the Pojomites to his doorstep.

But what if he did not sell it? What if he kept the dagger for himself? It was a fine bit of craftsmanship, and well, he deserved it. What was the point of being a thief if he never did anything for himself?

Moving as swiftly and silently as possible, Randall lifted the glass cases and removed the amulet and dagger. He paused holding his breath. He worried about this part. Everyone knew that the priests placed wards upon the crypts and catacombs to keep the spirits of the dead where they belonged. Could, or would, they place similar wards upon their valuables?

Nothing happened.

Randall released his breath and crept out of the room. His instincts ached to run and rush out of the temple. He resisted those urges. Haste would result in him being captured, or worse. He already broke one of his rules, he would not break another.

He backtracked as quickly as he could, ignoring the trappings and decorations on the wall. He could view hunting scenes at any time if he visited the temple during the day.

Vaulting over the balcony railing, Randall landed on a gargoyle and steadied himself for the meticulous journey back down the tower. Leaning out over open space while trying to lasso the gargoyles beneath him made the world spin. He was not scared of heights. He just did not like them. Who in their right mind would enjoy being this high above the safety of the ground?

He lassoed the first gargoyle and belatedly realized his mistake. He could not climb down the rope; he would plummet and free fall the instant he stepped off of his current gargoyle. He should have brought more ropes with him, and tied them to his current gargoyle, leaving the rope behind.

Randall's only option was to leap out into the empty space, parallel to the building, and swing beneath the gargoyle. Then he could climb up to the gargoyle, untie his rope, and repeat the whole process over again. The trick would be avoiding crashing into the temple or any gargoyles on the way down. Broken ribs and dropping the rope would be the result of that, and he could not fly.

Randall swallowed and closed his eyes hoping to steady himself. That did not help however. The spinning sensation only increased, making him feel as if he would vomit into the blackness. He reopened his eyes, took one last deep breath and stepped out into the night.

The air rushed past him as windows flew past. The rope snapped tight as he reached the bottom of its arc. He swung back and forth like a pendulum, cold sweat drenching his body. Mercifully he scrambled up the rope and wall. He clung to the gargoyle, his breathing rapid, panic threatening to consume him.

It was madness. Tears leaked down his face. Madness with only one way out. He could either climb back up and try to sneak out of the tower through more mundane means of transportation, or continue his series of freefalls. He did not like his odds of navigating every level of the temple without being detected. That left one other path down the building: continuing to toss his rope and trying not to smash into the temple. If he went quickly, maybe the nightmare would be over sooner.

He tossed his rope onto the next gargoyle and plummeted downward for a second time. He comforted himself with the thought that when the theft was discovered, no sane person would possibly consider his escape method as a possibility.

Randall rushed down the gargoyles as quickly as he could manage, stopping only at the final gargoyle. There was nothing else beneath him to anchor his rope. His only remaining option was to jump to the roof beneath him. It would hurt, but hopefully the power of his totem would help absorb some of the impact from the fall. Everything now hinged upon his legs not breaking. He would just pause for a minute and then—

"Thief! Robbery! Catch the thief!" the voices shouted from the street below.

Randall nearly jumped out of his skin. Was his theft discovered already? Someone just happened to look in that room? Maybe there actually were wards in there.

He could not stay near the scene of the crime, not as the bustle in the street was increasing. If one watchman looked up, or one priest ducked their head outside of a window, he would be in mortal danger perched precariously as he was.

Randall wrapped his rope into coils, slipped it over his head and shoulder and took one last deep breath and flung himself from the gargoyle. He flew through the air, but he figured out the trick of jumping between buildings years ago.

Do not look down.

The shock of the impact reverberated up his legs and pitched him forward in an awkward roll. He groaned as he scrambled to find his footing. The fall was a little bit longer than he anticipated. He distantly remembered that he had already gone shopping for food, and could lay about in bed all day if he managed to get back to the warehouse.

The voices and bustle in the street grew louder and Randall forced himself into action. It would not take them long to think to search the rooftops. Randall began running, leaping from rooftop to rooftop. He needed to vanish out of the Temple District as soon as possible.

He landed on the next rooftop and bounced into something hard. He landed on the rooftop, stunned, his nose sore and his eyes watering.

Randall blinked his eyes and looked up. He crossed this rooftop earlier, there was not anything on it then. But there was now. Standing on the rooftop was a cloaked man in black.

A few things began to make sense to Randall. The watchmen were not looking for him, but this fellow. And if the watchmen were looking for this man, that may explain the increase in crime throughout the city.

The hooded man reached a hand out, pulling Randall to his feet, and then took off at a dead sprint, leaping from rooftop to rooftop. Randall stared at the cloaked man in shock. The shouts from the watchmen broke him out of his momentary reverie.

Randall broke off at a run, following in the hooded man's wake. He would prefer to travel in a different direction, but the closest boundary wall for the Temple District was in the direction the hooded man was travelling.

The man travelled swiftly, quicker than Randall could manage to move. Randall reached the boundary wall, but by that time the man had already vanished into the night. Randall quickly did the same, heading towards North Market and putting as much distance between himself and the Temple District as he could. He would make sure that he had truly lost the watchmen before circling back towards the warehouse hideout.

The presence of the hooded man bothered Randall. Sure, he helped Randall up on the rooftop, but Randall's instincts said that the man would have no qualms about throwing him to the watchmen if it ensured his freedom. That was just life on the street. There weas no honor among thieves.

The thought gave Randall pause and he quickly patted himself down. Nothing was missing. He still had the amulet and dagger. At least he still had that. If tonight was any sign, money was going to be more difficult to come by in Loach.

Chapter Four

"And just like that they're to be married?" Dalton asked incredulously. Jeron rolled his eyes before answering. "Yes, just like that."

"But that's insane!" Dalton protested. "They barely know each other."

Jeron shrugged as he returned his gaze to Duke Havram, Prince Nelson, and Princess Iniza. The Duke held both of their hands in his and raised them above his head to the raucous applause of the nobles in attendance at court.

Princess Iniza was positively beaming at the match. A link between Talendor and Biona would prove quite advantageous to her family. And who would not like to move from the desert and its seasonal vampire assaults to a coastal city?

Prince Nelson response was more tepid. He smiled politely and waved to the crowd. It was also a good match for him from what Jeron understood. Nelson owned a fleet of ships, and pairing up with Duke Havram's caravans could make both of them wealthier.

As far as personality went, Jeron supposed the pair could do worse. Iniza genuinely liked Nelson. That much was obvious from the first time he saw them together. Nelson, well, Jeron did not think that the man liked anyone very much, except for himself. Every time he saw the man, Nelson had a scowl on his face. He did not speak much with Jeron, and with that ever-present scowl, Jeron was not disappointed by that turn of events.

Prince Darik looked pleased at the announcement. It was the one reaction that Jeron was fully certain that he understood. Biona and Talendor were Antier's greatest allies in the war against Loach. With the alliance between the two duchies solidified, the alliance grew stronger which was a great boon to Antier's depleted forces.

"Vernon, I mean Prince Irvin seems more uncertain about the engagement," whispered Dalton. Despite their location on the back wall, furthest from the pomp of court, it did not hurt to be careful. Especially considering the mysterious circumstances surrounding the destruction of Kelon. Conspiracy theories abounded over the event, and neither Jeron nor Dalton wished to be overhead discussing matters relating to Kelon. At court, any noble could potentially have been involved in the plot to destroy the duchy.

"Talendor neighbors the remains of Kelon," whispered Jeron. "Can you blame him for being nervous at a marriage between the child of its ruler, and the child of another duchy? Neither of whom are in line to inherit anything."

Dalton's brow furrowed. "Why would inheritance matter?" he asked. "Each family has plenty of money. Both Nelson and Iniza enjoy the finer things in life."

Jeron shook his head in disagreement. Dalton excelled in the moment, reading the surface of events. Planning far ahead in the future and in deeper intrigue? That was not his specialty. "Think it through, Dalton. How are Talendor's forces getting to the war?"

"Darik is leading Talendor's mercenary force, while their regular army remains behind to rebuild from the attack on the inner city," he replied. "That force is rather sizeable. We may actually stand a chance in the war."

"Not what I asked," said Jeron as his annoyance rose. "How are they going to get to the war? What route are they going to take?"

"They'll head to the King's Highway and march north into Loach," answered Dalton slowly, uncertain at that obvious answer.

"Passing through the ruins of Kelon on the way," supplied Jeron. "With an army. Prince Darik is going to need to pacify the ghosts in the area. Priests and their wards. Otherwise, the passing will be unsafe for the army, and they will be forced to fight the ghosts. The alternative is leaving a host of specters at your back, which is no way to fight a war."

"And part of Kelon will become pacified again," said Dalton as recognition dawned on him. "People will begin resettling the area, reclaiming the land."

"Right. Reclaiming Vernon's land, but maybe not for him," said Jeron.

"Hmm. And that would not be good for you or your lady," said Dalton innocently.

Jeron scowled at him. "My what?" he growled.

Dalton rolled his eyes in exasperation. "Oh please. After everything you two have been through, all the talking, whispering, hugging, and let's not forget that kiss. How could I forget the kiss?"

"She did that to prevent me from charging after the Loachian twins," protested Jeron weakly.

"Uh-huh," said Dalton unconvinced. "Oh, and I nearly forgot, she calls you 'dear'. I can't recall her ever calling me that."

"Oh, shut up," said Jeron.

Dalton grinned at Jeron unashamed. "Don't think I will. You never answered the original question. What are you going to do if someone tries to take her lands?"

"You never asked that question."

"I didn't?" said Dalton with a pause. "I suppose I didn't. But I'm asking it now."

Jeron paused before answering. It was an interesting question. A year earlier it would not have been a decision at all. His path was clear then. He would train, become as strong as he could, and protect Byron, Darik's little brother and Jeron's best friend, with his life. He would marry whoever he was instructed, and serve Antier and the Church as a paladin until his dying days.

Things changed with Loach's betrayal at Fort Hope and Byron's murder. After that, he had grown accustomed to making his own decisions. He had met Jayna and the others. Everything had changed then. He had changed. His future was no longer clearly visible. He now had options, which previously he had never had the time or inclination to fully contemplate.

"I don't know," he finally admitted. "I guess I'll figure it out if it happens. Right now, I have a war to focus on."

Dalton chuckled softly to himself, earning him a sharp elbow jammed into his ribs. "Oww," Dalton gave him a mock glare. "Alright. I'll stop. Hey, do you think they'll be serving any good food for this party?"

"I doubt there will be a party," said Jeron drily.

"What? Why not?" protested Dalton. "The vampires left days ago, there is an engagement, and we should be leaving for war soon. Why not feast?"

Jeron smacked Dalton upside the back of his head with an open hand. "Really? A feast after all those people in the inner city lost their lives to the vampires? When so many people need to rebuild?"

Dalton rubbed his skull and scrunched up his nose in discomfort. "Point. Alright, well instead of a feast, how about we run out of here and try to find some food?"

Jeron's stomach growled at the mention of food. "That doesn't sound too bad," he said. "Let me go and find—"

"If you say that you need to find Jayna, I will smack your brains in with my mace," said Dalton with his hands on his hips. He now wore the mace along with his customary spear. The man claimed that after all that they had been through, that he wanted options in his weaponry.

"You're that lonely, huh?" asked Jeron.

"Dreadfully bored," corrected Dalton.

"She is better company than you."

"I doubt that."

"Please don't try to kiss me," said Jeron.

"I make no promises. You know how I get when I'm hungry," said Dalton.

"Irritable and irrational. Prone to poor decisions," said Jeron as he moved towards the exit of the chamber.

"Yup. That's me," declared Dalton proudly as he pointed at his chest.

"You boys heading somewhere?" asked a voice from outside the chamber.

Jeron glanced over at the man and smiled. The voice belonged to Emkario, one of Prince Darik's friends, and a fine soldier. Emkario was joined by Vincent, another of Darik's lieutenants. In times before the war, Jeron hesitated to call them peace time, Vincent helped design structures, weaponry, and all sorts of other projects for Duke Cedric. Jeron respected that. In his younger days, Jeron wished to construct great buildings, castles and the like. Vincent was a kindred spirit as far as he was concerned.

"Just to get some food," said Dalton amiably.

"Enjoy it," said Emkario somberly. "It may be your last good meal for a while."

"I know," said Dalton as he waved him off. "We're marching to war."

"No, *we're* marching to war," emphasized Emkario. "*You* are accompanying Prince Nelson to Biona."

"What?" said Jeron. His heart raced; he did not want to go to Biona. Not when everyone else was marching to Loach.

"Not you," said Emkario dismissively. "You're staying with us. You get along too well with the Kelonians."

"Well so do I," said Dalton defensively. "Brukel and Marcela in particular."

"True," said Emkario with a shrug. "But it's not in my hands. Prince Nelson needs to be accompanied back to Biona. As they're our ally, Prince Darik wants him travelling with someone that he trusts. That means you, Atticus, Telwin, and Lentil."

"None of the soldiers from Prince Darik's unit, huh," said Jeron unhappily.

"Nope. We get to stay," said Vincent happily.

"At least I'll have the opportunity to go home before you guys," said Dalton.

"Wait a minute," said Jeron. "That means I'll be left behind."

"You're needed here," repeated Emkario firmly. "Irvin and his people trust you. Jeron, you have to stay, but you aren't being left behind. You're marching to war with us. Enjoy your meal. We need to speak with the prince."

Jeron scowled as they walked away until Dalton tossed his arm around Jeron's shoulder. "Well then. Time's a wasting. Let's go grab some food. We have tons of topics to discuss. Such as how there are multiple princes in our lives, why every child of a duke is a prince or a princess, and what Olivia's reaction will be when I tell her about you and Jayna."

The anger in Jeron's chest began to subside, and he started to laugh at Dalton's ridiculous behavior. At least his mane did not pop out with his anger this time. He was getting better at controlling that. "Do I have a choice?" he asked.

"Yup. Beer or wine," said Dalton as he pointed a finger towards the sky. "The only choice a man really ever needs to make."

CHAPTER FIVE

"Lieutenant Lorezzini, get in here immediately!" bellowed Olivia from the entrance to the command tent.

Calabella Lorezzini halted her attack mid-swing before turning her head towards Olivia. She nodded, and left the training yard without any further words. These days, she perpetually kept her boar tusks out on her face. The anxiety of waiting for battle was beginning to wear upon her. Everyone was nervous, waiting for the first engagement with Loach.

They had bunkered down for the winter miles south of Antier's border with Loach. A giant crater was located roughly two miles north of their position. The previous Duke of Antier perished there during a violent battle, the power of his totem exploding out of his body, and causing the crater.

"What's going on, Vivi?" Calabella asked calmly. She no longer breathed heavily after exerting herself. None of them did anymore.

"You have a mission," Olivia responded. "Follow me inside the tent, we'll go over everything."

The inside of the tent had been turned into a field command center. A makeshift table sat in the center of the tent with maps of the surrounding area, and stacks of reports covering it. Captains Levren and Iandrick were engrossed in the maps along with Masters Tyson and Maxus.

"Ahh ladies, welcome," said Master Tyson with a warm smile. "Please gather around."

Olivia bristled at the opening. The winter months had worn her patience thin. She had grown accustomed to being in command of the female units in the army. It was surprising how much not being in command of the entire army bothered her.

Rationally, she knew that she lacked experience. But something inside of her grew with each passing day, wanting more. Ambition mixed with something else. A desire to protect her people? Jealousy? All she knew was that she trusted her women to carry out her orders. No one else earned that level of trust.

"Sirs," Calabella said as she snapped a smart salute.

"Good. Everyone is here," said Captain Iandrick without looking up. "Master Sildun informs us that his scouts have seen signs of Loach sneaking forces across the border into the Flintwood. Lieutenant Lorezzini, you'll lead a patrol of our troops to the spot designated by Master Sildun. It was previously known as Flintwood Village. Be careful. The village is years gone, and the Loachians may have tampered with the wards left behind by the priests."

"Flintwood Village?" asked Olivia as she narrowed her eyes. "That is where Jeron was from."

"Indeed," said Master Tyson as he crossed his arms beneath his chest. "That's why you will be staying here Captain Gabrella."

Olivia gritted her teeth. "I am fine," she growled, scowling at the men. "I have moved on."

"Sure you have lass," said Captain Levren with a sardonic grin on his face. "You look the very picture of fine. The scowl really adds something in my opinion."

"Mark," admonished Master Maxus in a long suffering voice. "Do you always have to be so disagreeable?"

"Gentlemen," interrupted Captain Iandrick. "Please focus. Lieutenant, do you have any questions?"

"How many soldiers will I have under my command?" she asked.

"A squad of twenty-five," answered Levren. "Move fast. If there are only a few Loachians, feel free to engage. But please be prudent. Intelligence is more useful to us. If you die, we gain nothing of value."

"Understood, sir."

"Dismissed," said Captain Iandrick as he resumed staring at the map.

They left the tent with Olivia still fuming at Captain Levren's barbs.

"He's right you know," Calabella said. "You're not acting like yourself."

"I'm not in love with Jeron," Olivia hissed. "I don't know if I ever truly was."

Calabella snorted. "I'm not saying that you are. I'm only saying that you cared for him, and that you strongly desire vengeance upon the Loachians. Travelling to his home town where he lost his family? Vivi, you definitely have a strong sense of poetic justice. I'll give you that."

Olivia hesitated. Was that how people saw her. "I don't think that I am consumed by vengeance."

"Sweety, you have been gnashing your teeth and caressing that sword hilt all winter. Silas says that the troops are terrified of so much as squeaking in your presence."

"Oh," was all Olivia could muster, a feeling of awkwardness setting over her. "Wait. Silas says? Bella, do I even want to know?"

Calabella grinned wickedly at her. "I'm almost certain that you don't."

Olivia rubbed at her temples in a circular pattern, trying to ease the sudden ache in her head. "Are you taking him with you?"

"Of course."

Olivia sighed. "Be careful, Calabella. The Loachians are dangerous."

"We'll be fine," Calabella insisted. "Where is Atrisha? I'd like to tell her the news before I leave."

"She's on sky patrol. She said that she wanted to get an aerial view of the land, put the maps into context for her."

"Well tell her where I am," said Calabella. "It'll kill her not being in on the first encounter." Calabella looked around uncertainly. "Well I guess I should go gather my team and get going...should I salute you or hug you?"

Olivia pulled her into a bear hug, laughing as she tried to avoid the taller woman's tusks. "Just come back to us safe," she whispered. "And if you can, kill one of them for me too."

CHAPTER SIX

Fotlin gripped his bastard sword tightly as beads of cold sweat trickled down his face. He had taken up sparring with the City Watch in an effort to improve their skills. The dowesults were...measured. Some watchmen, like Bruce, Janul, and Zirkel showed marked improvements. The rest...well, not as much.

At least it provided Fotlin with an outlet for his stress.

He brought his blade up in a high guard, easily blocking the blow from Owen. He pushed the blade aside and kicked Owen right in the stomach. It would have been easier to disembowel him, but with the war underway, he would not be getting much, if any, reinforcements. He needed to make due with even the useless watchmen.

Fotlin spun, his blade whirling, disarming the two other watchmen with ease. While his brothers learned military tactics, and how to manage the duchy's economy, he spent his time learning the blade.

With a blade he did not have to rely on anyone else, he did not have anyone, or anything, under his command except for the blade. He was a soloist, accustomed to working alone. If he was to seize any titles or wealth for himself, it would be on the strength of his blade and his wits.

"That's enough," said Fotlin as he spotted Zirkel standing off to the side of the room. "Clean up and go about your duties." He motioned Zirkel over as he sheathed his bastard sword. "Report."

"The Temple of Annelu has conducted a full inventory after the break in," said Zirkel as he ran a hand through his brown hair. "They have stated that numerous texts are missing from their records. Histories, religious texts, and the like."

"And the names of these texts?" asked Fotlin, annoyed that he had to try to pry the information out bit by bit from the watchman.

"No names, sir," said Zirkel. "They said the texts are ancient leather bound things. Names were never etched into the leather."

"Well then how in the hell are we supposed to find them?" Fotlin demanded. Zirkel merely shrugged in response.

Fotlin seethed. How was he supposed to find the stolen goods if he did not know what they looked like? It was an impossible task. But he needed to stamp down on crime in Loach. His future depended upon it.

"There's more, sir," said Zirkel cautiously. The man had a fair grasp of Fotlin's mood.

"More?" hissed Fotlin. "How could there be more?!"

"The Temple of Pojomi was also burgled," replied Zirkel with a wince.

Fotlin felt the blood rush out of his face. His stomach felt like a bubbling cauldron. The Pojomites were not fond of thieves. They took it as a challenge to their power and authority. The Pojomites would certainly send their own cavaliers and hunters out scouring the city for the thieves instead of relying upon his City Watch. Before long the streets would run red with blood as they hunted down every thief they could find.

Innocents would inevitably die in the hunt. Acceptable losses to the Pojomites, but not to the populace at large. People would stay in off of the streets, hunkered within the safety of their homes. Money would not be spent, and merchants would become uneasy as their profits dwindled.

"Double the patrols," Fotlin ordered. "Do we know what was stolen from the Pojomites?"

"An ebony jaguar amulet with emerald eyes and a ceremonial diamond dagger," answered Zirkel.

"We need to find them and the thief immediately," said Fotlin. "Top priority. Otherwise, things are going to become terrible for all of us."

CHAPTER SEVEN

"Well, what do you think Randall?" asked Tiona, her large brown eyes wide in fear.

Randall patted her head absently. "It's okay little one," he assured her. "Nothing to worry about. Just more watchmen roaming about. See, there's Mister Faron at his stall selling meat pies. Everything is normal."

Internally, he harbored doubts. The watchmen were everywhere in the markets and around the city. They could not know that his little band was a bunch of thieves. They were too careful for that. But the watchmen could make things more difficult.

Randall and his crew needed money to survive. Hunger would eventually lead them to take risks. Whether that included robbing from merchants, burgling heavily guarded buildings, or selling some of their more obvious and recognizable plunder, Randall did not know.

It was not just the watchmen that made him nervous. There seemed to be a tension in the air, as if the entire city was holding its breath waiting to be pushed off of the gibbet. Merchants cast suspicious glances at every passerby, people clutched their purses tighter, and the watchmen no longer engaged in the same sort of small talk with the citizenry.

"Can we buy a meat pie?" Tiona asked as she hopped from cobblestone to cobblestone.

"Not today, Tiona," he said sadly. "We need the money for other things."

To her credit, Tiona did not cry. She accepted it and resumed bouncing back and forth.

Randall returned his attention to surveying his surroundings. While security was increased, it still could not be everywhere. Medium to smaller targets still existed. Smaller businesses, consortiums, and lending houses were ripe targets.

The institution of martial law would be the only true threat to their existence. Barring the streets at night would make their lives infinitely more difficult, and maybe make survival impossible. They could get by in the current environment. It would be uncomfortable, put possible.

Randall continued their stroll acting the part of brother and sister. Tiona played her part masterfully, acting just like the eight year old child that she was. Their purpose for today was to scout out the Central and Eastern Districts. Too many thefts in the Northern Market, and they might as well light a beacon for the watchmen to locate them. To do so would necessitate trespassing upon the territory of other Thieves Association crews. Randall instructed Tiona to wear her boots today, and not to steal anything at all. The disguises should help them avoid the rival crews. Unknown street urchins would draw their attention. Children who wore boots? Not so much. Children hardly ever made good targets for thieves seeking wealth.

The real danger lay in controlling Tiona. The girl was blessed with quick fingers and impulses. She was capable of making clean lifts of purses that the other members of the crew were not capable of even attempting. Also, like many of the children in their crew, she had yet to find her totem. If caught, she would not be able to defend herself if the situation called for violence.

The Central District was the oldest district in the city of Loach. The Loach family originally built a citadel there to defend its mining operations. A city slowly sprang up around the citadel over time. With space in the district at a premium, the ducal family built a new palace, in the Eastern District, larger, grander, and closer to the mines.

Randall and Tiona moved through the crowds of the Central District, careful not to disturb the natives. With their rich history came a sense of arrogance and entitlement. Two children bumping into an adult in the Northern District would not be much of an issue. The adult would pat themselves down, checking that all their belongings were still on them. An unfortunate reflex since pickpockets work in groups. That purse was already long gone; passed to another member of the crew. In the Central District, the adults were known to grab a youth and cry for a watchman. Not for theft, but for 'assault on their person'. Randall had no clue why they thought the children would be seasoning them, but adults were strange.

Every building was just a little bit nicer in this area. The blacksmiths made better equipment; commonly purchased by the nobility. The tailors used finer cloth and created the garish outfits worn at the balls thrown by the rich. The jewelers also utilized the finest cuts of gems from the mines. Which they used to supply the nobles and the wealthy with fancy accessories.

Randall was an admirer of their work. One or two well swiped pieces from any of the merchants of this district could feed his crew for a fair amount of time.

"Randy, look out!" cried Tiona as she tugged on his hand.

Randall let her drag him out of the way as he tore his vision from his surroundings. Fortunately for him, Tiona was paying attention. Otherwise, he would have walked into the blacksmith or the mercenary that he was conversing with.

Trouble would have certainly found them then. At the bare minimum, he and Tiona would become known to the watchmen that patrolled the Central District. News of their activities would certainly make it back to the Thieves Association crews that worked this portion of the Central District.

"Be careful!" demanded Tiona as she stamped her foot.

"Sorry, little one," said Randall as he mussed her hair again. "I guess I was lost in my thoughts. I promise I'll be more careful."

Randall grabbed Tiona's hand gently and navigated the crowds with her. He pointed out fountains and sculptures, laughing as he showed her the sights of the city. She had probably never noticed them or seen them before.

By the time they reached the Eastern District, Tiona was beginning to show signs of tiring. That was common for her, she always burst about expending all of her energy quickly. Randall stopped at a large fountain and sat down with her on the stone edging.

"Tiona, do you see that large building over there?" Randall asked.

"Yes," she said quietly as she tried to muffle a yawn.

"That's the duke's palace. Next to that are some of the society headquarters within the city," he said as he pointed out the structures. "And down that street are some very fancy expensive inns where the wealthy from Loach and abroad eat and sleep."

"Why do they stay at an inn if they're from Loach?" she asked puzzled. "Why don't they just go home?"

"I don't know," said Randall with a shrug. "I figure rich people get bored with sleeping in the same place all the time."

"I wanna go home," whined Tiona as she yawned again.

Randall suppressed a sigh and held her hand as they began walking north, back towards the warehouse. Tiona would not make it there without falling asleep. Randall knew that. He would carry her when needed, but for now he would conserve his strength. He wished they could have walked further today, but he saw enough.

He found his next target.

CHAPTER EIGHT

Vernon was accustomed to walking. After years of living as a mercenary it was his preferred method of transportation. Riding horses or wagons felt strange to him. All the swaying and bouncing made him feel uneasy. He preferred either solid ground beneath his feet, or a nice wind gusting against his wings.

Notwithstanding his personal feelings towards the beasts, he wished they had more horses with them. Talendor was renowned throughout the kingdom for its deserts and merchant caravans. It was most likely those deserts that caused the Talendorians to have so many caravans. They did not have enough green grass to properly feed and care for the horses in their homeland and needed to move elsewhere. Besides, who wanted to stay in a desert?

As a result, Talendor lacked a robust cavalry. That placed their army of Talendorian soldiers and mercenaries at a distinct disadvantage. They possessed plenty of pikemen, enough to deal with a Loachian cavalry charge, but they were not going to win this war by playing defense.

"What's on your mind, Your Highness?" asked Elfred as he marched at his side.

Vernon suppressed a wince. Elfred avoided calling him "Your Highness" for years. The sudden reemergence of the phrase was jarring. For years they operated as friends and comrades, not as prince and subordinate. By revealing his identity, a barrier had risen between them. It was not a large barrier, but the relationship was different now.

He did not regret revealing his identity. The siege of Talendor was raging at the time, and Prince Darik was horribly outnumbered in the sky by a horde of vampires. The Kelonians needed all the allies they could get, and Prince Darik of Antier was as strong as they came.

Darik was one of the favorites to succeed the childless King Ramon. That sort of power could hasten the restoration of Kelon. Restore Vernon's family land and holdings. Finally allow their dead to rest in peace.

"Winning the war," Vernon finally answered. "The lack of horses bothers me. Do we keep our forces split and force the Loachians to do the same, or do we consolidate with the Antierian forces?"

"Sounds like a decision that will need to be made once we get better intelligence," said Elfred as he glanced around at the trees. It was his habit when travelling. "Let's change subjects then. How do you think the restoration of the King's Highway through Kelon is going to go?"

Vernon scowled at Elfred. "Is it that obvious?" he whispered.

Elfred kept his face impassive. "Is what obvious, Your Highness? I have not noticed whether laying the ghosts of Kelon to rest was weighing on your mind."

Vernon's scowl deepened. "By the gods, Elfred. Stop trying to be indirect and sarcastic. Just be plain about it. Say what is on your mind."

Elfred frowned. "I cannot, Your Highness. That would be improper."

Vernon grabbed the man and pulled him off to the side of the road. "To hell with what is proper!" he hissed. "We have been travelling together for years, and our entire adult lives. What is proper went by the wayside years ago. I trust you. But only if you're actually going to tell me what is on your mind. So speak up!"

Anger flashed in Elfred's eyes as he flung Vernon's hands off of him. "Fine. You want the truth?" he said, his usual stoic expression gone. "I think this is a horrible idea. We're fighting Antier's wars for what? A hope that they will help rebuild our graveyard?"

"Darik is a good man. He will help," replied Vernon.

"If he is alive, yes," said Elfred. "But there is no guarantee of that, and our numbers are very limited."

"It's the only way we get Kelon back?"

"Who says I want Kelon back?" asked Elfred. "Do you think I followed you all these years out a sense of *duty*? No. I followed you because you are my friend and a good man. Kelon is gone. The people that destroyed it still live. So even if we restore it, there is no guarantee how long we'll be able to hold it. Aren't our lives more important than that?"

Vernon understood his position. He wrestled with it himself for years. Did he even want to go back to his old life? The thought still caused him to lose sleep at night. After all, he still thought of himself as Vernon and not Irvin.

Life as Vernon was liberating. He made decisions based upon what he wanted to do at any one time. His only objective was to keep the six of them breathing. It was a familiar and comfortable lifestyle.

And not what he wanted.

When he spread his wings and took flight after Darik, he knew what he wanted. He craved the responsibility. Not because he wanted power, but because he thought that he could do a better job than those who currently had it.

There was also the matter of the survivors of Kelon. They had fled, spreading across the kingdom searching for a place to call home. He was focused on the safety of his few friends for so long that he neglected his responsibility to his people. He had the strength and ability to protect them when they could not protect themselves. It took the appearance of Toran to remind him that he was derelict in his duties.

"A year ago, I would have believed that," said Vernon as the fire died out of him. "But then I was reminded that our land died, not all of our people. They need a home, Elfred. Someone to look out for their wellbeing, their prosperity. I cannot step aside any longer."

"See?" said Elfred as his stoic expression returned. "Still a good man."

"You have no objections then?" asked Vernon.

"I have plenty," said Elfred. He hesitated a bit before continuing on. "But I'll try to voice them from now on."

"Thank you."

"But if I am not to call you by your rightful title, I'll have to insist on calling you Vernon," said Elfred.

Vernon beamed at his friend. "I consider that particular name the highest of honors, my friend. It's worth more than any title."

Elfred adjusted his armor and turned his back to Vernon as he walked back towards the road. "Thank you," he croaked over his shoulder.

Vernon let him go. It would be in poor taste to acknowledge the man's sudden outward expression of emotion. Let the man remain reserved and in control.

Elfred was correct in some of his concerns. They were putting a great deal of faith in outsiders. Not just in returning Kelon's dead to their graves, but in protecting their duchy. Vernon lacked an army, and his resources were meager at best. That would change once Vernon was back in his palace.

The fall of Kelon was so sudden, swift, and complete, that raiders were not able to plunder the land. Kelon's fortunes still resided where they lay, hidden behind a fog of specters roaming the land. Once he recovered that fortune, they could begin rebuilding, relying on mercenary companies for security. It was not ideal, but nothing ever was.

With Darik's army beginning to put to rest the ghosts that inhabited the area directly along the King's Highway, commerce would begin to increase. Merchants and caravans would travel along Kelon's border. It would not be long before others remembered the forgotten wealth that lay within.

But that would not happen until after the war concluded. Travel was about to become perilous in the northern duchies of the Ochandor. And, if things broke his way for once, they would have allies after the war concluded.

"Brother! Care to join us?" Jayna called out to him. She was openly smiling with glee. She hated hiding their relationship over the years.

"Hello, Jayna. Enjoying being home again?" he asked.

"Yes. Although I was hoping we would be able to show Jeron around some," she said as she looped her arm through the younger man's.

Vernon liked Jeron. He was a good loyal man. A tough fighter from what he witnessed, and a powerful totem holder. While Jeron possessed a powerful totem, his familial titles did not reflect that power. From what he gathered from Dalton and Thiago over their journey, Jeron's hometown was a small village in

Antier along the border with Loach. The village was destroyed in a border raid by the Loachian forces, orphaning Jeron.

In Vernon's eyes that made Jeron a kindred spirit with the Kelonians. They all had homes that were taken from them. Jeron's totem would prove useful in reclaiming and resettling Kelon, but his titles would not precisely frighten any outsider. If Jayna insisted on marrying the man, Vernon knew he would not object. Circumstances dictated that the Kelonian survivors were not as strong adherents to protocol and rank as other duchies in the kingdom.

"Prince Irvin," said Jeron as he nodded seriously in greeting.

Vernon offered the young man an encouraging smile and patted him on the shoulder. "Jeron, you're one of the few in this army that knew me as Vernon first. Please. Continue calling me by that name. As I am sure Jayna has told you, our previous names might as well be a previous life to us. Irvin is a stranger's name to me. It's more of a title than an identity to me."

"Actually, she won't mention her previous name," said Jeron drily. "I have given up asking about it."

"A wise man," said Vernon as he ignored the self-satisfied smirk on his sister's face.

"Thiago says that he has not seen that many ghosts out there," ventured Jeron as he tried to change the subject to something less likely to land him in trouble.

"Nor would he," said Jayna. "We're on the border with the duchy of Ochandor. Most of the ghosts will lie in the interior of the duchy. I wouldn't expect him to encounter that many unless he comes upon a border town."

"Why not?" asked Jeron, a confused look upon his face. "I thought all of Kelon was destroyed."

"Mostly," said Vernon. "Any town of size was targeted that night. Only the smallest of villages were spared along with farms and homesteads. But when the surrounding towns are destroyed for days in each direction, survival becomes nearly impossible. Those surviving people made mad dashes to the borders of Kelon. Not all of them made it through the ghosts and the ahh...other inhabitants of Kelon."

"Other inhabitants?" asked Jeron apprehensively.

"Werewolves, dear," said Jayna as she patted his arm. "Don't worry though. Most of them fell to the ghosts as well."

"So Kelon is full of werewolf ghosts now?" Jeron asked. "Is that supposed to be better?"

"I-I...actually I have no idea," said Jayna. "But I'd take Kelon back no matter what is residing there."

"Me too," said Vernon. "But let's not worry about that until after we deal with Loach."

Vernon patted the two of them on the back, leaving Jeron muttering something about minotaurs, vampires, and werewolves. Vernon made his way steadily towards the front of the column where he was sure to find Prince Darik. The man certainly believed in leading from the front.

Vernon hurried his stride without running. Soldiers were watching. He needed to keep his calm and dignity. But they were in his lands now. He would also lead from the front.

Chapter Nine

The Flintwood was an oddity of nature. It was the only location in the kingdom where flintwood trees grew. Flintwood trees were thick trees, like oaks, except for one minor feature: their bark was made out of flint.

The locals harvested the bark and used it in the crafting of simple everyday tools. Iron and steel tools were rare and expensive in these parts. Iron was usually mined and sent elsewhere as the locals relied upon their flint. The tools made from the flint might have been slightly less effective than their smithy forged counterparts, but they were affordable and cost-effective.

After the flint was removed from the trees, the local lumberjacks would swoop in and harvest the lumber. The wood that came from flintwood trees was highly valuable. The wood was stronger than that of other trees. It had to be to support the extra weight of the flint bark. And it was usually undamaged by animals or the elements, neither of which were strong enough to penetrate the flint bark.

The locals harvested large slabs of thick, dark, and rich wood and used it in the crafting of large furniture. Flintwood tables were in high demand by nobles throughout the kingdom. Their egos demanded long sturdy tables that were one continuous unblemished piece of wood. The duchy generated quite a bit of revenue off of those pieces.

That revenue was nearly non-existent now. The constant border clashes between Loach and Antier rendered most of the villages in the Flintwood ghost towns. Some, such as Flintwood Village, were the sites of military battles. While others simply were abandoned by locals weary of the constant strife.

If only they had remained ghost towns, thought Calabella. Loach was hiding men and supplies in most of them throughout the winter. The last little abandoned village they encountered had a small outpost of three scouts. Calabella and her squad eliminated them ruthlessly, ensuring that they could not send a message off.

What she found in their supplies troubled her deeply. Poisons. And a lot of them. Clearly Loach was planning on sending all manner of saboteurs behind their lines. An army that was sick from poisoned water was an army that would die quickly.

Not that Calabella had any experience with actual conflict or poison. But eating bad food, and becoming sick, was something with which she was familiar. She did not wish that fate on anyone in their army, especially if her life may be in that hypothetical person's hand.

She dispatched Silas two days earlier to convey a warning to Olivia regarding the Loachian plot. In her mind, her orders changed. This was not a reconnaissance mission but a counter-attack. She needed to neutralize the Loachian caches of poison before the saboteurs mobilized from their winter camps.

"Nellandra," she whispered, trying to prevent her booming voice from carrying through the woods. "What did you see?"

Nellandra took a sip of water before answering. The woman had circles under her eyes. She had been sleeping well. None of them had. "I didn't see anyone, but that doesn't mean much. The village was not leveled. Not completely. They favored these massive long log homes instead of smaller homes. Multiple generations and branches must have lived together."

"And?" asked Calabella. Who cared how the villagers of Flintwood Village lived?

Nellandra sighed exasperatedly. "Calabella, think about it. Large, long wooden structures. They can hold a lot of men and we won't know if they're occupied until we go inside. And if they are, who knows how many men they could have!" She tossed her hands up in frustration. "This may not be an outpost like the last village. It could easily be a supply hub, or the center of the Loachian's poisoning operation. We could be hopelessly outnumbered."

Calabella drummed her fingers upon the shaft of her mace as he she moved her jaw back and forth, causing her tusks to sway in and out of her vision. "We don't have a choice," she decided. "We have to stop their poisoning operations."

"So we just charge in and hope we choose the correct building, and that we aren't outnumbered?" Nellandra asked incredulously. "That's not a plan!"

Calabella shoved her finger into the shorter woman's sternum. "I am in charge. Not you," she growled. "And I never said that we charge in. We'll smoke any Loachians out. Set fire to a few of the buildings. See what hole, if any, that they dart from. Then finish them off."

"And if they have more men? If the fire spreads?" persisted Nellandra. "Is there a plan for that."

"The fire won't spread to the flintwood trees. They won't ignite," said Calabella. "And we'll crush the Loachians, numbers or not. They'll be panicked. Now let's get into position. Groups of four. Set fires where you can and prepare to kill the Loachians as they rush out."

Calabella readied her mace and shield, and peeled off from the group with three other women close behind her. Sneaking was not her forte, she was better suited to a charge. She tried watching where she placed each foot, careful not to step on branches, twigs, leaves, and the like. They moved quickly from building to building, peeking around corners and into windows when they could. The outskirts of the village were quiet as Calabella expected. Any resistance would most likely be nearest to the village common grounds.

It was common in Antier to leave a community well in the center of the village, as well as open grass for community functions, dances, markets and the like. Proximity to the well would be important for an enemy force occupying Flintwood Village.

Calabella communicated with the other six groups via hand signal. Their movement was slow and methodical. Each group instructed to communicate whether they spotted any forces as they crept along.

They reached the ring of buildings encircling the common grounds without hearing or seeing any signs of Loachian forces. She hesitated before giving the order to set the buildings on fire. Part of her wished her reluctance was because she thought the buildings could house people resettling the area. But the truth was, she was worried that the Loachians were out on a patrol, and the fire would alert them to the Antierian forces.

Calabella gnawed at her lower lips as she thought. War required decisive decisions, but they needed to be the correct decision. Failing to act could potentially put the entire army at risk.

She motioned Nellandra to burn the buildings. She would rather take action and be wrong, than do nothing and suffer a catastrophic defeat.

Flames went up around the common grounds as the Antierians moved swiftly from building to building, setting them aflame. Calabella's instincts screamed at her to run away from the fire. That flame was nature's way of dealing out death. But she fought down that instinct and waited.

The silence was broken by shouts and yelling as a commotion grew within three of the buildings. Calabella motioned the Antierians into position and waited. This was the true opening skirmish to the war, and it was one she intended to win. The faces around her were nervous, the gravity of the situation slowly sinking in.

As the first men began to pour out of the buildings, a thought struck Calabella. She should have ordered the fires started at the entrances to the building. Make the Loachians have to flee through windows or create their own exit.

Her second thought was delayed in arriving. More Loachian men than she anticipated fled out of the burning structures. They were in various states of dress and combat readiness, but still outnumbered her troops by at least three to one.

Calabella was paralyzed as she watched her troops execute the plan and charge the Loachian men. She could not breathe, could not move. Her body was a prison, unwilling or unable to react to her commands. She could only pray as she watched the madness unfold.

Nellandra slashed an unarmed man across his arm. The man screamed as he clutched at his arm at the triceps. His comrades did not hesitate however. The next man tackled Nellandra, forcing her to the ground, as he slashed her throat with a belt knife.

The same scene played out over and over as the seasoned Loachian soldiers quickly adjusted to the surprise attack. Many of them died, but their numbers quickly overwhelmed the small group of Antierian attackers.

Calabella tried to scream the order to retreat. Spittle flew out of her mouth. It was completely dry and felt like cotton was shoved into her mouth.

The last Antierian fell in the ill-fated assault. A man, a boy really, one that she did not know that well, took a spear in his intestines. He howled in pain as the spear pinned him to the ground. By all accounts that was a very painful way to die.

Calabella's feet remained planted in the exact same spot where she gave the order to fire the buildings. A voice told her to charge, go down in battle with her troops. But a second more persistent and logical voice told her to flee. There was nothing more that she could accomplish here. If she left now, the smoke from the burning buildings would cover her retreat.

The second voice claimed victory as her body found its argument persuasive. She found herself taking a few hesitant steps backwards without her mind having consciously made that decision. Soon she was in the Flintwood, trees rushing past her in a blur as her tears and shame consumed her.

CHAPTER TEN

"Will you need any help out there?" Tigun asked Randall eagerly. "We can grab a lot more with two of us."

Randall shook his head in the negative as he slipped into his work clothes. Dark woolen trousers with a long sleeved tunic that he liberated from a tailor last year. He draped his body in a dark cloak as well. It was a thin material that would not help much with shielding him from the cold as it was too small for his body, but it covered his face. He would prefer wearing a mask, but if he did that he might as well walk up to a watchman and introduce himself as a thief.

"No, I don't," answered Randall as he double checked that he had his burlap sack, a dagger, and his lockpicks. "Two people increases the chances that we'll be spotted."

"But people travel in pairs at night all the time," Tigun protested.

"Not on the rooftops," said Randall.

Tigun sagged as his body deflated in disappointment. "Fine," he said. "I'll look over the rest of the kids while you work. I'll wait up for you to get home."

"No need," said Randall. "I'll either come home, or I won't. Get your rest. And do not wait up on the roof. We don't need people asking questions about why children are coming and going into this warehouse."

Randall scurried out into the night, leaping agilely from rooftop to rooftop. His target tonight was a jeweler in the Central District. The shop was mighty inviting. A large three story affair, with an easily accessible rooftop. Entering the building should not be difficult.

The first floor of the jeweler was visible from the street. It was open to the public and displayed many fine pieces of jewelry for the nobles and merchants that frequented the shop. That was not his target on this night.

The additional two stories meant that there was more to the jeweler's shop than just the first floor. Merchants in the Central District rarely lived above their shops. Randall overheard merchants drinking at an inn describe such accommodations as being poor for the general ambiance of the district.

Without living quarters, the two additional stories of the building would be where the jewelers worked. It would have the jeweler's inventory including completed pieces, to raw metals and uncut gemstones. The latter was Randall's target. Without defining features, the metals and gemstones would be impossible to trace. Trying to fence the finished products would be tantamount to placing his head in the hangman's noose. Only the incredibly rare artifact was worth that risk.

The mood in the city remained tense, the war hovering over every person. Most of the citizens had yet to notice the different attitude of the watchmen. Their presence was significantly more noticeable, especially at night, while the number of urchins roaming the street was also on the decline. While the city's inhabitants who were out and about during the day had yet to recognize the shift, those who roamed the streets at night certainly noticed the difference. Taverns were less raucous, whores were quieter and less outright in their propositions, and the rooftops saw less traffic.

Randall hoped everyone was staying at home and not vanishing. Thefts were increasing throughout the city; even in the mines goods were vanishing. The watchmen would crackdown eventually. He just needed to have enough money and supplies built up to survive whenever that occurred.

The Central District was quieter than the North and Northeastern Districts. It was a reputable area for the upper crusts of Loach. There were not taverns, but inns and hotels. Whores did not walk the streets or sell their services in dingy whorehouses. No, Central had brothels that were populated with courtesans.

Propriety ruled the streets at night in Central. Carousing at inns and brothels was not considered inappropriate, so long as one exercised discretion. Patrons routinely concealed their identities as they skulked from one location to the next.

The increase in watchmen was not as noticeable in Central. Harass the wrong wealthy person, and even the city watchmen could lose their heads. However, the trade off from city watchmen was that there were more private guards in Central. They were a more seasoned sort, the younger sellswords having already been hired to fight in the war or guard merchant caravans from unsavory characters, including those in uniform.

Randall landed lightly upon the jeweler's rooftop. It was relatively well maintained, with the remaining winter snow shoveled off of the rooftop and into an alley behind the shop. Luckily, the lack of snow would help conceal the fact that he was ever there.

He pulled gently on the trapdoor leading into the shop. Unlocked. Randall slipped inside, careful to stay on guard. He doubted he was the first person to ever encounter an unlocked jewelry store. People were notoriously protective about their jewels and precious stones. There was bound to be more security.

The upper levels of the store were less ostentatious than the fancy ground floor. Practicality ruled the day. Wooden walls and simple tile floors were used in the construction. Randall thought that it looked nice. A simple type of luxury. He crept slowly down the halls so as not to make noise upon the tile. One of these days he would rob a rich person with an affinity for soft plush rugs.

The upper floor was littered with workbenches and other equipment that Randall did not recognize. The jeweler must have kept this operation on the upper floor for a reason. Working with metal had to be noisy. Something that he probably preferred his clientele not hear.

Randall tried the door to the work room. It opened silently raising his hackles. Something was wrong. People did not simply forget to lock multiple doors. He drew his dagger and moved through the workroom as quietly as he could.

Metal bins lined the far wall. The jewelers must remove what they needed from the bins and bring it to their workbenches. Randall shuffled over and looked within. Various metals filled the boxes. Copper, silver, gold, platinum, and few other metals or alloys that Randall did not recognize. They were in various cuts and bound by wires, bands, rings, and the like. Everything was precut, most likely smelted down at a smithy and transported to the shop. But none of them had gemstones inset within them.

And none of the bins contained gemstones. Randall began to panic. He needed this score. His people depended upon him. He scooped up a few fistfuls of the smaller cut rings, earrings, and amulets. They were bound to weigh less. He quickly scanned the room, looking for the gemstones.

There was a small door along one of the inner walls. It was nondescript, and the only other possible place where the gems could be hidden.

Randall gently touched the handle and the door swung in softly without him twisting the handle. His palms began to sweat, and his heart beat like it was one of those drums at the prince's farewell parade.

He weighed the idea of backtracking and grabbing more jewelry, but dismissed the idea. The gemstones would fetch a far better price than the metals. Especially to a merchant that was not from Loach and lacked contacts within the mining company.

Randall snuck through the open door and into a small office. It was empty. A pressure released from his chest and he felt as if he could finally breathe again. A simple yet solid tdesk with books, probably ledgers, sat in the middle of the room. Behind the desk there was a safe. And its door was wide open.

Shock and depression hit Randall like a blacksmith's hammer. All that planning and work wasted. Someone already robbed the jeweler tonight! He should have left shortly after sundown instead of waiting until after midnight.

He hesitated and moved toward the safe. Maybe it would not be all for naught. The thief may have left something behind. After all, they had not touched the metal jewelry.

His jaw dropped as he reached the safe. Luck did not begin to describe his situation. The safe was full of gems. Both cut and uncut. He saw rubies, emeralds, sapphires, topaz, and others. All would sell well. He grabbed them by the handful and tossed them into his satchel. He was disappointed that there were not any diamonds in the safe, but it was still quite a haul.

Randall emptied the safe entirely. Everything went into his satchel. He would check his loot later. He glanced at the safe and felt a wave of relief wash over him. Behind the handle and lock was a system of stained needles. Poison was the most likely substance to be coating the needles. Randall never encountered a trap such as this. He would have died if he attempted to open the safe on his own.

He left the room in a rush. Well as quickly as he could without causing a racket. His satchel was significantly heavier than when he entered, yet he felt so much lighter. He closed the doors behind him as he made his way back to the rooftop. The hired guards did not have access to this floor from what Randall could tell. It really was his lucky day.

The trapdoor settled behind him quietly as he took a deep breath of night air. His mirth slowly dwindled as his senses caught up with him. Shouting filled the night air. Randall peered out from the rooftop to see if his higher vantage point could help him pinpoint the source of the disturbance.

Flames flickered in the night off to the east. Torches, and a lot of them. That usually meant the City Watch was in pursuit of a criminal.

Panic rose in his chest as he thought of the already burgled jewelry shop. It quickly subsided when he told himself that there was no way that they could be chasing after him. The shop was too orderly, and the watchmen were making too much noise. They must be chasing after some other thief.

Randall whispered a quick prayer of thanks to the gods and set off into the night. There was no need to tempt fate. Just because the watchmen were pursuing someone else, did not mean he should stand still and provide them with the opportunity to catch him. The sounds of shouting slowly faded as he fled towards home, a smile engraved upon his face.

Chapter Eleven

Some days Owen detested being a member of the City Watch. Long hours, high danger, and everyone looked at him like he was the criminal.

Tonight? Tonight was one of the worst. Sprinting after a thief in a prolonged chase was exhausting. But circumstances required the pursuit. The victim was not just a member of a high profile society, but the entire society itself. And the culprit, who managed a few murders in the process of his larceny, refused to stop, leading Owen on a merry chase through the streets of Loach.

The cry of theft and murder rang out half an hour ago from the Eldritch Society. Every watchman in the Eastern District rushed to the scene. The front of the Eldritch Society building occupied half of a city block. It was a large stone complex with multiple towers and spires jutting up into the sky. Wizards apparently needed all the space they could muster to perform their experiments and "magic".

Owen had purchased one of their flamesticks for his nephew. The little man nearly set a tenement dwelling on fire by igniting a pile of laundry. Owen's brother confiscated the flamestick immediately following the incident. The brothers had opened up the metal pipe and found that pressing the button on it merely cause some flammable oil to enter a separate compartment and ignite upon touching the air. Hardly magic, but it sold for a fair amount of gold.

The intruder had broken into the wizards' compound and swiped some objects. From the bits and pieces of second-hand reports that Owen overhead, he determined that the intruder stole some books, jewelry, and other wizardly garbage.

The compound was in flame by the time he arrived on the scene. The wizards in their infinite wisdom had determined that the perfect way to deal with an intruder was to incinerate him. Naturally, they never stopped to consider that using aopen fire inside of your home was a decent method to burn it to cinders all around you.

To make matters worse, watchmen spotted the intruder leaping out of a window. Owen had bellowed for the watchmen to pursue the thief. Prince Fotlin was already breathing down all of their necks to capture the thieves responsible for the upswing in larceny throughout the city. Tomorrow morning the prince would be receive a report that one of the wealthiest and most influential societies in the kingdom was burgled, had its members or guards murdered, and that their headquarters in the duchy was covered in ash.

Owen needed to protect himself from that report. He needed the thief in custody. He needed the items returned to the Eldritch Society. At a bare minimum he needed a description of this murderous brigand. On a more personal level, allowing the thief to escape would be disastrous for him. Fotlin was not known for his compassion.

He estimated that his pursuit of the intruder lasted five minutes and wound through numerous streets. The winding route made it difficult for his men to split up, anticipate the thief's route, and cut off his escape.

The man was fast, and the watchmen were unable to close the gap behind him. Owen struggled with estimating distance; it just was not one of his skills. He placed the thief's lead at maybe five seconds. Judging by the burning sensation in his lungs, that lead was not going to shrink any time soon.

The thief ducked down the alley just past The Royal Scholar inn. A sense of triumph surged through Owen's body as a menacing grin spread across his face. That alley ended in a dead end at the wall separating the Eastern and Central Districts. The thief would have nowhere to hide!

Owen rounded the corner and the smile vanished from his face. The alley was empty! That was impossible! There was nowhere for the man to run! People did not just vanish.

A flash of light appeared at the end of the alley. Two globes of orange fire flew past him, splashing against the watchmen flanking him. The duo screamed as the flames stuck to their uniforms, slowly burning leather, cloth, and flesh.

"Get behind cover!" Owen cried as he dove behind a barrel, absently cursing himself for shouting. He did not need to draw the attention of the thief, and make himself the focus of the next blaze.

Owen peeked out from behind the barrel searching for the source of the fireballs. But the alley was empty. That did not last long as another pair of fireballs shot over his head towards the watchmen just beginning to enter the alley.

He breathed a prayer as he traced the fireballs' trajectories with his eyes. No firestick could conjure that sort of flame. The source of the fire was not from the base of the wall, but originated from on top of the wall. The thief was standing there in his dark hooded clothing with both arms extended before him. The man's head turned towards Owen's general direction and he felt his blood freeze. His left hand twisted in Owen's direction. Owen's body locked up in fear as he prepared himself for a fiery death.

The fiery globe of death never sought him out. The man waved jauntily at him and ran off down the wall into the darkness.

Owen gaped at his departing target. There was no way the watchmen would be able to reach the top of the wall in time to stop the man. None of them had wings, or a totem powerful enough to strengthen their legs to jump that high. That the thief could reach the top of the wall made his hair stand on end.

"Quickly men, break up and head into the Central District," he shouted. "The thief has reached the top of the wall. We need to cut him off. Hurry!"

The men grumbled and broke off on the hopeless errand with muted enthusiasm. Owen could not blame them. They knew the height of the wall, and could estimate how strong the thief must be to reach those heights. By the gods, he managed to break into the Eldritch Society and murder some of the wizards. What hope did simple watchmen have against someone like that?

Owen closed his eyes in resignation. Tomorrow's report to Prince Fotlin was not going to be pleasant.

Chapter Twelve

D alton grumbled under his breath as he stretched the night's knots out of his body. He loathed sleeping on the ground. Especially when there were warm beds nearby. Prince Nelson in his grand magnanimous nature determined that guards, even if they were part of the nobility, did not warrant beds paid for with gold from his own purse. However, the miser was willing to spare a few coppers to let them sleep in the inn's stables.

And if there was one thing Dalton hated more than sleeping outside, it was sleeping in a stable. The smell of horse and manure clung to his clothing and remained in his nostrils for days. Atticus, Telwin, and Lentil took Nelson up on his generous offer last night. So instead of smelling animals on himself all day, Dalton was forced to endure the odors emanating from his so-called friends for the foreseeable future.

Making the journey even more difficult was that Dalton did not even know what they were supposed to do. Emkario said they would be escorting Prince Nelson to Biona. But Nelson led them off of the King's Highway days ago. They were currently travelling west through the duchy of Ochandor and Dalton wanted to know why.

Nelson refused to divulge their destination. Well not so much as refused, and more that he just did not deign to converse with his Antierian companions. Being newly engaged had not done any wonders for Nelson's already prickly disposition. The man was sullen, withdrawn, and entirely too concerned with maintaining his image. Dalton thought the man would execute a court bow to a cow if one merely convinced him that the cow was bovine royalty.

"I see that you are awake early," said Nelson as he walked out of the inn. The man walked stiff, upright. "I expected you to be the last awake. You strike me as the lazy sort. Tell me, why did you not sleep in the stable with the others?"

Dalton narrowed his eyes as he glared at the pompous idiot. "Stables are for animals," he said hotly. "Property. And no one owns me. Not even you, Your Highness." He sneered as he said Nelson's title. The man irritated him to no end.

Nelson arched an eyebrow at him. "I see," he said simply, his melodious voice making the statement sound as if it held some grand mythic importance.

Dalton's three comrades exited the barn brushing hay off of their clothes. Dalton felt some measure of sympathy for them. Hay always stabbed him through his clothes when he slept on it. His momentarily lapse of emotion quickly vanished as their scents assaulted his fragile nose. Dalton liked to channel that part of his totem at all times, but the three of them made him strongly reconsider that approach.

"Good morning gentlemen," said Nelson as he tossed a cloth-wrapped bundle to Telwin. "Breakfast for the four of you."

"Mmm bread," said Telwin without a hint of sarcasm. Dalton wished that he knew how the man managed that tone. Telwin was adamant that he was always earnest in everything he said. Dalton doubted that. They were constantly surrounded by morons, pretentious assholes, and moronic pretentious assholes. Sarcasm was simply unavoidable.

"How'd you three sleep?" Dalton asked. If Nelson was going to feign concern for their appetites, it was the least he could to ask about their sleep.

"Just like home," said Atticus behind a yawn.

"He has a horse totem," Lentil explained to Nelson.

"Well then perhaps I may ask you for a ride if this journey drags on," said Nelson as if carrying him was such a great honor.

"I thought your soon to be wife was the only one permitted to give you a ride," sneered Dalton.

Something struck the side of Dalton's head. It was large, solid, and caused reverberations to shudder throughout his body. It must have been an anvil.

An anvil? Dalton thought as he picked himself up off the ground. *Why would there be an anvil? And when did I hit the ground?*

"That was wrong," said Lentil as he flexed his left fist. He regarded Nelson while rubbing his bull horns sheepishly. "Sorry about that, Your Highness. Dalton isn't like this usually. Well, he wasn't like this before Fort Hope. Well, you understand. Things happened there. We lost friends. He had a minor dalliance with a wine bottle."

"Lentil," said Telwin calmly as he placed a hand gently on his arm. "That's enough. You're rambling again."

"Ahh, my apologies," said the large man sheepishly.

"Nothing to apologize for. Either of you. Times have been difficult for everyone," said Nelson while managing to look dignified. Dalton scowled as he brushed the dirt off of his clothes. But with effort he kept his mouth silent.

"Luckily, we should reach the capital this morning," said Nelson as he turned and headed down the road.

"What are we going to do there?" Atticus asked eagerly.

"First, we'll stop by the Talendorian embassy and drop off a letter from Duke Havram," explained Nelson. "We'll be entering Ochandor by the Talendor Gate and will already be in their district. It will save us some time."

"Makes sense," agreed Telwin. Dalton doubted the man had ever visited the capital in his life, or even knew of its layout.

"After that, we'll head to the Bionan embassy. I'll send aerial messengers to my father, and confirm the whereabouts of our forces. If they're already en route to Antier, we'll meet up with them there. While at my embassy, I'll gather an honor guard and we'll head over to the Antierian embassy. I'll speak with the ambassador, and at the very least we'll restore the four of you back to life."

"What about Prince Darik and Jeron?" asked Dalton skeptically.

Nelson hesitated before answering. "I'm not sure," he said. "Prince Darik entrusted me with a letter. I am unsure of its contents. I'll deliver it to the ambassador and see how events unfold. Prince Darik's actions in Talendor are sure to spread through the kingdom like wildfire. But until they do, it may be safer for Darik and his companions if the kingdom is not made aware of his survival at this time."

"I can live with that," said Lentil.

"Me too," chirped Atticus from behind a mouthful of bread. "Besides, the duke and duchess should probably be informed first."

Nelson merely nodded solemnly, apparently at a loss for words. Dalton saw the wisdom in that course of action and decided to keep his mouth shut.

Returning back to life troubled him. How did one go about doing it? One day everyone assumes you are dead, and the next day you are alive again? How would people react to that? How would the duke react to that news? Dalton swallowed the rising lump in his throat as he realized that he would have to be the one to describe to the duke how his youngest son died.

Dalton glanced at his companions. They were silent with somber serious expressions upon their faces. He assumed they were weighing the same thoughts. Unlike Dalton, the three other boys had families back in Antier. Families that must have been devastated, and suffered untold grief at the news of their passing.

Dalton's family was years deceased. His only family left in the world was Jeron. And unlike Jeron, he arrived an orphan at the palace later on in life. He did not have that surrogate parental relationship with the duke and duchess.

The group of boys remained silent for the rest of the morning. Preoccupied with their own thoughts and fears. Atticus brightened as the sun rose in the sky. Apparently, he was fine with his return from the dead. Dalton envied him for that.

Just shy of midday they arrived at the city of Ochandor. It was the capital of both the kingdom and duchy of Ochandor and was built to match that reputation.

The city sat on an island in the middle of a lake. White stone walls surrounded the outer shore of the lake, with gates in the walls to allow in boats from the southern tributaries. Eight bridges extended over the lake. One for each duchy. Buildings, towers, domes, and other magnificent structures dotted the horizon.

White stone and marble were prominent in the construction of Ochandor, causing the light to reflect brightly upon the city.

"Your jaw is hanging open, Dalton," observed Nelson with a smile.

Dalton began to glare at the man until he saw that the man was not mocking him. Dalton barked out a harsh laugh. "I guess it is an impressive city."

"It is certainly that," agreed Nelson. "My first time seeing it, I couldn't fathom how anyone could live in a city without a grand port built for deep sea vessels."

"I see plenty of boats though," said a confused Atticus.

"Smaller boats," said Nelson dismissively. "Built for hugging the shore, or navigating a river. Not the real thing."

"Don't know much about boats or cities," said Lentil. "Now farming. I could tell you a bit about that."

"Maybe later," said Nelson. "Until then, let's try to make it to the Talendorian Embassy."

Nelson led them through the masses entering the city along the bridge. It was packed with people trying to travel to and from the capital. Surprisingly, Nelson did not try to force his way through the mass of humanity. He calmly waited his turn and allowed the crowd to dictate their pace.

Dalton and his fellow Antierians gawked at the sights as they walked through the gate. The city possessed an atmosphere unlike any he experienced before. The buildings were more beautiful than those in Antier, and less alien than those in Talendor. The citizens of Ochandor walked about with an air of contentment about them. The sense of desperation that was omnipresent in Antier and Talendor was absent. The people did not live their lives in fear of the next war, or of monsters invading their lands. It all seemed surreal, like a dream that Dalton knew could not be true.

"Be careful in Ochandor," whispered Nelson to the Antierians. "It isn't as peaceful and quaint as it appears. Plots and intrigue run rampant throughout the city. And not just between the duchies. Merchant guilds, the Church, the temples, and the societies are all trying to best each other at one thing or another."

"And we're at risk?" asked Telwin.

"Everyone is at risk," said Nelson. "You four more than most once you return from the dead."

"We're used to danger," said Dalton with a sense of resolute determination that surprised even him. "Nothing changes for us then."

"Oh, and be wary of pickpockets. The city is rife with them," advised Nelson.

After an hour they arrived at the embassy. The Talendorian embassy was an impressively large building constructed from the same red clay bricks common in the duchy. It certainly provided the building with a certain flavor and flair absent within the rest of the city.

The interior was as lavish as the Talendorian palace, complete with colorful murals and engravings. The guards barely paid any attention to them. Nelson bid the Antierians to wait in the foyer while he met with an unnamed diplomat. Dalton noticed that Nelson did not introduce himself by title, only as a messenger recently arrived from Talendor, carrying a letter from Duke Havram.

Dalton felt himself growing impatient quickly as he waited for Nelson. His anticipation and dread at returning from the dead was mounting as the day dragged on. But nothing happened inside the Talendorian embassy. Nelson returned and they left before Dalton could truly grow bored.

The Bionan embassy was more exciting. The water was a recurring motif inside of their embassy. Fountains dotted both the exterior and interior of the building. Columns resembled ship masts, and the walls were richly decorated in horizontal wooden planks that resembled a ship's hull.

Nelson again made them wait in the foyer. He cited the need to preserve Bionan state secrets. Dalton figured that the man was just being petty by forcing them to twist in the wind. Revenge for all of Dalton's snide comments most likely.

This time the other men shared in his trepidation. They fidgeted as they waited within the foyer, drawing the attention of the guards who kept glancing in their direction, hands inching closer to the swords hanging next to the colorful sashes worn around their waist. Even Atticus seemed worried. The boy's previously optimistic expression was gone, his teeth chewing furiously upon his lower lips.

"So what happens next?" asked Lentil. "I guess I am not heading back to my father's lands and growing corn?"

"Doubtful," said Dalton as he shook his head sadly. "I am fairly certain that we're going to be having a conversation with the duke about how Byron died. Then there is the matter of Darik being alive, and marching an army into Loach."

"So we're going back to war?" asked Telwin as he absently paced in a circle. "Seems that we've crossed the kingdom twice now to participate in what? Three wars now?"

"We have to talk to the duke?!" exclaimed Atticus, his eyes widening with shock and worry. "But we didn't do anything wrong! We fought hard against those monsters."

Dalton rubbed absently at his face with his hands. "I doubt you'll have to say much of anything," he said. "Me? Well, I'll have a lot of explaining to do. So would Cole and Jeron if they were with us." Dalton paused, his face still buried in his hands. Did Cole have a family? He must have mentioned it at some point. God, was he going to have to speak with them too?

Nelson took much longer with the Bionans than he did with the Talendorians. He rejoined them after an hour or two. He returned flanked by a group of ten soldiers clad in chainmail and bearing the tabards of Biona.

"My honor guard," said Nelson. "Men, allow me to introduce Dalton, Telwin, Atticus, and Lentil of Antier. Despite their appearances, all are noblemen and I expect them to be treated with the proper respect."

The men saluted, looking very formal and precise. Hardly the look of battle hardened soldiers. Dalton glanced sidelong at Telwin who was staring at the Bionan troops with a frown. Likely his thoughts mirrored Dalton's. Despite the age difference, the four Antierians were probably the most seasoned soldiers in their little company.

"Gentlemen, it appears that we will be travelling together for the foreseeable future," continued Nelson. "My father left a message in the event I arrived here first, ordering me to rendezvous with our forces in Antier. Are you ready to head to the Antierian embassy?" he asked to a chorus of groans and half-hearted responses.

Nelson frowned at them before leading them out of the embassy. It was a relatively short walk from the Bionan District to the Antierian District. Dalton welcomed the journey. The sight of familiar architecture interspersed with the white stone common in Ochandor helped set him at ease.

"Noticing the buildings, aren't you?" asked Nelson. "It's a fair observation. Antier was the last duchy to really see a surge in population and human settlement. For generations it was mainly farmland with hardly any people living in it. The Antierian District in the capital reflects that bit of history. Out of all the districts it has retained the most of the original Ochandorian construction. Some Antierians have slowly been remodeling the district to match their homeland, while others have preferred the more elegant original construction."

"I like the normal Antierian look," declared Lentil. "It feels like home."

"I do like the white stone," mused Telwin. "Looks fancy."

The Antierian embassy was a large stone building, essentially a miniaturized castle shrunk down in size and scope to fit into the district. The guards glared at everyone that passed by. War was causing everyone to see enemies lurking in every corner. Nelson identified himself to the guardsmen and one ducked inside to relay who he was.

"They're not letting us inside?" Atticus asked quizzically.

"Can't blame 'em," answered Telwin. "We're at war after all." One of the guardsmen looked at Telwin strangely. Dalton nearly smacked him upside the head for saying "we". They just needed to stay quiet for a little bit longer.

The door to the embassy creaked open as the guardsmen returned. "Please enter and be welcome, Your Highness," he said. "Ambassador Grigory will see you now." The guardsmen hesitated as the group stepped forward towards the door. "I am afraid that your guardsmen will have to wait outside. We are at war after all, and the ambassador is not permitting armed outsiders to enter the embassy."

Nelson bristled at the man's response. Dalton could not help but grin. Antier's status of the frontier caused its citizens to have a gruffer nature. Polite manners usually found in court were conspicuously absent in Antier. While Nelson may find their straightforward manner insulting, Dalton knew that was just the way things were back home.

"Very well," said Nelson behind a forced smile. "Men, you stay here. Gentlemen, come along now."

"I'm sorry, Your Highness. But outsiders are not permitted," the guardsmen insisted.

"Outsiders?" asked Nelson with a raised eyebrow. "My dear man, these are not outsiders, but members of Antier's military. Noblemen to boot."

"These scruffy guys are supposed to be Antierian soldiers and nobles?" asked another guardsman.

"Indeed," said Nelson. "All four are survivors of Prince Byron's forces at Fort Hope."

The guardsmen spluttered and stared in shock. Most of them. The one standing in the doorway seemed to grow enraged. "Fort Hope! You insolent little bastard. I lost a cousin there. Prince or no prince, I'm going to—" the man doubled over as Dalton buried a totem-backed punch into his stomach.

"Try to show some respect," said Dalton as he tossed the doubled over guardsman to his compatriots. "You are talking to our allies after all."

Dalton strode into the embassy with Nelson hot on his heels. "That was incredibly rude and not the way diplomacy works," insisted Nelson.

"It's how we do things in Antier," retorted Dalton. "Saves everyone the time of pretending that they aren't offended."

Nelson elicited a wonderful harrumph as he pushed past Dalton and strode towards the waiting servant. "Prince Nelson Wilcox to see Ambassador Grigor," he said stiffly.

The servant led them up a few flights of stairs and down a long hallway. The decorations in the embassy were fine, but not as extravagant as the palace back in Antier. The servant opened a door to a conference room while announcing "Prince Nelson Wilcox of Biona."

The ambassador was a reedy man with a wispy ring of white hair around his bald head. The whites of his eyes gleamed a dark yellow, nearly gold. And while age had ravaged his hairline and body, his skin remained young and fresh, as if newly grown.

"Welcome, Prince Nelson," his eyes narrowed as his tongue, surprisingly not forked, darted out to wet his lips. "And just who are these four distinguished...gentlemen?"

"Thank you, ambassador," said Nelson as he bowed with a flourish. He lifted his arm towards Dalton as he introduced the Antierians. "Allow me the pleasure to introduce four of your own. My travelling companions, Dalton, Lentil, Telwin, and Atticus. All Antierian nobility, and all recently served with Prince Byron at Fort Hope."

The ambassador's eyes widened at the news. "Prince Byron and Fort Hope?" he stuttered, momentarily caught off his guard. "My my. That must be quite a story."

"It is," said Dalton, annoyed at the diplomat's obsequious tone of voice. "But we'll be telling that news to the duke first. Directly."

"Of course, of course," said the ambassador in a silky smooth voice. "But please understand, just because you say you are who you claim to be, does not make it so. I must confirm your identities before I let you see the duke."

"They are who they are," said Nelson firmly. "Unless you are calling a prince a liar?"

"A liar? No no. Of course not," Ambassador Grigory said quickly. "Mistaken? Perhaps mistaken. You are a prince from another duchy. How would you know if these young men are who they say they are?"

"Because Prince Darik confirmed their identities himself," said Nelson with a hint of a smirk on his face. "Or hadn't you heard about the dragon that appeared during the siege of Talendor?"

The wall panel along the far wall slammed open at Nelson's words, revealing another room beyond. A large man with a gray hair and eyes strode forth from the other room. He was richly dressed in fine clothes and a cape.

Dalton recognized him. Panic immediately set in as Duke Cedric glared at him. "Darik is alive?" he demanded without preamble. "Speak now, Dalton."

"Yes, Your Grace," stammered Dalton. "He survived the Loachian attack at Fort Hope. We ended up meeting in Talendor."

Dalton felt the sweat beading on his forehead underneath the duke's gaze. He was vaguely aware that everyone else in the room had stopped moving. Except for the ambassador. He was sitting back in his chair leveling an appraising glance at Dalton.

"Why Talendor?" the duke demanded.

Dalton shrugged. "Jeron said that you told Byron to go there if he was ever in trouble."

"That's true," said Duke Cedric as a pained expression crossed his face. "Is Jeron alive then?"

"Yes, Your Grace. He is with Darik and the mercenary force Duke Havram provided."

"Mercenary force?" asked the duke. "And who else survived?"

Dalton recounted events quickly for the duke. Summarizing the Loachian twin princes attempts on the lives of Prince Nelson and Prince Bondoril of Talendor, and Duke Havram pledging his support in the war with Loach. "And that is everyone," finished Dalton as he counted off the remaining survivors. "Your Grace, about Byron—"

"I already know what happened to Byron," said Duke Cedric sharply. "A few of the masters survived the betrayal by seeking refuge in the crypts. With what they told us, it was not difficult to determine that Barith and Timver were spreading lies in court. Once discovered, they were quite eager to tell the truth of what happened."

"Yes, Your Grace," said Dalton with a sense of relief. All of Byron's murderers lay dead. That was one less thing to worry about. "If you don't mind me asking, why are you in the capital?"

"King Ramon asked me to come," the duke said with a wry grin. "Apparently it bothers him when dukes wage war against each other in his kingdom."

"Excuse me, Your Grace," said Nelson as he stepped forward. "I am Pri—"

"Nelson of Biona," interrupted the duke. "Yes. I know. Thank you for bring-ing Dalton here. He is like a son to me after all." He paused to flash a quick smile in Dalton's direction. The budding sense of dread vanished from Dalton. The duke did not blame him for Byron's death! And he thought of him like a son. He never said that before. All sorts of buried emotions began to bubble up inside of him.

"But enough of that," said Duke Cedric. "Time is short, and we need to get you all out of here. Only rumors of events in Talendor have reached the capital. If the king learns that he has witnesses to both events in his city, he'll never let you all leave. Prince or not."

"What do we do?" asked Dalton.

"You leave immediately," answered the duke. "Take some food from the embassy, and gather some horses. I will send five members of my guard to accompany you. Along with Prince Nelson's men, you should have enough numbers to avoid trouble with bandits. Now go. The Antierian and Bionan armies are making camp near the Flintwood, just south of the border with Loach."

The duke did not wait for an answer. He motioned for the ambassador to follow him as he retreated back through the hidden door in the paneling.

"We met the duke," whispered Lentil reverently.

"Yes, you did," said Nelson has he patted Lentil's shoulder. "Now let's take his advice and leave town quickly. I don't want to be a 'guest' of the king."

CHAPTER THIRTEEN

Matlin poured over the maps while Clara read him the day's reports. It was early in the war, but they could use a victory. True, there had been that skirmish in Flintwood Village. His forces destroyed the smaller Antierian force, but not before the Antierians set fire to their supply of poison. That plan was effectively ruined, and ensured that a quick and decisive resolution to the war would not happen anytime soon.

"Aerial reports state that the mercenary force is moving at a steady pace through Kelon," Clara reported. "Our scouts and wraiths have not been able to approach while the force is in Kelon. The scouts say the ghosts make the forests too treacherous, and the wraiths state that the army would be too suspicious of any newcomers that arrived in ghost-infested lands."

Matlin grunted. "And they would be less suspicious of anyone that joined in Loach?" he said drily.

Clara shrugged. "People follow armies all the time. Seeking their fortune and profiting off of the soldiers' needs."

Matlin sighed. "Rhetorical question Clara. You don't have to be so literal all the time."

"I see," said Clara as she pursed her lips. "Moving on. Do you still believe that Prince Darik is leading that force?"

"It makes sense," said Matlin. "Our agents have not spied him anywhere else. And our reports state Duke Havram remains in Talendor caring for his injured son. Someone has to be leading the force, and Darik is the logical choice."

Clara tossed the stack of reports down on the table. "Well then, Your Highness, that brings us back to the same issue that we've been stuck on."

"Whether to split our forces or not," he agreed. It was a familiar argument, and one that they debated since hearing of the Talendorian force marching towards Loach. Alone, they could beat either force, eventually. Together, well, that was the risk. The Antierian force was green, and the mixed force of Talendorians and mercenaries lacked horses and conviction. Matlin doubted that they would stick around for a long grueling conflict. Well, he doubted it before Dedlin tried to murder their prince.

The poisoning plan was his idea to deal with one of the forces quickly. It was frustrating how one small group could cause him so much trouble.

"We can't stay here," Matlin said. "The Talendorian forces will appear from the east eventually. If they hit us from our flank while we are occupied with the Antierians..." he let his voice trail off.

"So we let them join forces?" Clara asked. "That seems risky."

"It is," replied Matlin. "But at least we get to choose the terrain. Pick a defensible position."

Clara grimaced. "Are we to turtle for the entire war?"

Matlin shook his head. "No, not that. We fight wisely." His finger hovered over the map. "Here," he said as he jabbed his finger down. "We fight here. The mountains will prevent them from attacking our supply lines. If we move our engineers immediately, and support them with some of our physically strongest totems, we may be able to fortify the position with a crude fort."

"And the Antierians will just sit back and allow us to construct defenses?" Clara asked skeptically.

"Of course not," said Matlin as he waved his hand dismissively. "Don't be absurd. They'll harass us at every step of the way. That's why a portion of our army will frustrate them every step of the way."

"And you will be leading the men in these battles?" Clara asked with a disapproving scowl on her face. "I don't like it. You should have the full backing of our armies behind you at all times."

"I agree," said Matlin. "And I need to remain here to protect our forces from an attack by Darik. I am the only one we have who can fight him on even footing. That is why you'll be the one leading our forces."

Clara gaped at him. "But who will watch your back?" she asked. "And will they actually follow me?"

Matlin nodded. "The men will follow you or suffer the consequences. As to the other..." he held his claws up before her with a predatory smile on his face. "Well I pity the assassin who tries to attack me."

Chapter Fourteen

Fotlin paced around the large circular table in his father's planning room. Everything was being ruined. The murders and theft at the Eldritch Society had sent the city into a turmoil. Everyone with any influence whatsoever was howling about the crime rate.

Murders had increased throughout the districts. Each morning his men found more people lying dead. So far, they were all urchins and street ruffians. No one missed them exactly, but no one liked finding their corpses in the street each morning either.

Fotlin assumed the Pojomites were behind the murders. He lacked any proof of their involvement. However, with the rise in successful crime it made sense. The thieves had too many targets and spoils to risk their lives fighting each other. And the Pojomites had been awfully silent following the break in at their temple. The only conclusion Fotlin could draw was that they were taking matters into their owns hands.

"Stop pacing. You're making me dizzy," drawled Yutlin as he slouched back in his chair, his feet up on the table.

Fotlin scowled at his little brother. He turned fourteen and suddenly he knew everything. "Be quiet," he growled as he stalked towards his little brother. "You don't actually know anything or have the first idea how things are run in this city. So shut your mouth and let me think."

Yutlin's face darkened with anger as he rose from his chair. He paused halfway out of his seat before he started chuckling. "No. I don't think I'll fight you," he said with a smirk on his face. "*I* haven't done anything to earn father's wrath. You on the other hand...well let's just say I want to see how things play out."

Fotlin gritted his teeth and clenched his fists. One of these days he would deck his little brother. He was old enough to take the beating without complaint. Fotlin hesitated as he was also old enough to take the beatings from both of his parents. And mother would not take it kindly if someone laid a finger on her baby boy.

That bothered him more than Yutlin's impertinence. It was always the baby boy, or Matlin was the eldest, or how pretty and sweet his sisters were. But when it came to him, it was always disappointment. Do better Fotlin. Stop picking on them Fotlin. He had no idea how Setlin dealt with all of it.

"Enough," bellowed his father's voice from the entrance to his quarters. "Both of you sit down and be quiet. Comport yourself as befits one of my children."

Duke Camen took his seat without bothering to confirm that the boys followed his orders. He expected compliance. And in Fotlin's experience, what the duke expected, he received.

"Now, Fotlin. Let's talk about Loach's crime problem," began the duke. "What are you doing to combat the problem?"

"Increasing patrols and watchmen stationed throughout the city," answered Fotlin. "Pickpocketing and market thefts have decreased drastically."

"Is that so?" said his father with an arched eyebrow. "Then explain to me why every noble, merchant, society member, and priest is battering down my door complaining about thefts and murders."

"Those are happening inside their buildings, within their security perimeter," said Fotlin as he felt his anger rising at the constant criticism. "We can't patrol inside every building within the city."

"I see," said the duke. "And barring that, what viable options are open to you?"

"Increased punishments for breaking the law?" answered Fotlin. "I'm not sure. Arrest any known or suspected criminal?"

"Hmm," said his father thoughtfully. "And you Yutlin? What would you do?"

Yutlin leaned forward, placing his elbows on the table. "That's easy," he said. "The people are no longer frightened of the law. We hang anyone who breaks the law. That will restore order."

"Are you insane?" Fotlin demanded angrily. "If we start killing people for every minor offense it won't be long until they start killing us. We won't have any watchmen left once that starts."

Yutlin shrugged unconcerned. "Then we only do it once or twice. Make a big show of the hangings and order will return. And if they get upset? Well, who cares? We can hang them too."

"And you think a few hangings will deter the thief who broke into the Eldritch Society, murdered the few wizards who stumbled upon him, stole their artifacts, and fled the City Watch while flinging fireballs from his hands and leaping up onto city walls?" asked Fotlin incredulously. "I've already hanged some people for serious thefts. It won't work."

Yutlin dismissed him with a wave of his hand. "Not our problem," he said. "He is obviously a wizard seeking revenge against his own society. The fireballs prove that. Let the wizards deal with their own."

"A bold plan," said Duke Camen, his rocky face impassive as usual. "I look forward to seeing its successful result."

"Father!" protested Fotlin, as Yutlin smirked in contentment. "This plan is madness. It's doomed to fail. We'll be hanging street urchins. I don't want to do that!"

"You won't son," said his father stoically. "He will." Yutlin's jaw dropped as their father pointed at him.

"Me?" Yutlin stuttered. "But I have never been a part of the City Watch before. I don't know anything about catching criminals!"

"Learn," said Duke Camen. "Your brother will remain in command of the City Watch, but will provide you with three patrols of watchmen to implement your plan. Remember Yutlin, if you come up with the plan, you better be prepared to see it through to the end. To reap the rewards, you also have to deal with consequences of your actions."

Their father left without another word. He rarely wasted time on goodbyes. Said it was energy he could exert thinking of something worthwhile.

Fotlin rounded on his brother, he could feel his temper rising at the sight of the insolent twerp. "Okay you little rat," he said. "Head down to the City Watch headquarters. Ask for Watchman Bruce. Tell him I said that his patrols are working under your command until I say otherwise."

"Don't you mean until father says otherwise?" Yutlin shot back.

"You are out of your mind if you believe father is going to micromanage the City Watch patrols," said Fotlin with an older brother smirk. "Now get down there and begin implementing your doomed plan. I won't have you blaming it on me. Just this once, father is going to see you for the rat that you are."

Yutlin extended his middle finger with a bratty superior smirk that all younger siblings seemed born with, and departed the planning room with a snicker.

Fotlin collapsed exhausted into his chair. He managed to survive another meeting with his father. Of course, matters in the city were only going to become worse once his brother implemented his foolish plan. And despite everything that transpired, they failed to compose a plan to deal with the intruder at the Eldritch Society. That was a problem that was not going to take care of itself.

Fotlin disagreed with his brother regarding the man. He did not believe the man was some rogue wizard out for vengeance. That idea was simply too fanciful and farfetched. But what did he expect? The idea came from a teenager after all. The simpler explanation was that he was the man behind most of the high profile thefts within the city. And Fotlin had no idea how to catch him.

Chapter Fifteen

R andall darted through the crowd with Tigun hot on his heels. Everything had been so simple. Steal the gemstones and then just wait things out until the right opportunity to sell them came along.

All they had to do was not steal anything. Wait out the authorities. They had enough money and supplies to do that. Their main enemy would be boredom. But boredom could be conquered.

Just not by children.

He and Tigun had tried their hardest to keep the young children occupied. The other children in their early teens had pitched in every now and then, but they mainly wanted to sleep. Randall should have seen it coming. He should have boarded up the exits. Done something.

Tiona had slipped out. Randall did not notice right away. It took him a few hours to find the loose board covering the old smugglers tunnel beneath the warehouse. Fear found him in that moment. Fear for Tiona, fear for himself, and fear for all the other children that called the warehouse home.

If Tiona was captured, she would squeal if put to the question. She would not survive imprisonment for long. She was too tiny and sweet of a child to handle the poor conditions and lack of food.

He and Tigun scoured the city searching for the girl. Randall left the other teenagers in charge of the children. Otherwise, they would all bolt and scatter throughout the city. Boredom was a terrible thing after all.

Tiona had strolled through the city with him a lot. But he had always led her through the city, and she rarely was awake on the return trip home. If she wandered throughout the city, she would be hopelessly lost. He could only pray that Tiona stuck with the areas that she knew well.

That meant the North Market. His lungs burned as he raced to the market. He ignored the stares from the merchants and watchmen. Hopefully, the latter assumed he was a bored child and not any sort of threat.

"You don't think she'd actually do anything stupid do you?" asked Tigun.

"No. I'm sprinting for the fun of it," replied Randall.

"She knows the rules, man," said Tigun. "She knows better."

"She's also eight years old," said Randall. "Knowing better doesn't always mean anything."

Tigun said nothing as they made their way through the market, careful not to jostle anyone. "This is pointless," Randall muttered. "How are we supposed to find an eight year old girl in these crowds?"

"We could search all day and never find her," agreed Tigun.

"Let's get to some high ground then," suggested Randall. "Maybe we'll be able to see her that way."

"Over there," said Tigun as he nodded to some crates leading up to a rooftop.

The boys scrambled up the crates quickly, and flattened their bellies against the rooftop. They crawled to the edge and peered out over the crowd.

"Do you see anything?" Randall asked hopefully.

"No. Should we move?"

"And do what?" asked Randall. "Shout out her name over the crowd and explain to the watchmen how we're looking for a lost little girl?" Tigun grunted in acknowledgement. "Where are her parents? How does she survive?" he said with a grimace. "We'd all be in prison."

"We'll just give it another few minutes," said Randall, his voice tinged with worry. "See what we can see."

They did not have to wait long. Within minutes a commotion broke out in the marketplace. Watchmen darted towards the disturbance, and the boys scampered across the rooftops seeking a better vantage point.

The watchmen gathered around someone, and judging by their body movements, that person was struggling against them.

"Can you see? I can't," said Tigun.

"No. Nothing."

"Randy! Help meeee!" shrieked a tiny voice from the marketplace. Randall gasped. He was unable to breathe. Panic set in as he buried his face into the rooftop and began sobbing.

The watchmen had Tiona. There was nothing he could do about it either. Stab all the guardsmen with his dagger? Unlikely.

"Randall," whispered Tigun sharply. "Randall. Something is happening. You need to see this."

Randall wiped the tears from his eyes and crawled back towards the edge of the rooftop. The watchmen gripped Tiona as she thrashed and wailed against them. A well-dressed kid that looked similar of age to Randall and Tigun stepped on top of a crate and held his hand up to the crowd. He was finely dressed and groomed. Those two attributes alone caused the marketplace to go silent at his command.

"Hello everyone," the boy shouted, his still high pitched voice struggling to carry over the crowd. "I am Prince Yutlin Loach, and I am in charge of implementing the duchy's new policy towards crime."

"What's policy?" whispered Tigun.

"I don't know. Police stuff? Isn't that another name for watchmen?" answered Randall.

The young prince cleared his throat before continuing his oration. "From now on. There will be zero tolerance for thievery of any kind. Who the thief is it does not matter. This young girl," he gestured down at Tiona. "A nobleman, a priest, it does not matter. If you commit a theft in Loach, you hang. No exceptions."

A strangled gasp rose from the crowd and just as quickly the crowd fell completely silent, not a word was spoken. Tears streaked down Randall's face as he watched frozen in horror. Tigun curled up into a ball and rolled away from the ledge, sobbing as his body convulsed in pain.

"The first hangings will be tomorrow at noon in the Old Plaza in Central District," the prince continued, no longer needing to struggle to be heard over the din of the crowd. "Your presence is requested. The duke wants you to know that we are all very serious about ending the crime spree that has beset our great city. Come and see. The truth will be revealed. Remember this girl's face. You will see this thief meet the gods tomorrow. Good day."

Prince Yutlin stepped down from the crate and walked calmly out of North Market, his cadre of watchmen dragging Tiona along in his wake. She screamed the entire way, her ragged voice tearing at Randall's soul with every scream.

Sounds of life slowly returned to North Market after the prince departed. But they were muted. The entire market felt depressed. Hearing that a young girl was to be hanged ruined the joy of shopping. Randall wanted to hate them. Hate them for not speaking up, for not preventing Tiona from being dragged away. But he had remained quiet too. He had not done anything.

"Randall, we still have a whole day," said Tigun, desperation lacing his voice. "We could do something."

"What can we do?" asked Randall. "Break into the city prison?"

"Well, maybe," said Tigun uncertainly.

"That would be a death sentence," whispered Randall as he closed his eyes. "Tiona knew the rules...she...I mean..." he fell silent, his voice failing him. Eventually he was able to gasp words out through his labored breathing. "We can pray to the gods. And we can attend tomorrow. Maybe we'll think of something. But – excuse me – it's the least we can do."

"Yes, it is," agreed Tigun. "We'll have to be extra careful tonight and tomorrow. If they're cracking down on crime, they may get Tiona to talk."

"We store the extra blankets, cloaks, and clothes in one of the extra rooms. We all sleep in the tunnel for the next few days," answered Randall, a bitter taste rising into his mouth. It was not five minutes since the watchmen dragged Tiona away, and they had already moved on to planning their survival.

Randall hated himself for that. He hated Prince Yutlin for what he planned to do. He would hate the city watchmen too, if he only knew their names.

Chapter Sixteen

The Old Plaza was a salute to Loach, complete with a plethora of flags, battle standards, and banners hanging above the grounds below. It was the site for great celebrations. The people and the nobility put on plays, parties, feasts, and great ceremonies in the Old Plaza. It was synonymous with great cheer and victory.

Today, the erected gibbet felt out of place. A dark spot shoved up against the cheery mood of the plaza. Stone buildings were built around the plaza grounds, encircling them and stretching as high as fifty feet into the sky. Banners and flags jutted out from these buildings; their poles firmly secured in the stone walls. Usually, their presence was forgotten, the only reminder they were even there was when they broke up steady beams of sunlight like man-made tree limbs. However, today, the ripple of their fabric in the wind was audible over the low buzz of the crowd.

People from all over the city had arrived at the Old Plaza. A difficult feat as only four narrow roads fed the plaza from the north, south, east, and west. The crowd was of all walks of life. Randall saw a pair of fat nobles wearing puffed out colorful sleeves chatting amicably in low voices, some merchants in well-crafted clothes that were still suitable for a day's labor, a gaggle of priests from various temples, a variety of mercenaries, and surprisingly, a mixture of beggars and urchins.

Randall bumped into everyone as he walked around in a haze. People muttered and patted at their purses, but no one raised a fuss. Even the adults did not want to draw attention to themselves. Not here.

Being short was both a blessing and a curse for Randall. There were many things and places that he simply could not reach. But there were also many tight places that he could sneak into that a larger person could not. However, seeing over a crowd was not one of the benefits of being short.

He was trying to reach the front of the crowd, provide Tiona with a reassuring face before the end. It seemed the least he could do for her. The crowd however was impenetrable, an unyielding mass of humanity. He could not bump, squeeze, or jostle his way through it. These people had arrived early and they were not about to miss the show.

Randall's eyes itched and burned. He could not stop yawning. His reactions were half a second late on everything. Staying up late was a necessary part of being a thief. But usually, he slept in and recovered from his nights out on the city.

Last night he tried everything he could think of to help Tiona. He scouted out the prison and the Old Plaza. The prison was a nut he simply could not crack. Patrols of watchmen marched along the walls and at every gate. And that was only from the outside. Who knew what was on the inside. Given time, he may have found a way inside the prison. A loose sewer grate, an old mining shaft that somehow connected to the prison. But there was no way to find that in one night.

He attempted to scount the Old Plaza, find some way to secure an escape for Tiona. However, the watchmen locked the area down tightly last night. No one was able to enter the plaza from the street or the rooftops. The watchmen were paranoid now. Archers were posted along the rooftops. How effective they would be with the flags and banners in their sights, Randall did not know. He also did not want to find out.

He was helpless in this situation, and he knew it. He could not even try to give Tiona some comfort. He was a failure.

"This way," said Tigun as he tugged on Randall's sleeve. "We can climb on top of that wooden awning over there. It looks sturdy enough to support our weight."

"And if the watchmen see us?" Randall asked wearily.

Tigun shrugged. "We're just two more people in a crowd. Everyone is trying to see the...everyone is trying to see."

The duo labored their way through the press of humanity. They moved slowly, in no particular hurry to reach their destination. They climbed the rickety stack of crates and pulled themselves up on top of the awning. They drew their knees to their chests and sat and waited. Neither of them feeling the urge to speak.

The crowd milled about waiting for the arrival of noon. Some enterprising vendors set stalls up outside the plaza. The nature of the proceedings ensured that no one would be bold enough to attempt to steal from the makeshift stores. The smells of food enticed the crowd into buying. They were already on edge, and they calmed their nervous energy by eating.

Noon came sooner than Randall expected. Trumpets and drums announced Prince Yutlin's arrival long before he came into view. A parade entered the plaza by the eastern road. Randall frowned at that fact. The city prison was in the Western District. Did they house the prisoners in the palace, or transport them in that direction so Prince Yutlin did not have to travel to the prison?

The parade was smaller in size and scope than Prince Matlin's military send-off. Yet it still had the same trappings. Trumpeters, drummers, priests from various orders, and a gaggle of court ladies too old to be attracted to the young prince.

Watchmen led the procession carrying chains that dragged the prisoners behind them. Randall counted ten prisoners, all dirty, and all wearing clothes that marked them as street urchins or beggars. Prince Yutlin rode behind them on a grand white horse. He was bedecked in fine silks and jewelry, glimmering like a hero out of one of the temples' stories.

"He sure has a high opinion of himself, doesn't he?" spat Tigun.

"I hope he falls from that horse and breaks his neck," said Randall bitterly.

They watched the procession make its way to the center of the plaza. The immovable crowds parted for the prince. The watchmen marched their shackled prisoners up the steps of the gibbet and led them each to a noose. Ten nooses awaited the ten prisoners, the ropes already measured to the prisoners' heights.

Which meant that they did not even need to lift Tiona up into her noose. The watchmen reluctantly tightened it around the whimpering girl's neck, trying hard to ignore her existence as if her cries had no effect upon them.

Prince Yutlin dismounted off his horse and bounced jauntily up the steps of the gibbet. His merry attitude was in sharp contrast to the somber pall hanging over the city folk. The beaming prince raised his hands up to the crowd, imploring them for a silence that already existed.

"Welcome everyone!" he exclaimed. "I am thrilled to see that so many of you have shown up to witness the restoration of justice to Loach. Lest you forget, we are at war. Capital punishment will remain in effect for theft for the duration of the war. The city will remain safe and prosperous while our forces deal with the Antierian heathens!"

Silence greeted the boy until he began to scowl at the crowd. Nervous applause began with those at the front and slowly swept its way back through the crowd. The prince flung out his arms in exuberant joy as he basked in the crowd's adulation. He gestured towards one of the watchmen and the rope supporting the gibbet was cut.

The paneling beneath the prisoners gave way, and their bodies dropped. The ropes around their necks snapped taut. A few snapping sounds were audible as some of the prisoners mercifully had their necks snapped. Tiona was not one of them.

She struggled against the noose, her face turning red and then finally a shade of blue and purple. Her legs kicked as her mouth tried unsuccessfully to scream. Randall tried to stand, tried to lunge towards Tiona, but Tigun was faster. He restrained Randall until Tiona ceased to struggle.

Her tiny body hung in the air, lifeless, suspended only by the rope attached to the crossbeam. Randall stared at it blankly. He felt hollow inside. He could not muster any rage or sorrow. He let himself just go away for a little while. He did not have words to describe it, and he did not care.

Tigun guided him home from the plaza. Randall vaguely noticed the press of the crowd around them. Part of him was accustomed to death. Living on the street taught him that life was short and fragile. But it was different with Tiona. The little one was so sweet and innocent. She did not deserve the gibbet.

And why was she dead? Because of the thefts in Loach? Because of him? He was only trying to survive. Make a better life for their miserable little group.

Well, if stealing was what was making Prince Yutlin's life more difficult, he would increase his efforts. He did not care about any war. He had never even met anyone from Antier. But if it was war the prince was concerned with, he would wage war. And the City Watch would lose.

Chapter Seventeen

Atrisha scowled as the Bionan patrol departed the camp. Ever since the Bionans arrived, Captain Iandrick was assigning the majority of the dangerous missions to men, whether they be Bionan or Antierian.

Iandrick and Levren insisted it was because the men were more experienced, but Atrisha knew the truth. Ever since Calabella returned alone from her patrol, the captains had been withdrawn. Their reluctance to use their female soldiers was palpable to everyone in the camp, and it made Atrisha furious.

"They have no right to keep us from the battles," she insisted to Olivia and Calabella.

"Yes, they do," said Calabella softly from the rock she was sitting on. She was quiet and meeker since her mission. She no longer walked around with her tusks protruding from her skull. Worse, she agreed with the captains' refusals to send them out on missions, preferring to sit on that rock and stare off into the distance.

"That was one time," said Olivia, her face locked in determination. "One time. Was it a mistake? Sure. But when our reinforcements reached the village and searched the burnt out houses, they found cauldrons that had held that poison." She grabbed Calabella's chin and jerked it up until they were looking eye to eye. "You did the wrong thing for the right reasons. Yes, people died. But you also saved a lot of lives. Stop feeling sorry for yourself."

Anger flashed quickly in Calabella's eyes as she leapt up from her rock. "Damn right I'm feeling sorry for myself," she shouted. "But at least I can still feel! That's something Nellandra can't do anymore. And why? Because I was stupid. I thought I would just charge in there and roll over the Loachians." She snorted out a scornful laugh. "There I was acting like some fool in a story. Like the enemy would fall before us because our cause was just. Idiot."

Atrisha rolled her eyes and let Olivia handle the outburst. Atrisha handled Calabella's previous outbursts; it was only fair that Olivia pitch in this time.

"Don't be ridiculous," said Olivia, her voice filled with scorn. "You were forced to make a judgment call without experience. You think I don't know how you felt? When we charged those bandits as trainees back on the way to the capital, who was in charge? It wasn't you. It was me. I made the decision back then knowing full well that I might be sending you all to your deaths." She brushed a few strands of hair back off of Calabella's defiant face. "I was lucky. None of you died. You weren't as lucky. Learn from it. The decisions aren't going to be getting any easier."

"They still should let us fight," said Atrisha as she gazed up at the clouds. She was sorely tempted to spread her wings and search out isolated Loachians on her own. "There's no reason to keep us all here."

"They aren't keeping all of us here," said Calabella hotly. "Just us. Only the officers."

"What?" hissed Atrisha. She kept her voice pitched low as she turned slowly on Calabella. "What do you mean just us?"

Calabella shrugged, unconcerned at Atrisha's frigid behavior. "They take female soldiers with them. They say it's so they can get seasoning and experience."

Olivia picked up a small stone and tossed it out into the tall grasses. "They don't trust us," she said angrily. "Otherwise, we would be out there too. Learning from our mistakes, becoming more experienced."

Atrisha frowned as thoughts of her father flooded through her mind. He was a kind loving man, always trying to protect his daughter from harm for as long as he could. He always said it was his job to protect her from danger. Eventually, and after a lot of convincing, he admitted that she was capable of protecting herself.

"Maybe," Atrisha said slowly, her voice uncertain. "They don't trust themselves. They placed Calabella in command of the patrol. That was their decision, and it had terrible consequences. Maybe they are simply holding us back, trying to protect *us* from *their* mistakes."

Olivia snorted. "Protecting us from getting better," she said. "And making us look ineffective to the troops."

"Oh, I agree," said Atrisha. "I am only suggesting that their intent might be in the right place. We just need to convince them that they are wrong. We are not dolls that need protecting. We're trained. Let us lead."

Calabella sighed but remained silent. Olivia narrowed her eyes at the tall woman. "Oh, I agree," she said. "Anything is better than this constant waiting around."

"Let's go talk to them then," declared Atrisha. "I mean they're both walking right there...they're both walking right there? But why?"

Even Calabella stood up to look at the sight. Captains Levren and Iandrick rarely left the command tent. They ate and slept there. If they left, there had to be an important reason for it.

Atrisha focused, changing her eyes into an avionic shape. The camp itself was in order. Nothing was out of place. She looked at the captains, and there was a slight man with them. Lightly armed and armored. A messenger.

"Hmm, there is a messenger with the captains," she mused out loud. "They all are staring down the road to the south."

"Can you make anything out?" Olivia asked.

Atrisha stared down the road. Far in the distance a cloud of dust was hovering above the rode and moving towards them. Multiple riders. "Multiple riders are coming up the road from the south. A small group is peeling off and heading to the Bionan tents."

"That's strange," said Calabella. "Bionans and Antierians travelling together? We haven't seen any mixed unit reinforcements."

Olivia frowned. "No, we haven't. And there haven't been any reports or notices of reinforcements. Trish, can you make out their identities?"

"Just give me a minute," said Atrisha, her voice tinged with annoyance. Olivia was tempestuous and demanding. When she wanted something, she wanted it that instant. It was not one of her better qualities.

Atrisha counted nine riders, all male. They looked rough, dirty, and unshaven. Five of them wore Antierian tabards and rode as if they were guarding the other four. Not guarding them like they were prisoners, but as if they were allies. Atrisha kept her eyes on them as they made their way up the road, they were still too far out of sight for her to make out their features.

"Masters Tyson, Sildun, Richard, and Maxus have joined the captains," Olivia observed. "I think it is safe to say that something serious is happening. Trish, do you have anything yet?"

Atrisha flicked her hair back in annoyance. "Nine riders heading this way, five in Antierian tabards protecting the other four. They're almost in eyesight. Give me a minute," she grumbled. The riders slowly came into focus and she felt her heart leap into her throat. Electricity shot through her body. Surprise, and a nearly forgotten emotion, hope, rushed through her.

"Dalton," she breathed before spreading her wings to fly straight towards him. If Dalton was alive, then Cole may be as well!

Olivia and Calabella snatched her and pulled her back down to earth. "Where do you think you are going?" demanded Olivia.

"And what do you mean by 'Dalton'?" asked Calabella.

"One of those riders is Dalton!" declared Atrisha. "He survived the Loachian ambush at Fort Hope!"

"That-that is unbelievable," whispered Calabella.

"Indeed," agreed Olivia. "And it explains why the captains and masters are gathering. I think we should be joining them. We are officers after all."

"I say we should just go ahead and speak to Dalton ourselves," said Atrisha. "The captains didn't invite us after all; they can wait their turn."

"And that is going to get them to trust our judgment for missions how?" asked Olivia. "You can pepper Dalton with questions in their presence as well."

Atrisha did not sulk or complain. That was not her method, no matter what outrageous claims Olivia made. She simply reevaluated her options and decided that Olivia's plan was the most likely to succeed.

A thousand questions danced in Atrisha's head. Nearly all of them relating to what happened at Fort Hope and Cole's whereabouts. Her stomach turned itself into knots just thinking about it. She had the chance to live again. Maybe be happy again. Or maybe finally allow Cole's memory to rest in peace.

Captain Levren grimaced as the women arrived. Atrisha could not say why, but Levren's reaction pleased her.

"Captains, lieutenant," greeted Captain Iandrick with all the warmth of a Loachian winter. "What are you doing here? If you're not too busy, I am sure we can find something else for you to do."

"Like lead soldiers into battle?" Atrisha asked sardonically. The captains glared at her while Master Tyson knuckled his nose, trying to hide a grin behind his fist.

Olivia quickly stepped in and broke the silence. "And since we have not been assigned any duties, an oversight I am sure, we thought we would greet our friend. Especially since we thought he was dead."

Master Maxus stared at Atrisha and Olivia with sympathy in his eyes. "Ladies," he said, his voice nearly overwhelmed with compassion and emotion. "Don't think for an instant that we are unaware of your relationships with Cole and Jeron. Perhaps it would be for the best if you let us question Dalton about these matters first."

Olivia planted her hands on her hips with a huff and a glare. Atrisha decided to forego fury, and level her best emotionless glare at the paladin.

"Perhaps we can make that decision for ourselves," said Olivia hotly.

"And perhaps we don't need you all deciding when we need protection," said Atrisha as she drummed her fingers on her sword hilt.

The masters did not react how Atrisha expected. Tyson and Sildun burst into laughter, while Richard muttered some disgruntled curses underneath his breath. Maxus, Iandrick, and Levren varied their expressions between angry and impassive, unsure of whether to berate them for their remarks.

Dalton reined his horse in; sparing them from extending the awkward moment. He grinned an insolent smirk at them. "So be honest," he said without preamble. "How many of you thought I was dead?"

Silence greeted him.

"What?" he asked innocently as his eyes darted back and forth, unable to make eye contact with any of them. "It was a near thing many times. By God, I even crossed the kingdom twice in order to get here."

"Dalton," said Maxus coolly. "We are all quite surprised to see you. However, we have heard some stories about what happened at Fort Hope-"

"Right," interrupted Dalton. "Duke Cedric mentioned Barith and Timver confessing." His face grew more solemn as he regarded them. "Byron is indeed dead," he turned and looked at Olivia and Atrisha in turn. "Jeron is alive, and I have no idea about Cole. I'm sorry, but we became separated on the battlefield."

"Maybe we should take this inside," said Captain Levren. The man looked annoyed, as if a fly was buzzing around his head. "Leave your horses with those men over there. Dalton, you and the three other lads with us, you five find a billet." Levren turned and walked back towards the command tent without bothering to check if anyone followed.

Dalton dismounted from his horse looking dismayed. "I travel across the kingdom twice, only to find myself back under Captain Levren's command," he grumbled to himself. "How does that happen? So unfair."

"Most of our experienced captains died at Fort Hope," Atrisha said as she turned up her nose and gave him her most haughty look. "Be thankful that we have him."

Dalton deflated, the joy on his face dying as his eyes turned downcast. "Yeah. That does make sense," he said softly.

Atrisha grabbed Dalton by the shirt and yanked him forward, nearly pulling him off his feet. "How did you let yourself become separated from Cole on the battlefield," she asked, careful to keep her voice devoid of emotion. She would not let these boys see how furious she was.

Dalton was a tall man and her pulling him along by his shirt made quite an awkward sight as he hunched over trying not to lose his balance. He brushed her hand off of him and drew himself to his full height, scowling down at her. "I didn't let myself do anything," he snarled. "When three different armies are fighting in a narrow space, and there are large explosions all around, you tend to lose track of things while trying to survive. You'd know that if you actually had any sort of experience what so ever."

"We have experience," declared Olivia with an air of defiance about her. "After you all abandoned us on your way to Fort Hope, we fought against scores of bandits as we cleared the roads."

"Bandits," said Dalton flatly as the three other boys behind him snickered none too softly. "So no minotaurs, cyclopes, centaurs, satyrs, vampires, or even a Loachian?"

"I've fought the Loachians," Calabella said softly.

"And how did that go?" asked Dalton, his voice somewhere between angry and genuine curiosity.

Calabella did not say a word. She just shook her head sadly.

"I see," said Dalton, the anger vanished from his voice and strangely filled with compassion. Atrisha nearly punched him for that tone of voice. How dare he be condescending about this!

Dalton glanced around. "Where is Nellandra? As I recall the four of you are rarely apart." Atrisha's voice caught in her throat as she was unable to speak. Calabella coughed back a sob, and Olivia stared down at the ground. Dalton grimaced. "I see," he said without any smugness. "I'd tell you that it gets better, but it doesn't. Just...try not to drink too much wine, okay?"

"Why would she drink wine?" asked Olivia puzzled. "We're an army. We don't carry wine. Always obsessed with your finer things in life, eh Dalton?"

"Grow up," agreed Atrisha. "You're in the army now, not a tavern."

"That's not what I'm—gah, forget it," protested Dalton before giving up after the other three boys started laughing.

They reached the tent without further conversation. That was not entirely true. The four boys kept talking quietly to each other, pointing out things of interest in the camp.

"What are you boys doing here?" asked Captain Iandrick after they all squeezed into the tent.

Dalton shrugged. "Prince Darik had us escort Prince Nelson back to the Bionans before arriving here. We made it to Ochandor, where Nelson was ordered to join the Bionan forces here, and Duke Cedric ordered us to follow."

Captain Iandrick sighed and ran his hand over his face. Master Maxus placed a hand on Dalton's shoulder. "Son, Prince Darik sent you all from where exactly? To protect this Prince Nelson who is...?"

"Oh, I'm sorry," apologized Dalton. "We left Talendor after the seasonal vampire siege. Nelson is the son of the Duke of Biona, and is now currently engaged to Iniza, the daughter of Duke Havram. From what we heard, he helped thwart the vampire's tunneling into the inner city within the mesa. Nasty place. The inside of the mesa is dark and the subterranean lake makes it very humid."

"Dalton," interrupted Master Tyson. "Start from the beginning. This is all very difficult to follow."

Dalton paused and conferred with the other three boys. "Okay. New plan," he said. "Me, Telwin, Atticus, and Lentil here will fill you all in on everything that transpired since Fort Hope."

Dalton began recounting their tale and Atrisha felt her fists clench. How did they just lose track of Cole on the battlefield? It sounded more to her like he was making excuses for not being with Byron during the confrontation. And worse, they ran off and left Cole behind! Calabella nodding her head in agreement did nothing to soothe Atrisha's anger.

The rest of the story just sounded like nonsense. They encountered a group of strangers, one of whom happened to be a beautiful priestess that took a liking to Jeron? Atrisha found that highly implausible. But at least Olivia's posture made the story worth it. After all of her insisting that she was over her feelings for Jeron, it was pleasant to see her vacillate between anger and depression, her body shifting between the two extremes as she managed to pace without actually walking.

"Wait wait wait," interrupted Tyson. "Your travelling companions included a prince and princess from Kelon."

"Yup," agreed Dalton.

"Did they say how Kelon was destroyed?" Tyson asked.

"Nope," answered Dalton simply. After everyone glared at him, he sighed and continued. "They don't like talking about their earlier lives. Only Vernon, excuse me, Prince Irvin, has even said what his name used to be. The rest all remain silent and refuse to answer. So no, they didn't speak about what happened to the duchy."

"Carry on then," said Tyson with an amazed chuckle.

Dalton wound up describing the vampire siege, and concluded with Prince Darik marching an army of mercenaries and Talendorians through Kelon and onto Loach.

"Prince Darik has an army? And it is marching on Loach's eastern border?" asked Captain Levren.

"Yes," said Dalton impatiently. "And before you ask, no I don't know when they'll arrive or anything like that. After that, all we really did was accompany Prince Nelson to Ochandor. That is where we met with Duke Cedric. Who sent us here. You're all caught up now."

"Thank you," said Captain Levren approvingly. "You've done a good job. That information changes everything."

"Indeed, it does," agreed Captain Iandrick. "I'd expect Loach to withdraw its forces from our border. Drop back more into their own land to avoid being caught between our forces."

"We should harry their forces the entire way," chimed in Maxus. "Force them to cover their rear while retreating. Make them speed up, and they will have to leave some of their supplies behind."

"Agreed," said Iandrick. "Atrisha, Calabella, you two are up. You two will be in charge of our first harrying force. Sweep the area in a wide band. If you engage their forces, attack so long as they are not a superior force. The goal here isn't to kill them to a man, but force them to bleed while retreating."

"Understood. We can handle that," said Atrisha approvingly. Finally, she had the opportunity to extract her revenge. If the captains wanted to make it a slow drawn out process, she was fine with that. The Loachian army deserved to suffer for its treachery. Better that it last.

"They are bound to have some surprises for us," said Calabella softly as they exited the tent.

"We'll handle them," said Atrisha confidently. "We were trained by the best."

"If you say so," said Calabella, thoroughly unconvinced.

Chapter Eighteen

The air remained cold this far north. Atrisha's breath turned into fog each time she exhaled. She swayed easily in her saddle, scanning the horizon for any sign of the Loachian forces.

Their scouts said that Loach had employed a rear guard. It was a smaller force, slightly detached, and hanging back from the rear of the main force. Even with her avian sight, Atrisha could not see any sign of the forces, but if she were the Loachian commander, she would have them on the other side of the small mountains that were just up the road. Lookouts surely should have spotted their force by now. With any luck, the Loachian force would already be prepared to retreat further up the road.

Sunlight had abandoned this desolate land. Everything was gray, drab, and monotonous. Atrisha flexed her wings, aching to soar above the clouds. Maybe she would be able to find sunlight up in the skies. Unfortunately, her duty bound her to her saddle.

Calabella had not said much during their patrol. She was content to smile and giggle with Silas. Atrisha disliked the boy. He was uncouth, very forward, and always speaking in innuendo. Atrisha doubted that he was even a nobleman.

"Stay alert," she snapped at Calabella. "I don't like the look of the road ahead."

"You've said that five times already," said Calabella drily.

"Just pay attention," said Atrisha. Did every officer have to deal with so many annoyances?

They did not have to wait long. One of their scouts galloped back down the road to them, kicking up a prodigious amount of dust. The men and women around Atrisha tensed, hands checking weapons and securing armor. A scout galloping back to the force meant only one thing, and her soldiers knew that.

"Captain, the enemy is straight ahead," said the scout as he reined in his horse just before her.

"Numbers?" Atrisha asked.

"I couldn't get a count," he answered. "Those mountains to the left of the road could easily be concealing some of their forces. From what I could see, their forces were of similar number to our own, but not mounted. All infantry."

"Very good," said Atrisha as she tried to squint her eyes and peer up the road. "Fall back into the column. Calabella, pass the word that our troops are to prepare for a charge at the enemy forces. Easy gait for the horses until the signal is given. And by all means, have them be alert for a flanking attack from the mountains on the left."

Calabella nodded in acknowledgment, as her tusks slowly began to emerge. Atrisha suppressed a smile. It was the first time since Calabella's failed mission that she openly displayed her tusks. That had to be a good omen.

The Loachian forces were indeed prepared for their arrival. Pikeman stood across the road, with archers standing just a bit further behind them.

It was a tempting target. Everything that Atrisha learned about tactics ran through her mind. Such a formation against a cavalry charge should be easy to defeat if she only swung some cavalry out to her right to come crashing in on enemy forces' flank. She could rout the enemy in one fell swoop.

But that was exactly what everyone warned her not to do. Just engage the enemy and cause them to run. No vengeance. No glory. Atrisha gritted her teeth in frustration. She would send out the flanking force, but if the enemy retreated, she would proceed with caution.

"Hold some of the forces back, giving them a clear path to charge down the right flank," ordered Atrisha. "Make sure the Loachians can see them. Do not pursue if they flee. I think they have something unpleasant cooked up for us, and I want to dissuade them."

"Done," said Calabella as she passed the orders back to some sergeants. The soldiers would be in the proper place. Atrisha had faith in them.

Atrisha steered her horse backward deeper into the lines. She had paid attention to her tutors. Only a foolish captain led a cavalry charge from the front. The army always had more soldiers capable of riding a horse, but it did not have more officers capable of planning an attack, while also keeping an army fed and supplied.

As they drew closer, Atrisha kept her eyes on the mountainside. It would be just like the Loachians to have extra archers hidden within the rocks.

Two groups of cavalry broke off from the Antierian formation and moved off to the right of the road. One was the flanking group, led by Calabella, the other the reserve group. Atrisha prayed that they would not need the latter.

Atrisha nodded to a sergeant and the cry went up for the charge. Her horse surged beneath her as it picked up speed, causing her to fold her wings back behind her. It would have been easier to put her wings away, let them sink back into her back. But if this was to be a protracted retreat fought in stages, she wanted the Loachians to recognize her. She wanted them to know when death was charging at them.

Arrows fell into their ranks, striking man and beast. Disappointment and regret settled within Atrisha. Casualties were avoidable in war, she knew that. Still, she entered the battle hoping that she would not lose any soldiers. She did not want to be responsible for someone else losing their loved one, however inevitable that may be. Atrisha knew the pain of that loss.

The first wave of horses crashed into and through the Loachian pikemen with a sickening crunch and a chorus of screams. Atrisha reached the line within moments and swung her sword in a downward strike and felt a satisfying tug as a spray of blood flew into the air. Whether the Loachian died or not was irrelevant, she drew first blood in her crusade against the treacherous murdering bastards.

She burst through the line of pikemen in time to see Calabella's group crash into the archers from the flank. Atrisha could see Calabella swinging her mace as she lay into the Loachian forces with savage fury. Atrisha smiled to herself. While she had planned on breaking off after the initial charge and reforming, things were going too well. Maybe they would eliminate this force, however small it may be with one charge.

She continued on towards the archers, leaving the remainder of the pikemen to the swarms of cavalry in the area. With their lines broken, the Loachian pikemen were of no great threat.

Calabella's force moved through the archers quicker than an axe through a log. The archers lacked the weapons and armor to resist a cavalry charge. Atrisha nearly smiled as she watched the bodies fall.

The first arrow struck Atrisha's horse in the neck, causing it to cry out in pain and fall to the ground. Atrisha barely removed her feet from the stirrups, narrowly avoiding being crushed beneath the horse's weight.

She stumbled to her feet and looked around. Arrows plummeted from the sky, from the direction of the mountains. The arrows fell scattered amongst the battlefield without a pattern or clustering. Atrisha frowned as she raised her shield up over her head. That meant that the archers were not firing a concentrated volley, thereby making their shots less effective. But why would they do that?

Atrisha did not have to wait long for an answer. The thundering of hooves shook the ground. The Loachians also had a reserve force of cavalry waiting to strike. Atrisha swore at herself. She should have anticipated that. Who would fail to have cavalry of some sort covering their retreat?

The Loachians charged straight into Calabella's flank, breaking straight through the ranks and causing the battlefield to devolve into a mounted melee. Atrisha spotted Calabella in the thick of the action. Blood covered her tusks, and...was she laughing?! At least Silas was with her. He would try to keep her alive. The man needed an audience for his innuendos after all.

Much to Atrisha's surprise, the Loachian force was led by a blonde woman in teal robes. She rode upon a black stallion, controlling the fractious beast with ease. The woman swung a longsword with ferocious grace, felling numerous Antierian soldiers as she charged through the battlefield.

Calabella took notice of the woman and steered her horse toward her, Silas close on her heels. Atrisha could only cheer her on as she watched. Caught between the pikemen and archers without a horse did not leave Atrisha with many options. Entering either fray would most likely see her trampled by a horse. She dared not take to the sky with the Loachian bowmen watching over the field.

The Loachian woman smiled cruelly, the corner of her mouth turning up in a sneer as she saw Calabella heading in her direction. That expression caused a jolt of dread to radiate throughout Atrisha's body. Something was wrong.

The robed woman lifted her left hand, fingers spread apart and palm facing out towards Calabella. Her hand glowed briefly and lightning erupted from her palm and fingers.

The lightning bolt shot across the field of battle and coursed through Calabella, causing her body to convulse in her saddle. It passed through her and struck through the Antierian soldiers, passing from one to the next. Smoke rose from their bodies, their armor charred. Many did not stay in their saddle. They fell from their horses, bodies jittering. Whether with life, or an aftereffect of the lightning, Atrisha could not say.

The archers bombarding the battlefield ceased firing while the robed woman fought. Atrisha seized the opening, spreading her wings and taking to the sky. Part of her wanted to dive at the woman, striking her before she could fire lightning again. But that was a rash decision, and she could no longer entertain those.

She took the brief respite in the battle to survey the field. The Loachians were slowly pulling back while the Antierians scattered about in chaos, their discipline shattered by the barrage of arrows and lightning.

It was a perfectly timed retreat. The Antierian reserve cavalry would not be able to reach the Loachians before they withdrew from the battlefield. Atrisha did not wave them off though. The horsemen would help secure the battlefield and their wounded; finishing off any Loachians that were unable to retreat.

She spared a glance over at the mountains, finally spotting the archers. Small groups were moving across the mountainside, parallel to the retreating cavalry. Their movement was the only reason she could see them. They did not wear standard military uniforms, or a scout's greens. Their armor was a mottled mess of grays, browns, and blacks. It made it difficult for even her eyes to distinguish them from the dreary backdrop.

Atrisha diverted her gaze back to the battle, searching desperately for Calabella. She found her, still mounted on her horse, riding aimlessly on the battlefield. Atrisha dove down, gliding down next to her.

Calabella's skin was charred, blackened really. It was cracked in numerous places with red lines of dried blood breaking the surface. Atrisha grabbed the reins of the runaway horse and pulled on them, forcing the horse to a stop.

She dragged Calabella off of the horse and held her in her arms. Checking for a pulse felt pointless. Calabella's chain mail was melted, and her eyes were a smoking ruin, steam rising from the melted...stuff...that used to be her eyes.

Despite the obvious damage to her friend's body, Atrisha placed her hand to her friend's neck and searched for a pulse. Nothing. She was dead. Atrisha rocked her back and forth in her arms, tears trickling down her face and sprinkling upon Calabella's desiccated skin.

Atrisha sat that way for a long time. She lost track of the time, vaguely aware of someone placing her on Calabella's horse and leadng her back to camp.

Chapter Nineteen

C lara dug her heels into her mount as she led the retreat. The mission had been a disaster. She lost too many men. Matlin said to bleed them, make them earn every step forward through Loach.

She could not keep this pace up as they fell back. The lightning trick would only work once. Next time they would inevitably have archers on alert for a robed woman. She would need to vary her appearance, make it more difficult for the Antierian heathens to spot her on the battlefield.

Her tactics also needed improvement, and she could not ask Matlin for advice. He was too busy, and she certainly did not want him viewing her as weak or incompetent.

That left the other officers. People whom she did not know or trust. Any of which could be involved in an assassination plot against Matlin. Or, through her interaction with them, become the perfect avenue for a potential assassin to exploit in order to reach Matlin.

No, she would need to become more intelligent. Pick her battlegrounds carefully. Study them beforehand. Control every aspect of the battle.

She was not a soldier, but she was clever. That could be her advantage. The enemy would be expecting conventional tactics. If she was clever, she could keep them off balance. She did not need to win the campaign, merely delay them until Matlin's fortification was complete.

By the gods, she could do that.

CHAPTER TWENTY

D arik gazed at the village for a second straight hour. Its existence irritated him to no end. It was a puzzle that he was not certain how to address. Solving it was easy. There were multiple methods he could select. But what factors should take precedence? Morality, expediency, or some combination of the two?

The village was in Loach. It paid taxes to the duchy, supplied the duke with levies, and contributed to the local economy. The easy and expedient thing to do would be to march on the village, dispatch its defenders, seize their supplies and valuables as his own, and fire the village. That way the villagers would no longer be able to support Loach in any of its efforts, war or otherwise.

But even entertaining that thought made him travel back in time to Fort Hope. He felt helpless then, watching the Loachian force slice through his men from behind. Should he engage in that same sort of treachery to win the war? Could he?

What was the alternative? Marching his army through the dense forests so as to avoid the village? That would add days onto their journey. Antierians and their allies would die and suffer as a result of the delay. Were their lives worth less than the villagers?

"Well something is bothering you," said Vernon as he stood shoulder to shoulder with Darik. "Can't figure out how to deal with the village?"

"Burn it to the ground and take everything they have, or bypass the village completely causing more of my people to die?" asked Darik as he absently stared at the village. "There has to be a third option, but I can't really see one that would work."

Vernon nodded in agreement as he stared at the village. "I know what you mean," he said. "When Kelon fell, many innocents died. We never found out the reason why, and it probably does not matter. But what was the perpetrators' objective? Kill the ducal family, or extinguish all life in Kelon?"

"It seems they chose the latter," said Darik darkly. "That doesn't exactly make this any easier."

"Well that is because you think of it in terms of numbers," Vernon pointed out. "Not everything is a matter of numbers. Emotion comes into it as well."

Darik looked at his fellow prince skeptically. "What are you getting at?"

Vernon shrugged. "You could try talking with them first. Offering them a choice."

"And what would that choice be?"

"Step aside, hand over some of their supplies," said Vernon. "Not enough to starve them of course. And ask that they throw down their weapons and surrender."

"And wouldn't the duke take umbrage at that?" asked Darik.

Vernon shrugged. "That is a possibility. But it will take quite a bit of time until he can respond. By then the war could be over. Who knows? But that would be his decision, not yours."

Darik barked out a laugh. "Just like that? A people who have hated mine for generations will just willingly surrender?"

Vernon smiled sadly. "I never said it would be easy. But there are some factors in your favor."

"Such as?"

"These people have bordered my dead land for years," he said. "They are probably more worried about ghosts than your people."

Darik narrowed his eyes. "And they probably count Kelonian refugees amongst their number?"

"The thought had crossed my mind," said Vernon with a slight smile. "But maybe I am just tired of the land being populated by ghost towns."

Darik sighed as he gave the village one last look. "We'll try it your way then," he said.

The sad smile came back to Vernon's face. "It's your way too, my friend," said Vernon. "You just haven't admitted it to yourself yet."

"So that's why I haven't razed the city to the ground yet?" asked Darik. "I'm just too good of a man?"

"Maybe you don't like death," said Vernon.

"Maybe," said Darik. "But what were you thinking of when you came here?"

Vernon chuckled softly. "Perceptive. I can see why people claim you are cunning," he said. "My thoughts were less noble or interesting. I was merely wondering why when the king does not have an heir, every child of a duke must be a prince or princess? Could you imagine either of those twins from Loach as king?"

Darik chuckled. "No, I couldn't," he admitted. "I imagine the playwrights would have a ball with that. The people, not so much. And besides, the Talendorians don't always refer to Iniza as a princess. So maybe the princely epidemic is contained."

"Perhaps," said Vernon. "But should we really pin our hopes on people who willingly choose to reside in a desert?"

"Good point," said Darik. "Now I get to inform Renaldo of the plan. I guarantee you he insists on being there with us. He never could resist a wild and reckless plan."

"We?" asked Vernon with a single chuckle. "When did this plan become 'we'?"

"Your idea, you get to go," said Darik. "You just haven't admitted it to yourself yet."

CHAPTER TWENTY-ONE

"Your prince is an honorable man," Jayna whispered to Jeron.

"You should have seen his brother," retorted Jeron drily.

Jayna pushed him back holding him at arm's length. "Are you saying his brother would have razed the village? Because the way you speak of him, I just don't see it."

"Hardly," he scoffed. "He would have brought some casks of ale and wine. There would have been a party worthy of song. And at the end he would have befriended all of them...or fought them all. Much the same thing really."

"And you followed such a man?" asked Jayna skeptically. "A drunkard, a lout, and a ruffian?"

"And a good man," insisted Jeron as they followed Darik into the town. "You would have liked him. By God, at the end he even showed a responsible streak."

Jayna glanced around the town uncertainly. "And offering these people peace makes you think of him why?"

Jeron shrugged. "I miss him. So do Dalton and Darik," he said. "And this reminds me of him. A plan that was not the easiest, but definitely was what any religion would classify as 'good'? He would approve."

Jayna shook her head in disbelief. "If you say so. I still find it hard to believe."

"He hated seeing anyone mess with the little people," explained Jeron. "He still hadn't found his totem when he died. But he suffered for that his entire life. His experiences...well let's just say that Prince Darik was well aware of what Byron went through. And he is a rather protective older brother."

"I can relate to that," said Jayna with that warm smile of hers. "Now hush. It looks like they're going to speak."

Darik paused on the village common grounds next to a well. He leaned against the well and waited. The village folk slowly gathering along the outskirts of the common ground. They were rightfully scared. Uncertain of what was to come next, but slowly overcoming their fear to see what was transpiring.

"Hello good people of the village," began Darik after enough of a crowd gathered. Jeron winced. Darik was a good man, but an orator he was not. "Now you may be wondering what this large army on your doorstep, arriving out of a ghost infested land, has to do with you. Well allow me to introduce myself. I am Prince Darik Villa of Antier."

The crowd gasped in shock and fear. Darik waved them down. "Easy now. I am not here to kill you. My disagreement lies with Duke Camen, not you fine folk," he said as he turned while speaking in an effort to draw in the entire crowd. "But I also can't let an armed force, no matter how small, remain at my army's rear. What I will have to do is confiscate your arms, armor, and some of your supplies."

Anger answered his proclamation. Darik waved them back down. "Easy. I will leave you with enough to defend and provide for yourselves," he said. "I won't let you starve or suffer banditry. I believe that is more than fair. But I will allow you all with time to decide for yourself. You have an hour. Choose wisely."

Predictably, the crowd burst into panic as they ran amongst each other. Jayna leaned in towards Jeron. "That went well," she said.

"Give it time," said Jeron. "They'll realize they are hopelessly outnumbered and do the wise thing."

"Jeron, sweety, dear," said Jayna in her most patronizing voice. "You forget sometimes that I am a priestess. The conflict between Antier and Loach goes well beyond mere geographic and political matters. It is rooted in religious belief. While Antier may have both the Church and the temples, Loach only has the temples. The conflict between your two duchies spans both this life and the next. You can't expect people will just set that aside easily."

As if bidden, a villager charged at Darik with a knife drawn. "Die you heathen Antierian!" he shouted as he leapt at the prince.

Renaldo intercepted the man easily. His greataxe cleaving the man in two. Pandemonium ensued as the village reacted to the death.

Villagers charged their force with whatever was handy. Fists, knives, cleavers, it did not matter. Darik held his hands up trying to forestall the violence. But it was too late. The mercenaries did what they were paid to do. They killed. Without mercy. Villagers of all ages died, and quickly too. Jeron tried to place himself between Jayna and the violence, but she shoved him aside. Disbelief and horror engraved upon her face.

The fighting, if you could call it that, was mercifully short. The villagers did what innocents were prone to do during war. They died.

Darik stared at the death with disgust on his face. Emkario promptly emptied the contents of his stomach. Vincent followed him shortly thereafter.

Jeron softly rocked Jayna back and forth in his arms. His mind shouted at his body to close his eyes, but it would not listen.

Jayna sobbed quietly into his chest. "I told you," she gasped. "I told you."

Jeron stared at the destruction in disbelief. Darik shook his head sadly as he rubbed his hands on his face. "Take the supplies," he whispered to Renaldo. "Bury those who died, aid those who didn't. Let's at least make this atrocity worth something."

Chapter Twenty-Two

R andall groaned as small hands tried to drag him out of bed. He brushed them off as he tried to fall back into that blissful dream world.

There was no need to wake up. He already knew what the world held. A bunch of children were worried and would ask him about food. Tigun and the few other children old enough to have found their totems would ask him about selling the goods he had stolen. And at the end of it all, Tiona would still be dead.

And why was she dead? She was a smart girl; he doubted that she would randomly steal. Well at least not from a merchant. The only explanation he had was that the watchmen assumed that she would not be missed. It did not make any sense. But then again, he just did not care.

None of that mattered. The little hands persisted. Shaking him without cessation.

"Wake up, Randy!" cried little voices.

"What is it, you little rats?" mumbled Randall as he tried to roll over, pulling his blanket over his head.

"You promised you'd buy food today, Randy!" they complained. "We're getting low and the others old kids won't go out and buy any."

Randall tried to ignore them, but the damage was done. They succeeded in shaking and talking him into consciousness. He was awake and he would not be finding sleep again easily.

He complained under his breath as he pulled his boots on in a haze. Randall did not know what the children wanted out of him. He was not their parents.

Clearly, he could not protect them from what was out in the world. They would be better off facing the world without him. He paused with one boot on his foot and amended his thinking. Loach was a dangerous city. The children most likely would not be better without him.

Randall climbed out of a window and wandered throughout the city in a haze. The mood of the city was somber after Tiona's execution. Perhaps he should have cared about the other nine dead people, but he did not.

Suspicious looks were common no matter where you went or who you were. The other day Randall witnessed a merchant giving a nobleman the twice over. The merchant was fortunate that the nobleman had little experience with that expression. Otherwise, the nobleman may have beat him for his impertinence.

Paranoia was on every lip and every corner. That friendly beggar who knew you by name and heaped the praises of all the gods upon your head? He had vanished. All the familiar faces disappeared. It was as if he woke up in a different city.

Three more public executions had taken place. All overseen by young Prince Yutlin. Randall detested the boy, but there was nothing he could do about it.

A thief killing a prince? Unheard of. Randall doubted the priests even had a story of a similar nature. Even the diamond bladed knife he pilfered from the Pojomites would not do him any good. It was not like he had any training on how to use a dagger. He merely attempted to poke people with the pointy end. And those "people" were all imaginary foes that he fought in the air of his bedroom.

The North Market was quiet. People hurried about their business, striving to return home as quickly as possible. Everyone walked about with their hands outside of their pockets and cloaks. It was a habit ever since the hangings began. If your hands were visible, merchants were less likely to accuse you of theft.

Randall purchased some bread from a nearby vendor. He coaxed his face into a half-smile. No one would have believed a full smile. The joy of shopping and seeing the sites of the city was gone.

Bodies were found in alleyways and on rooftops throughout the city. Randall had no way of knowing if there were fewer thefts following the hangings, but murder was certainly on the rise. Either people felt that they could kill anyone they suspected to be a thief, or there were groups of people, maybe watchmen, dedicating their nights to murdering any suspected unsavory elements.

Randall scratched at his scalp while he tried to remember what they needed. His hair was incredibly greasy. A bath would be one of the things he needed. But as for food, bread would not be enough for all of the children. They would need some beans, maybe some dried meat, and maybe even fruit and vegetables. Otherwise, the children would get bloody gums. Again.

He had not always been capable of providing good food for the children all the time, but with the implementation of his rules, money was now normally available for that sort of thing. Once he managed to fence the stolen goods from the temple and jeweler heists, they would be flush with gold. But that was never going to happen in the current environment.

A commotion rippled through the North Market. Randall turned his head lazily and stared at the noise with a mixture of apathy and boredom. A young boy dashed amongst the stalls trying to outpace the City Watch.

The youth was frail with wan pallid skin. Regular meals or semi-regular meals did not appear to be a part of his diet. Merchants and customers alike looked at the pursing watchmen with disdain. Everyone knew how the chase would end for the boy, or for anyone who interfered.

Randall winced in sympathy as the watchmen tackled the boy to the ground. He had tripped and fallen to the ground numerous times in his life. But his bones had never made that brittle cracking sound.

The watchmen hauled the young thief to his legs. The boy screamed and cried. Whether the broken bones or the thought of imminent hanging was causing his panic was irrelevant. The boy was a dead man. Especially with the young prince's love of hangings and public spectacle.

"What was that about?" asked Randall as he looked over a merchant's supply of apples.

"That's how they're dealing with crime now," answered the merchant skeptically as he watched over Randall like a hawk. "Bunch of rich people got themselves robbed. So they hanged every beggar and street urchin they caught thieving."

"I'll take a dozen apples," said Randall absently as he showed the merchant the coins first. "So they're hanging the little children?"

"Yup," said the merchant as he spat on the ground. "A pox on them all. The gods don't like killing children. Mark my word. They'll get what is coming to them."

"Has anyone tried to help the urchins? Give them some food?" asked Randall as he placed the apples within his satchel.

The merchant gaped at him as he clutched Randall's coins tightly in his fists. "Give it to them?" he asked befuddled. "Why would we give our stock to them? We have to make do for ourselves."

"Of course. Just a stray thought," said Randall as he hefted his satchel. "Good day, sir."

Randall roamed the market purchasing a few odds and ends that they would need. More thread, needles, and the like. Every alleyway haunted his steps; pairs of hungry eyes staring out, stalking him. He tried to ignore them and finish his shopping, but they persisted.

A little voice in his brain kept nagging at him. Saying that Tiona could have easily been one of those urchins, abandoned, and having to weigh their fate. Starvation or risk the gibbet.

The watchmen and the merchants did not seem to care. And it was not like the Thieves Association to provide for needy children. That left only him, Tigun, and the others. And their warehouse simply was not large enough.

Randall sighed as he meandered his way back to the warehouse. This new endeavor was going to be a lot of work.

CHAPTER TWENTY-THREE

Fotlin did not bother to hide the smile dancing on his face while Yutlin paced a circuit through the planning room. His little brother had been a nervous wreck since the executions. Crime had not decreased in the city. The thefts on the nobility, temples, merchants, and societies had not ceased. They had increased.

Worse for him, crime in the markets had also increased. Beggars and urchins became emboldened by hunger. Yutlin did not realize that fear of death only lasted so long as the people were only terrified of dying by your hand. Let hunger gnaw at their stomachs for a while, and hanging did not seem quite so bad.

"So, what are you going to tell father?" asked Fotlin with a smirk on his face. "What are your results?"

Yutlin spun around, his face red and his breathing just a little bit fast. He was nervous. Fotlin let his smirk widen just a bit more.

"Tell him?" demanded Yutlin in a near shout. "What is there to tell him? I kill the thieves and they still steal. They actually steal even more!"

"They're hungry you idiot," sneered Fotlin. "What did you think would happen?"

"That they would stop stealing!" yelled Yutlin, his voice rising as it echoed off the walls.

"Riiiight," said Fotlin as he dragged the word out for maximum annoyance. "Young children will stop stealing food and maybe go work in the mines. Oh, but they're too small and weak for manual labor. That rules out farming too. Well that and none of them have any money to own a farm. Oh I know! Maybe they'll open a business! Wait, no. That wouldn't work. They still don't have any money. They don't have any assets either. So they can forget loans. Hmm. I wonder where they're going to get money or food from. I can't quite figure it out."

Yutlin knocked one of the chairs over. "Do you think this is funny?" he screeched in a most satisfying high pitched voice.

"Tragic really," said Fotlin. "Unfortunately, I'll be the one cleaning up your mess."

"Both of your messes," corrected their father as he entered the room. He glided into his chair, staring imperiously down his noise at both boys. "Fotlin, you could not stop the string of high profile robberies. Yutlin, you misdiagnosed the situation. People who rob the incredibly wealthy do not need to worry about stealing food. You sentenced children to die for no reason whatsoever, resulting in an angry and scared populace, an increase in theft, and a downturn in commerce. Congratulations."

Fotlin possessed the good sense not to speak in his own defense. That always earned his father's wrath. You took your punishment with dignity like a man.

"That's not how it happened!" protested Yutlin. Fotlin winced at the outburst. Yutlin taking his anger out on their father was not going to end well.

Duke Camen chuckled softly. "Is that so?" he said. "Well then. You have a chance to redeem yourself. Yutlin, you will be in charge of handing out food to the populace throughout the markets. Call it the Ducal War Relief Effort. Blame the food shortages on Antier, and feed the citizens before things become out of hand."

Fotlin's mouth nearly dropped in shock. His father was providing Yutlin with a second chance to prove himself? And he laughed at his rebellious streak? Fotlin gripped his fights tightly in anger, hiding them beneath the table. He never in his life received such favorable treatment!

"Fotlin," said Duke Camen, the mirth gone from his voice, replaced with his more familiar grave tones. "You will see to it that the City Watch oversees these distributions. The populace needs to see them aiding the people, not only executing them."

"And you're afraid someone might try to kill Yutlin for the executions?" said Fotlin without amusement.

"I don't fear anything, child," replied his father as he stood from his chair. "See that it is done correctly. I cannot continue to waste my time overseeing the pair of you while also trying to manage a war with multiple duchies."

The duke departed without wasting another word on his sons. Fotlin took the opportunity to glare at his little brother. His father had moved deftly to cut him off. Making Yutlin's safety during these charity events his problem was quite clever. Now he could not move on his brother in public.

Had his father known that he was planning it? Yutlin was becoming quite a bit too ambitious for his liking. Soon he would recognize that Fotlin was in his path and needed to be removed. Fotlin saw it happen in numerous other Loachian noble families. His younger brother would not be killing him and usurping his position.

Clever on his father's part, but not on Yutlin's. Cunning would win the day. He would need to be creative in how he dispatched Yutlin.

"I expect your best men to be on the detail," said Yutlin as he straightened his tunic, trying to regain some semblance of composure.

Fotlin barked out a sharp laugh. "Oh please, brother," he said in his most patronizing voice. "You've worked with the watchmen. What makes you think there are 'best men' in the detail?"

"Every group has people in it that are better than the rest," protested Yutlin.

"Oh, I agree," said Fotlin as he sauntered over to his little brother. He leaned down placing his nose inches from Yutlin's own. "And those men left with Matlin to fight a war."

Yutlin's eyes widened, the whites growing increasingly large. "But that means...only average men would be protecting me?"

Fotlin patted his brother's shoulder in mock sympathy and condolence. "Mediocrity can be such a terrible burden," he whispered before pivoting and walking towards the door.

He exited the planning room feeling incredibly joyous. He had grown accustomed to living with his father's disapproval. But seeing his brother squirm under his gaze, and seeing the fear take up residence in his eyes? Oh, that made everything worth it.

Fotlin grinned as he walked through the stone hallways, finding comfort in the pillars and symmetry of the blocks used in the palace's construction. The order of the palace architecture eased his mind. There was planning to do and that worked best when he was in the proper frame of mind.

Chapter Twenty-Four

There were days where Owen enjoyed being a watchman. Those days were a distant memory, and they grew dimmer with every passing day.

Danger was always part of the job. But thieves that murdered and shot fire from their hands? That was something entirely new. And arresting every urchin and beggar accused of theft? Even for swiping some food? Sending them to the gallows? It turned his stomach thinking of those children walking to their death over a loaf of bread.

Owen muttered a prayer to the gods for the souls of the children. If the rumors were true, the duke would be handing out food. No more children would be acquainted with the gibbet.

It was a pleasant thought, and a good distraction for his mind as he ran up the spiraled staircase in the Temple of Espira. The thief had a lead on Owen and his watchmen by at least a few floors. If their previous chase was any indication, they would not catch the man. He could probably just leap over to the next rooftop.

The priests of Espira contacted the watchmen immediately after becoming aware of the intrusion. Apparently, private guardsmen were not employed at the Temple of Espira. The priests said there was a time and place for everything, and they would not stand in the way of events.

Owen swore as his legs stiffened up. Why could tonight not be the time and place where the thief did not get spotted by the priests? For such a successful thief he sure was terrible at the whole not being noticed part of the job. At least he had not killed anyone this time.

Yet.

Owen pushed through the door, staggering out onto the rooftop. Every temple's architecture was as different and unique as the gods that they worshipped. The Espiran temple had spiral staircases spread throughout the temple, each leading to the rooftop. It made the flat rooftop look like it was decorated with little stone and tile huts.

He motioned for his men to fan out. The intruder could be behind any one of the huts. At least there was moonlight tonight. That way they could clearly watch the thief as he fled into the night.

Owen crept up to the next hut as silently as he could. His heart was pounding in his chest. Thoughts of his body being roasted did nothing to calm his nerves.

He told himself that the intruder could be anyone. It was not necessarily the same thief that could leap impossible heights and shoot fire from his hands. Just your run of the mill criminal.

Who was standing mere feet away from him, staring at the wall of the hut behind Owen's.

Owen pulled his head back behind the hut and took a deep breath. This was it. If it was the same intruder, he could be roasted alive before he could blink. He waved his arm as he tried to attract the attention of his fellow watchmen, but it was too dark.

Now was not the time to be a hero, he admonished himself. But if he did not make an honest attempt at capturing the thief, one of the two princes would see him to the gallows.

Owen slowly and carefully drew his simple broadsword from its scabbard, careful to make as little noise as possible. He was a fair hand at the sword, as far as the watchmen were considered. That mattered little to Prince Fotlin, who claimed he was just a hair above incompetent with a sword. Tonight would put those opinions to the test.

He rounded the corner with his sword held ready to strike. One quick blow and it would be all over. His blade barreled downwards as he swung it with all of his might. Sparks shot up from the stone as his sword came in contact with it. But it never sliced into flesh.

The man was gone.

Orange scripts glowed in the stone, wisps of smoke still rising from the wall. A book lay at his feet. Owen picked it up. It was an old leather bound tome, but he did not see any writing on the cover. An uneasy feeling settled in his stomach. This book matched the description of those stolen from the Temple of Annelu.

"Can you read?" asked a voice from behind him.

Owen leapt into the air, the book dropping from his hands while he smashed his head against the tile roof of the hut. His heart nearly burst, as it beat rapidly. Pounding harder and harder. He spun around; the voice had come from behind him.

The thief slouched against the wall of the hut Owen had been hiding behind. His body language screamed insolence, like he was laughing at Owen. A sword hilt protruded over his right shoulder, but the man made no move to draw it despite Owen's bared steel.

A fireball danced between the thief's hands. Back and forth it swam in some sort of looping pattern. Owen was mesmerized by it, as well as being scared to death. But the thief did not so much as spare a glance at the flame.

"I asked if you could read," repeated the man with a hint of mirth in his voice.

"No-no," stammered Owen as he tried to keep his blade between the two of them. "And you're under arrest for theft."

"I don't think so," said the thief unconcerned. "Show that to someone who can read. They're going to want to see it." He said it so casually, as if he were simply inviting Owen out to a tavern, an easy invitation to reject.

"Well, I must be going," he said as the fireball slowed, its orange glow changing to blue as it seemingly hardened. "Catch you later." The fireball leaped forward, speeding towards Owen.

Owen raised his blade in a feeble attempt to block it. He did not want to die, but he was not trained for this. The fireball struck his blade and shattered. Pieces of it scattered around Owen.

He turned his head each way, searching desperately for the thief, but he was gone. The man meant the fireball to distract, not to kill. Owen bent over and picked up one of the shards of the fireball.

It was ice. His mind struggled to wrap itself around that fact. The man turned fire into ice in a heartbeat. Owen stared at the shard until it melted in his hand. He glanced around desperately, but all that remained of the fireball was a puddle of water.

Owen looked down, searching frantically for the book. He snatched it back into his hands and clung to it. Between the book and the writing seared into the wall, he would have no choice but to bring the matter to his superiors. He highly doubted that this would be one of the days he enjoyed being a watchman. Not after the prince read what the thief had to write. It could not be anything good.

Chapter Twenty-Five

A pair of soldiers intercepted Jeron, trying to block his path. He snarled, picking up the pair by their collars and tossing them to either side of the road.

Soldiers gaped at him, stunned at his outburst. None of them had ever seen him lose his temper before. Mainly because he had not been fighting with them. And that was the source of his anger.

Renaldo stood just down the road, his axe in his hands. The axe head rested against the ground, casual, but ready to burst into action. His usual jovial expression was gone, his lips pursed, making his already narrow face seem even leaner.

"Stop right there, Jeron," commanded Renaldo, his hands tightening ever so slightly on his axe haft.

"The hell I will," growled Jeron. "This is madness and you know it. Now get out of my way."

"I can't do that," said Renaldo, his muscles rippling as his totem surged into him. Jeron knew very little about the man's totem, he kept it a secret as far as Jeron knew. A not uncommon practice in the kingdom, but Renaldo had more reason than most to be paranoid.

What Jeron did know was that Renaldo's totem made him strong. But not fast. Jeron was strong, both with his natural human muscles and his totem infused strength. Outside of their time on the walls of Talendor, Jeron had never actually witnessed Renaldo let loose his full strength. Which made it impossible to know beforehand who was stronger.

Jeron's mane sprouted from his face while he smiled menacingly at Renaldo. The older man might be strong, but Jeron was fast and quick. His muscles bunched and tensed, energy building up within them. Renaldo raised the head of his axe, and Jeron pounced.

He leapt forward covering ten yards in the space of a heartbeat. Jeron could hear Renaldo's heartbeat. Fast, and rapid. He was uncertain of the fight. Good.

Renaldo swung his axe in a diagonal stroke meant to decapitate. A mildly surprising tactic. Jeron thought Renaldo would attempt a backhand blow with the shaft of his great axe. A debilitating blow; not a lethal one. Especially considering that Jeron had not even drawn a weapon. Jeron had to give him credit, despite his carefree manner and blatant disregard for the gravity of every situation that he found himself in, Renaldo actually took his job seriously.

Not that it would do him any good.

Jeron rolled to Renaldo's offhand side, easily passing by the descending axe head. Renaldo lifted the axe to strike again, his eyes locked in determination. Jeron swept his legs through Renaldo's, toppling the smaller man over. Jeron rolled on top of him and with two quick totem-powered blows, knocked Renaldo unconscious. He may have dislocated the man's jaw in the process, but in his defense, Renaldo had tried to kill him first.

Jeron picked up Renaldo's greataxe in one deft motion. It was heavier than he anticipated. He heaved the axe, tossing it end over end, burying the axe in the wall of the inn. Jeron kicked the door open and walked into a room filled with naked steel pointing in his direction.

"Hello gentlemen," he said with an insolent smirk. "If you will excuse me, I'll be beating some sense into the prince now."

"What did you do to Renaldo?" asked a weary Darik. His eyes were bloodshot and he looked like he was not sleeping much. That pleased Jeron. No one should be sleeping well after what transpired.

"He's sleeping off a small headache," answered Jeron. "Jayna can heal it for him. In fact, everyone that isn't Darik should leave now and go bring Renaldo to her for healing."

Emkario and Vincent placed themselves between Jeron and his quarry. "Do you really think we're going to let you through after you were fighting with Renaldo?" asked Emkario incredulously. "We're not that stupid."

"Well, I'm not," quipped Vincent. "He is."

Emkario glowered at the shorter man while Vernon chuckled. "And I don't follow your orders," Vernon said as he poured over a map of what Jeron assumed was the local area.

"Then maybe you should all rethink your position unless you want to make this a group discussion?"

"What do you want?" asked Darik, clearly exasperated.

Jeron gritted his teeth in rage. What did he want? Darik was not that stupid. "What do I want?!" he bellowed. "How about for this army to stop destroying villages. People live there you know! We're ruining children's lives!"

"You think I don't know that!" shouted Darik, smoke puffing out of his nose. "I have tried to keep them alive! I have! Every village we pass on the road we warn in advance that we are coming. And still the people don't leave. They choose to fight. And we are forced to fight. Do I wish there were another way? Of course I do!" he continued his voice rising to a crescendo. "But what choice do I have? Go off road, delaying us for days, weeks? And leaving the rest of our allies alone to fight Loach by themselves? Best case, they suffer terrible casualties. Worst case, we lose the entire force and Loach chews up each of our armies one at a time. So tell me Jeron, what would you have me do?"

"Better. Do better," thundered Jeron. "We don't murder innocent people to avenge other murders."

"And who do you think supports those murderers you despise so much?" asked Emkario, folding his arms beneath his chest. "Tell me, who provides them with food, weapons, armor, gold, and more soldiers for their murdering?"

"They're innocents. Just trying to make a living in this world," said Jeron, his knuckles popping as he clenched his fists even harder.

"They can be both," said Emkario. "Those are not mutually exclusive things. Notice that we don't set fire to their homes and shops. We could. But we don't.

We take what we need, and move on. We give them fair warning in advance. They choose to make the decision to fight, not us."

"This is ridiculous," shouted Jeron as he tossed over a few tables. But he did not advance towards the prince.

"You'll just have to accept how things are," said Emkario.

"I don't have to accept a damned thing," snarled Jeron as he stalked towards the older man. "And if things continue like this, don't expect me to act so civilized."

"Enough," shouted Darik as he finally broke his silence. "It's not ideal, and I don't like it any better than you do." His voice was strangled, as if his emotions were warring for control of his voice. "But we are fighting a war. And it may well be for our very survival. If you have a better plan, tell me."

Jeron remained silent as he seethed.

Darik nodded as if expecting the silence. "That's what I thought," he said bitterly. "No one ever has an idea of their own."

"Would everyone stop posturing already?" asked Vernon. He was tracing his finger along the map. "It is rather pointless. Darik, you're not trying to kill villagers. And Jeron, you know that he isn't. So would you please stop your whining so that we can figure out the least damaging route to take."

"I still think we should cut off of the King's Highway and move cross country as soon as possible," said Vincent.

"No," said Vernon and Darik in perfect synchronization. The two glanced at each other in surprise.

"Look at the map, man," said Vernon with impatience. "We've been over this. See, this is a road. Armies travel faster along them." Vincent rolled his eyes while Vernon continued his lecture. "That means we get where we're going quicker. Whereas who knows what can happen on a cross-country march. We may get stuck behind a mountain ridge and lose even more time."

"Or have to run through a ghost filled ruin!" chimed Vincent with a smirk. "That one was fun."

Jeron looked at the man completely bewildered. "A ruined city filled with ghosts? What are you talking about?" he asked.

Vincent shrugged unconcerned. "Just part of our flight from Fort Hope," he said. "It's not that important, but it got you to calm down." The man grabbed a seat and began whistling, unconcerned as if everyone else in the room was not present.

"You're insufferable sometimes," remarked Emkario with a roll of his eyes.

"I know, mate," said Vincent smugly in a faux Nuquanian buccaneer accent.

"Hush you two," admonished Darik. "Vernon, do you agree? Should we have encountered any Antierian scouts yet?"

Vernon scrunched up his face. "Maybe one or two under normal circumstances," he said. "But with the loss of so many troops, I assume your commanders are keeping the perimeter rather tight. We probably should start making contact with aerial scouts soon. Especially if word from Talendor has reached the army."

Darik rubbed at his chin absently. "Nelson did say he was going to stop by the Antierian embassy in Ochandor," he said. "If he did that, the message should be arriving soon, if it hasn't already."

"And that matters why?" asked Jeron, his mane slowly retracting into his body.

"Because we would prefer for our allies to know that they have another army coming to reinforce them," said Darik drily. "Which you would have figured out for yourself if you could control your temper."

Jeron felt his mane shoot out and heard his knuckles start popping again. But he did not step forward or say another word. And they thought he could not control his temper.

"Did the Loachians split their force up with our arrival?" asked Emkario, pointedly ignoring Jeron's presence.

"Our scouts do not report any sign whatsoever of the Loachian army, only a few skeleton garrisons and household guards in the vicinity," answered Vernon as he pointed to the map. "At least here, here, and here."

Darik nodded. "I expect they're falling back to a more defensible position. Try to lure us in where they can face both armies at once."

"What makes you think that?" asked Jeron skeptically. "They don't strike me as a particularly passive sort."

"It's what I would do," said Darik absently. "Set traps along the way. Bleed everyone slowly. Making this a war of attrition will act in their favor."

"Why is that?" asked Vincent. "Why is so time pressing?"

"Gold," replied Darik. "Well, more iron and everything else that comes out of the mines of Loach. Eventually, the three duchies, four if you count Ochandor itself, not involved in this war will tire of the economic impact it will have on them. And then who knows what will happen. Maybe they get involved for one side or the other."

"Each time I've passed through the city of Ochandor there are rumors that the king's health is getting progressively worse," said Vernon. "The dukes almost certainly have better intelligence on the king's health than we do. But if something happens to him, there is going to be a power struggle. Maybe even a civil war."

"Okay, so we move quickly," said Jeron. He paused. But where were they moving? He actually had no idea. "Umm. This may be a silly question, but what are we moving quickly towards? What is our actual goal outside of revenge? Are we going to overthrow all of Loach?"

Emkario grinned broadly and began clapping his hands in mock applause. "Bravo, bravo. Everyone give the brave paladin a hand," he said sardonically. "Welcome to command my boy. It's more than just whether or not we burn Loachian villages to the ground."

"Then what is it?" Jeron asked, the heat back in his voice.

Darik sighed wearily as he finally took a seat. "Well, we could try to defeat the Loachian army in combat, that is one option. Another is we kill Prince Matlin, avenging the betrayal at Fort Hope while simultaneously removing Loach's best option at having someone named king. Or, perhaps we try and lay siege to the city of Loach itself. Or we raze the entirety of the duchy, every city, town, village, farm, and mine. Make it impossible for them to wage war or continue on as they have."

A sick feeling took hold in Jeron's stomach. He felt queasy just listening to the options. "I don't particularly care for that last one," he said. Jeron already had nightmares of the death and destruction at his childhood home of Flintwood Village. He did not need to add any more fuel to those nightmares. Sleep was rare enough already.

"Neither do I," said a resigned Darik. "Unfortunately, it will have to remain an option. Eventually, we will need to pull our forces back. Another massive buildup by the monsters at Fort Hope could be disastrous. Or, a civil war for the crown could also require our forces to be elsewhere. If we can't kill Matlin, then what? It's not a pleasant thought, but one that we'll have to entertain."

"We better not," said Jeron as he glared at everyone in the room. "Now if you'll excuse me, I think I am going to go elsewhere. You know, somewhere where there is good company." He sneered as he said the word "good" hoping that his barb landed on at least some in the room.

Without another word he stormed out, slamming the door behind him. He left Renaldo's axe buried in the wall. The man was strong enough to pull it out himself. A less generous man would have broken the weapon out of spite. And they said he did not know how to control his temper.

CHAPTER TWENTY-SIX

D alton took a deep breath before entering the command tent. Things were tense in the camp recently. The soldiers were wound up tightly with all of the harrying missions. Half of the troops were worried of dying in those missions, while the other half were worried that they would go out on a mission and find the entire Loachian army lying in wait for them.

He did not mind either so much. No one asked him to participate in the harrying missions, and he was fine with that. No one in their right mind would actually want to go out on those missions. And after two grueling sieges on either side of the kingdom, against two different armies of monsters, he thought he deserved a little break.

The commanders of the army however were somber for a completely different reason. The girls were distraught over Calabella's death. The men clearly felt guilty, as it was their plan that went awry. Now every detail of every engagement was second guessed to the extreme. The horses could not be fed without an extreme debate breaking out within the tent.

Dalton found the meetings tedious. Make a decision and follow through. If he learned one thing about battle, it was that things always went wrong. Your enemies always do something that you did not anticipate. You just had to have a plan and adapt as necessary. It was less the plan and more the habit of planning that kept him alive.

His standard battle plan was simple. If things went poorly, he would channel his totem and run as fast as he could. Leave all this war nonsense in the dust. Find a nice tavern or inn, and drink himself silly. It did not matter which city. Maybe

Ochandor. He enjoyed his time there, and it was doubtful any army would be marching on the capital.

Dalton entered the tent and stood next to Prince Nelson. The Bionan's presence, while not enjoyable, was easily more tolerable than the others in the tent. He could only handle so much morose behavior. The stiff-necked Bionan was a brief respite from that.

"Did I miss anything?" Dalton whispered.

"If you were punctual, you wouldn't need to ask," said Nelson from behind a glower.

"If I was punctual, I wouldn't have been able to snag that bit of blackberry pie from the chef's tent," responded Dalton with immense satisfaction. It had been the perfect blend of sweet and tart. A rarity for army chefs.

"Blackberry pie?" asked Nelson with a hint of intrigue creeping into his voice. "I do not suppose you have any left? I have not had the opportunity to leave the tent all day."

"That depends," said Dalton. "Do you have that flask of whatever on you?"

"Bionan brandy, and yes," said Nelson cautiously.

"How about a trade then," said Dalton as a pulled a small cloth wrapped bundle from beneath his cloak. "My food gets you through this meeting. Your brandy gets me through it."

Nelson stiffened himself, stretching his body to his full height. "That hardly seems a fair trade," he said. "My brandy is much more expensive and–"

"We split it then," said Dalton.

"Deal," agreed Nelson quickly.

The pair quickly exchanged parcels as surreptitiously as possible. Dalton glanced down at the flask and quickly looked about the room. Even if he took a quick pull, the captains and masters would see it. Unless he had an excuse to turn around.

Dalton feigned coughing and politely turned his back on the military brain trust. He took a swig from the flask and began coughing in earnest. Bionan brandy, whatever was in it, burned. It burned pleasantly all the way down his throat. He choked and coughed, barely able to appreciate the warm sensation in his belly.

Someone smacked him on the back. Hard. "There, there, let it out," said Nelson. "You'll be okay. Just breathe."

Nelson leaned down and lowered his voice to a whisper. "Nice acting. I'm going to take a bite, hand me the flask in just a minute."

Dalton nodded weakly as the prince stuffed his face with a fistful of pie. He handed off the flask and Nelson took a small sip along with the pie. Who knew that the formal prince had a sense of fun about him. Maybe he would not mind...no no. That was a bad idea. Dalton quickly abandoned that train of thought. Nelson would not become his drinking partner.

"You alright son?" asked Master Maxus as he walked over and patted Dalton on the back.

"Yes, sir," coughed Dalton. "Just a little something caught in my throat."

Maxus sniffed at Dalton and frowned at the boy in disappointment. "I should certainly say so. Now if you young men don't mind, there is a war to be about."

"Are we ready now?" demanded Captain Levren with a scowl. "Good. So have we made contact with Prince Darik's forces yet?"

"Not yet," replied Master Sildun. "My men have kept their scouting to the limits you prescribed. We have not ranged out on any long expeditions to date. We could send an aerial unit on a reconnaissance mission if you like."

"No. We'll give it some time still," said Levren. "We'll make contact eventually. Have there been any sightings of the robed Loachani witch?"

"Wizard I believe, Captain," said Master Richard as he smoothed his brown robes.

"Yes, her," said Master Tyson. "And a few of the men believe to have spotted a robed figure. The color of the robe has changed, and they only have seen glimpses."

Captain Levren harrumphed in acknowledgement. "But the lightning attacks still occur?"

"Indeed," said Tyson. "She varies her tactics. She does not always come to each battle. And when she does, she arrives at random and in disguise."

"She must be well studied in the art of war," observed Captain Iandrick.

"Or maybe she is getting lucky," said Olivia with her arms crossed and a frown on her face. "If we never received a military education, what makes you think she has?"

"Are you suggesting that you and Atrisha have been thwarted repeatedly by an untrained wizard?"

Olivia and Atrisha both bristled at the captain's words. Dalton found it refreshing to see that. No matter how far he traveled, those two girls remained defiant and prideful at every turn. Although it had been disappointing to hear of Calabella's death. He enjoyed her company. She was a quality drinking partner. Capable of enjoying fun and revelry without causing a brawl. Pity. A real waste that was.

"No, she is not," said Atrisha darkly, her face flushing red. "We're suggesting that if we get another opportunity at this woman that she is dead."

Dalton arched an eyebrow. Olivia had said that Atrisha was cold, distant, and angry since hearing of Cole's death. If that was cold, then he could not rely on Olivia's impressions. That was as angry and passionate of a response as he had ever seen.

"Perhaps I have an idea," ventured Master Richard. "Let Dalton accompany them. He's a smart boy. I've met him before on the way to Fort Hope. Let me speak with the lad in private, give him a few tips on combating magic."

"Accompany us?" demanded Olivia. "We are perfectly capable of leading the forces without a minder."

"I agree," said Atrisha as she glared at the masters and captains. "And if you know so much about fighting magic, why aren't you going?"

"I am not a warrior, my dear," growled Richard, the vein in his temple beginning to bulge.

Dalton suppressed a grin. His prior relationship with Master Richard involved that same look on the master's face while Dalton held a spear to his throat.

Those were good times. Things had only barely begun to descend into madness at that point.

"Yeah, uhm, maybe I shouldn't go," Dalton said uncertainly. "I mean, Olivia and Atrisha seem to have a great grasp on things."

"Shut up. You're going," said Captain Levren angrily. "Everyone else here has been dragooned into doing something outside of their comfort zone. Welcome to the war boy. Now go with Richard."

Nelson patted Dalton on the back, gently pushing him towards Richard. Dalton followed the wizard out of the tent past the withering glares of Olivia and Atrisha. That hardly seemed fair. He was not the one to suggest that he accompany their force. In fact, he argued against it! They had no reason to be upset with him.

Richard glanced around the camp looking irritated. "I don't belong here you know," he said before pointing towards a wooded area off the main road. "That way. Common folk tend to become nervous around magic. Things they don't understand always cause them to succumb to fear. Never underestimate human stupidity, boy. It is one of the most predictable things in this world, and also the most terrifying."

"Yes, sir," said Dalton as he tried to interject a sense of gravity into his voice. He recalled Master Richard being a demanding teacher, with a short temper and no tolerance for foolishness. Which was a pity, as Dalton was rather fond of foolishness. Especially, when it paired with a nice red wine.

Richard scowled at him. "Watch your tongue beanpole. Now tell me, have you been practicing what I taught you."

Dalton shrugged. "Little things. I heated food while travelling, cooled drinks while in Talendor, you know, simple things that wouldn't draw any attention to me."

Richard twisted his face into a look of pure disgust. "You used magic to make your food taste better? For such simple things?"

"Man, you don't get out much, do you?" asked Dalton. "When you're travelling in harsh environments, a good meal is the most divine thing in the world."

Richard hesitated before responding. He looked around the bleak Loachian frontier before bowing his head in acknowledgment. "I'll admit that there may be some truth to that. Now show me what you remember."

Dalton focused, reaching out with his mind and will, and grabbed hold of the world around him. Ice formed in the space between his hands. It crystallized, growing larger and larger, until it was the size of a human head.

"Very good," said Richard as he ran a hand through his hair. "Some rust is to be expected. But you need to do it faster. Now hit those trees in order."

The ice shot across the clearing in the woods faster than an arrow. It slammed into the tree with a loud crack. Shards of ice and wood filled the air. Dalton focused his mind as he struck at the trees. He pictured them as enemy soldiers, training his mind to become used to the action.

"Switch elements," instructed Richard.

And so it went. Dalton shaped fireballs into existence, conjured lightning bolts, threw boulders, and formed structures out of dirt and stone. Master Richard put him through the paces until sweat drenched Dalton's clothing.

His brain hurt, the result of fatigue. Dalton wanted nothing more than to sleep, rest, and recover from the effort. But the strain of using so much magic, especially after such a long time, left him with a throbbing headache pounding behind his eyes. It struck against his brain in rhythm with his heart beat. Dalton assumed it was nature's revenge against him for damaging so many trees.

"Not bad," admitted Richard reluctantly. "You never were the most creative with your use of magic. You're more a work mule boy. You can generate a lot of power for long periods of time. Handy for what you're going to be doing."

"Some special technique to fight against the Loachian wizard?" asked Dalton.

"Oh, that? No," said Richard with an amused expression on his face. "That was merely an excuse to get you out of the command tent and see what you remembered. Your special training is what you just did. You counter magic with magic. The better your imagination, the better the results."

"Have any good examples?" asked Dalton from behind a yawn that he did not bother to conceal.

"Hmm. I once saw a wizard conjure up an impressive wall of flame before a cavalry charge," said Richard. "The opposing wizards extinguished the wall with a sudden deluge of water directly overhead of the wall of flame. The opposing wizard then conjured up a gale of wind, blowing the smoke and steam back into the eyes of the first wizard and his army. The cavalry charge was quite effective against defenders who had trouble seeing and breathing."

"That's downright devious," said Dalton. "But I don't know if I can think of that on the fly."

"Of course not," scoffed Richard. "Few are great at improvisation. It's easier use that thick skull of yours in advance. Conjure up enemy tactics in your head and devise multiple ways to defeat each one. That way your brain can reach for an acceptable choice even if you forget the correct one."

"That sounds an awful lot like the sort of training Master Maxus and Captain Levren put me through," groaned Dalton. "It's a lot of work."

"Good. Then you'll be accustomed to it," said Richard in satisfaction. "Now get some rest. Your mind needs it more than your body. I am not sure when the next patrol will be going out, but try to practice when you can. When you are sure you are not going out on patrol, push yourself. You'll never grow stronger if you don't push yourself."

"Are you going to teach me more than I already know?" asked Dalton.

"Maybe," said Richard as he stared off into the distance in thought. "I've already taught you more than the Eldritch Society will be pleased with. You may have to learn to accept being the paladin who can control the elements."

"There are worse fates," agreed Dalton. "Please tell me that eating and drinking helps the mind recover from using magic."

"Of course," laughed Richard. "Why do you think so many elderly wizards are fat?"

Dalton sighed in relief as they walked the short distance back to camp. At least practicing magic would give him something to do when not on patrol. Something told him that Olivia and Atrisha would not be the best of company, and Nelson was still best in small doses.

A smile crossed his face. Those cooks who made the pie were still in the camp! Perhaps he could hunt them down before going to sleep or riding off to battle.

CHAPTER TWENTY-SEVEN

Matlin inspected the dirt bulkhead that his soldiers had constructed along the road heading north from the King's Highway. It was a simple, yet effective fortification. It was not defensible for a long period of time, but then again, that was not its purpose.

His men were constructing defenses every few miles along the road for Clara to use in her retreat. They would slow the Antierians, delaying their arrival at the fortress his engineers were constructing a few days further up the road. Every hour the Antierians spent trying to break through the dirt fortifications would allow him to reap the rewards of the engineers' work. Higher and stronger walls on the fortress, maybe even a few siege weapons if he was lucky.

Clara required all the aid he could provide to her. She was not a military mind and it showed. She was bleeding troops at a higher rate than he was comfortable. But she was bleeding the Antierians as well.

He would replace her if he had another acceptable option. Matlin would much rather that she ride with him and help manage the army. However, he lacked subordinates that he could trust with the delaying force. Any of his officers could be assassins, or nobles bribed by one family or another. He was not about to place the dagger that stabbed him in the back into the hands of his enemies that quickly.

Something collided into his back hard. The suddenness of the attack surprised him as he tumbled off of the dirt bulwark and fell to the ground below.

A man wearing the uniform of one of his men leapt down after him. His sword pointing straight down as he plunged through the air, clearly intent on skewering Matlin. A poor decision. The man would not be able to adjust his trajectory if Matlin moved.

Matlin did not oblige his attacker. He rolled to his right. The odds were that his attacker was right-handed, like most in the kingdom. That would place Matlin on his offhand side, giving Matlin an instant longer to react.

The would-be assassin slammed into the earth, his blade missing Matlin by mere inches. Matlin swiped at the man, raking his claws through the man's lower spine like a knife through freshly baked bread. The assassin shrieked as his bones gave way. He thrashed his body against the ground, flopping like a fish of out of water. No matter how hard the assassin tried, his legs did not move.

A cold smile spread across Matlin's face. He kicked the sword out of the man's hands and casually snapped both of his arms. He would get some answers from the man. Whether they were the truth or not, well, that was no longer the assassin's problem.

Matlin chided himself for letting the man get so close to him. He was so absorbed in his own plans that he neglected his own personal safety. He would need to recall Clara after all. His mind was not going to become less burdened as time went on. He would just need to risk placing the retreat in someone else's hands. If fear of Matlin did not keep the men in line, fear of the advancing Antierians might just do the job.

Chapter Twenty-Eight

F otlin rubbed at his head while he read the words over and over again. The writings in the book matched those inscribed within the roof of the Temple of Espira. Worse, the Temple of Annelu confirmed that the book was one of the tomes pilfered from their libraries.

Much to the Anneluites chagrin, Fotlin had retained the tome as part of his investigation. Once he showed the book to his father, then he would return it to the temple. It was best that his father saw the tome with his own eyes. The words within were troubling to say the least.

When the dragon rises from the wyvern's treachery,
The seas and the desert will war against the mountains themselves,
And ghosts shall return to exact their revenge.
Mines shall close, and walls shall fall beneath their fury,
And the downtrodden shall rejoice at the return of justice.

Fotlin tried interpreting the words in multiple ways, and had come up with only a few possibilities. But no matter how he tried to convince himself, one interpretation rose above the others. That the current war was predicted by some old tome. It added credence to the reports that Prince Irvin of Kelon was alive and fighting at Talendor alongside Darik. What other returning ghosts could the book possibly be referencing?

And how did this thief fit into things? Did he fancy himself as some champion of the downtrodden? An instrument of prophecy? He seemed more interested in stealing from temples, societies, and anyone else with ancient relics. Owen's stories about the man were farfetched and fanciful. Fotlin would never have believed the man without the book, or the inscription etched into the temple. However, having seen those items with his own eyes, it lent credence to the watchman's reports.

Catching this man was almost certainly on his list of responsibilities. His father would see that this man would become a priority for Fotlin over all else. With watchmen and an entire temple having access to the thief's message, it would not take long for it to spread throughout the populace like a sickness.

Finding a man that supposedly used fire to write in stone should be fairly easy. But no one knew the man's face, and he easily could be using one of those contraptions that the Eldritch Society crafted to alter his appearance. He could be anyone.

Fotlin exited his office with the book as he began his trek from the headquarters of the City Watch to the palace. He wracked his mind while he walked, trying to determine a way to deduce the identity of the thief, assassin, freedom fighter, or whatever the man was. His father would want more than ideas; he would demand a plan.

That meant entertaining even Yutlin's previous hairbrained idea that the man was a dissatisfied member of the Eldritch Society. While it was possible that the man was a wizard, Fotlin retained his reservations. The man was highly athletic if reports were to be believed. There just was not a good explanation for the man's varying set of skills. Strong, athletic, and sneaky?

A thought struck Fotlin as he walked through the common grounds of the Central District. Maybe he did not need to identify the man. He had the man's goals did he not? Steal things, kill things, and maybe aid the commoners. If the man had goals, then he had a plan. And men made plans. Plans could be thwarted, and men could be caught in a trap.

He needed more information for his plan to work. He needed to know what his older brother knew. Setlin ran the mines which were also suffering from a string of thefts themselves. Maybe those events were linked. Maybe not, but it would help him convince his father that he had formulated a plan.

The mood of the city had yet to change since the executions. Tension was felt everywhere, even in one of the wealthiest districts in the city. Yutlin's food giveaways had not worked particularly well. People were scared, and were avoiding the markets as the watchmen were certain to be there. News of the free food stagnated in the markets, and those who needed it the most either never heard of it, or were not attending from fear of a trap.

Fotlin could not blame them as he spared a look at the gallows. It did seem too good of an opportunity to be true. If you're afraid of being arrested by the watchmen, why willingly deliver yourself into their arms? There was a reason many of the thieves, urchins, and beggars possessed totems that were prey and not predators. Their survival instincts tended towards finding ways to survive those more powerful than them.

Yutlin's attempts at charity had accomplished one thing. They spread anti-Antierian sentiment throughout the city. Embellishment was not even needed. The truth of those Antierian heathens and their allies was terrible enough. An army of mercenaries arriving out of duchy of the dead, that massacred and looted any village or town that stood in its path? It was too horrible to comprehend.

Fotlin took the steps leading up to the palace two at a time. He did not want to be late for today's meeting. His position was already perilous, and Yutlin was still young enough to try something rash, impetuous, and stupid.

The atmosphere inside the palace was not much better than out in the city. Servants hustled quickly and quietly through the corridors, unwilling to speak to each other, or risk looking their betters in the eyes. Guardsmen stared suspiciously at every unknown face, seeing daggers and threats everywhere. The court ladies did not even roam the halls as they used to. Instead, they huddled in groups in their rooms, or within the palace museum, staring and chatting over the art.

It made Fotlin's hair stand on end. The war just made everyone feel unsettled. Which was not the feeling he needed before confronting his father.

He entered his father's planning room without being announced. There was not even a person to announce him had he desired it. If someone was mad enough to enter his father's planning room without his father desiring their presence, that was their problem, and most likely their head.

Both Setlin and Yutlin were already in attendance. The former's face had smudges of dirt and dust on it. Setlin was prone to actually inspect issues within the mines personally. The thought made Fotlin shudder. Being cramped and confined in those narrow corridors was simply unnatural. No rational person could possibly enjoy it. He should know, he had tried it once. The entire experience made him feel as if the walls were creeping in on him with every step. Fotlin found it difficult to breathe in the cramped confines. He had not panicked. Panicking was what others did.

Fotlin took a seat across the table from Setlin. There was plenty of room at the table without his other siblings present. Of course, the twins would not be returning, but he hardly counted that as a loss. There was something not right in their heads. That mixture of cunning and cruelty made their presence unbearable.

"Setlin, I have a question about the mines for you," asked Fotlin as he flexed his calves beneath the table. Walking long distances always made his calves and ankles sore.

"What is it?" asked Setlin, his voice neutral except for a hint of weariness in it.

"What exactly is being stolen from the mines?" Fotlin asked.

"Why do you want to know?" said Setlin warily.

Fotlin steepled his fingers and tapped his index fingers together while he spoke. "I'm trying to establish a pattern behind all the thefts in the city. One thief in particular, with a habit for pilfering high value items. Maybe there is a pattern there."

Setlin nodded in understanding before speaking. "Diamonds," he said as he exhaled loudly. "And a lot of them. All colors of them too. Gray, white, blue, yellow, orange, red, green, pink, purple, brown, and black. Doesn't seem to matter to our thieves."

"And that's it, only diamonds?" asked Fotlin excitedly. If he had a lead, he could comb over his reports searching for stolen diamonds. Discover which places had not been struck yet and lay a trap.

"No," admitted Setlin as he ran his hands through his dark brown hair. "We've had other precious gemstones stolen as well as gold, silver, platinum, and other mundane metals such as iron. Only small amounts though."

"Interesting," said Fotlin as he drew out the word. His mind raced as he tried to recount the reports that entered his office.

"You have something?" asked Setlin eagerly. A fire came into his eyes as he leaned forward on the table. Fotlin suspected their father was riding him hard as well to stop the thefts in the mines.

"Who cares whether they're linked?" asked Yutlin as he paced the room. "What does stopping one thief mean when crime is running rampant throughout the city? Food merchants are being robbed daily; their warehouses looted despite me giving away free food. None of this makes sense."

Fotlin and Setlin shared a wry smile at their little brother's consternation. He would learn eventually that being able to claim any victory at these meeting with their father was a necessary accomplishment.

"Maybe you shouldn't have hanged the urchins and beggars," said Setlin as he closed his eyes waiting for their father's arrival. "I don't know little brother, but I think some of them might be angry at that."

"Just a little bit," agreed Fotlin. Seeing Yutlin scowl at them was worth witnessing the pending tantrum. But his little brother would grow out of it eventually. Even Duke Camen would lose his tolerance with Yutlin's tantrums, youngest child or not.

"You little—" Yutlin snarled.

"Little what?" asked Setlin as his eyes snapped open and he glared at Yutlin menacingly. "What exactly are you going to do about it *little* brother," he sneered. "Have the watchmen hang me? I think not."

"But—"

"Grow thicker skin," advised Setlin. "Especially around us. You may be our adorable little brother, but dealing with your temper is wearing thin. Learn to think with your brain and not your emotions."

"I don't have to—"

"Yes, you do," agreed Fotlin, unable to resist the opportunity to badger his little brother. "Otherwise, you'll take it from father. And trust us, you don't want that. But if you don't believe us..." he let the threat trail off as he extended a hand to the door leading back to the ducal apartments.

The duke entered at that moment and Fotlin yanked his arm down hoping that his father did not see it. Yutlin however was not as lucky. His pacing left him standing awkwardly, and alone, the full gaze of their father brought to bear upon him.

"Father—" began Yutlin.

"Sit down, son," commanded Duke Camen. "Now."

Yutlin dashed into his seat, nearly knocking his chair over. He sat there, silently for once, his wide eyes darting about looking for refuge.

"Very well," began the duke without further preamble. "What do you have to report today."

Fotlin repressed a sigh and a wince before speaking. This was going to be a bad one.

"Father, the thief who struck the Temple of Annelu has struck again," said Fotlin with as crisp and steady of a voice as he could manage. "He broke into the Temple of Espira this time."

"What did he steal this time?" his father asked while glowering at Fotlin. "The temples are going to be in a fine fit over this."

"Nothing that the priests are willing to disclose at this point in time," said Fotlin.

"If he didn't steal anything, why are you wasting my time son?" said his father, his implacable face drawn into a frown.

"Because he left behind something," answered Fotlin. "Two somethings, actually." Fotlin pulled the two items out and set them on the table. "First is this tome. The thief left it behind. It is one of the books he stole from the Temple of Annelu. The priests at the temple confirmed it. The second is an inscription that he inscribed into the roof of the Temple of Espira. I have a copy of it here." Fotlin slid the two documents across the table.

"He inscribed it? How?" asked the duke as he read the document, his expression darkening. "This is a copy."

"He ahh, burned it into the stone," said Fotlin uneasily. "The watchman says he used fire. He was not close enough to see with what, but he reported that when he tried to apprehend the thief, the man conjured a fireball between his hands and turned it into ice."

"Did he now?" mused the duke as he turned his head and full attention to Fotlin. He appeared genuinely intrigued by the theft. Fotlin's mind conjured up all the curses that he had ever heard. His father intrigued by one of his cases? And it had to be a case where he had few leads? Fotlin felt that familiar feeling creep into his stomach.

"Yes, sir," replied Fotlin. "And the inscription matches a passage included in that tome. I have already marked the page for you." His father picked up the book and flipped to the marked passage. His eyes flickered briefly over the pages.

"I see. And how many people know of this...prophecy?" asked the duke slowly.

Fotlin tried to hide his wince again. "Ahh too many father. Some watchmen and many priests in the Temples of Annelu and Espira. The inscription is still in the stone on the temple roof. By now? Who knows how many people have viewed it."

"And you didn't think to have the inscribed stones removed?" demanded the duke in a cold, low voice. Despite speaking softly, the duke had a deep voice that carried easily throughout the room. Fotlin envied that. He had to shout to generate that sort of power in his own voice.

"Not without your approval father," replied Fotlin. "After the robberies at the temples I thought it best not to risk angering the temples without your approval."

A slow satisfied smile crept onto the duke's face. "Wise, my boy. Very wise. Now what leads do you have on this thief?"

It was the question Fotlin dreaded all morning. He tried to ignore the sweat beading above his temples. "Not many, father," he admitted slowly. "No one has seen his skin, much less his face. The best the men have managed is dark clothing, a man's body, and one capable of performing powerful physical feats. We have deduced at the very least the man has a powerful totem."

"His voice?"

"Watchman Owen thought he sounded amused while speaking," said Fotlin. "Beyond that, he couldn't make out too much. The voice was muffled by the clothing."

"I see. What are your plans on catching this urban bandit?" His father casually rested his chin in his left hand while he waited for an answer.

"Well father, I am operating under the theory that this man is responsible for some, if not all, of the other high profile thefts that have occurred throughout the city. I compared notes with Setlin to see if there was any overlap in the crimes. And we uncovered a possible link," said Fotlin. It was best to provide his brother with some credit. Setlin would remember if he did not, and it let their father know that they were working together and using all of their resources. Besides, Setlin was not all that bad. His only bad trait was that he stood in Fotlin's way of promotion.

"Diamonds," continued Fotlin. "They have been swiped from the mines as they have throughout the city. Items and stones alike. My plan is to stakeout some of the jewelers in town that peddle expensive jewelry and try to apprehend him there."

"Your entire plan is a stakeout?" asked his father, his face blank with emotion.

"No, father," said Fotlin. "I plan on interviewing the Eldritch Society and a few of the temples regarding this man's ability to use fire. While my watchman may believe he witnessed magic, I will need more convincing. It could easily be a device, and if it is, such a contraption is certain to have a weakness."

"And if it is magic?" asked his father.

Fotlin hesitated. Magic was not his expertise. "I cannot say that I know much about that," he admitted. "But I will explore that possibility with the wizards and priests."

"Good. Do that," commanded the duke. "Setlin, are you adhering to our plan involving the mines?"

"Yes father," said Setlin simply. Fotlin fidgeted in his chair. Setlin made sure never to let his little brothers know what was happening with the mines. And worse, his father permitted Setlin his secrecy. The mystery gnawed at Fotlin's curiosity. He chased thieves and solved crimes. He absolutely needed to have these answers.

"Good. It is imperative that the mines are operating at full capacity," said his father. "And Yutlin, how about you, my boy."

"The ahh, charity work is going smoothly, father," said Yutlin with trepidation on his face. "Few commoners have accepted our generosity however. I believe they are afraid of being hanged."

"Predictable," said his father. "Continue your work. Be seen around the better parts of the town as if all is fine. But do not execute anyone else for the time being. Let things die down and they will accept the food."

Duke Camen stood from his chair and regarded all three of his sons. "You have your orders boys. See that you carry them out. Dismissed."

As soon as their father exited the room, Yutlin made a mad dash for the door. Any semblance of restraint and decorum forgotten.

Setlin chuckled. "I remember when I was like that," he said.

"Angry and impetuous?" asked Fotlin.

"No, a teenager who was terrified of father," said Setlin. "Eventually, he'll grow out of it and find his own way."

Fotlin grunted. He was not as convinced. The twins had soured him on that front. "Tell me brother, have you received any word of the diamonds being smuggled out of the city?"

Setlin shook his head. "No. And believe me, we've been searching. If you catch wind of anything let me know. I'll have some of my men over to help as quick as I can."

"I'll keep it in mind," said Fotlin as he moved towards the door. "But if you'll excuse me, I have to interview some wizards and priests. Odds are they will be less then cooperative."

Chapter Twenty-Nine

L ynn smoothed her dress as she waited patiently next to the other girls in the common room of the Blushing Lady. She glanced in the mirror checking her reflection for the umpteenth time that night.

Her face was heavily powdered, the rich men seemed to fancy that, and her long black hair was done up in long flowing locks. She wore a short blue and black satin dress exposing her long legs. Her smile was both coy and friendly, a combination that took years to perfect. Business should do well tonight.

The customers in the Blushing Lady were mainly wealthy merchants with a few minor nobles sprinkled throughout. Money would be decent tonight; she just needed to avoid Squire Mervin and his ilk. One black eye from them could mean little food for the next week or so. Although some men did like their women skinny.

Some of the other girls preferred to walk around the common room and mingle with the patrons. Not Lynn. Her style was to lounge upon one of the soft couches throughout the common room, placing her long legs on display. It was all about power. She wanted to draw them into her, make them want her. That was the business after all.

The minstrel played a jovial bawdy tune while the patrons engaged in some drinking before participating in their revelry. Lynn saw the young man walk in during the middle of the song. He was young, maybe in his middle teenage years. He was a pretty thing, with dark well combed hair, and decent size to his gangly form. He would most likely fill out to be a decently strong man.

It was his clothes that jogged her memory. They were fine garments made of silk and bore the colors of House Loach. He wore them and strode about with a sense of pride that young men have when their parents have accomplished something. Worse, she knew him. He was not one of her previous customers. She remembered most of those. No, this man was something worse.

He had killed her sister.

That moment was frozen in her mind. That young man, Prince Yutlin, standing upon those gallows, puffed up as arrogantly as humanely possible. He preened and droned on and on about crime and justice. Then he snuffed out little Gemma's life as if she were less important than a cockroach. And for what? Because she was hungry?

Lynn stared at the man as she tried to conceal her hatred. She would not hang like her sister, but she would not sleep with her sister's murderer for all the gold in the city.

Unfortunately, the swaggering youth took her stare as one of interest. He stalked towards her with an oily smile on his face, and a burning lust in his eyes. Lynn felt her stomach turn over in revulsion. The preening fool actually thought she was interested in him. Gods, her luck was terrible.

The princeling stopped before her, that vomit inducing smile of his stretching out even farther. "How much?" he asked, contempt dripping from his voice.

Lynn blinked in shock. Every patron always tried to engage in sweet talk with her. It was part of the dance. A charade they put on to pretend as if they were not in a brothel, and to try to ease the girl's feelings, as if they could convince the girls that they truly were honorable gallant gentlemen. This little shit did not even have that decency.

"You can't afford me, young one," said Lynn in as sweet of a voice as she could muster.

The prince laughed. "I have more money than you'll ever see in your lifetime, whore."

Lynn stiffened as did everyone within the Blushing Lady. The minstrel stopped playing, and the patrons stopped drinking. The other girls stared at the boy in obvious discomfort. The word "whore" was anathema in the common room of the Blushing Lady. It ruined the fantasy for the patrons. Fantasy and escapism were part of what they were paying for after all.

But no one moved towards the prince, or said a word. If they were not present at the hangings themselves, they were quickly informed by others in the room who had.

Lynn dropped her smile and put on her most patronizing voice. "It's very sweet of you to express interest, but I don't work with people of your age. I like my men to be men."

"Too bad," said the prince as he grabbed her and pulled her off of the couch. "I've had a rough few days and I'm in the mood to show you how much of a man I am. Now show me to your room."

Lynn struggled against him as the room stared on in mute silence. One merchant made a beeline for door as he tried to extricate himself from the situation. When no one moved a muscle to help, she stopped fighting. She was not prepared to meet the hangman. At least not for slapping a young prince.

Every girl had her own way of dealing with unruly clients, and Lynn had hers. Some small needles that were spread out on her table next to her makeup and brushes. She arranged them carefully to disguise their appearance as part of her makeup kit. A quick dab at a vial and a prick later, and the troublesome client was no more.

Part of her wished she could bypass the poison and go straight for the dagger secreted in the wall behind her bed. A little leather patch that was hard to see in the dim room covered the hole in the wall. She could easily remove the patch, grab the dagger, and end the threat that way. But a slit throat left behind a body, and the killer would not be in doubt. So far, she never had to resort to using the dagger.

Lynn opened the door to her room slowly and entered reluctantly. The prince brushed past and began undressing from his elaborate ensemble.

"Hurry up and get naked," he said brusquely. "I don't have all night."

"Of course," said Lynn sweetly, her fake smile plastered upon her face. "Let me freshen up for a moment. I am a professional, and I'll be damned if I don't give you the most memorable experience of your life."

"Make it quick," he grumbled as he sat on her bed and yanked off his boots.

Lynn picked up a brush and began patting randomly at her face. The brush had nothing on it, but the boy did not notice as he was busy meticulously removing and folding his clothes. Lynn grabbed one of the needles and quickly dabbed it with the poison. She slipped the needle into her hair, using it to bind it up.

She slipped out of her dress and walked smoothly to the bed, her hips swaying with every step. A ravenous hunger was in his eyes. She kissed him forcefully on the lips, pulling him down on top of her while being careful to keep her legs closed.

The young prince kissed her back with a fiery one-sided passion. It was a short uncomfortable kiss, his teeth bumping into hers. And like all young men, he quickly disengaged and focused on sucking upon her breasts. Lynn had no idea why breasts fascinated men so much, but in that moment, she was eternally grateful that they did.

While the prince was busy looking down at her bust, his eyes were not focused on her face. A feature Lynn was certain he cared very little about once she was naked. She took the opportunity to remove the needle from her hair and plunged it into the back of his neck.

Prince Yutlin howled in pain, his teeth biting into her breast in shock. The prince swung his fist, striking Lynn in the face. She refused to cry out, to give the vile boy what he sought.

"What did you do?" he demanded as he struck her with a backhanded slap.

Lynn never had the chance to answer. The window to her bedroom exploded inwards in a hail of glass and wood shards. A dark clothed man stood in the room, looming there with a sword strapped to his back. The prince lurched to his feet and tried to swing at the intruder. He missed horribly, his punch coming nowhere near the man. The prince stood unsteady on his feet, looking about groggily.

Lynn smiled. She had multiple poisons. Both slow working poisons that took hours to set in, and fast acting poisons for the very dangerous clientele. She gave the prince the latter. Otherwise, a man of his station could afford a cure from an apothecary or priest. A vengeful prince was not something she wanted to encounter at a later date.

The intruder threw a combination of punches striking the prince's ribs before landing a final blow upon his jaw. A sickening crunch filled the room as the final blow left the prince's body limp as the naked little lord collapsed and shriveled up on the floor.

"What did you do to him?" the newcomer demanded.

Lynn looked at him impassively as her mind tried to determine whether or not to trust the man. "Poison," she whispered. "He killed my sister."

"I'm sorry," the man said softly. "When the watchmen come, blame it on me. They know me by my clothing and my weapon." A small stream of fire shot out of his right hand as smoke curled up from her wall. "And show them that. It will convince them without a doubt that I was responsible."

"Wait," whispered Lynn, quick and harsh as the man picked up the prince's unconscious body. "What will happen to him? I want him dead."

"Don't worry," said the man as he tossed back his hood. A gleaming shining skull grinned at her. Its eye sockets were covered in the same gleaming material as the rest of the skull, and she had the strangest sensation that fire was burning within those eyes. The skeletal mouth moved as he spoke. "Standard punishment."

The terrifying man with the strange skeletal skull said no more as he leapt out into the night with the naked Prince Yutlin tossed over his shoulder.

CHAPTER THIRTY

O wen hated being a city watchman with a passion. As he gazed at the bruised face of the pretty young prostitute, he tried to remind himself of why he continued to don the uniform.

It was for the gold.

Without money his own daughter would be in the same position as the young prostitute. The woman was barely older than his daughter. His girl would not be whoring to survive so long as he continued to breathe.

The young girl's story had the ring of truth to it. One of the princes took a liking to her, and smacked her around some. That was common enough. Owen supposed that young Yutlin had some of the twins' tendencies about him. He was the right age for those feelings to begin to creep out.

Owen cleared his throat before asking the next question. It was one of his least favorite. "Excuse me miss, but did the prince ahh...finish having sex with you?"

The woman's back stiffened and she ceased weeping. She shot him with an imperious glare that he may have expected from a queen sitting upon her throne. "We never had a chance to have sex," she said hotly. "The intruder interrupted us and abducted the prince before that could happen."

"I see," said Owen absently. At least he would not need to be escorting this young woman to the Temple of Illis. The Sisterhood took its vows of chastity rather seriously, and was a common dumping ground for possible princely bastards.

Owen scratched at the stubble on his chin as he tried to piece the events together. Fotlin would have his hide if he did less than that. His thief arrived quickly at the Blushing Lady. That meant he was either stalking Prince Yutlin, or he was working with this Lynn.

His brow furrowed in thought. That did not make sense. For the man to be working with the prostitute he would have to know that Prince Yutlin would show up at the brothel, and choose Lynn. Yutlin did not have the same reputation as the twins, so that possibility felt remote. But he was not paid for assuming the unlikely.

"That seems awful quick," noted Owen. "The man just happens to break in that soon?"

"Yes," insisted the prostitute.

"Be honest," said Owen. "You're working with him!" An accusation always loosened up tongues, no matter how flimsy it may be.

"Absolutely not!" replied the prostitute as she placed her fists on her narrow hips. "I would never work with a monster like that!"

"A monster? You mean that you've seen him?" asked Owen eagerly.

"After he burned the wall, he pulled back his hood," said Lynn.

"Burned the wall?" asked Owen as a sinking feeling entered his stomach. She pointed in response and Owen glanced at the wooden wall. Words were etched into the wood, and Owen had no doubt what they would say.

"What did he look like?" he asked as he averted his eyes from the message.

"He was hideous," declared the prostitute. "His face was not a face, but a skull. It gleamed of some sort of shiny material. It wasn't stone, nor metal. It looked like a gem, or a crystal, or something like that."

"I've never heard of skull shaped crystals," said Owen uncertainly.

"Me either," whispered the young woman. "But that is what I saw."

Owen thanked the woman for her cooperation and warned her not to disturb the writing left behind by the intruder. He exited the brothel feeling weary and exhausted. Prince Fotlin was going to lose his mind when he heard about the night's events. Owen berated himself for not arresting the prostitute. The prince would want someone to blame. But he could not bring himself to see another innocent hanged.

"Owen," called out a young watchman as he raced through the street. Owen scrunched up his brow as he clawed through his memory trying to remember the lad's name. Terrel, he thought.

"There's something in the Central District common grounds that you need to see," said Terrel. Sweat coursed down his face, and his breathing was rapid, heavy. Owen assumed the lad must have ran directly to the Blushing Lady with the news.

"How did you know to find me here?" Owen asked suspiciously. With the way things were going lately, he was not prepared to take any chances.

"Huh?" asked Terrel bewildered. "You're the senior watchmen on duty tonight. Everyone said there was an incident at the Blushing Lady, and that you were here. I ran straight here."

"I see," said Owen. "And what happened in the Central District?"

"Umm sir," stammered Terrel. "It really is something you should see for yourself. I uhh don't want to be spreading any rumors."

Owen wanted to scream. After tonight only one thing could possibly raise that sort of reaction from the lad. He pushed the thought away and tried to banish his fear. Maybe it would just be another robbery. His string of bad luck needed to break at some point.

Terrel did not speak as they walked through the district. The dawn hours were already quiet as people slowly stumbled into their morning routines. Conversing on the streets during that time period was frowned upon when on duty in the Central District. Prince Fotlin loathed receiving reports from angry wealthy merchants that his watchmen were causing a ruckus in the early morning hours resulting in taxpaying citizens losing sleep.

Without the normal pedestrian travel, they arrived at the common grounds quickly. Multiple watchmen stood guard at every entrance barring the area off from the public. Owen nodded to the men as he walked onto the common grounds. Soon the area would be bustling with people and not even the watchmen would be able to keep them out.

"What am I looking at?" asked Owen. "The place seems deserted."

Terrel gulped before answering. "Up there," he said, his finger quivering.

Owen followed the young man's trembling finger and his stomach turned to acid at the sight. High above the common grounds a naked body dangled from one of the many battle standards. The body hanged by a rope, undoubtedly in a noose.

"Get the body down without damaging it," ordered Owen. "And quickly. Keep it covered with a sheet. Scour the area for clues as to who did this and where they went. I'll go to the palace and inform Prince Fotlin."

Owen closed his eyes as he said a prayed to the rising sun. "And may the gods preserve us all for what will come next."

CHAPTER THIRTY-ONE

D alton's horse swayed while he rode out on what felt like his hundredth patrol. If he was being honest, it was closer to ten, but the lack of appearance by Loach's wizard made him restless and uneasy. His orders were to accompany the other riders, fight if he must, but hold back at all costs until the Loachian wizard showed herself.

He scowled at everyone in sight. There was little doubt in his mind that the last order was a result of Master Richard. The man simply did not wish to confront the enemy wizard. Not because he feared her in combat, but Dalton suspected the forty-something year old man did not enjoy travelling, or being on a horse at all.

Olivia and Atrisha however found the order humorous for reasons they did not deign to share with him. The perks of command they said. Dalton scowled even harder at the memory. Two sieges in two separate wars, and no one thought it fit to make him an officer? Master Maxus merely frowned when Dalton raised the issue, and changed the subject, lamenting the fact that he did not have a set of full platemail on hand for Dalton.

Dalton knew better than to argue at that point. His previous experience marching through southern Antier in full platemail had been brutal. The smell was horrid. He still had memories of that stench. Disposing of the armor had been one of the most satisfying moments in his life.

While he was ordered to stay back, Olivia and Atrisha found it frustrating to try and enforce that order. There was very little they could do. He was essential to fighting the opposing wizard. Without him, they would not stand a chance.

It was not like Dalton wanted to fight on the front lines. He hated it. But sitting back while others fought in his place bothered him. He hated feeling useless. But as he sat on his horse heading towards possible death, useless and boredom did not sound terribly unappealing.

"So are you actually going to stay back this time?" growled Olivia. Master Richard had not informed her of his own instructions for Dalton. He suspected that being omitted from that portion of the plan bothered her greatly. Apparently, the perks of being an officer only extended so far.

"Unlikely," said Dalton. "Someone has to keep an eye on you two."

"Oh, like how you kept an eye out for Cole and Byron?" asked Atrisha venomously. There still was such anger behind her eyes as she spoke. Dalton thought that after a few weeks she would have softened towards him a little bit. It was unsettling when one of your allies most likely wanted you dead more than your enemies.

"Yup," agreed Dalton with a little nod. "I lost sight of them for a little bit and look what happened. I am not prepared to let that happen again."

"We can take care of ourselves," snarled Atrisha, her blue eyes burning bright.

"I never said that you couldn't," replied Dalton as he rolled his eyes. "But since you can take care of yourselves, I assume the rest of this army is just for show? You two will be doing all of the fighting?"

"Don't be ridiculous," scoffed Olivia. "Of course they will be fighting too."

"I see. So your problem is only if I fight," said Dalton.

"Because you're trying to protect us, and we don't need protecting," declared Atrisha.

Dalton snorted. "Of course not. You're invincible," he said sarcastically. "And who gives a damn why me or anyone else in this army fights, so long that we actually do it? Everyone has their own reasons. Your only concern should be that we actually pick up weapons and fight. Beyond that, it's none of your damned business."

"It matters to us," insisted Olivia. "And so long as you're under our command you'll follow orders like a good soldier. Now be quiet, we've almost reached the next bulwark."

Dalton shut his mouth and rode quietly. He was not sulking, no matter what the two girls might say. It was not his fault that he was the only one with common sense in this army.

The bulwark was just like the previous three that they had encountered. A large thickly packed dirt wall stretched across the road. There would be platforms on the other side for Loachian defenders to strike at them. They never stayed long enough for a fight. Merely to kill Antierian soldiers. Once it became apparent that the Antierians were going to seize the bulwark, the defenders would disengage, hop on their horses and ride off. The Antierian horsemen could not easily climb the bulwarks, allowing the Loachinas to make a clean getaway.

It was slow and bloody work until the previous bulwark. The Loachians had set a nasty trap. Archers hid in the woods alongside the road, peppering the assaulters with a blindside attack on their flanks. Dalton assumed the trap would only work once. You could only lure an enemy into a false sense of security once before they took precautions.

That was why he was riding with their forces after all. To counter the magic of someone who almost certainly had been practicing for years longer than him. A brilliant strategy. No wonder he could not be an officer. There was no way he could think of such an intelligent strategy on his own.

Dalton watched lazily as the Antierian forces dismounted to prepare for their assault on the bulwark. He would not participate in the attack. It was too easy to take a stray arrow, and he preferred to be on horseback in the event of a retreat. There was no reason to take unnecessary risks.

He held back a yawn as the soldiers prepared their charge. At this pace they could be plowing through these dirt mounds for weeks before engaging the enemy. The soldiers charged, hollering out battle cries praising their religions and duchies. Dalton found it silly. He never thought of either of those things when fighting. His thoughts were mainly focused on his battle mantra of "don't die."

The first wave of Antierians hit the wall, leaping onto the bulwark, their hands and weapons digging into the dirt seeking hand and footholds to climb. It was at that moment that the Loachians sprung their trap.

The bulwark exploded in a giant fireball sending the dirt and wood used in its construction flying. The explosion flung Dalton from his horse with a force he had not felt since the ambush at Fort Hope. Dalton tried to lift himself from the ground, focusing his thoughts through the pounding in his head.

No, not his head. Not entirely. That pounding reverberated through the ground. Those were the strike of hooves beating against the ground.

Dalton swore as he tried to focus his blurry eyes through the dirt and the smoke. But try as he might, he could not see the Loachian cavalry charge that he felt coming. He glanced around nervously at the Antierian forces. They were scattered, the foot soldiers near the bulwark were in a daze from the explosion, while the cavalry behind were struggling to regain control of their frightened mounts. They would be hopelessly slaughtered by a cavalry charge in this condition.

He tried to focus, reach out his senses like Richard taught him and grab hold of his surroundings, and mold them to his will. Everything was a blur in his mind. His thoughts were foggy and sluggish. He dimly heard Olivia and Atrisha barking out orders at the top of their lungs, but he could not make them out.

Power from his totem surged into his body. His muscles bulged as his body surged. It was an incredibly joyous feeling, like he had unlimited energy and could sprint for days. It was a feeling he had felt only once before in his life. Back home, when centaurs raided his village and slaughtered his family and friends. Everything became a blur as he ran back then, his speed faster than his mind could handle.

His legs twitched, desiring nothing more than to run like he had back then. But he gritted his teeth and sank his fingers into the hard earth. He had run twice in his life. Once, when he was a child and his village was destroyed, and the second at Fort Hope after Byron died along with their army. He would not run for a third time and leave his friends to die. Even if they were on the prickly side.

Dalton's mind may not have been able to handle the speed when he fled from his village. But he was a child then, unaccustomed to such power, and suffering from the traumatic loss of everything and everyone he ever knew. There was no reason why his mind should not be able to move as swiftly as his body when powered by his totem.

He blew past the fog in his mind, parting through it like a spider's web. Beyond that web lay clarity, peace, calm, and a sense of determination that felt foreign to him.

Dalton reached out, grabbing hold of the ground in the direction of the Loachians. He clenched his fists together, pulling at the ground beneath him as he pushed all of his will into forcing the earth to do the same. He strained, and clenched, sweat pouring down his face as the pounding began to grow louder.

But as it grew, he sensed the rattling pick up. The pounding was not only the horses, but the ground itself rumbling. Dirt flew into the air as the earth itself protested its movement. The area shook, animal and horse cries rising from the settling dust cloud. Waves and ripples shot across the ground, knocking over trees and pulling up roots in a tangled mess.

The Antierians gaped at the scene, unable to make sense of why the ground itself was aiding them in the battle. Their calm was restored as they looked on at the scene of madness in the road. Loachian soldiers lay scattered upon the ground. Some tried to regain their feet, while others cried from broken bones.

Dalton distantly heard Olivia cry "Charge!" before the Antierian horses lurched into motion, reversing the trap and replying to the planned Loachian cavalry charge with one of their own.

He tried to regain his footing, but his body refused to listen to him. Events swirled around him but they were happening to others, not him. Dalton was merely a distant observer. As his consciousness slipped into blackness he was left with one lasting image. Atrisha standing above him, her face a mixture of wonder and concern.

And to think he had thought she was prickly.

CHAPTER THIRTY-TWO

"I thought they'd be more excited," observed Jeron as he scanned the Antierian forces.

"It's not like they knew we were alive," said Renaldo darkly. Ever since Jeron pummeled him, he had been nothing but glowers and frowns. Jeron only felt slightly bad about the incident. But only slightly. Renaldo had drawn his weapon and tried to kill him after all.

"Also, the prince's armor isn't colored as it usually is," continued Renadlo as his face brightened with cheer. "Why how would the men recognize the Jewel of–"

"Finish that sentence and die," growled Darik. Renaldo tossed his head back and laughed in response.

Jayna bounced up to Renadlo, beaming at him. "I'm afraid I've never heard this story," she said mischievously. "Do tell."

"Nor have I," echoed Vernon. "I am most intrigued to say the least."

Darik threw up in hands in exasperation. "It was morning, I had dew on my armor when I showed up to court. The ladies said I looked like a jewel. The name stuck. I hate it. End of story."

Jayna burst into a fit of giggles while the rest of the men struggled to choke back laughter. "I like it," she declared. "It fits you. You do have a sparkling personality."

Darik groaned and buried his face in his hands.

Jeron placed a hand on the prince's shoulder, ignoring Renaldo's stiffening body language and glare, and leaned down. "Not in front of the troops, Your Highness," he said amiably. "It's bad for morale."

Darik looked up at him distraught. "Be a prince. Be in the command. Why does everyone want that?" he asked. "It's a terrible burden."

"Oh, it's not that bad," observed Vernon.

"You live in anonymity under an assumed identity," scowled Darik.

"Well, yes," replied Vernon without a trace of a smirk. "That's because I'm smart."

Jeron grinned as Darik grimaced in distaste. "Why does everyone around me think they are a jester?" the prince moaned.

The group chuckled softly at the prince's displeasure. Few villages had tried to fight their army since Jeron confronted Darik. The lack of dead civilians rose the spirits of those in command. Things had returned closer to normal since then.

The laughter died on Jeron's lips as he saw who awaited them. Captain Levren. The man who enjoyed making training as miserable as possible. He took great delight in tormenting Jeron and his friends. Jeron should have known the man would have been too disagreeable to die in the ambush at Fort Hope.

"Your Highness, welcome," said Levren with a respectful bow of his head mirrored by his companions. Jeron felt his jaw drop. This was not the same man. Respectful and without a trace of condescension?

Another older gentleman in armor stepped forward and Darik threw decorum away as he wrapped the old soldier in a hug.

"Who is that?" asked Jayna.

"Harold Iandrick. Captain of the duke's household guard," answered Jeron. "Good soldier, good man. Very strict though. Believe me when I say that you don't want to cross him."

"I won't," said Jayna with a thin smile. "But I'm also not a wild teenage boy prone to getting into trouble."

"I-I-that's true, I guess," said Jeron in resignation. "However, I'm not a teenager anymore either."

"We have an advance party out," said Captain Iandrick to Darik. "The Loachians have built dirt bulwarks across the road to slow us down. We should be encountering the next one while we speak."

Darik nodded in understanding. "I saw the remnants of a few after we turned north," he said. "I assume since you all are not surprised to see me that Dalton arrived?"

"Indeed he did, sir," answered Captain Iandrick. "Along with the Bionan prince. We sent a messenger to fetch him from his camp. The lad would be inconsolable if he were not here to greet you."

"He does like his ceremony," agreed Darik. Jeron snorted in derision. Ceremony was about all that Nelson loved.

"Dalton is out with the advance party," said Captain Levren. "He should be back soon."

"And what about Atticus, Lentil, and Telwin?" asked Vernon.

Captain Levren furrowed his brow and glared at the man. "And who the hell are you?" he asked. "And why the hell should I tell you where my troops are?" Jeron felt himself smiling in relief. Levren was still the same surly crusty man.

Darik lightly smacked himself in the forehead with the palm of his hand. "Ceremony, right. I forgot," he said. "Captains Levren and Iandrick, Masters Maxus, Tyson, Sildun, and Richard, please allow me the honor of introducing Prince Irvin of Kelon, his sister Jayna, and their companions Elfred, Marcela, Aron, and Brukel."

"My apologies, Your Highness," said Levren gruffly without a hint of apology in his voice. "Those three boys are also with the advance party."

"Excuse me captains," said Darik with a hint of wonder in his voice. "But is this army comprised mainly of women?"

"Not mainly, Your Highness," said Captain Iandrick. "But we do have a large number of female soldiers. Your father's idea."

"Replenishing our losses at Fort Hope, I assume," said Darik. The prince turned to Emkario. "Keep the mercenaries away from the women. They will almost certainly cause trouble after a long march."

"Yes, Your Highness," said Emkario as he darted off to comply.

Captain Levren rubbed his chin thoughtfully. "That probably won't be necessary, Your Highness," he said hesitantly. "We have only had a handful of incidents so far, and they have been dealt with rather strongly."

"As it should be," said Darik. "But I won't risk it. I am not familiar with the training and temperament of the mercenary force. Best not to take chances this far along. We'll keep them separate from the Antierians, just like the Bionans are."

Horses galloped into the camp from the north. Jeron craned his neck trying to catch a glimpse of the advance party. Dalton would almost certainly find a way to position himself near the front of the column. If there was a way to be first in line for food, that man would find it. How he remained so slender remained a mystery to Jeron.

Darik folded his arms and waited patiently, displaying years of court bred training. Jeron and Thiago did not have that same training.

"Do you see them?" whispered Thiago. "I can't wait to tell them about Kelon."

"Oh, you barely saw any of it," said Jeron. "You hardly scouted far from the road at all.

"Further than you," muttered Thiago.

"Boys, hush," said Jayna. "If you want stories of Kelon, I have more than either of you. And they're not only ghost stories."

Heat crept up Jeron's neck as his shame and embarrassment rose. At that moment he wished his skin was as dark as Thiago's. He disliked other people knowing how he felt inside, even if it was normal.

Jeron was saved further embarrassment by the arrival of the horses. The group of riders reined in before the command tent. They were led by a beautiful woman in chainmail. Her dark brown hair bound back in a pony tail showing off the sharp angles of her jaw and her burnt brown skin.

Jeron's eyes widened as he recognized Olivia. He scarcely could believe she was here. She looked more beautiful than he remembered. Her eyes met his for a brief instant and passed by him without a flicker of recognition. Her expression tightened slightly at the sight of Jayna, but she said nothing. Jeron winced ever so slightly.

"Captain Olivia, report," said Captain Levren as he stepped up to the girl's horse.

"The Loachians are routed after suffering heavy losses, sir," she said crisply. "It was a trap. The bulwark exploded as our ground units tried to take it. Most likely a surprise by the Loachian wizard. The Loachians were mounted behind the bulwark, prepared to charge our forces."

"How did you survive then?" asked Captain Levren. "Don't look at me like that. You just described a clever tactic that should have worked."

"We don't know," said Olivia as she gestured to Atrisha. "The ground started shaking, cracking and falling to pieces beneath the Loachians. They were tossed from their horses or killed outright by the earthquake. We aren't entirely sure how it happened, but we have our suspicions."

"Such as?" asked Levren.

Atrisha pushed her horse alongside Olivia's. A familiar body was slumped across the horse, tied down tightly. "I found Dalton passed out on the ground, clutching the earth tightly. He must have been squeezing as hard as he could as his hands were broken and bloody," she said as she glared in the direction of Master Richard. "What we want to know is what *he* told Dalton to do. We know there was some sort of plan he was supposed to execute in the event the wizard showed her face. But this?"

Jeron tried to move toward Dalton, but Thiago grabbed him by the arm. "Wait," Thiago hissed. "Something is going on here."

Reluctantly, Jeron waited with fists clenched. He felt helpless waiting. All he could do was stare at Master Richard and wait for an answer.

"I have no idea why he is like that," said Master Richard defensively. "Nothing we discussed should have left him in that condition."

Atrisha stared daggers at the robed wizard. Jeron did not recall her as being one prone to screaming when she raged. She always kept her emotions tightly reined in. But not now. Something changed in the girl.

She scanned over the crowd, her eyes widening ever so slightly at the sight of Jeron before stopping to rest on Jayna. Atrisha appraised the woman coolly before speaking. "You there. Dalton mentioned travelling with a priestess that could heal wounds," she said as if accusing Jayna of murder. "Is that you?"

Jayna smiled sweetly at Atrisha. "Yes, I am she, child," she said in as friendly a voice as she could muster. Jeron saw his wince mirrored on the faces of the captains and masters. They must have learned quite a bit about Atrisha since he had been gone.

"Child?" said Atrisha acidly. "I'm no child. I'm a soldier. Now can you help my friend or not?"

"I meant no offense," said Jayna as she tried to placate Atrisha. She spread her arms out wide in an open, inviting gesture. "And you forget. He is my friend too. Please get him off the horse and into the tent please."

Jeron rushed forward, Thiago a step behind him as they worked to untie Dalton from the horse. Jeron heaved as he tried to lift Dalton from the horse. How the man could be that heavy while remaining so slender, was a mystery. Perhaps all the food he consumed only impacted his weight while he was unconscious.

Master Maxus led him into the tent and Jeron lay his friend gently down on a bedroll tucked away in a corner. The remainder of the group filtered into the tent slowly, parting gently to make way for Jayna.

"Jeron, and Master...Richard, is it? Would you two please lend me a hand?" she asked in a stern direct voice. Jeron raised his eyebrow in surprise. She had never acted this way before. Jayna was always laughing and having fun. Serious was a rare expression for her, usually reserved for battles.

Jayna lifted Dalton's eyelids and peered into each of his eyes. She analyzed his wounds while Jeron and Richard hovered over her shoulders, their backs to the rest of the people in the tent. "Tell me if there is anything I should know before trying to heal him," she whispered as she slowly turned his hands over in hers.

"I'm not so sure that is wise," whispered Richard.

"He can use magic, can't he?" Jayna said flatly.

"Well, now that could—" stuttered Richard.

"Yes," interrupted Jeron. He glared at Richard, daring the older master to say anything. He was not going to let his friend be hurt over Richard's secrets.

"That's what I thought," Jayna said. "I don't see or sense any physical wounds with the exception of those on his hands. And those wounds are self-inflicted."

"Meaning?" asked Jeron as he tried to nudge her towards an answer.

"Meaning he is most likely mentally exhausted," said Jayna. "Using any magic is an exertion of willpower. If you over extend yourself, you usually become tired. If you extend well past that threshold, this is what happens. Your mind shuts down as it tries to recover."

"Are you trying to say that Dalton caused that earthquake?" asked Jeron skeptically. He had witnessed Dalton create fireballs and other small objects, but an actual earthquake? That was magnitudes beyond what he believed Dalton's capabilities to be.

"Impossible," said Richard. "He's never been that strong."

"Unless he channeled his totem while focusing his willpower," said Jayna. "His is particularly strong after all."

Master Richard's face paled. "I hope not," he whispered. "That is highly dangerous. Passing by the limitations of the human mind. The Eldritch Society discourages the practice."

"Wizards having closed minds and being stubborn? Perish the thought," said Jayna sarcastically. "Priests do it all the time. Your totem is a part of your soul, and lets you do a lot more."

"Sometimes limitations are necessary," said Richard defensively.

"Is that so," said Jayna flatly as her hands began to glow. She carefully lay them upon Dalton's brow. "Please tell me more."

Richard clenched his fists as his face flushed red with anger. Jeron stared at him in amazement. And people said that he had control issues.

"Have you ever heard of soulfire?" asked Richard.

"No," admitted Jayna absently. Jeron shrugged his shoulders, but neither of them paid heed to him.

"It's magically conjured fire," Richard explained. "Looks and gives off heat just like real fire with one or two exceptions. It's a deep violet in color and does not burn flesh. It burns the soul."

Jayna frowned. "That seems dangerous. Why haven't I heard of it?"

Richard blew out a deep exasperated breath. "It's highly dangerous. Wizards don't like to speak of it. Removing a person's soul? It just shouldn't be done. That's why we discourage using a totem in conjunction with magic. If the animal instincts take over, there is no telling what sort of destruction could be wrought."

"Purple fire huh?" asked Jeron skeptically.

"Violet."

"Violet. Whatever. But Vernon, excuse me, Prince Irvin said the vampire queen assaulting Talendor shot purple fireballs at him and Prince Darik."

Richard's face paled. "Soulfire," he breathed. "Wielded by vampires? The implications..." his voice trailed off as he ended the thought in a shudder. He said no more.

Jeron shrugged it off. He was competent with the basic rudimentary skills of magic thanks to Richard, but this soulfire stuff held no interest to him.

"Jayna, what are you doing to Dalton if his wounds are mental?" he asked.

"I'm trying to heal the fatigue from his mind. Speed up his recovery," she said as her hands stopped glowing. "He'll still need to rest, but it should help some."

Dalton groaned as if bidden to wake up. His eyes flittered open, blinking rapidly as he tried to focus. "Where am I?" he asked groggily. "And who are you? Can't see."

"Shh, easy now. You've been through a lot," said Jayna. "It's Jayna, Jeron, and Richard here to see you."

"Richard is an ass," mumbled Dalton.

"I agree," said Jeron as the wizard's face darkened anew.

"Enough," said Richard curtly. "Dalton did you see the enemy wizard?"

"No sir," he answered as a bout of coughing struck him.

"Did you cause the earthquake or did she?" asked Richard.

"I did," admitted Dalton.

"I see," said Richard as he unleashed a flurry of curses underneath his breath that were highly unfitting for someone with the rank of master.

"Get some rest," said Jayna as she patted Dalton's arm gently. "We'll talk when you wake up."

Dalton mumbled something incoherent as he slipped back into sleep. Jeron and the others stood up and returned to the planning table.

"I assume Dalton was the source of the earthquake," stated Darik as if it were already established fact.

"Your Highness, I don't know what you mean," spluttered Master Richard as he searched aimlessly for an excuse. The prince glared at him, and for once the color drained from his face. He looked meek, scared. Jeron wanted to cheer at the sight.

"Master Richard. Allow me to tell you a story," said Darik as he kept his gaze focused on the maps and reports spread out on the table. "When I was a child, my little brother wanted to do everything that I did. Even if he was too young, or physically incapable."

Jeron found himself listening intently. This story was from before he was orphaned and sent to the palace. Before he ever met Byron. Those stories were rare. He glanced around the room and saw the others staring in rapt attention, but for entirely different reasons. Many were paying attention simply because the prince was speaking, others because Byron became an infamous figure throughout the ducal court as a teenager, and stories of him as a child were a rarity.

"Even as a child my little brother was never fond of being told what to do," continued Darik. Captain Levren snorted and the prince looked up from the map and shot the older man a withering glare. The captain gulped audibly causing Jeron to snort with laughter.

"As I was saying, he hated being told what to do. And when the captain of my father's guard, Iandrick's predecessor, forbade Byron from studying the sword, Byron took extreme measures," said Darik. "He stole the captain's ceremonial sword and refused to return it until after the captain agreed to train him."

"He blackmailed him?" laughed Brukel. "What a kid."

"Indeed he did," said Darik with a wry, sad smile. "He always found a way to get what he wanted. And since Dalton here is not a wizard, yet he caused an earthquake, I think it is safe to assume that Byron blackmailed our dear Richard here into teaching them some magic."

Master Richard looked like he was going to be sick. Jeron wanted to laugh and tease the man about focusing his willpower on calming his stomach. But he did not dare interrupt Darik with that look on his face.

"You don't need to say a word Master Richard," continued Darik. "I know my brother too well. It's also why you're going to continue training Jeron. We'll need both of the boys if we're facing a Loachian wizard."

"Train Jeron, Your Highness?" asked Richard. "I don't think that is permitted."

Irritation flashed across Darik's face. "Jeron. Did Byron blackmail the master here into training the four of you boys on how to use magic."

"Yes, Your Highness," said Jeron as he ignored the stares of disbelief pointed in his direction.

"Fantastic. You all may continue training when Dalton wakes up," said Darik.

"Darik, if I may," said Vernon. "You say that we're facing a Loachian wizard? Why don't we bring Toran in here and see what he knows. The man did serve under the ducal family."

"Do it," said Darik, his jaw clenched.

Elfred ducked out of the tent and returned moments later with the stocky young cavalier. His gray eyes looked bewildered, but he remained silent.

Jeron did not care for the man. While he may be a refugee from Kelon, that did not erase the years of service he provided to House Loach. Nor could Jeron easily forget Toran riding alongside the twin princes from Loach as they placed four arrows in Byron's chest.

"Your Highness, how may I serve you?" Toran asked as he executed a bow that would make Nelson proud.

"A female wizard is with Prince Matlin's forces. Do you know who she is?" asked Vernon.

"Most likely the lady Clara," answered Toran. "She is the prince's cousin, and the only person he may consider a friend. She is his constant companion. Beyond that, I don't know anything else about her. Edlin and Dedlin did not like spending time around her. She enjoyed being cruel to them, so they stayed away, and since it was my duty to protect them, I stayed away."

"Thank you," said Vernon. "If Prince Darik does not have any objections, please go with Jeron and Master Richard and tell them every detail that you can remember." Darik absently waved his hand in acknowledgement; his focus returned to the maps.

"Yes, Your Highness," said Toran with a deep bow.

Jeron gave Jayna's hand a quick squeeze and flashed her a smile as he ducked out of the tent. There were worse things than questioning Toran about a deadly adversary. Worse things like speaking to Olivia about what had happened in his life since they parted.

"Hello there Jeron," said Prince Nelson as he strode towards the tent. "It's good to see you again. Have I missed anything?"

Jeron threw his head back and roared with laughter. "Just head inside, Your Highness. And keep an open mind."

CHAPTER THIRTY-THREE

Clara clung to her horse as her scattered forces retreated up the road. The Antierians rendered the bulwarks nearly useless after the battle. Blood still clung to Clara's robes. Whose blood it was, she had no clue. There were so very many options. Horses fell all around her as human and animal limbs cracked under the assault.

The earth itself had opened up beneath her troops. First cracks ran through the ground. Then the horrible shaking and quivering began. The cracks enlarged as the soil tore itself apart. Rocks crumbled, and trees split and collapsed under that terrible force. If she had any luck at all the Antierian army would have difficulty crossing what remained of the destroyed road.

Clara had never seen magic of that magnitude in her life. She had not even known that it was possible. Granted her training was self-taught through tomes she and Matlin had acquired. The Eldritch Society had a strict no female policy. Still, she was able to find rogue wizards, witches, and other types willing to impart little nuggets of wisdom. None of which involved moving the very earth itself.

She had instructed some of her forces to remain behind. They would place traps around the remaining bulwarks and have the soldiers serve as scouts. Their orders were to flee at the first sign of the enemy. She would not waste more resources fighting someone that strong without a plan.

By the gods she did not even know who she was fighting. The Antierians had yet to display any magical competency. Her scouts had not made note of any robe wearing soldiers in the Antierian forces. Their wraiths had only made mention of the one wizard, the master who never left the camp. This did not feel like his handiwork.

Clara rode to Matlin's camp without stopping. Not having to fight at each bulwark certainly made the trip quicker.

Matlin's camp was inside a hastily constructed fortress of stone and wood. Clara's heart sank as she gazed at the fortifications. All this work and it was for naught. The Antierians with their new weapon would make short work of those walls. One magical earthquake and the walls would crumble.

Clara worked her way through soldiers who were acting as makeshift miners, carpenters, and laborers. Many of them probably were experienced in those professions prior to their military service. Their work was fast and sloppy, but it was still their work. None of them were going to be thrilled about leaving it all behind.

The fortress was incomplete. It consisted of one large wall and gate stretching across the road at the tree line. Siege platforms were constructed further behind the wall. Catapult platforms and crude ballistae rested on the platforms. The rear of the platforms consisted of ramps so that the defenders could roll or carry ammunition up to the higher vantage points. A pulley system and lifts would have been ideal, but they did not have time for that.

Clara tossed her reins to a cavalier standing guard. "Care for my horse, and care well," she said. "If there is anything wrong with him, I am holding you responsible. And my boy, I never forget a face." She patted him on the cheek and walked into the command tent carrying herself with more confidence than she felt.

A table dominated the center of the room. Matlin stood alone on the far side of the table with an unobstructed view of his captains and the entrance. He smiled as she walked into the tent. "Ahh Clara, to what do we owe the pleasure?" he asked, suspicion briefly flickering across his features. "Aren't you supposed to be with our rear guard?"

"Cousin, there's been a development," said Clara as she tried to explain herself. "One that you're going to want to hear for yourself."

"I see," said Matlin flatly. "Gentlemen, leave." The captains saluted smartly and beat a quick exit out of the tent.

"Cousin—" Clara began.

"Stop right there," Matlin commanded. "I gave you specific instructions, and yet you are back earlier than you should be. The truth now."

Clara looked at him in shock. He never spoke to her this way. Something in him changed. His eyes were dark and hooded, constantly shifting around the room. Matlin was never this nervous. Something had him spooked.

"Magic," she said with difficulty. "Antier has someone, or multiple people, capable of using powerful magic."

"Bah," said Matlin dismissively. "Magic, technology. What's the difference between some lightning when compared to some catapults? I thought you said this was important."

"They caused an earthquake that tore the ground asunder and ruined our cavalry in a matter of seconds," said Clara. "And they'll do the same thing to these walls you've built."

Matlin roared in anger, tossing the table through the tent, tearing a hole in the canvas. "What would you have me do? Retreat?" he bellowed. "When that story gets around to the rest of the nobility, I'll never be king. All of this will have been for nothing."

"I don't know," said Clara stoically. "I am not a tactical genius. I just know a problem when I see one. And this is a big problem."

"Of course it is," agreed Matlin, his claws slashing a fresh rent into the canvas. "We have no other choice but to retreat, make them chase us back to the capital. Darik has been destroying towns and villages throughout southern Loach in an effort to draw me out, Clara. He'll do the same until we reach Loach. More will die and lose their homes."

"I'm sorry," said Clara. "We can try to warn those on the way. But we don't have any chance of stopping that sort of force without the city and its populace behind us. We'll need all the numbers we can get our hands on."

"And our forces can harry their supply lines, make a siege difficult," he said in resignation. "Thankfully the rings of walls in Loach will make it more difficult for them to knock the walls down and advance. It'll be street to street fighting if they break through."

"Then we don't let them break through," Clara declared stubbornly.

"And how do you presume we do that?" asked Matlin.

"We plan," said Clara. "Between the two of us we have time to come up with a plan. Maybe even delay them here for a little while."

"I thought the wall wouldn't be of much use," said Matlin.

"Only if they send their wizard in the first wave," said Clara. "Like I said, we have time to plan."

Matlin smiled grimly, his face still creased with worry. "Well then let's get to it."

Chapter Thirty-Four

R andall dangled high above the warehouse floor suspended only by one of his silk ropes. The warehouse was stuffed full of crates of various foodstuffs. Vegetables, dried meats, potatoes, wheat, and other items he could not name. The wheat would be ideal if only they had means to transform the wheat into flour, and then bake that flour. But they did not have that luxury.

He would stuff the silk satchels he brought with him full of food and tie them to the rope dangling from the roof. Three quick tugs on the rope and Tigun and the other children would haul the loot up to the roof. There the younger children would disperse with the satchels, heading back home by varying routes. They would repeat the process until every child had as much as they could carry.

Randall worked as quickly as he could, stuffing the satchels with all sorts of food. He did not know how much time they would have. This particular warehouse was in the Southwestern District, far from home. He was unfamiliar with the watchmen or the patrol schedules in this area. Not to mention he had little idea what was in all of these warehouses and shops. This was not his territory. In his entire life he had only been here a handful of times. Part of him worried that the children would become lost on their way home.

This warehouse was newer than his home, or maybe just kept in a better state. The point was academic, and one Randall did not care to indulge in too much. In fact, he preferred to steal from clean warehouses as opposed to filthy.

A *thud* echoed across the warehouse, causing Randall to leap on top of some crates. Randall took a calming breath and tried to slow his heart rate. He eased his mind and tried to focus on what he heard, while also seeking for other sounds.

The sound was of something striking the ground. Most likely a crate. Randall frowned, a guardsman familiar with area would know where the crates were, and would not be knocking them over when patrolling. Unless he was making unnatural movements, like if he were searching for someone. Other options included stray animals, or another thief.

The latter option frightened Randall. Thieves were notoriously territorial creatures. The Thieves Association frowned and discouraged poaching. The fact that Randall and his group needed food was not an excuse to those people. Randall had to know which it was. If another group of thieves saw him here, he needed to know.

He leapt off of the crate, landing as quietly as he could. He tied his remaining satchels of food to the rope and gave it three sharp tugs. No reason to let his curiosity waste good food.

Randall waited for the rope to return and climbed up, pulling himself up onto the rafters. He crept silently amongst the wooden beams, looking down and searching the warehouse floor. His heart raced as he clutched to the support beams. He doubted that he would ever again enjoy staring down over any significant distance. He was sane after all.

The warehouse remained silent. Whoever was in the warehouse with him was also taking pains to remain silent. Randall fingered the ceremonial dagger he had liberated from the Temple of Pojomi. Things had grown worse in the city over the past few days. More bodies were dropping, and not all of them were found in alleyways. He had discovered a few bodies on rooftops when trying to search for a warehouse that stored food. With the way things were in the city, if anyone caught him, he was dead, regardless of what dagger he was carrying. Meaning he might as well use the best weapon available to him.

The smart play would be to leave the warehouse now. But Randall needed to know. Multiple people depended on him, and if they angered someone, he needed to know.

He crept over rows of crates piled high on wooden pallets. The smells were interesting to say the least. Cleanliness did not always equate with dutiful. Some of the food was rotten. The smell infuriated Randall. He saw people starving every day, and the owners of the warehouse let the food rot? That was outrageous.

The rhythmic slapping of bare feet on stone drew Randall's attention. A small form darted between a stack of crates making a beeline for the front door. The child dropped an apple but continued running to the door. Fear must have overridden the child's hunger, because there was no stopping the boy or girl in their flight to the front door.

Randall winced in sympathy as the door creaked open. If any guards or watchmen were about, they would surely notice the front door creaking open. He hastened back to his rope and climbed up onto the roof.

Tigun helped pull him up out of the skylight and onto the roof. "What happened?" he whispered.

"A child was also in there stealing food," answered Randall. "Couldn't see their face. Don't know if they saw mine. Child left by the front door."

Tigun swore. "That's a fantastic way to bring the watchmen about."

"Sure is," said Randall. "Are those two the only satchels left?"

"Yeah. Let's take them and get out of here quickly."

Randall nodded and grabbed a satchel. The two boys left across the rooftops moving as quickly as possible to the northeast. His instincts told him to skirt the Central District and avoid all the trouble brewing in that area, but to do that he would have to pass the Western District or the Eastern District. The jail or the palace. Not places a thief wanted to spend too much time around.

He dashed across the rooftops, giving the common grounds a wide berth. It made his route more looping than he preferred, but he had bad memories of that area.

Everything was going swimmingly until he reached a rooftop about three streets south of North District. Something snagged his foot causing him to trip and fall to the ground. Tigun yelped as he too fell to the ground. Something fell down upon them causing Tigun to burst into a new round of curses.

Randall grabbed the offending object. It was netting, probably rigged to drop the instant he made contact with the tripwire. Randall tried pulling the netting off, but he was hopelessly tangled, and its ends were most likely weighted down.

"Daggers. Cut out," Randall whispered to Tigun trying to keep communication to a bare minimum. Who knew what was beneath them. Their fall could have disturbed the sleep of any number of good citizens. There was no reason to cause more of a commotion and draw more attention to themselves.

"Way ahead of you," whispered Tigun as he sawed furiously at the ropes.

"Well, well, what do we have here?" asked a voice from across the rooftop.

Randall jerked his head in the direction of the voice. A slender man stalked across the rooftop. Not skinny like some men, but slender like a tight rope. He moved gracefully, his heels barely touching the ground as he walked. He carried a spear with a tear shaped blade. His clothing consisted of hides and furs, yet did not look rough and poorly fashion. The outfit was held together with beads and colored threads woven together in intricate patterns.

The ensemble was topped off with a headdress fashioned from the head of an alligator. Inside the headdress a feline face grinned victoriously in the pale moonlight. Randall suppressed a groan. He had bad experiences with feline totems. Quick and cunning, many of those humans enjoyed setting traps for their prey, and toying with them after they were caught. Randall did not have high hopes that this man was any different. People who openly walked around exhibiting the physical features of their totem usually were prone to exhibiting that behavior. It crept in on their human instincts, slowly influencing them and replacing them with the animal within.

The man's eyes widened in shock as he saw the diamond blade in Randall's hand. The man threw his head back and roared with laughter. "A child?" he said in disbelief. "I expected the thief to be the man that killed Prince Yutlin and is giving Prince Fotlin fits. I even set up a trap to catch him," he threw his arms out encapsulating the net and tripwire. "And it has netted me quite a few of you misbegotten thieves. None of them knew anything, but that doesn't matter now. You have the dagger, and I assume the amulet as well. Hand them over and Pojomi will be merciful."

"What amulet?" stammered Randall. "And this dagger? Found it. If you want it, it's yours. Just let us go."

The man shook his head while making a *tsk tsk* sound under his breath. "Now now, boy," he said patronizingly as he placed his spear tip beneath Randall's chin and lifted it ever slow slightly. "I was not born yesterday. There is no way you just found that dagger. Tell me, how did you get in and out of the tower? Avian wings?"

Randall squeezed his eyes shut in anger. If only he ignored his fear and travelled through the Western District, none of this would have happened. Instead, he found himself on this rooftop. If what the man said was true, they were dead either way. Just two urchin boys whose bodies would be found on a rooftop when they began to stink. His only option was to string things along and hope an opportunity to free them presented itself.

Randall looked up at the Pojomite hunter defiantly. He would not succumb to pity and resignation. "I climbed the gargoyles with silk rope," he said.

"Brave. But how did you make it back down?" the man asked.

Randall smirked at him and remained silent.

"No...you didn't," said the man aghast. "That means...you swung down with the rope?" He burst out into a deep belly laugh, clearly unconcerned about unwanted attention. "Kid you are more courageous than any boy has a right to be."

"I agree," said another voice, causing the Pojomite to jerk around in surprise.

Randall nearly swallowed his tongue at the sudden movement. He could have had his throat cut if the Pojomite yanked his spear in the wrong direction. Randall pushed the thought from his head and quickly resumed sawing at the ropes with his dagger. This was precisely the sort of distraction they needed to escape.

"Please don't look so surprised," said the newcomer. "After all, you did set this trap for me."

While Randall wanted to escape, he also was curious as to the identity of the second man. He glanced up from the ropes to see a familiar figure. The man in black from the night he burgled the Temple of Pojomi stood on the roof, a sword in his hand.

"My my," purred the hunter. "Two prizes in one night. Pojomi truly smiles upon the faithful."

The hunter lunged at the thief who easily danced aside from the thrust. The Pojomite was relentless in his attack, launching a series of stabs, thrusts, and slices while only occasionally using the shaft of the spear as a quarterstaff. The black-clad thief dodged, ducked, or parried all of the strikes. He did not appear to be exerting himself too hard, or taking the fight that seriously. But Randall did not know terribly much about sword fighting. He only knew body language.

"I'll have you soon," declared the hunter. "There is nowhere to run."

"Who said anything about running?" asked the thief. "And you're getting tired. Sloppy. So much for a hunter's stamina."

"I am not!" shouted the hunter as he lunged forward trying to skewer the thief.

The thief twisted his shoulders, causing the spear to pass right by him, and leaving the hunter overextend. In one smooth motion the thief removed the hunter's right arm at the elbow. Spear and hand bounced softly upon the ground with a clatter.

The Pojomite screamed, grasping his bicep as blood shot from his stump. "You never should have hunted children," said the thief as he raised his sword a second time.

Randall never saw the blow land. His dagger cut through the final rope, rending a hole in the net large enough to climb out. He pulled Tigun out after him, and the pair dashed off into the night, still clutching their satchels.

A blood curdling scream split the night before ending abruptly. Randall vaulted over the wall and into North District leaving the murder in his wake. Just because the thief killed the intruder did not mean he would not also kill Randall. He had probably seen the diamond ceremonial dagger as well. Randall cursed himself for a fool. It might be a better weapon, but the blade certainly marked him as a target for theft and violence.

He sprinted until his lungs burned. And then he ran some more. He did not stop until he reached the warehouse. He slipped in through the window, leaving his satchel in the main room and bolted into his bedroom. Randall closed the door and curled up into a ball, rocking himself quietly to sleep. He would return the dagger to its hiding place in the morning. There the amulet and dagger would be safe and secure. And he would only need to worry about a black-clad figure hunting him on the rooftops at night.

CHAPTER THIRTY-FIVE

Find him, Fotlin. Find him. The words echoed in Fotlin ears. It was all anyone said to him these days. Immediately after they found Yutlin's naked corpse, everybody went into an uproar. His parents and his sisters in particular badgered him about finding the murderer.

Sure enough, the writing in the whore's room matched the prophecy etched into the temple. And it spread quickly throughout the city. There was no containing it this time. The prophecy sprang forth from people's lips like an epidemic.

Then there were the temples. One Pojomi hunter was found dead and naked on a rooftop this morning, and now they wanted the murdering thief found as well. Fotlin barely escaped the meeting with the temple clergy with his hide intact. He did not even have the chance to voice his theory that the Pojomites and their hunters were responsible for all of the bodies being found throughout the city.

Fotlin found himself torn over his younger brother's murder. It enraged him that someone would, and could, murder one of his family members in their own city. Sure, he was planning on doing the deed himself, but that was different. Yutlin was his brother, his family, and his problem. If anyone was going to gut the little snot it was going to be him.

And then there was the manner of Yutlin's death. Hanged like a commoner. It was unthinkable. And to make matters worse, the killer left a trail linking Yutlin to a brothel. He did not just kill Yutlin, but also his reputation, staining the honor of the entire family. Fotlin grimaced at the thought. Visiting brothels was perfectly acceptable amongst the nobility. Letting those visits leak out to the public? Not so much. It was a mark of unrefined and crude behavior for such visits to reach the commoners. The twins were bad enough. But Yutlin made it a pattern, and whispers were spreading about the ducal family.

All of that added up to Fotlin following his only lead: diamonds. He sat in the shadows of the jewelry store in the Central District on the main throughfare two blocks away from East District. He sat in the same shop nearly every night waiting on the intruder. This jewelry store was one of the few remaining stores in the Central District that had not yet been robbed by the thief.

The waiting was horribly dull. It allowed him plenty of time to brood over every situation bothering him. Yutlin's death, the war, his inheritance, and catching this thieving murderer. Fotlin frowned as he pondered the thought. With the way the man was stockpiling thefts and murders, he would soon need his own name. Reciting a list of his crimes as a reference was becoming too arduous.

There remained one bright spot through all the hassle of the man's crime spree. One of the duchy's food warehouses had been robbed last night. The people had refused to accept the food from Yutlin. But plunder it from the duchy after his death? There was some irony in the situation. That was one problem his father should not be able to lay at his feet.

"What if he doesn't show up, Your Highness?" asked Watchman Zirkel. The man was fidgeting all night. Fotlin wondered how effective the man actually was during a patrol. Did he jump at every shadow in every alleyway?

"Then we keep waiting," said Fotlin. "Eventually he will strike one of the stores with diamonds. Then we'll have him."

"Umm sir. What if he doesn't need any more diamonds?" asked Watchman Bruce.

Fotlin scowled at the man, even if his expression was wasted in the darkness. "Who ever heard of having too many diamonds?" derided Fotlin. "He'll be back."

The watchmen wisely did not say another word to Fotlin. They remained silent and fidgety. Like Fotlin, they wanted to catch the perpetrator, but for different reasons. Right now, the focus of the search was on Fotlin himself. Soon, the duke and everyone else with any power would start questioning them and their abilities. That could mean their jobs, or being sent off to the army.

Fotlin had other concerns if this did not go well. His entire life depended on having accomplishments. Because sooner or later his father would die, and so would the king. At this rate, Matlin could either become King of Ochandor or Duke of Loach. If the former, Setlin was still in line to become Duke of Loach. Either way, Fotlin would be a prince no longer. No titles to his name unless one of his brothers kept him on as head of the City Watch. A glorious future that would be. Throwing street urchins and beggars in dungeons. He soured at the thought. There had to be more to life than that.

Like most of the jewelers in the city, this store stored its diamonds in a safe. The safe was kept in an office in the center of the building. There were no windows, and only one door led into the office. Fotlin had a clear view of that door from the shadows of the store's workshop.

A soft clicking noise caused Fotlin's head to jerk up. The noise came from inside the office. But that was impossible. The door never even opened. Unless their villain was an actual ghost, he would need a door to enter the room.

Fotlin crept across the room, careful not to cause a ruckus and scare off their thief. If it was indeed him. He cracked the door open and peeked in. The safe was wide open.

"Thief!" he bellowed as he flung open the door and charged into the office. The safe still had many items in it, but Fotlin did not see any diamonds inside. He cursed under his breath. At least the owner would not be destitute from the robbery.

If the door was open, what made the noise? Fotlin quickly glanced around the room and saw the answer. A hole was cut, maybe burned into the ceiling. The noise had to be caused by the thief stepping on the safe to pull himself back through the hole.

"To the roof!" cried Fotlin. "The thief is fleeing to the rooftops!"

Fotlin darted out of the room past a stunned Zirkel and Bruce. He dashed up the stairs trying to stare into every shadow along the way. Nothing. He hit the narrow wooden staircase leading to the roof and flung open the trapdoor. It was unlocked. He had personally confirmed that it was locked when he arrived for the stakeout.

The rooftops were usually deserted in Loach. No person up to any good spent time on their roof at night. Which meant that the shadowy figure Fotlin saw running a few buildings over was almost certainly his intruder.

Fotlin took off at a sprint. It was reckless, he acknowledged that. One wrong step could send him tumbling over the roof, or crashing through one. But he had one advantage over the thief. He had his totem.

He hated resembling a wolf when he used his totem. It made him look so undignified. Fotlin spent years learning how to suppress the fur and snout from appearing. He did not want to resemble those lupine abominations from Kelon. But the fangs and the eyes? He did not mind those so much, they made him look fearsome.

Fotlin howled as he sped across the roof. It was more fun when the prey knew they were fleeing from you. His prey changed directions at the howl. He leapt off to his left, crossing the street below and landing in a roll. The man sprang up and bounded off into the distance.

A wolfish grin spread across Fotlin's face. He had not participated in the other pursuits of this criminal. While it was pleasant to see that his men had not exaggerated the rogue's abilities, it was also reassuring to know that he could accomplish the same feats.

Fotlin's legs bunched beneath him as he sprang over the gap. He skidded across the rooftops, kicking up tiles as he regained his footing. He scampered across the buildings, rapidly closing the gap between him and his prey. It was only a matter of time now. He would pounce on the man's back and drag him to the ground. He would need to kill him. He could not risk the man escaping.

The man must have made the same calculation as Fotlin. He leapt off the rooftop and landed in front of the entrance to the cemetery, drawing his sword as he spun around, preparing to fight. Fotlin howled with glee as he crossed the roof, leaping to the ground; drawing his blade as he landed.

Fotlin launched a ferocious series of cuts at the man. The thief's blade danced lightly as he intercepted every blow. Fotlin gritted his teeth as he launched another combination of attacks. Same result. The man parried every blow without so much as moving his feet. Fotlin clenched his jaw in frustration, sweat trickling down his face. He had met few people who were able to keep up with him in battle. And the man had the audacity to act bored? It was a terrible insult that his pride could not bear.

"You killed my brother," he shouted as he swiped at the man's head. He hated talking when he fought. It seemed so childish. However, he had never fought his brother's murderer before either.

"Two of them actually," replied the man, his voice laced with amusement. Fotlin stared at the man in shock, missing a beat. The pause nearly cost him his life as the man's riposte slashed across his chest, breaking the rings of his chainmail and leaving a shallow furrow in his skin.

Fotlin glared at the man, wary of his blade. "Who are you?" he demanded.

The man bobbled his head back and forth. "That depends on the time and place," he answered. "But your twin brothers knew me as Irving Mire."

Fotlin howled, swinging a vertical two-handed blow at Irving with all of his totem-enhanced strength. Irving danced nimbly out of the way as the blade plunged into the street. The blade stuck in the cobblestones for an instant. Fotlin yanked at his sword hilt, pulling the sword free, but the hesitation cost him.

Irving's blade bit into his leg from behind the knee and up into his buttocks. Fotlin screamed in pain as his leg gave way beneath his weight. Tears blurred his eyes as he rolled onto his back, his blade wavering in his blurred vision.

"I wonder, do I get anything special if I collect the whole set of you?" asked Irving. "Pity. I only got one of the twins though."

"You'll die you bastard," screamed Fotlin.

Irving shrugged. "You don't know how little that concerns me," he said as he pulled back his hood. A gleaming skull grinned down at him. "Maybe I'll look prettier in my next life. Now if you'll excuse me, our dance partners are catching up to us. I really should be going now. Don't forget to get to plenty of bed rest. A limp can really cripple your social life."

The insufferable thief pulled his hood up and walked calmly into the cemetery, vanishing into the darkness and swirling mists of ghosts wandering the cemetery. Half a minute or so later, Zirkel and Owen were the first to arrive, their chests heaving.

"Your Highness, reinforcements are on the way," said Owen. "Our men outside the store are pursuing along the street – by the gods! Your leg!"

Fotlin gritted his teeth in pain. "Bring me to the palace and send for the priests. If I lose consciousness, send word to my father. Our thief is called Irving Mire. He claims he killed one of the twins. He ran into the cemetery. Send the men in after him."

The two watchmen paled in fear. Neither apparently were very keen on delivering that message, nor on entering the cemetery at night. The ghosts were wandering about; their moans clearly audible from street. Fotlin had no intention of bleeding to death and joining their number tonight.

"Yes, Your Highness," said Owen cautiously. "Now hold still, we'll wrap your leg and get you moved as quickly as possible."

Fotlin collapsed onto the street in agony. "Just be quick about it. If I lose my leg, I'll hold it against you."

CHAPTER THIRTY-SIX

O livia tapped her foot impatiently. The boys always appeared to enjoy making her wait. They received some sort of secret magical training, and what did she get to do? Stand watch with Atrisha and the priestess. All because they had to keep the circle of knowledge small.

"And then tens of vampires, the entire family from the homestead, charged out of the barn!" said the priestess, Jayna, as she waved her arms about. The woman loved talking with her hands. Olivia hated that habit. If you could not say something using only your words, you should not say it at all.

"Why were they in the barn?" asked Atrisha as she leaned forward, intent on hearing the end of the story.

"Because it was dark," said Jayna. "A vampire had attacked the homestead and turned the adults into vampires. I nearly pissed myself when I noticed that."

"You did not," laughed Atrisha. Olivia felt her face darken. No matter what she felt about the priestess, it did her heart well to see Atrisha show emotion again. Something in Atrisha had changed when Calabella died. She had cried for days after her death, but after that she seemed unable to remove her emotions, and journey back to that cold emotionless place where she had resided since hearing about Cole's death.

"I did too," protested Jayna. "I never lived on a farm! I had no idea that something was out of place." She giggled at her own stupidity. "You should have seen the Antierian men fight. They were the only ones who were not caught unprepared. The fought like lions, ending the misery those poor people must have been in."

"And the vampire?" asked Atrisha eagerly. "Did they kill the vampire too?"

"Elfred dueled the vampire," said Jayna. "He has the most experience with that sort of thing. Thiago place an arrow in the creature giving Elfred the opportunity for a killing blow. An incredible man he is. Do you know him well?"

"Not really," admitted Atrisha.

"He's a nice man," said Jayna. "Very quiet and solemn. But a good heart. I'll introduce you."

Olivia rolled her eyes. Who cared about silly things like vampires? They had an entire army of actual Loachians to worry about, and they wanted to exchange horror stories.

"Oh give it a rest, Vivi," said Atrisha. "They'll be done soon. Learning anything takes time and practice. I don't see why magic should be any different. And personally, I don't mind not having to charge the Loachians again. I could use the break."

"So you *have* seen actual combat," said Jayna gleefully. "You simply must tell me about it."

"Surely, you've seen combat as a mercenary," said Olivia drily.

Jayna nodded her head in agreement. "Of course, but that is different," she said. "You're mainly trying to keep yourself and your company alive throughout it all. Your cause is money, not something higher."

"Oh you're being too hard on yourself," said Atrisha. "We're each fighting for someone or something we love. And that's the important thing."

"I thought the important thing was winning," said Olivia as she tossed a twig into the bushes.

"Don't mind her," said Atrisha dismissively. "She and Jeron used to have a thing back in training. She's not taking your presence, or his, well at all."

"Atrisha," gasped Olivia. "That is simply not true."

"It's okay," said Jayna with one of her easy smiles. "People have pasts. I don't see why you Antierians should be any different." She walked over to Olivia and held her hands. "Please forgive me. I did not know. I feel terrible now considering how I have prattled on in front of you. I meant no offense."

"It's nothing," said Olivia quickly. Too quickly judging by the frown on Jayna's face. "Not like that. I'm just. I don't know. Embarrassed?" Olivia rubbed at her eyes. "See the last time I saw Jeron I gave him this little speech about how I was an independent woman and needed to be free. I told him that I cared about him greatly, but since we were going to be apart that we shouldn't be together. I patted his cheek and left him standing there gawking." She shook her head. "It's embarrassing. I'm mortified even thinking about the experience."

Atrisha winced. "I said something similar to Cole," she said. "Except instead of patting his cheek, I kissed him." Her face darkened as she started to slip into one of her more morose moods. "I guess that is why I was so angry. Not just because he died, but because I didn't tell him how I really felt."

Jayna pulled Atrisha and Olivia into a big hug. "Oh hush both of you," she said. "You two are some of the strongest, bravest women I have ever had the pleasure of meeting. Look at what you have accomplished. Do you honestly think those two are the only men who will love you? I don't." She released them, but kept her hands on their shoulders with a gentle squeeze. "So look on those memories fondly. I am sure you all cared about each other greatly, and I doubt that will ever change."

"That's easy for you to say," said Olivia.

"What does that mean?" asked Jayna, her usual smile turned down into a slight frown.

"Well what do we have here?" asked Dalton, his usually pleasant tenor booming throughout the camp. "Why Jeron, I believe this is your nightmare."

"Shut up," said Jeron as he punched Dalton's shoulder. He glanced over at Jayna. "It's not, I swear."

"Are you all done?" asked Olivia, annoyance creeping into her voice. She was not jealous. Of that she was certain.

"For now," said Jeron. "Master Richard is tidying things up a bit."

Horns blared throughout the encampment. Olivia sighed. "Okay everyone, back to the command tent," she said. "It seems we're on alert for something."

"You think we can grab a bite to eat along the way?" asked Dalton. "All that work made me hungry."

"Me too," said Jeron. "You all run ahead, we'll be right there."

Olivia opened her mouth to protest, order them to return to the command tent, and thought better of it. Now was not the time to push the issue of them not respecting her rank. They just finished some grueling training, and strategically speaking, they would need those two boys at their best if there was to be fighting. Also, she was not entirely certain what rank, if any, that the two boys held. Everything was murkier on that front since Darik arrived.

Atrisha shook her head sadly. "They're never going to listen to orders, are they?"

"I doubt it," said Jayna gently. "They were on their own for so long that they learned to make decisions for themselves. It's hard to backtrack from that. In fact, Jeron got into an argument with Prince Darik on our way here. Knocked Renaldo out with his fists."

"He did what?" asked Atrisha in a scandalized voice.

"He's prone to getting into fistfights," said Olivia smugly.

"Oh I am sure of that," agreed Jayna. "But Renaldo wasn't using his fists. He was using his axe."

Olivia snapped her mouth shut. That did not sound like Jeron at all. Sure, he got into trouble and fought a lot. However, it was usually Byron who caused the trouble, and Jeron was merely pulling his friend out of the fire. Jeron threatening the prince? Surrogate older brother or not, that just did not sound like the Jeron she had known.

"They changed, didn't they?" she asked softly.

"Yes, they did," said Jayna, her voice filled with compassion. "When we found them, they were only days removed from the massacre at Fort Hope. There was a hardness in their eyes. Something desolate lay there. Like they had just watched the world end. It took weeks of travel before they all showed signs of having emotions or a sense of humor. It took Dalton the longest. He drowned his feelings in the bottle." Jayna looked sad as she stared off into the trees. "Prince Darik fixed that though. Please forgive me for prattling on. I hope I am not drudging up unpleasant memories for you two."

"Oh not at all," said Atrisha. "We reacted quite differently to the news.""How is that?" asked Jayna.

"We didn't sulk," said Olivia with a sense of satisfaction. "We persuaded Duke Cedric and the nobles to allow us to fight and raise an army of female warriors."

"That is amazing," gawked Jayna. "In all my travels I have never seen anything like that. Tell me. How did you do it?"

"Well, Atrisha started wearing her sword to court every day, and knocking every closed door off of its hinges," said Olivia.

"Off their hinges?" giggled Jayna with glee. "That is incredible. I am so glad to have met you two! I hope we can be friends. You truly are astounding women."

"Aww thank you," said Atrisha as she looped her arm with the priestess. Olivia's mouth dropped. Was she...skipping?

Olivia did not say another word as they made their way to the command tent. Atrisha and Jayna prattled on about all sorts of things. Religion, the other duchies, the difference between growing up in a small city versus a large city, and wine.

They entered into the command tent with smiles plastered on their faces. Prince Darik glanced up from his report as they entered. "Ladies," he said in greeting. "Good to see you. We have news. Our scouts have found the main Loachian encampment." Darik's voice trailed off as his eyes narrowed, glancing around the ring. "Where are Jeron and Dalton? They are important to this."

"Apparently their stomachs rank higher than their commanding officers," said Olivia.

"Ahh I see," said Darik. "Smart lads. We'll need them at their top strength for this."

Olivia gaped at the prince; her mouth wide open, perfect for catching flies. If she had tried that stunt, she was certain that there would be comments about her weight, a demotion, and spending the next week or two digging latrine trenches.

"Captain Gabrella? Are you okay?" asked Prince Darik, concern on his face. "Do you need a day or two off? I know you have been pushing yourself hard. Captain Melango is more than capable of filling in for you."

Atrisha beamed at the praise while Olivia scowled at the prince. "I am fine," she said through clenched teeth. "I don't need any sort of special treatment."

"Oookay," said Darik, his hands raised in supplication. "Moving on then. The Loachians have set up a makeshift fortress. Walls on three sides blocking the road right here," he thrust his hand down at the map. "We have a chance to break them here. Send them scattering back to the city with their tails between their legs."

"And if we succeed?" asked Master Maxus. "Are we looking at a siege of Loach then?"

Prince Darik hesitated before answering. "Maybe," he said. "That depends on a lot of factors. How the battle goes, et cetera. We are still walking a dangerous political situation here."

"What do you mean?" asked Atrisha.

Master Tyson cleared his throat before speaking. Prince Darik waved the man forward. "We have reports that things are not going so well in the city of Loach," said the wraith. "Crime is up and food shortages are running rampant throughout the city. The city is close to igniting and burning itself up. The other duchies are watching, and a slaughter of civilians in retaliation for a slaughter of military forces will not sit well with the other duchies."

Prince Nelson nodded in agreement. "I can attest to that," he said. "Biona would not look favorably upon the killing of innocents." He hesitated before continuing. "By the gods. Not even the Nuquanian buccaneer captains would stomach it. And that is saying something."

"So we can't exact our vengeance because of...politics?" spluttered Atrisha heatedly. "That's not justice."

"No. It isn't," agreed Prince Darik grimly. "But it is reality. A combined force from the other duchies could easily crush us. Especially if Biona and Talendor withdraw their support. No offense, Nelson."

"None taken," said Nelson. "Biona will act in accordance with her own conscience. Those are just facts."

"There is also the matter of the king," interjected Master Tyson. "Reports from your father do not paint King Ramon's health in a favorable light. If the king finally succumbs, everything will change. Haste is imperative."

"Agreed. Now circling back to the fortress," said Darik. "We have been marching on the road for so long that we haven't made any siege weapons. Normally, that would be a problem. However, Master Richard has assured me that Dalton and Jeron can make short work of any small fortifications."

"He certainly was not happy about it," scoffed Captain Levren.

"No. He wasn't," said Prince Darik. "And he wouldn't say why. And since he isn't speaking, we'll just have to carry on."

"They're using their totems to power their magic," piped up Jayna. "What?" she asked the stunned room. "I am not a wizard, and am not beholden to their 'secrets' and 'mysticisms'. Dalton used his totem to power his magic. That's why the earthquake was so strong. He has a powerful totem, as does Jeron. Apparently, the Eldritch Society frowns upon that practice. It's superstitious nonsense, but that's why he won't mention it."

Olivia along with everyone else in the tent gaped at the priestess in shock.

"Excuse me," said Master Sildun, his voice shaky. "Wizards can power their magic with their totems."

"Of course," said Jayna nonchalantly. "Priests and priestesses do it all the time. It isn't that big of a deal."

Captain Iandrick threw up his hands in frustration. "Then why won't Master Richard tell us about it?" he demanded.

"Because wizards are more superstitious than the temples?" said Jayna rhetorically. "I don't know for sure. No one ever credited wizards with wisdom."

"As I was saying," said Prince Darik, the volume of his voice rising. "Dalton and Jeron should be able to destroy at least part of their fortifications. From there, we inflict the maximum amount of damage upon the Loachians as possible. The more of the walls that they bring down, the more damage we can inflict. After that? Who knows."

Dalton and Jeron entered the tent at that moment with very satisfied smiles on their face. Olivia glared daggers at them.

"So what did we miss?" asked Dalton flippantly.

"The battle plan," answered Emkario in a deadpan.

"I assume the two of us are taking down any fortifications and targeting the enemy wizard?" asked Jeron with a lazy yawn.

"Essentially," said Prince Darik. "Are you two up to it."

"Of course," said Dalton as he feigned mock outrage. "The chefs had a nice rabbit meat pie ready. After eating one of those, I could fight for a full day. Maybe two."

"Rabbit pies?" asked Darik. "Emkario, go fetch us a couple."

"Must I?" asked Emkario woefully.

"Send Vincent."

"An excellent plan," agreed Emkario as Vincent exited the tent with a grin on his face.

Someone nudged Olivia in her side. She turned and frowned at Jayna. "Easy dear," whispered Jayna. "They are taking things seriously. They're only using the food to distract themselves from the prospect of dying."

Olivia glowered at the woman. How dare she assume that she was upset about the food. Of course, she knew people had to eat and that they would be scared. She was upset that the boys were wasting all of their time.

"Thank you for pointing that out," whispered Olivia through a clenched jaw. Atrisha frowned at her, but Olivia did not care. She had to keep her jaw muscles tight in order to whisper that low. It was nothing personal.

"The Loachians know that we are know where they are," continued Prince Darik. "It's their trap and they have been waiting to spring it. We're not going to charge in right away without any sort of intelligence. Master Sildun, have your scouts try to spot any traps. Jeron, Dalton, get some rest boys. We're going to move you soon. Everyone else, prepare your weapons, your troops, and be ready to move. We march on the Loachian fortress tomorrow."

Olivia nodded brusquely to the prince as she departed the tent. No direct orders for her or Atrisha. That meant they would be with the troops on the front line. A captain without orders and limited authority was really no different than any other soldier. She would just have to make sure she killed enough Loachians to dispel that idea.

Fortunately, Jayna did not receive any orders either. That meant she would be behind the battle lines. Maybe caring for injured soldiers, but not gaining honor.

"Will you be okay?" whispered Jeron as softly as possible, his voice still loud enough for Olivia to make out.

"Of course," laughed Jayna softly. "It might surprise you, but I actually prefer healing to cracking skulls. Gives me a sense of accomplishment."

"Not at all," beamed Jeron. "You have a good heart. That doesn't surprise me in the least."

Olivia gnashed her teeth as she exited the tent. Things had been so much simpler when Jeron was dead.

Chapter Thirty-Seven

J eron whistled as he walked alongside the Antierian column. He had grown accustomed to trusting his feet while marching across the kingdom. Riding a horse at this point in time would just feel wrong.

Besides, he had never practiced using magic while on horseback. This battle was too important to leave anything to chance. Master Richard assured them both that they did not need to touch the ground in order to cause an earthquake.

During their practice, Jeron had found that advice to be true. However, in the heat of battle, things changed. Men stank of fear, plans changed, and in that chaos a person's will could falter. What if his horse bolted at the first sign of an earthquake? What if enemy archers were able to pick him out easier from a horse?

No. There were too many variables. He would not leave such matters to chance. He and Dalton even decided not to fight side by side. It felt strange to Jeron, but it made sense. They could not risk both of their wizards being killed in one lucky barrage. Their friends however, were not prepared to let them fight alone.

"This feels strange," said Telwin as he rubbed the sleep from his eyes. The man always tried to sleep in as late as humanly possible. "I've trusted Lentil to have my back in all of our fights. Say what you will about him, but the hayseed is a great warrior."

"He certainly is that," agreed Jeron. "Which is why I am glad that he is watching over Dalton."

"You think you can actually do this?" asked Telwin skeptically.

Jeron shrugged his shoulders. "I have no idea," he admitted. "Dalton is the one with experience at this. But he only blew up an earthen bulwark. Stone walls that are defended by bowman? This could be an entirely different monster."

"Yeah," said Telwin. He paused as they marched on. "Good thing we have experience fighting monsters."

"Damn right," agreed Jeron. "And these will even do us the favor of staying still."

"Our victory is all but assured then."

"Women cheering our arrival? Feasts thrown in our names?" asked Jeron with a laugh.

Telwin gave him a sidelong glance. "Ehh, that's your dream," he said finally. "I would not mind some peace and quiet. That and no one telling me what to do. Maybe a nice farm somewhere."

"There are worse fates," said Jeron. "Only one problem. You'd miss all the food and wine. You're almost as bad as Dalton."

Telwin snorted. "Please. It would take a squad of men to be as bad as him." He paused thoughtfully. "But maybe the farm doesn't have to be too far away from a city."

Jeron barked out a laugh drawing sidelong glances from the soldiers. They clearly did not find the humor in the upcoming battle. They continued their chat as they marched along. It was good for his nerves to bleed some of that excess energy out.

They arrived at the Loachian fortress a few hours before noon. The sight of it did not inspire awe or fear within Jeron. He had seen real fortresses in Antier and Talendor. This mess was not one of them. It was a jumbled collection of stone and wood. It would slow defenders down and provide defenders with solid footing, but it would not stand up long to a siege.

Jeron felt his hopes buoyed at the sight. He had been terrified of seeing something like the walls of Talendor on the horizon. His confidence that he could knock those over with his fledgling skills was nonexistent. This craftsmanship? That was another story. He could have built better walls himself years ago.

"Doesn't look that intimidating," mused Telwin. "Of course it isn't the walls that scares me."

"What is?"

"The men with bows standing on top of them," Telwin said.

"With that sort of insight, they ought to name you captain," observed Jeron.

"And miss out on all the fun of charging one of those things?" asked Telwin. "Perish the thought. Besides, they'd never let me retire to my farm and live out in peace."

"Always another war to fight," agreed Jeron.

Telwin nodded his head in agreement, his sandy blonde hair dancing in the wind. "By the gods, ain't that the truth," he said. "After what we've been through, I consider myself a lucky man. But eventually, even the gods' own luck won't save us."

Jeron glared at the man darkly. "Just to be clear. You're the one who turned this conversation dark," he said sourly.

"Dark? You find seeking eternal glory in Ormun's name and an eternity of residing in his keep, prepared to engage in glorious combat dark?" asked Telwin.

"Bah, you temple worshippers are all the same," retorted Jeron. "One minute you want to live out your days on a farm, the next, everlasting war at the side of one of your gods. It is so much easier to just pick one."

Telwin held out in his hands in mock surrender. "These things are out my control, Jeron," he said apologetically. "Can I help it if the universe is ordered in strange and confusing ways?"

"There is order to the universe," insisted Jeron. "One God. It really is simple."

"Well hopefully today we won't find out which one of us is correct," said Telwin.

"There you go making it dark again."

"It's an epidemic," agreed Telwin. He scratched his chin thoughtfully. "I have to stay next to you the entire time, right? While you do whatever it is you're supposed to be doing?"

"Those are the orders," said Jeron as he studied the walls, searching for his point of attack.

"Meaning I'll be out of the main battle," said Telwin. "Hmm. It may be that if I die it wouldn't be in Ormun's good graces since I was not in the thick of it. On second thought, let's not seek glory in Ormun's name."

Jeron looked at the man as if he had sprouted horns and declared himself a peacock. "Are all temple worshippers this crazy, or is it only those of you that belong to the Fist of Steel?"

Telwin grinned maniacally at Jeron. "The society of warriors is known for its prowess in battle," he boasted. "We make no claims as to our sanity."

Horns started sounding, blaring out their harsh notes across the field. Jeron took a series of deep breaths. He needed to calm his heartbeat and clear his brain before the chaos came. Normally his temper seized control during a battle, and his lion instincts rose to the forefront of his mind. He could not allow that to happen today. If he stalked the battlefield, his mind would not be focused on providing magical cover. However meager that might be.

The first wave of Antierian soldiers began a slow march to the wall. They would pick up their pace before coming into range of the defender's bowmen. It was Jeron's job to time his assault so that the walls were down and the ground was stable before the Antierian forces reached the wall. Friendly fire was a very real possibility, and one that he wished to avoid.

Jeron calmed his mind and stared off at the point in the wall that he wanted. He grabbed at the ground with his mind, picturing giant hands constructed out of his willpower. He pushed, and pulled...and nothing happened. Sweat poured down his face as he strained against the earth. Nothing. The ground began to tremble to the left of the where he was focused. Dalton apparently was not having trouble.

What was he forgetting? Jeron growled under his breath. Growling. That was what he forgot. He was supposed to use his totem to charge his magic. Jeron kept his focus on forming those invisible hands of willpower and let the lion surge through him.

The ground shook and split open underneath the wall. He unclenched the hands and moved to a different spot. He kept grabbing and tearing up the ground beneath the Loachian defenses like a farmer tilling the soil.

The fortress walls began to crumble and give way under the combined earthquakes. Stone tumbled and wood cracked as the hastily built structure collapsed. Men screamed as the ground beneath them gave way, and debris ground up bones like millstones.

The expected volley of arrows never came. The archers simply were not there. More horns sounded and the next wave of Antierians charged across the field.

"You did that?" asked Telwin, his mouth hanging open in shock.

"Part of it," admitted Jeron.

"Well then why didn't you do that before?" demanded Telwin.

"Honestly, I didn't really know how," said Jeron. "And I really can't do any more than I have already done. I'm more likely to harm more of our soldiers than theirs."

"Okay then," said Telwin enthusiastically. "Let's get in the thick of things then. We could definitely do some good in there."

"We can't," said Jeron.

"What? Why not?" demanded Telwin. "We followed our orders. We kept you safe and out of danger while you conjured up those earthquakes. Mission accomplished. Now we kill some of the enemy."

"Whatever happened to you not being prepared for meeting Ormun after a glorious death?" asked Jeron drily.

"That was merely me coming to terms with my orders," said Telwin. "Those orders have been completed."

"No," said Jeron firmly. "Our orders are clear. And even if they aren't, I can't go risking myself like a common soldier. We'll almost certainly have need of what I can do later. I'm sorry to say, but I can't die right now."

"Someone has a high opinion of himself," grumbled Telwin.

Jeron smacked Telwin upside the back of the head. "Where is Prince Darik?" he asked angrily.

"Overseeing the battle," answered Telwin.

"Why isn't he fighting?"

"He's too important. We can't replace him—Oh," said Telwin as he slumped his shoulders. "I see. I guess I'll have to look forward to the food and wine from now on and not the battles."

"That's what gets me through the day," muttered Jeron.

"Oh really?" asked Telwin mischievously. "I guess you won't mind if I tell Jayna that?"

"Why don't you go charge the Loachians by yourself," grumbled Jeron as he turned around to search out Darik.

It was hard to tell how the battle was going from his current vantage point. And if he was not going to be in the heat of the action, then he would at the very least be where the decisions were made.

"Umm, Jeron, where ya going?" asked Telwin in a lazy voice.

"To Prince Darik," said Jeron simply.

"The prince?" said Telwin nervously. "Umm am I allowed to be there?"

"Don't see why not," said Jeron. "The prince did not have an issue with you guarding me. So there is that."

Prince Darik was sitting astride a horse, surrounded by his usual cadre of advisors. Jeron frowned ever so slightly at the sight. Darik only used horses for travel. He hated fighting upon them, claiming that dismounting slowed him down in his transformation into a dragon. Jeron's brow scrunched up as he thought on the matter. That meant that Darik was using the horse as a vantage point. Why not use his wings to see the fight?

"What's the matter?" asked Telwin.

"Just wondering why Darik is on a horse instead of in the skies," said Jeron.

"Because he can still see, but it makes relaying orders easier than if he were in the skies," answered Master Tyson from behind him. Jeron felt his body jump involuntarily. He hated when the insufferable man did that.

"Also, it removes the temptation," continued Tyson. "It would be very easy for Darik to settle things with Matlin in the skies. However, that doesn't do the rest of us any good at all. Army or duchy. The prince resists the urge to do it all on his own by sitting in that saddle."

"I can relate," grumbled Jeron. "Next time don't sneak up on me though."

Tyson laughed softly. "I promise nothing," he said as he strode past the boys and towards Master Sildun who was holding a horse for him.

Dalton and Lentil appeared from the other direction. Apparently, they were bored as well.

"Gentlemen," greeted Prince Darik. "Nice work on the walls. Almost didn't think you could pull it off. Well done."

"Thank you, Your Highness," answered Jeron. "But Dalton did his job very well. I'm the one who needs to work on things."

"I see," said Darik. "Try to figure it out. This war isn't over yet."

"Things not going our way in the battle?" asked Dalton. "Couldn't really see from our vantage point."

Darik kept a blank impassive face as he monitored the battle. "Not as well as we hoped," he answered. "Loach did not commit their entire army to this battle. It's another stalling force. A sizeable one meant to bleed us." He frowned and paused for a handful of seconds before continuing. "If I had to make an early guess, I'd say that Dalton's earlier demonstration frightened them out of using fortifications in a battle."

"Then where will they fight us next?" asked Dalton.

Prince Darik, the captains, and the masters burst out into laughter. "One thing at a time son," laughed Master Maxus. "How about we finish this battle first."

Dalton blushed and remained silent. The battle lasted a few more hours without incident. The Loachian wizard failed to make an appearance in the battle. Jeron was eternally thankful for that. What would he have done if she showed up? He had trouble taking down a wall. A large stationary object incapable of fighting back against him. A living, breathing, moving person with years of experience? What would happen if he tried to use magic against her and nothing happened? Would he die or have time to close in for melee combat?

The thought completely ruined his post-battle meal. Jayna stared at him strangely while he ate. She probably thought the killing bothered him. That was not it. Killing Loachians did not bother him at all. They deserved it after what they did to Byron.

Failure is what bothered him. It ate at him. Always had. He failed Byron at Fort Hope, and he almost failed the entire army today. That failure gnawed at him and kept him awake that night.

Jeron tossed off his blankets and searched out a clearing. He would train until the sun rose if he had to. This war was far from over. and Loach was not going to wait for him to improve.

Blowing up some trees sounded like a relaxing exercise.

CHAPTER THIRTY-EIGHT

F otlin hated his bed. He hated having his leg in that stupid sling all day. However, the priests forbade him from rising, walking, or doing anything that a living capable person might enjoy. Instead, he was confined to his chambers while the City Watch tried to manage the utter disaster that was the city.

Rumors spread about his encounter with the man called Irving Mire. Reports said that the watchmen were incredibly nervous, and Fotlin could not blame them. The man had killed two princes, could have killed a third, and he walked into a cemetery in the middle of the night, unconcerned of the specters floating about.

Truth be told, Fotlin was not particularly enamored with the idea of continuing the chase. That gleaming skull woke him up at night, his body in a full sweat. But the alternative was worse. Laying around in bed until one of his family members decided he had zero utility to the family and needed to be put down? That was not going to happen.

Fotlin lifted his right leg, straining as the weak muscles struggled to respond. He grabbed his leg with his hands and heaved it out of the sling. He grunted with the effort. It was either grunt or scream, and he was not prepared to show weakness.

Thankfully, the priests kept him clothed during the day. He had to protect his dignity during meetings. Fotlin grabbed his hiking stick, a long hickory affair, and hobbled out of his chambers.

Surprisingly, his leg seemed to work almost perfectly. There was a little stiff-ness to it, but it appeared that the priests knew their business well. He should be back to his old self in a matter of days.

Fotlin walked, he certainly did not hobble, to his father's planning chamber. He pushed the doors open and strode into the room. Every head in the room turned to look at him. His father, Setlin, and a handful of captains. Every chair in the room was full.

Setlin slid out of his chair and gestured for Fotlin to sit down. Fotlin smiled at his brother, grateful for his kindness. His leg was a mite bit sore, and standing for the remainder of the meeting would truly be uncomfortable.

"Son, you're supposed to be in bed resting," said Duke Camen gravelly.

"And the Antierians are supposed to be in Antier," retorted Fotlin. "Some-times we don't get what we want." Fotlin cut himself off before going any further. There was no need to test his father's patience, and he preferred leaving his statement ambiguous as to who wanted him to remain in bed.

Duke Camen snorted. "Took you long enough," he said. Fotlin stiffened, ready to snap off a scathing retort, but Setlin squeezed his shoulder with one hand, warning him off.

"Fotlin, can you tell us more about this Irving?" asked Setlin. "Both your report and your watchman's say that this Irving has a gleaming skull for a head? Pardon me, but that sounds absolutely incredible."

Fotlin blew out a deep breath before answering. He hated that damn grinning skull. "That's what I thought when I first heard about it," he said. "But I can confirm that his face was a skull and it gleamed. I've given this matter a lot of thought, and I have some theories about why."

Duke Camen frowned ever so slightly. "Please by all means. Continue."

"I'm not sure how, but I believe that skull is the byproduct of all the dia-monds this Irving has been stealing," said Fotlin.

"Explain yourself," said the duke.

"Well think about it," said Fotlin. "What is he going to do with all of those diamonds? Sell them off? It would take him decades to sell that many diamonds.

Smuggle them out of the city? Maybe. But that would be nearly impossible. It's almost a certainty that he would be caught."

"Right. We deduced that," said Setlin.

"But if he isn't selling them or smuggling them, what is he doing?" asked Fotlin. "He has to be putting them to some use. Why not make a skull or something else, I don't know what."

"There's a problem with your theory," said Duke Camen. "The amount of heat that he would need to generate to melt all the diamonds down."

"We've already seen him use fire," said Fotlin defensively.

"Not the same thing," said his father sternly. "We're talking two completely different magnitudes of heat here. That sort of heat would have consequences and would be noticed. Something would have caught on fire by now."

"Oh," was all Fotlin managed to say.

"Keep your head up son," said the duke. "You may be wrong, but you're on the right track. Selling and smuggling does not seem to be the motive. And the only way we are going to catch this man is if we figure out his motive."

"We already tried staking out the jewelry stores," said Fotlin.

"Not that," interjected Setlin. "The diamonds are part of his plan, but not his motive. This Irving has admitted to killing two of our brothers. And the twins died months ago in Talendor. Well before the diamonds were stolen. And Yutlin was not killed during a robbery."

"No he wasn't," said Duke Camen darkly, murder in his eyes.

"Irving is after our family," said Fotlin. "That's why he's stealing diamonds. To drain our coffers?"

"But why?" said Setlin. "Why go to all that trouble? Some of our reports said that the twins tried to kill him once. Do you think he holds a grudge over that?"

"We could debate why forever," said Duke Camen. "But for now we know what his motive is. And we can use that to our advantage."

"What is our plan then?" said Fotlin eagerly. "We set a trap for him?"

"Indeed," said Duke Camen. "And we are the bait."

"What?" asked Setlin. "How is that going to work?"

"It's simple," said the duke. "We allow ourselves to be seen in public. Setlin engaging in commerce, Fotlin running the City Watch, and myself meeting with the society and temple heads that have been robbed. Matlin will be arriving at the city soon, and he can also join us. We'll throw another parade or ceremony of some sort."

"So he comes after us. Then what?" asked Fotlin. "The man is very good with a sword. And he'll attack us when we're at our weakest."

"That's why we won't be alone," said the duke with a menacing smile. "We'll be shadowed by cavaliers, soldiers, watchmen, priests, wizards, hunters, wraiths, and anyone else we can wrangle to our cause. If he tries to strike at us again, he will die."

"Fantastic plan father," said Fotlin. "But if you'll excuse me, I think in order for it to work I am going to need that bed rest the priests ordered."

"No," commanded his father. "You made it this far on your own strength. You can make it further. You're not required to fight the man. Others will do that. You're merely the lure to get his attention."

"You mean he'll go after the weakest man," said Fotlin drily. "Fantastic."

"I'm glad you see it my way. Now why don't you go into the city and have yourself a nice meal?"

Setlin helped him stand as Fotlin walked silently from the room. His father wanted him to be the bait? Probably retaliation for not catching this Irving before he killed Yutlin. A wounded prince that the man already bested would be a tempting target.

Fotlin paused at the door. "Father, there's one problem," he said. "The man already had the perfect opportunity to kill me and he didn't take it. Why would he come after me again?"

"Maybe he has something else in mind," said his father, his voice booming off of the stone pillars. "Or perhaps, maybe you'll be lucky and he won't attack you. Either way, go enjoy your meal."

Fotlin exited the room muttering a prayer or three under his breath. Go get something to eat? Like he had any appetite remaining. Not when he was the bait. Not when he was the meal.

Chapter Thirty-Nine

O wen yearned for the days when he merely despised being a part of the City Watch. Those were simpler days where psychopathic killers did not duel princes outside of cemeteries. Where killers did not walk calmly into a horde of ghosts as if they were right at home among them. Days where he did not have to provide security for the duke himself.

Even worse, he was providing that protection within the Temple of Pojomi. The place gave him the creeps. The Pojomites were not content with merely hunting animals. They relished the opportunity to pursue human beings. They commonly derided the City Watch as a half measure. According to the Pojomites, the true pleasure in the hunt was in slaying the prey, not bringing them to prison. Owen thought that they must have adored Prince Yutlin's take on combating crime.

The Pojomite cavaliers were amongst the worst. The hunters were bad enough with the bodies they left scattered throughout the city rooftops. But the cavaliers were downright fanatical. Their armor was fashioned to resemble the predator totems they embodied. They all kept their human shapes, but from what Owen could tell, every single one of them wore their animal features openly and with pride.

It was disconcerting standing next to lizardmen, snakemen, catmen, and every other type of animal-men that the mind could conjure up. Talking to them was worse. To say they were socially deficient was an understatement. All they talked about was the hunt. How to hunt, when to hunt, who to hunt, and stories about their hunts and the glory they brought to Pojomi.

Owen was not surprised to find out that the men lacked families.

So long as he was in their temple, he would play nice. Owen was a religious man, but he was not terribly fond of Pojomi. He said all the benedictions, but that was it. His heart just was not in it.

Today the duke had travelled to various temples and societies drumming up support for something. Owen was never allowed within the meeting rooms. He was told to stand guard and be on alert for the man terrorizing the city. This Irving Mire.

Owen would be on the lookout alright. He would lookout for the man and scream. He had seen the fireball with his own eyes. Watched it turn to ice. Watched that man walk into the cemetery in the middle of the night. He would not stand a chance against Irving. Not even with all the City Watch as backup.

No. He would raise the cry and stand back and watch as the others fought. Owen had a family to think about.

Besides, the man would have to be insane to attack the duke. Especially with all of this protection. So far, the man had numerous opportunities to seize that opportunity and he had not. Up here on the highest floor of the temple they would be safe.

"Excuse me gentlemen, could you please point me in the direction of Duke Camen?"

Owen turned in the direction of the voice and felt his jaw drop. The darkly clad man, Irving, was standing in the doorway to the antechamber, leaning nonchalantly against the doorframe. Owen's tongue felt dry as he tried to shout out a warning.

The cavaliers and hunters pushed past Owen, drawing their weapons and shouting battle cries loud enough to be heard a few streets over. Irving stepped casually into the antechamber, seemingly unconcerned about the charging Pojomites. He drew his blade and danced into combat.

Owen pushed himself back against the door leading to the conference room. He was merely giving the Pojomites the space necessary to fight such a man.

Irving seemed to move quicker than Owen recalled. He slid underneath a horizontal slash from a cavalier and removed the cavalier's right leg just beneath the knee. Irving sprang to his feet pirouetting around a thrusting spear, his blade slicing neatly through the attacking hunter's throat. He moved effortlessly. Prince Fotlin referred to some swordsmen as artists, but Owen had never understood the sentiment until that moment.

A hulking warrior charged Irving with his steel tower shield held before him, intent on bowling the thief over. Irving dropped his sword and pushed his hands out towards the shield. Flesh met metal with a large groan. The shield bent inwards in the shape of Irving's hands. The warrior slammed into his own shield and fell to the ground, still clutching his shield; without budging Irving an inch.

Owen swallowed involuntarily. He knew from the first time he pursued Irving that the man had to have been strong to leap from the ground to the top of the wall. But bending a shield in? How was Owen supposed to compete with that?

Irving struggled against the shield; his hands still caught within the metal. For a brief moment Owen contemplated charging across the room and impaling the man. Visions of his own messy death halted that idea very quickly.

It was a good thing too. Not a second later, steam and smoke began to emanate from the tower shield. The metal began to warp as it melted. The warrior howled in agony as the molten steel dripped down his hand and arm, coating them in metal. The smell of burning flesh filled the air as the warrior mercifully ceased screaming. Whether he died or merely lost consciousness, Owen did not care to know.

Irving stood alone in the center of the antechamber over the fallen warrior. He flexed his hands as steel still dripped steadily from them. The man bent over and picked up his sword, flipping it end over end one time before sheathing it with a flourish.

"Ahh. I remember you," said Irving as he walked towards Owen. "Be a good man and introduce me to the duke would you?"

"Uhh. I can't really do that," squeaked Owen.

The door open behind Owen causing him to fall backwards. Strong hands stopped his fall and moved him out of the way.

"No, he can't," said Duke Camen as he strode out of the meeting room, in full armor that bore the resemblance to a giant bulldog. "But allow me to introduce myself. I am Duke Camen Loach. You murdered two of my children and wounded a third. You are a dead man."

Irving laughed as he drew his sword. "How disappointing. I was hoping for some witty repartee. Maybe a monologue. A speech about how my actions have hurt your wealth." Irving shook his head sadly in disappointment. "And yet, you're only upset that two murderous brats got what was coming to them. So disappointing."

"I would tell you that I am sorry to disappoint you, but I am not," barked Duke Camen. "Perhaps you'll find my swordplay more to your liking."

"If it's anything like your wordplay, I doubt it," retorted Irving. "Your Grace, I hate to hound you about this, but you simply have less personality than the stones in your mines."

Duke Camen growled as he swung his giant claymore at Irving. The thief danced nimbly away from the blade. The duke heaved again, and again, his sword tracing a deadly arc throughout the room. Irving moved too quickly for the duke, always one step ahead, ducking, diving, and bouncing off walls. The duke could not hit him with such a massive and slow weapon.

But the same could not be said for Irving. His blade flicked out whenever he saw an opening. Steel met steel as his sword scored hits upon the duke's armor. Owen saw flecks of paint missing from the bulldog armor, but did not see any blood. Irving's strikes lacked any sort of real power as he was constantly moving and could not get his full bodyweight behind them.

Owen was far from an expert, but it seemed like the two men were at a standoff. The duke was unable to hit Irving, and the thief was unable to hurt the heavily armored man. One of them was bound to get tired first. But which one would it be? The man expending all that energy dancing around, or the man wearing the heavy armor?

"You move pretty well for an old guy," said Irving without a trace of heavy breathing in his voice.

"I move as well as I need to," growled the duke as he tried to impale the thief on the end of his claymore.

Irving easily rolled to the side, chuckling as he regained his footing. "That move again?" asked Irving. "I guess you can't teach an old dog new tricks. Your boys on the other hand. Now they had some imagination."

The duke roared in rage and flung himself into an all out barrage on Irving. Swing after swing wrecked the furniture in the room and threatened to cave in the walls. Owen inched closer to the open doors. Hopefully there would be a way out through the meeting room, because there was zero chance that he would survive crossing that killing field.

"Getting warmer" shouted Irving as little balls of flame struck the duke's armor. They barely singed the painting of the armor, sending the usually reserved duke deeper into a blind rage.

"I'll tear you in half!" bellowed the duke. Owen winced in sympathy. Maybe there was a reason the duke did not speak often.

"Oh why not. This farce has gone on long enough," said Irving as he spread out his arms in a welcoming motion. "Take your best shot."

The duke did not hesitate. He cocked his sword back behind his right ear and brought it down on Irving's head. A large crack echoed in the room making Owen feel sick. But Irving did not falter. The duke's sword shattered, shards of steel embedding themselves in what remained of the furniture, walls, and ceiling.

Irving rolled his head around as he stretched his neck out. "Well, that was not pleasant," he said as he tossed back his hood.

The gleaming skull with black eyes scowled at the duke. The lighting in the temple let Owen see more of the skull than he could the first time. The eyes, while dark, also sparkled. And his eyes had not deceived him; there was a warm flame radiating behind that black gleam. Unlike a real skull that should have had gaps between the bones, this skull was completely covered in that gleaming material. It looked like one solid piece with different colors filling in the gaps between the bones.

There was more color than white or black, causing the skull to sparkle and seem more alive. The mouth opened and closed when Irving talked, but Owen could not discern any hinge or contraption allowing for the movement.

"Impossible," gasped the duke, fear creeping into his voice. "There is no way you could have forged the diamonds into anything resembling armor."

"Who said anything about forging it?" asked Irving.

"But why fight if we couldn't actually harm you?" asked the duke.

Irving smiled. A very unpleasant sight that made Owen back into the conference room with only enough remaining courage to peek out into the antechamber.

"Ahh Your Grace, you seem to be under a misconception," he said smugly. "I didn't come here to explain anything to you. I came here to kill you. All part of the plan. You understand."

Irving moved in a blur, bringing his sword above his head and swinging it downward in a mirror strike of Duke Camen's. The duke's head split like a log in a spray of blood and brain. Owen shrieked at the sight.

"Don't worry, watchman. I'm not going to kill you," said Irving. Gleaming crystalline wings sprouted from his back as he spoke. He flexed them twice as if trying them out for the first time. The wings started to glow as fire coursed through them. The fire brightened as it picked up intensity and erupted on the outside of the wings. Owen's eyes watered as he tried to look at the sight. It may have been his imagination, but it appeared that the flames were taking the shape of feathers. Madness.

"Watchman, if I were you, I would think about leaving the city as soon as possible," said Irving as his wings fluttered behind him. "The city is going to ignite after this, and I am sure you don't want to be blamed. Your family is what, in the Southern District? Take them and get out of town immediately. If you hurry you should have time."

Owen stared at the man in fear and astonishment. He knew where he lived? He needed to get his wife and daughter out of the house as soon as possible. Owen spared another glance at the duke's lifeless corpse and amended his thinking. He needed to get them all out the city as soon as possible.

Flames covered Irving as he ran past Owen and leapt out of the conference room windows in a hail of glass shards. He glided for a few seconds before plummeting to the ground. A bright flash of light accompanied a large explosion that made the tower shudder.

Owen staggered uneasily over to the window and stared out. Loach was on fire. And not only the Temple District. Flames covered the north and central portions of the city. They were localized for now, but the flames would spread. Soon almost the entire city would be aflame. There was very little anyone could do to stop it.

He fled out of the room and took the stairs at a dead sprint. He could rest later. Owen had no intention of letting his family roast in the flames.

Chapter Forty

M atlin smiled as he rode towards the city gates. According to his father's missive, he would enter the city tomorrow to a grand celebration. Today, he would ride in through the Palace Gate without fanfare. A day of meetings and briefings awaited him along with Fotlin's sullen gazes.

There was no place like home.

Matlin walked through the palace towards his father's planning room. What he really wanted was a nice bath after all the days out on the road. But that could wait. At least until he found out if his father was home or not.

The palace was eerily quiet. Few people wandered the hallways and the guards seemed uneasy. Either people were more concerned about the war than they had any right to be, or something was happening within the city.

He entered the planning room to find Setlin and Fotlin already there. Fotlin had a bandaged leg resting on the table, a walking stick next to him. Matlin felt a flash of sympathy for his little brother. Leg wounds could be a painful thing.

"Hello brothers," he said in greeting. "Will father and Yutlin be joining us?"

Fotlin grimaced while Setlin slowly closed his eyes while looking up from his stack of reports. Matlin felt his heart sink. Those expressions did not portend good news.

"What is it," Matlin asked, his voice soft and reserved.

"Yutlin is dead," said Setlin, his voice strangled. "A few weeks back a thief and a killer named Irving Mire, the same man who killed one of the twins in Talendor, kidnapped Yutlin out of a brothel. He hanged our brother, naked, in the Central District common grounds."

"I'll kill him," said Matlin, his throat thick and hot.

"Good luck," muttered Fotlin. "I tried and he nearly took my leg off. And quickly too."

"Where is father?" demanded Matlin. "He should be here."

"He's off trying to trap this Irving," explained Setlin. "We've all been exposing ourselves as targets trying to goad him into attacking. Oh, don't give me that look. He's supported by some of the finest cavaliers and hunters in the city. He's been going from temple to temple collecting them."

"Tell me everything that has happened," instructed Matlin as he sat down. He could take a bath later.

Setlin gestured vaguely in Fotlin's direction as he went back to reading his reports. Fotlin mumbled under his breath before launching into a long and simply unbelievable tale. Thieving, hangings, murders, and a man with a skull for a face? Matlin felt bad for the lad. Clearly fear had addled his wits and he could not remember events clearly.

A sudden force struck the palace causing everything to shudder. Matlin leapt to his feet and drew his sword. How could the Antierian wizards have conjured up an earthquake from this far away? That should be impossible.

"What was that?" asked Fotlin quizzically. "And put your sword away Matlin. It's embarrassing just looking at you."

Matlin ignored his brother and darted out of the room. He needed windows and quickly. He sprinted past the guardsmen in the hallway as he searched for the proper window. He was vaguely aware of their feet pounding on the floor after him. Good men to follow their prince without needing to be told to do so.

Matlin gazed out of the south facing windows. In the distance he could vaguely make out the Antierian forces on the horizon. They were too far away for any sort of combat. Those tremors could not have been caused by them.

Matlin dashed off again past the guardsmen who were just beginning to catch up with him. He found an east facing window and stared out. His army was fine.

He frowned. That only left the north and west facing windows. Which meant that the source was from within in the city? That did not make sense.

Matlin took off again, passing the same group of guardsmen that were now breathing heavily. He gazed out the north facing windows to a sight straight out of a nightmare. The city was on fire. Flames stretched to the sky throughout all of the northern districts. He hoped the flames had not spread to the Central and Western Districts. One would cripple the economy; the other could possibly result in a horde of prisoners flooding into the city if the jail was significantly damaged.

"What happened?" called out Setlin as he rushed up to the window with Fotlin well in his wake. Setlin's face paled as he stared out the window. "By the gods," he breathed. A moment passed before his eyes widened. "Matlin. Father was supposed to be at the Temple of Pojomi today. And that area, it is all..." his voice trailed off.

"On fire," Matlin supplied. "Father is strong. He'll manage for himself. Right now, we need to put out all the fires. Mobilize every guardsman, soldier, and watchman that we have. Form bucket lines and put those fires out. And send word to the temples. Maybe they can help."

"Still think I was making it all up?" Fotlin scoffed.

Matlin glowered at his brother and ran off to organize the saving of the city. Winning the war was irrelevant if in the end he wound up holding only a smoking ruin.

Chapter Forty-One

R andall awoke with a start. Living on the street taught him to sleep lightly. It was a necessary skill for survival.

He bounded through the door and looked around. But the warehouse was fine. The children glanced around uncertain of what was happening, but nothing seemed out of the ordinary. If the watchmen were raiding their hideout they were doing a poor job. They should have just knocked in the doors and been done with it.

Randall scrambled up through one of the side windows, intent on scouting out the area. He never made it though. The window let him see everything that he needed to know. The city was burning. Even the warehouses in the Northeast District were on fire.

"Everyone gather your things!" bellowed Randall. "Quickly. Food is the most important. Fill up every satchel and bag that you can carry! And don't forget your boots!"

"What's going on?" asked Tigun.

"The city is on fire and we need to get out of here!" shouted Randall.

"Where are we going to go?" asked one of the smaller children.

"Out of the city," answered Randall. "We'll need food and coin to help us. Now move!"

Randall darted into his room and began packing. It did not take long. He did not own much, and he always was prepared to run. The most important thing would be retrieving the gold he had secreted throughout the warehouse.

Randall stuff the ceremonial dagger and amulet into a sack and tossed a cloak around his shoulders.

"And don't forget to grab a cloak or two," bellowed Randall as he darted throughout the warehouse retrieving the gold.

"How are we exiting?" shouted Tigun. "Through the tunnels? We should be safe from the smoke there."

"Too dangerous," hollered Randall. "Those tunnels aren't the most stable things around. And suppose we make it through. Where would we exit? The mines? We would be arrested on sight."

"Where do we go then?" asked Tigun.

Randall's mind raced as he thought. "We exit to the south. The fire hasn't spread there yet."

Tigun herded the remaining children up. Each carried at least two satchels on their back and looked scared out of their minds. "Stick together now," said Tigun. "Hold hands and speak up if someone becomes separated. Now be careful, and stay close."

Randall heaved against the warehouse doors. They did not want to budge. Years of dirt jammed the doorway. Tigun slammed his body against the doors causing them to shudder. Even the little ones threw their weight against the doors. Eventually, inch by inch the doors opened.

"Everyone out. Now!" said Randall as he squeezed out the door.

The warehouse section of the Northeast District was nearly deserted. People did not live in the area, and those that worked there were already leaving to save themselves or their family.

"Remember, hold hands and follow me," shouted Randall.

The city had descended into madness. People rushed about, shoving and pushing, trying to make their way in any direction that was not on fire. Others stood still or staggered about, a vacant expression on their faces.

Randall wished he could take to the rooftops and flee out of the city, but he could not take that chance. The smoke was billowing up, obscuring the rooftops. One wrong leap would send them all into a fiery grave.

Fire was bouncing from building to building at an alarming rate. Randall and the others were barely staying ahead of the inferno. Eventually, they reached the Eastern District, but it was no better there. While the flames had not yet reached the district, the people had. The crowds surged, pressing against one another. The true threat was a stampede with everyone trying to flee. Hopefully by moving as one large mass, the little ones would not be trampled.

Soldiers were darting about everywhere, on foot and on horseback. They did not bother to instruct the populace to get out of their way. They shoved and charged their way through the people, heedless if they left the people dead or injured. Randall tried to keep their group on the edge of the street for safety, but it was slower going. They took risks daily to survive. None of them were strangers to danger. They would just have to shoulder more risk if they wanted to escape the city.

Randall led them through the masses trying to make use of their smaller size to squeeze into the gaps. People jostled him and a few even tried to cuff his head, but he kept his people moving. He just had to get them south. Exiting east near the palace was never going to happen through the mass of soldiers.

"Randall," cried Tigun over the noise of the crowd. "The fire hasn't spread here yet."

"I know!" said Randall. "We need to hurry."

"Then let's do it from higher ground," said Tigun.

Randall nearly smacked himself in the head as he ran. He should have seen it sooner. They were outpacing the fire. That meant the rooftops were available to them again.

He ducked down a nearby alley and looked at the tiny faces staring back at him. "Okay everyone," he said as patiently as he could manage. "You all remember how to run across rooftops? Good. Now the same rules apply. Stick together. Hold hands when possible. We're going to get out of here."

Tigun scrambled up the building and helped Randall boost the children up on the rooftop. It was more difficult for the children to climb while they were weighed down by all of their clothing, bags, and satchels. But those items were necessities, and unless he was wrong, were going to be in short supply for the likes of them.

Randall pulled himself up last and stared out across the city in horror. Shades of red, orange, and yellow greeted him. The fires had spread since he last viewed the city. The north, central, and western portions of the city were a raging out of control inferno. And the south? The south was a teeming mass of humanity flowing out of the gates. But from what he could tell, the people were not stopping after they reached the gates. They kept running, allowing those still trapped inside to flee.

"Okay people, Southeastern Gate," said Randall. "Let's move. Once we're through the gate we go south, southwest. Away from our army. They'll recognize us for thieves. Now move!"

Chapter Forty-Two

O wen did not miss being a watchman. Trying to bring order to the city while it was in this heightened state of chaos would be nearly impossible.

He had stripped off his watchmen's tabard and pulled a coat on over his armor when he arrived at home. There was no going back to the City Watch after today's events. He was on duty when the duke was murdered. Even worse, he had survived while the duke had not. There would be no forgiveness for that.

Irving's advice had been accurate. He barely had enough time to get home and get his wife and daughter to safety. But just barely.

The Southwestern Gate was clogged by members of the populace. The press of humanity bumped against him and bounced off harmlessly. Standing his ground in a crowd was one of the few skills of a watchmen that was actually useful in this situation.

"Excuse me," said a low female voice.

"No problem, miss," began Owen before his eyes widened in shock and recognition. It was the young prostitute from the night Prince Yutlin was murdered. Judging by the shocked expression on her face she recognized him as well.

"I'm sorry, please don't mind me," she said as she moved away. Owen snagged her by the arm. He could not let her leave. Not when she recognized him and knew he was leaving the city. He wanted to escape the princes' vengeance, not lead them straight to him.

"I'm not going to tell anyone about you," he hissed. Judging from the look of relief on her face she was having similar thoughts. "Look. I have a similar problem as you. We're in the same boat here. Let me help you get away."

"Oh? And do what? Be your wife?" she asked sarcastically.

"No," snarled Owen as he held his hand out to his wife and daughter. "This is my wife Margaret, and my daughter Kendra." The prostitute frowned at him in confusion. "Look. You resemble my daughter enough that you could be sisters. Stay with us and we'll get you out of here."

"No. I couldn't," she protested.

Margaret wrapped her arms around the trembling prostitute. "Sweet heart, trust my Owen," she said sweetly. "If he says it's dangerous out there, then it is. If you're in some sort of trouble, no one will be looking for you with us. And I know Kendra always wanted another sister."

The prostitute started to cry. "I-I-I had a..." her voice trailed off as she broke into a messy bout of tears. "My name is Lynn," she gasped.

"It's a pleasure to meet you Lynn," said Kendra timidly. Owen was proud of her. She was such a sweet girl. "We're heading southwest of here. It's like an adventure! It's the only place that we may actually be safe."

Owen prayed silently to the gods as he looked over the three women. They would be a target out on the road. But Antier was their only chance. Maybe he could gain some sympathy there with his story regarding Duke Camen's death. Or vanish into the wild frontier and start a small farm. Either way, it beat burning to death, or whatever the princes had in store for him.

Chapter Forty-Three

C ole winced as the metal pierced his skin. He hated sewing. It was such a tedious activity. But it had to be done. It would not do to go out in his clothes with tears in them. People would notice.

He moved the needle deftly in and out of the dark green, almost black, material. The tear was not that large, but it would grow if he did not fix it now. He finished it and tossed it on top of the pile of clothing.

Blacksmith's clothing, nobleman, mercenary, bravo, sellsword, butcher, innkeeper, miner, merchant, he had it all. The different outfits allowed him to move about the city with ease. He picked them up and tossed them into the last chest. He left it open as one more outfit needed to be placed inside of it.

The hideout was hardly luxurious. A stone room, probably a basement of some sort that was nearly completely sealed off from the world above. The only entrances and exits were through the sewers, a crypt within the graveyard, and a trapdoor that led into a deserted alleyway between some warehouses in the Southwest District.

It was in the alleyway that Cole had secreted the wagon. It was stronger than most wagons, with reinforced axles, hidden compartments, and a canvas covering. Which was a good thing, as there was a duchy's ransom in loot that needed to be smuggled out of Loach. Only one last chest remained in the hideout.

Cole leaned his chair back against the stone wall and kicked his feet up onto the table. He tried to relax, but he was feeling anxious about moving on. The entire plan depended on chaos tearing the city apart, and the guardsmen being too distracted to search the wagon.

"Well you certainly look comfortable," said a man's voice from the sewer entrance. He wore a dark green outfit, identical to the one that Cole had just finished sewing. He tossed his hood back revealing that hideous skull face. "Shall we be going?" he asked.

"Not so long as you look like that," answered Cole as he slid the chest across the table with his foot. "Pick an outfit. I went for the travelling merchant look. How'd your disaster go?"

The skull winced as the diamonds slowly seeped back into his human skin. "The phoenix is stronger than I anticipated," answered Byron with a sheepish grin. "I may have set more of the city on fire than we planned."

"How much of the city?" asked Cole with his eyes narrowed.

"Umm, the entire northern portion of the city, as well as the Western and Central Districts," said Byron as he stripped out of the Irving disguise.

Cole rubbed at his eyes. "That is going to make the stampedes worse than we expected," he said. "It's going to make getting the wagon out of the city even more difficult."

"We'll manage," said Byron as he tossed on one of the mercenary outfits. "After everything we've already accomplished, I doubt a minor thing like a crowd will stop us."

"Maybe you," said Cole as he folded the disguise and placed it within the chest. "My totem doesn't let me come back from the dead."

"That's only happened once," protested Byron. "Okay, maybe twice. And I do try not to die. It's not exactly like I know how this thing works. I'm not even sure that I actually died."

"Well you should work on learning to control that thing before you manage to incinerate me," grumbled Cole. "Now pick up the chest and let's get out of here. At least on the bright side we won't have to walk all the way through that narrow passage into the crypts."

"Aww, but I liked that passage," said Byron. "Made everything feel more mysterious."

"We had to walk halfway across the city. Underground," said Cole as he jimmied open the trapdoor.

"True," admitted Byron. "But you didn't see the look on the Loachians faces when I walked into the graveyard. It was the stuff of legends."

"What happened to the serious responsible version of you?" asked Cole.

"He's on vacation I think," said Byron as he pulled the chest through the trapdoor. "Or maybe you forgot to pull him out of the river."

"Oh, so it's my fault now?" muttered Cole as he leapt up onto the wagon. "Do you know how difficult it was camouflaging myself while I climbed down the entire cliff side?"

"Nope. I took the quicker way down," said Byron as he secured the final chest in the wagon.

"And did you take the quick way down again today?" asked Cole as he moved the wagon into motion.

"Nah. I grew wings," answered Byron as he climbed out of the back and next to Cole.

Cole grumbled a few nasty phrases as he navigated the wagon into the crowd. The people were still moving frantically, but none of them tried to stop their wagon. Most likely they were frightened that the wagon may run them over, breaking limbs. That was not part of Cole's plan, but if left with no other recourse, he would take that path.

It took a few hours, but they made it out of the city before the flames could reach the southern districts. Soot and smoke covered the countryside. The Loachian people looked tired and haggard. Many of them appeared to have aged years in only a matter of hours. Byron looked on at them grimly, his usual cheer gone.

His moods toggled like that recently. Whether it was dying, or whatever actually happened to him with his totem, losing the men under his command, the thieving, or the murdering, something ate at the prince. He put on a brave face and tried to hide the pain with jokes, but Cole saw it. This war was eating away at Byron's soul.

"I wonder if the others had that look in their eyes when they fled," Byron whispered.

"Don't know," replied Cole as he kept the wagon heading down the road to the southwest. "I imagine it must have been different. Witnessing people die is different than the abstract knowledge that they perished."

"Abstract?" asked Byron skeptically. "Since when do you talk like that? How many of those old books did you read?"

"All of them," answered Cole. "I was bored."

"Stop the wagon," said Byron abruptly. "I recognize these people."

Cole reined in the wagon as they approached what had to be the largest family he had ever seen. There was a husband, a wife, two girls in their late teens, and about eleven children carrying multiple sacks over their shoulders.

Guilt washed over Cole as he looked at the terror on the children's faces. Terror he helped wrought. He did not need to look over at Byron to know that his expression was mirrored on his friend's face.

"I think I recognize the eldest boy," whispered Cole silently.

"Me too," whispered Byron. "As well as one of the teenage girls, and the older man."

"Excuse me, good sirs," said the man as his wife wrapped one of the children's legs in a makeshift cloth bandage. "We don't mean to be in your way. The child has an injury. You understand."

"Not at all," said Byron. "I was talking to my partner here, and he suggested that you all join us. Seeing as we're all travelling in the same direction. It breaks our hearts seeing children in this condition."

The man narrowed his eyes. "Is that so?" he asked suspiciously.

His wife slapped him on the shoulder. "Owen," she said the name in a tone of admonishment. "Is that any way to treat someone trying to help the children."

"We don't need anyone's help," declared the boy Cole recognized.

Cole frowned at him, causing the man to begin speaking over himself. "Oh, please don't be angry good sir," he said. "He's not my child. We found this band of children walking around unsupervised and injured. My wife and daughters insisted that we help them."

"Very generous of you," said Byron. "And after today, that would not offend us at all. The offer still stands if everyone, the little man included, is in agreement."

The boy scowled at Byron, but the expression softened as he surveyed the other children. "We don't have a problem with it," the boy said softly. "We would appreciate the ride."

Cole smiled gently at the boy. That had to be hard on his pride to admit that. "Okay then," he said. "Everyone climb into the back, and please don't open any of the containers."

Everyone mumbled their agreements as they climbed into the back of the covered wagon, collapsing in tired sighs.

"So what is your plan? If you don't mind me asking," Owen asked, hastily adding on the qualifying statement.

"Not at all," answered Byron. "We're going to catch up to that army over there and follow it out of Loach. The locals are going to be consumed with that fire back there and won't be able to adequately patrol the roads for bandits and people who have become desperate. Better to be protected by an army."

"You mean the Antierian army?" asked Owen skeptically. "You think they would let Loachians follow their army?"

"I don't see why not," answered Byron. "I've done a bit of travelling in my life, and can't say that I know of any people that would turn a group of children such as these away."

"Ahh I see," said Owen as certainty mixed with a touch of cynicism entered his voice. "I was wondering why you invited us to travel. You need us so that you can travel safely with the Antierians."

Cole snorted at the thought. "We invited you because you looked like you needed help," he said defensively as his annoyance began to rise. "If you haven't noticed, the two of us aren't Loachians. We'd be more easily accepted by the Antierian forces without you."

"Enough," said Byron. "Listen. We're glad to have your company. Truly we are. It feels good to feel like you're helping someone throughout all of this madness. But it has been a long day for everyone. Especially the children. Why don't you all get some rest, and we'll wake you when we stop to make camp."

Owen opened his mouth to protest, but his wife grabbed his arm and silenced him with a quick look. "Very well then," said Owen reluctantly. "Thank you for your generosity."

The Loachians all settled down and were asleep within minutes. Owen included.

Cole glanced back at them as jealousy crept into his mind. The worst was over for them. The future may be terrifying and uncertain, but at least they had hope. He and Byron had no clue what awaited them at the Antierian army. Hopefully good news and open arms. But anger was a real possibility. All it would take was one loose arrow or hastily swung sword before they could explain themselves.

It was a bleak possibility, and one Cole did not relish dwelling upon. Nevertheless, Cole considered himself lucky that he was travelling with a man so adept at returning from the dead.

Chapter Forty-Four

D arik gazed silently out over the burning city. The fires raged for a second day, and did not show any signs of relenting. From his vantage point, it was impossible to determine if the inferno consumed the entire city.

"Any word from Master Tyson?" asked Darik as he forced a neutral tone onto his voice.

"Not yet," answered Renaldo as he idly stripped the bark from a fallen branch.

Darik seethed. The wraith vanished shortly after the fires began without asking Darik's permission. Master Sildun reported that Tyson claimed his sources would be nearly impossible to contact in a situation such as this and that he needed to gather intelligence in person.

Tyson's recklessness could cost him dearly. And at such a delicate time too. How Darik handled this situation could determine the succession. Attacking a city whose populace had just been turned into refugees would make him look like a monster to most of the nobility. But allowing House Loach to escape justice for their attack on Fort Hope would make him look weak to those same nobles. It was a fine line to walk, and one that he would prefer to traverse after being fully advised by his master of intelligence.

Instead, he stood in their camp, looking down on the burning city, waiting. If he was going to strike, the time would be now. Loach's gates were wide open, and its army was preoccupied with battling the blaze.

The only problem was the wave of refugees between the two of them. Darik had sworn to himself that he would minimize civilian casualties after his earlier follies in eastern Loach. But was his morality a situational construct? Did the ends justify the means? The citizens were not innocent per se. They supported House Loach and fought willingly in their military. They were the base of Loach's power and wealth and they reaped the benefits of it. But did they deserve death?

No matter what decision he made everyone would second guess him. He could be crowned king as well as the greatest monster in the history of the kingdom, all at the same time. Or he could desist, letting his brother's murderers live and hope honor would carry the day. By God it would help if he only knew what had occurred in the city.

Jeron and Dalton were in a panic and had been ever since they saw the fire explode over the city. They were convinced that the Loachians developed a new weapon to counteract their earthquake assaults. From what Master Richard reported, the two were looking into methods of saturating an area with water and using a dome of ice as a defensive shield.

Which begged the question. Could he send his army down there if the Loachians could turn such a destructive force against his men? Questions were all he had, and he was quickly running out of time to formulate answers.

"Your Highness," said Emkario as he walked up to the vantage point. "Our scouts estimate that the first of the few refugees heading our direction will arrive in a few hours."

"Is Thiago one of those scouts?" asked Darik.

"Yes, Your Highness."

"Send him here," ordered Darik. "I'd like to hear his thoughts on the matter."

Emkario bowed his head and departed without another word. He was a good soldier and friend. Darik could expect him to voice an opinion if he thought Darik was erring. Until then he would give Darik space to think.

Darik had little time to continue his musings, as Prince Nelson and Prince Irvin filled the void left by Emkario.

"Have you made up your mind yet?" asked Irvin, his voice solemn as he stared out at the burning city.

"Not yet."

"Don't attack the civilians," said Nelson brusquely. "I'm warning you. Things will not go well in Biona if you do."

"Some history there that I don't know about?" asked Darik.

Nelson nodded. "Nuquanian buccaneers are prone to raiding towns along the coastline and kidnapping people. Rumors are that they keep the women, and sell the men into slavery across the sea," explained Nelson. "Naturally, attacking non-military forces does not sit well with my people."

"It shouldn't sit well with anyone," whispered Darik.

Someone coughed clearing their throat. "Excuse me, Your Highness," said Thiago. "I was told to report to you."

"Ahh Thiago. Just the man I was looking for," said Darik. "Emkario tells me that you have been out scouting and have observed the Loachian populace. Are they a threat?"

Thiago shook his head in the negative. "No, sir. Many of them are armed, but they aren't travelling together. The weapons are for their own personal protection. The people are looking at each other very suspiciously. Like they expect all of their neighbors to turn to banditry at a moment's notice."

"That's very likely," said Irvin. "Once their food runs out, people turn vicious very quickly. It's easy to justify banditry when you're starving."

"Your Highness!" shouted Master Sildun as he sprinted through the camp. The master was breathing heavily, sweat pouring into his salt and pepper beard. The man had given up shaving at some point during their march.

"What is it?" Darik asked as the man tried to catch his breath.

"One of our messengers arrived from Ochandor just now," panted Sildun as he handed Darik a letter. "All the messenger knows is the contents of that letter. King Ramon is dead."

Darik closed his eyes as the pounding headache returned. Of all the times, he had to die now. That decided things.

"I've made up my mind," said Darik. "We'll pull back slowly, providing cover for those citizens that want it. Nelson, I assume you and your men need to get back to Biona?"

"Indeed, we will," said Nelson appreciatively. "Every noble worth their title will be converging on Ochandor. I'll meet my father there with our men."

"Bringing an army to the capital?" asked Irvin skeptically. "Are you looking for a fight?"

Nelson shrugged helplessly. "I assume everyone else will. No one will want to be standing by and let someone else seize the throne through force."

"He's right," said Darik. "I'll be bringing my forces there, and I expect Matlin will too. At least once he has a handle on this burning city situation."

"You sound as if there'll be a battle," said Irvin disapprovingly. "In the city."

"No," said Darik. "Not in the city. There isn't enough room for the armies to fight within the city. It will be the nobles who do the fighting."

"Count me in," said Irvin. "There are a few nobles that I would not mind killing."

"Such as?" asked Nelson as he leaned forward with interest.

"Neither of you," said Irvin grimly. "But there are still a few more that deserve what is coming to them."

Darik sighed. "Irvin. You've proven yourself to be a good friend. So let me say this as a friend. Don't do anything stupid. You're a good man, and there are plenty of people that would miss you."

Irvin did not reply. He just kept staring out at the inferno with those sad brown eyes.

Chapter Forty-Five

B yron groaned as he tried to ignore Cole shaking him awake. The sun was barely peeking out over the horizon. He still had at least a good half hour of sleep left.

"Wake up," hissed Cole.

"Why?" groaned Byron. "We're going to catch up to the army today. This could be our last good sleep."

"That's exactly why you need to get up," insisted Cole. "Everyone is going to have questions for us. It'll answer a lot of questions if we both show up as Irving."

"That...doesn't make much sense," said Byron. "Our faces and names should work."

"Well at least your brain is awake now," said Cole. "But our faces and names coming from a ragtag group of refugees? Come on. What soldier is going to believe that?"

"And you think Irving would work?" asked Byron from behind a groggy glare.

"Maybe," said Cole. "But at the bare minimum it should get us to see Nelson, and we can go from there."

"And frighten our travelling companions," pointed out Byron.

Cole shrugged. "We've both helped the Randall boy, and you did save that young woman," he said. "They may be grateful."

"I doubt Owen will feel the same way," said Byron as he let Cole manhandle him to his feet. "I'm going. I'm going."

Byron climbed into the wagon and unlocked the chest with their disguises. "Why don't you just admit it," he said as he tugged off his studded leather armor. "You only want to be in disguise so that you'll have time to figure out what to say to Atrisha."

Cole bristled at the response. "And what's wrong with that?" he demanded. "Like you aren't worried about explaining yourself?"

Byron gestured down at the four scars decorating his chest. "Nah. I have these," he said while grinning. "It really helps sell the whole I came back from the dead story."

"I wish I had some of those," Cole grumbled. "It would make my explanations a lot simpler."

"No, you don't," said Byron as he rubbed at his scars absently. The memories of that day were horrible. He could still remember the power surging through him on that day. He almost dropped his sword in shock when he parried the first direct blow from a minotaur. It should have torn the sword straight from his hands. But it did not. Nor did the next three or four minotaurs.

He had never felt more alive, more energized. And then the twins shot him full of arrows. Byron did not remember much once he fell from the cliffs. He recalled a vague warm sensation filling his body, and then nothing.

Byron had woken up to Cole's concerned face standing over him. He thought he had been losing his mind when the trees started to move. He was too tired to move or say anything though. All he could do was watch in horror as they transformed into humans.

Truth is rarely as exciting as legend. The swamplands were not a death trap because of any horrible monsters living there. Travelers from Ochandor always made the mistake of trying to chop the trees for firewood. They had no way of knowing that instead of an animal totem, the swamp folk possessed tree totems. Their efforts were always doomed to fail because they kept trying to kill the residents for firewood.

Byron and Cole were in too poor of condition to attempt a similar mistake. They got lucky. The locals took them in, nursed him back to health, and provided them with the strange dark green clothing. He was also fortunate that his new totem helped him heal quicker than usual.

"What's on your mind?" asked Cole. "You stopped getting dressed."

"How to explain the swamp," replied Byron. "How do you tell people that their ghost stories aren't real?"

"That's the part you think will be a problem?" said Cole drily. "Here I thought everyone would be upset that we let them think we were dead."

"There was nothing we could do if I came back from the dead," protested Byron as he tugged on the dark green clothing. "It would have been war right away. A war we couldn't win."

"I know that," chuckled Cole. "We just have to hope everyone else views your path of mayhem the same way."

"My mayhem?" asked Byron. "What about your little murder spree in Ochandor?"

"Your plan," insisted Cole. "Your mayhem."

Byron grinned before pulling his hood up over his face. "So who do we wake up first?" he asked with an evil laugh.

"Oh, that's cruel," said Cole. "I say all of them at once. Although the children will probably bolt if they wake up to a scream."

"Fine," said Byron as he tossed back his hood. "We'll keep our faces visible. I don't feel like chasing down all the little munchkins."

"And because they could get hurt out there," supplied Cole.

"Yes, yes," said Byron impatiently as he buckled the strap holding his scabbard across his back. It felt so much more natural there than at his hip. "That goes without saying."

Byron leapt to the edge of the wagon and stared at the sleeping forms on the dirt ground. They all looked exhausted, dirty, and haggard. He really wished he could let them rest, but they lacked that luxury.

"Good morning, everyone," he called out. "Time to wake up. We have a busy day ahead of us."

The Loachians woke up slowly. They must have all been in a deep sleep. The boy, Randall, was the first to notice their changed outfits. He gaped openly at them. Byron tossed the kid what he hoped was a reassuring wink. The prostitute smiled at him in satisfaction. He would need to catch her name before reaching the army. All of their names actually.

And Owen. Poor Owen. His reaction did not leave anything to be desired. "You!" he shouted as his eyes focused on Byron and Cole. His face froze in shock as his mind tried to process the two of them standing there in their Irving outfits with the hoods down. "You two killed the duke! And set the city on fire!" He kept jerking his head around in panic. The man had witnessed Byron fight and knew he did not have a prayer if he chose to stand against him.

"The duke is dead?" asked the prostitute with a hint of a smile on her face.

"That was me," said Byron simply. "I owed him that for trying to murder me."

"And setting the city on fire?" demanded Owen's wife Margaret with her hands on her hips, a disapproving frown on her face, and a glower in her eyes.

"That was for killing my men," said Byron simply. "There is a war going on if you hadn't noticed."

"Your men?" squeaked Randall. "Who are you?"

"Prince Byron Villa of Antier," said Byron with a flourish and a courtly bow. "At your service."

"A prince huh," said the prostitute sounding less than impressed. "Of course, you thought the lives of us poor city folk were beneath you."

"If I thought that, then why did I save your life?" asked Byron.

"I don't know," she said. "But there is no way you could have known that the fire wouldn't kill me."

Byron sighed in defeat. That was true. "I never meant the fire to be that large," he admitted. "It was only supposed to be a distraction, not a calamity."

"And that makes it okay?" said Owen angrily. "We had to flee the city!"

"Owen, you were going to have to leave the city eventually," said Byron. The older man's shoulders slumped in defeat. "And not just for failing to catch me. You can't tell me that the child hangings didn't bother you."

All of the Loachians flinched and looked down at the ground at that. Byron frowned as he glanced over at Cole.

"I am guessing they all knew someone who died," he whispered. "Or they just don't like murdered children."

"Can't say as I blame them," whispered Byron. He turned back to the people and raised the volume of his voice. "I'm sorry for bringing up bad memories. But if you'll recall, I killed that little child-hanging psychotic myself. If you would like to needle me for that, can we please do it on the road?"

The prostitute blushed, and lowered her head in shame. That needle quip had stung. Good.

"I'm sorry," she said. "I know we haven't been introduced, but my name is Lynn." She took Byron's hand as he helped her into the wagon. Her eyes narrowed as she glared coolly at him. "But don't think this means that I forgive you."

"Not at all."

The remainder of the refugees poured into the wagon. They were too tired and terrified to complain beyond that. The children's sacks were filled with food. Byron was impressed. Running for their lives and they had the where-withal to think to bring food with them? Not everyone would have done that. Strangely enough, the children shared their food with those in the wagon. Byron smiled as he took the reins and lurched the wagon into motion.

A small hand tapped him on the shoulder. "Sir," said Randall as his eyes darted about nervously. "Umm, would you two care for some food?"

Byron smiled graciously at the child. "I would be honored," he said.

"Here is some, umm apples I think," said Randall. "I uhh, just wanted to thank you. For saving me."

"From the Pojomite?" asked Byron. "It was my pleasure. Why was he after you?"

The boy blushed and remained silent.

"He robbed the Temple of Pojomi," answered Cole. Randall looked at the flame haired man in shock. "Don't deny it," said Cole. "We ran into each other on the rooftops that night."

"Wait," interrupted Owen. "You were the thief?"

Cole shrugged. "Sometimes."

"Well which one of you evaded the City Watch by leaping up onto the wall after robbing the Temple of Espira?" asked Owen. "That night has been bothering me for a while."

"I robbed the temple," said Cole with a twinkle in his eyes. "As for jumping onto the wall..." his voice trailed off as he channeled his totem and vanished. Their passengers gasped and Byron could not help but chuckle.

"And I was already on the wall when he did that," laughed Byron.

"So there were two of you?!" concluded Owen with satisfaction and puzzlement.

"Of course, dear," said Margaret as she patted his arm. "We can all clearly see that."

Their passengers quieted down after that. They were content to eat their breakfast and ride along in silence. Byron knew the feeling. When he was recovering from his wounds, he did not want to talk much. He had too much on his mind. His future, his plans. It had all been so much to handle, and he could not focus on all of it immediately. He needed time to process what happened.

Byron kept his hood raised while travelling. It was not long before that tactic paid off.

A solitary miner was walking along the road. He was a sturdily built man with short cropped hair and a goatee. He did not openly carry anything. Not a bag, and not any visible weaponry.

"Excuse me, sir," Byron called out to the miner. "But what are you doing over here? Aren't the mines on the Northeastern side of the city? Shouldn't a miner be over there?"

The man flinched in a very satisfying manner as his hands drifted towards his belt. Cole and Byron burst out laughing as they threw back their hoods.

"Excuse me, Master Tyson," said Cole. "Can we give you a ride back to the army?"

Master Tyson stared at the two boys in shock. Tears began to well up in his eyes as he choked out a few chuckles. "Well I'll be damned," he said as he shook his head in amazement. "Can't say that I've ever turned down a ride from a pair of dead men before. May I?"

Byron and Cole shuffled over, making room for their old teacher. He leapt up spryly onto the wagon, squeezing Byron in a one-armed hug before ruffling Cole's hair. "You two have a lot of explaining to do," he laughed. "And I hope you can explain what happened in that city. I've only been able to put bits and pieces together."

"Byron killed the duke and set the city on fire," said Cole. "There you go. All caught up."

Tyson's face went slack as he shook his head in silent disbelief. "Somehow I'm not surprised. No, Byron. Don't make any excuses. Just tell me what happened."

Byron rolled his eyes. "I think I'll wait until we get to camp," he said. "That way I only have to tell it once."

"You just want to keep me in suspense," grumbled Tyson.

Byron smirked as he kept his eyes on the road. There was nothing wrong with that.

"Trade secret," he said with a friendly smirk.

Chapter Forty-Six

C ole yawned while reclining on the wagon seat. His efforts to remain calm were only making him feel sleepy.

Master Tyson remained tenacious in his pursuit of their story. Like Byron, Cole also did not have any desire to repeat himself and merely shook his head. Then Owen had the misfortune to open his mouth and speak. Cole felt extraordinarily sorry for the man. Master Tyson had climbed into the back of the wagon and began interrogating the man for the past few hours.

The other occupants had remained quiet after witnessing the barrage of questions that Master Tyson buffeted the watchman with. However, it was not very long before their involvement in events was uncovered by the wraith. The spy had them all speaking and spreading tales in no time.

"Boys, you know that with me here you don't need to wear those outfits," called Master Tyson from the wagon bed.

"And miss Nelson's reaction?" scoffed Byron. "I don't think so."

"Wait. That was you in Talendor?" asked Tyson. "Cole where were you?"

"Whoops," said Byron.

Cole let loose an exaggerated yawn and closed his eyes. There was plenty of time for interrogations later.

His eyes were only closed for a second or two before someone was shaking him. "Wake up, Cole," said Tyson. "We're at the first lookouts."

Cole blinked his eyes at the bright daylight. He must have nodded off in the shade from the hood. At least he did not have to answer any questions during that time.

"What did I miss?" asked Cole sleepily.

"Byron was explaining your grand plan to me," Tyson replied.

Cole snorted. "I must still be dreaming."

Tyson sighed in defeat. "It was worth a shot."

The first lookouts, as Master Tyson referred to them, were more of a rolling checkpoint. A mixture of soldiers and scouts stood at the road. From the looks of things, they were questioning and directing the refugees.

A look of disgust crossed Tyson's face. "Boys you owe me for this," he said with great distaste. "I hate announcing myself or letting myself be seen, but I guess time isn't on our side anymore."

Master Tyson cupped his hands to his mouth. "Thiago!" he bellowed. "Over here you lout."

The solemn faced scout walked over, a rare ivory smile splitting his dark face. "Ahh Master Tyson, your arrival has been anticipated...for quite a while," he said with meaning.

Master Tyson spread his hands out disarmingly. "Ahh Thiago. I have missed you too," he said smugly. "Now if you don't mind, please show us to Prince Darik."

"I do mind," grumbled Thiago. "A wagon full of Loachian strangers brought to the prince without being checked? Are you out of your mind?"

Cole felt a grin stretching across his face. He had liked Thiago while they travelled together. Seeing his reaction would be grand.

"Gentlemen, if you would?" said Master Tyson with a smug superior grin on his face. Cole and Byron crossed their arms and stared at the master. His smug expression faltered as he threw up his hands in exasperation. "Ha. Ha. Very funny. Just do it." Byron nodded at Cole and the two pulled back their hoods simultaneously.

Thiago did not so much as flinch. He continued staring at them, bored and unimpressed. "That's it?" he asked. "Two mercenaries? Well done, sir. You truly are a credit to your craft."

Cole jaw dropped at Thiago's expression. He had expected shock and maybe joy. But no recognition at all.

Byron burst out into laughter. Thiago met that laughter with a smile. "Still trying to figure out how much I weigh, Your Highness?"

"Too much for me, Thiago," chuckled Byron. "Bless you man, but that was fantastic. Can you show us to my brother? I promise I'll suggest that you stay for the story."

"Of course. Right this way," said Thiago. "And how could I miss a story about you being too dumb to stay dead? And Cole being stupid enough to follow after you?"

Byron roared with laughter as Cole looked on befuddled. People confused him sometimes. He slipped the hood back over his head, and noticed that Byron doing the same. Thiago's presence notwithstanding, their reasons for wearing the disguises had not changed.

Thiago led them through the checkpoint and pointed at a messenger. "You there," he called out. "Send word ahead that I'm returning with Master Tyson." The messenger nodded and ran on ahead.

"Just Master Tyson?" asked Byron.

"And miss everyone else having a heart attack?" replied Thiago. "I think not."

Cole felt his forehead bunch up. "Wait. That was your shocked face?" Cole asked.

"Yes. I'm a chameleon," Thiago said indifferently.

"Really? Me too!" said Cole excitedly. He had never met another chameleon.

"No. Not really," said Thiago in that same solemn monotone.

Cole shut his mouth in frustration. He knew there was a reason he never spoke much with Thiago. The man made him feel dumb and uncomfortable.

The Antierian army was a sight to see. It was nothing like Cole's memories of their forces at Fort Hope. The most obvious difference were women walking around clad in all sorts of armor. But there was something else about the force. This air of hopefulness. These soldiers had tasted victory, and even more important, they expected to win.

Prince Darik was awaiting their little wagon outside of his command tent. Soldiers were already packing the tent up for travel. Cole sighed in relief. They caught up to the army in time.

The prince was flanked by many faces that Cole recognized. Jeron, Dalton, Olivia, Atrisha, Renaldo, Captain Levren, and Masters Maxus, Sildun, and Richard. A few others that Cole did not recognize were also standing there, but that mattered little to him.

Atrisha was standing there looking absolutely beautiful. She confused him to no end. He still did not know what her true feelings for him were. The last time he had seen her, she gave him what could best be described as conflicting signals.

She looked tired and maybe a little lean. And when had she taken to keeping her wings out at all times? That seemed unlike her.

"Master Tyson, I am so glad you could be bothered to show up," said Darik with a glare that could melt steel. "Why when we received news that the king had died, we searched everywhere for you. I am so very relieved to find you here and not in the capital."

"The king is dead?" Tyson asked in shock. Cole felt his mouth drop. Very little surprised the man.

"Yes," said a very annoyed prince. "So the intelligence you have for me better be good."

"Excuse me, Darik," said a wide-eyed blonde man. "But if I could interject? Thank you. Irving. Why are you here, and why are there two of you?"

Recognition dawned on Cole. The young man in question had to be Prince Nelson.

"One of these men is Irving?" asked Prince Darik, his eyes narrowing. "Which one? I owe him thanks for killing the brat that murdered my brother."

"Ahh that would be me," said Byron as he rose from the wagon. "As for killing your brother," Byron tossed his hood back to a chorus of very satisfying gasps. "Well it didn't take."

The reactions from the group were varied. Prince Darik's face was caught between a mixture of a scowl, glare, and broad smile, all warring for supremacy. Prince Nelson looked shocked and scandalized. Jeron and Dalton roared in celebration and begin charging the wagon. The rest of the group looked merely stunned, unable to process the scene.

Except for Atrisha. She was staring at Cole. Her face frozen without expression. Fear gnawed at Cole and lightning rushed through his body. This was the moment he had dreaded for months. He locked his gaze on Atrisha's eyes and stood, slowly pulling back his hood.

Jeron and Dalton roared in excitement again. Slowly diverting their angle. Master Tyson wisely hopped off the wagon before the pair leapt up engulfing Byron and Cole in bear hugs and backslaps.

Cole tried to push the pair aside so he could find Atrisha. She looked distant. His stomach plummeted. She did not seem to care one whit that he was still alive. Cole supposed that answered his questions.

"Enough," said Darik with a scowl on his face. "We can all catch up later. But first we need to know what is going on with Loach."

"Well that's a long story," said Byron unabashedly. "Do you want to know about our crime spree, my killing Prince Yutlin and Duke Camen, or when I uhh kinda destroyed the city?"

The celebration and mirth died in the area as everyone stared at Byron in shock. "What?" he asked innocently. "I didn't mean to destroy that much of the city."

Darik pinched at the bridge of his nose in frustration. "But you meant to destroy part of the city? By all that is holy, why?"

Byron shrugged. "It was the only way to get our wagon out of the city," explained Byron. "With all of the people fleeing, they didn't have time to search it."

Darik closed his eyes while clenching and unclenching the hand that was not holding his nose into a fist. "And why did you need to get that wagon out?" asked Darik in a measured voice, biting off each and every word.

Byron looked at Darik as if he were dense. "Because that is where we stored the loot? From the crime spree I mentioned?"

Darik clenched both fists, his patience visibly running thin. "And why did you need to go on a crime spree in Loach?"

Byron dropped his innocent expression, his lips twitching hard to conceal a grin. "Well one reason was to rob the city of its easily transportable and highly valuable items," said Byron. "With so much of the city damaged, and so much of the populace having fled, there really aren't enough people to work the mines and run the businesses in the city. All they really can do is rebuild. And since most of their wealth burned up, they really won't be able to afford to rebuild, run their economy, and wage war."

Darik gaped at his brother while Renaldo broke into a fit of laughter. "Since when did you become so clever?" asked Renaldo.

"You waged war on their economy?" asked an incredulous Darik.

"And bolstered our own. That was part of it," admitted Byron. "The other part was killing the man behind the plot that killed me and my soldiers."

"Killed you?" scoffed Olivia. "You seem rather alive to me."

Byron smiled wickedly at her. "Well you see that was the other reason I robbed the city. I needed the diamonds."

"Why don't you just tell us," growled Darik. "And not make us drag the story out of you bit by bit."

"Tell what?" asked Byron with his faux innocent expression back on his face. His eyes were dancing. He clearly enjoyed harassing his brother.

"Why you needed the diamonds," said Darik curtly.

"Ahh part of my totem," said Byron offhandedly. "I needed to absorb the diamonds so that I could get the skin and bone structure just right."

"You found your totem?" blurted out Renaldo as he clapped his hands in glee. "What is it? Another dragon?"

"Nope. A phoenix," said Byron.

"Well that explains the coming back from the dead," remarked Nelson darkly. Cole doubted that the prince was pleased that the Irving identity was a disguise.

"Oh, lighten up Nelson," chided Byron. "I've died twice you know. And the second time was a result of saving your life."

A smile finally crossed Darik's face before he suppressed it. The prince was clearly happy for his little brother, but struggling to balance that with maintaining some sense of duty and discipline. "Why didn't you tell anyone you were alive?" demanded Darik with simmering anger hiding beneath every word. Cole amended his previous thoughts. The prince was both happy and furious. The plan was going swell.

"How would I manage that?" said Byron. "A duchy wanted me dead, and I had no army of my own. Father always said to go to Talendor if we needed help. So I did. Things kinda got out of hand there. I couldn't think of a good way to broach the subject with the duke before the twins tried to kill Nelson. After that, I did not have any other choice than to flee Talendor and head off to Loach."

"Sounds reasonable to me," said Renaldo as he fiddled with his axe.

"Except for one part," said Darik. "Cole, why don't you tell me where you were while Byron was in Talendor?"

Cole bit his lip nervously at the question. He really did not want to answer in front of everyone. "Umm," he said as tried to stall for time. Prince Darik glared at him and he wilted under the pressure. "I was in Ochandor," he admitted.

Atrisha bristled at the answer. Olivia grabbed her arm and whispered something into her ear. Cole frowned at the sight. Why would she be angry that he was in the capital?

"You too?" sighed Darik. "Just tell me what happened."

Cole shrugged. "I gathered information there and ahh removed certain Loachian nobles and merchants."

"You mean you killed them," Darik said flatly. Atrisha looked like she was going to be sick.

"It's my job," said Cole stoically.

"And how did you wind up in Loach?" Darik asked. Byron flinched at the question.

"Because that was part of the plan," answered Cole. Recognition dawned on him too late. Prince Darik had been manipulating him into answering the question honestly.

"So the plan all along was to go to Loach?" Darik demanded.

"Of course it was," said Byron in a tone just beneath a yell. "They had me killed and killed countless others!"

"Oh and Prince Yutlin?" asked Darik. "Was he part of the scheme to kill you."

Byron's expression darkened. "He murdered innocent children. Hanged them for stealing food. He deserved death."

"And since when did you get to decide who lived and died," snarled Darik.

"Since I had four arrows placed into my chest," retorted Byron. "I have the scars to prove it."

"Do you realize what you've done?" asked Darik.

"Justice."

"You may have handed the crown directly to Matlin Loach," answered Darik.

"We'll have to see about that," said Byron, his face an emotionless mask.

Darik flung his hands up in disgust. "Have your wagon fall in line with the rest of the army," ordered Darik. "I'll be wanting to speak with you and your companions later."

The prince turned and left, his captains, masters, and men following him. Cole breathed a sigh of relief. That could have gone a lot worse.

"And why didn't you tell us you were alive?" demanded a feminine voice as a shadow obscured the sun.

Cole glanced up and saw Atrisha hovering above him, her wings beating furiously. Her blue eyes burned with emotion. Cole glanced around nervously, looking for a way out. All he found was Dalton and Jeron failing to hide their amusement while Byron looked preoccupied with his thoughts.

"I uhh, didn't know what to say?" asked Cole cautiously. "How do you tell someone that you aren't dead after months have gone by? Especially when they confuse the hell out of you?"

"I confuse you?" shouted Atrisha as she yanked him out of his seat and pulled him into the air. "Do you have any idea what you put me through?" she demanded.

Cole glanced down nervously. He did not like heights. "Umm no," he said uncertainly. "I'm sorry?"

Atrisha glared at him before pulling him forward. Her lips met his and rational thought fled. "Now do you understand?" she asked, her voice wavering.

For once, Cole thought he did.

Chapter Forty-Seven

M atlin walked through the ruins of what had been the Temple District. It was a charred husk. Embers still flickered days after the conflagration. Smoke still streaked to the heavens with no foreseeable end in sight.

Blackened bits of what had once been tile crunched under his boots. Not every temple had been burned to its foundation. Matlin had been shocked to learn that. Instead blackened empty shells scattered the area, the benefits of stone construction.

"Your Highness," said one of the attendants, a fat bearded man who walked with the hunch of someone who had spent their early years in the mines. "Structurally speaking, I doubt these buildings are salvageable. The stones have seen too much heat and damage."

"And how do we fix that?" asked Matlin.

The man dabbed at the sweat on his forehead. "Your Highness, all the stone and rubble will need to be cleared. The district will need to be completely rebuilt."

Matlin did not immediately answer. He squatted down and scooped up a handful of ash allowing it to slowly trickle through his clawed fingers. This was more than just an attack on Loach. It was an attack on its people and everything for which they stood.

Every temple was in tatters and ruins. Countless priests and priestesses perished in the flames. This was an attack on Loach's religion and its people's very way of life. Only a heathen could have launched such a callous and brutal attack. And if witnesses were to be believed, his father was in the Temple of Pojomi when the flames began. Aerial and insect totems were carefully scouring the building for a sign of his survival, but Matlin held little hope. The outer shell of the building remained, but the interior was an unstable wreck, with many of the floors damaged or collapsed.

Citizens had started to trickle back into the city over the past few days. Only four of the districts remained comparatively free from fire damage, including the Eastern District that housed the palace. Food and roofs were becoming a problem. Merchants and nobles were rendered homeless, and soon would have to resort to the very thieving they condemned.

Matlin cursed Yutlin for the fourth time that morning. If only he had utilized his brain, they would still have generous stockpiles of food. Instead, they had given the food away, or had it stolen from their warehouses. Idiot.

"Clear and rebuild the other districts first," ordered Matlin. "People need places to live and jobs to work. The temples can preach the good word at any common ground or market in the city."

"Yes, Your Highness," said the attendant as he rushed off to start on rebuilding the city. Smart and efficient. Traits that Matlin valued. He would need to find out the man's name and track his progress.

Until then, other matters required his attention. "Setlin, have any other messengers confirmed the news?"

"Yes, Your Grace," said Setlin. Matlin stiffened in anger. He had yet to give up on their father. "The king has expired. Every duke will be descending upon Ochandor in force."

"I am not the Duke of Loach," insisted Matlin.

"Yes, you are, Your Grace," said Setlin calmly. "If father had survived, we would have heard from him. The people need a leader, and it is you. Consider this your coronation." Setlin stared resolutely at his older brother. "Now what are your orders."

"Fotlin, you're in charge of the city and duchy in my absence," said Matlin as he tried to hide his apprehension. Fotlin had ambitions. Leaving the city in his hands was a risk, but it was not like it was the most defensible city in the kingdom at the moment. He could recapture it if need be. "Clara, please gather our army. The forces that fought against Antier. And have Catalina and Olina join us. My sisters need to be present for the coronation. And have them bring their swords."

Matlin looked at Setlin and nodded grimly. "You're also coming with us," he said. "I trust you know what to do?"

Setlin bowed his head. "As you wish, Your Grace," he said solemnly. "I will pack my things and meet you with our forces."

Matlin gazed out over the rubble of his hometown. It had been his life's ambition to become king. But now he weighed that dream against his heart's newest desire. Vengeance. He would hunt this Irving Mire down and exact his revenge. For his father, for his city, and for his religion.

And he would do it looking like a duke fit to be king. Matlin focused and the wings sprouted from his back, sliding through the slits in his armor designed specifically for them. Red, silver, and black scales glistened in the daylight.

Matlin flexed his claws and wings as he took to the sky. The view was worse from the higher vantage point. He could see the entire city and the devastation the fire had wreaked. It made his blood boil, but first he had something he needed to do.

He folded his wings back and dove down at the Temple of Pojomi. He glided through an open door, careful to keep his wings beating. If the structure was as unsound as his men said, he would heed their warnings and not set foot on the ground.

If he was to lead the duchy, and seize the crown, he first needed to know his father's fate. The damage to the upper floor was quite severe. He frowned as he looked at the broken furniture and damaged walls. It was not fire that did this. This damage was caused by heavy impacts. By humans. In battle.

Matlin hastened his search, focusing his search towards the epicenter of the destruction. The remains of what may have been an antechamber lay at the center of damage. Nothing remained in one piece. Metal shards studded what remained of the walls, sparkling in the light streaking through the rents in the building's walls.

A body lay in the middle of the room. Matlin's vision went red. He would recognize that bulldog armor anywhere. But not the body that lay within it. His father was dead. Whoever had murdered him had cleaved his head in two, and then left the body to be roasted.

Matlin howled in anger and burst through the damaged walls as he flew towards the palace. Someone would die for this. This Irving Mire, as well as the Antierians that kept Matlin from being there for his father. Even if he had to kill every noble that arrived in Ochandor, he would have his revenge and the crown.

CHAPTER FORTY-EIGHT

Randall gazed in wonder as they crossed the bridge. He had never seen a bridge before. Or all of this water. The men called it a lake. From what he knew of the world outside the city, lakes were not the sea. That meant there existed even larger bodies of water in the world. It was difficult to imagine that even being possible.

The kingdom had been disappointing. At first the trees were a novelty and an exciting adventure. But as the days and miles dragged on, he grew accustomed to them. He no longer jumped at every noise or shadow. In short, he was bored.

He missed the thrill of the heist. The planning, the break in, the never knowing what was around the next corner, lifting the goods, and of course, the escape. Of course, he hated actually being chased. But another few days on the road and even that might change.

This new city looked simply grand. Sitting out on the water. And everything was so bright. He could find all sorts of new fun. The little ones were not going to feed themselves after all.

"Whatever you're thinking of boy, don't do it," scowled the watchman, Owen. "If you haven't noticed, we're arriving to the capital in the company of princes."

"So?" said Randall. "I'm no one."

"Not anymore," said Owen. "Nobles play all sorts of games, and we're just pawns to them. They will notice you, and they will follow you. If you engage in any of your old tricks, you will be caught, or worse."

"I have to do something," said Randall. "I can't just sit here and do nothing!"

"Yes, you can," said Lynn with a frown on her face. "All of us arrived together and your mischief could get us all killed."

Owen frowned disapprovingly at the girl. "So far they have not treated us poorly, and have even provided food for us," he said.

Lynn shrugged unimpressed. Randall found the movements mesmerizing for some reason. "So?" she asked. "These are the same people who burned Loach to the ground!"

Owen hesitated. "You mean person," he said. "One man did that. And from what I understand, he also saved both of your lives while sparing mine."

"And?" Lynn demanded. "What now? Can we leave? Are we to serve out the rest of our lives in servitude to him?"

"You'd like that wouldn't you?" asked Owen. "Don't think we haven't seen the way you look at him." Randall giggled. That was certainly the truth.

"It's not like that," Lynn insisted. "I only want to know why. Why he did what he did."

"Perhaps I can answer that," said a man as he jumped into the rear of the wagon.

He was a middle aged man with short cropped brown hair and a beard that was more gray than brown. He was built like a bull with a face like cracked stone. Randall remembered him from their initial trip into the Antierian army. But try as he might, he could not remember the man's name.

"Prince Byron does what he believes to be right," said the man. "Whether it was saving your lives or burning a city."

"Burning a city is not right," insisted Lynn.

"I never said it was," said the man. "I merely said that the prince believed it was right at the time. Most likely he was weighing the lives of those he lost and those he had sworn to protect against those who supported his enemy."

"I agree," said Owen. "Still doesn't make it right."

"No," said the stranger. "But it makes it understandable. As I am sure some of your actions would be if we all viewed them through your eyes."

Randall looked at the man confused. What the hell was he talking about? Why did adults always speak in riddles? It would be so much easier if they just said what they wanted plainly. It irritated him. Clearly the man was trying to speak over his head. Just because he was not educated, did not mean he was stupid.

"Who are you?" he demanded. "What do you want? And what is going to happen to us?"

The man threw back his head and laughed. "Randall is it?" he asked rhetorically. "You have spirit boy. Remind me some of myself when I was your age. I am Tyson Orgun, Master Wraith of the Brotherhood of the Dark Flame, in service to His Grace, Duke Cedric of Antier." The man flourished what Randall assumed was a courtly bow to a wagon full of unimpressed faces.

"Nothing?" Tyson asked drily. "Ahh so be it. Anyway lad, your questions are intertwined. Your futures and what I want are the same thing."

Randall stared venom at the man. "Stop speaking in riddles!" he said hotly. "Just say what you want."

Tyson raised an eyebrow warily at Randall. His demeanor shifted. Randall felt a surge of fear spike through his body. His "spirit" was not as amusing as it had been.

"What I want is for you all to work for me," Tyson said. "The princes will almost certainly offer you new lives. Most likely in service to the crown, or maybe a farm of some type. I on the other hand want to put your talents to good use."

A farm? Randall frowned. He did not know anything about growing food. Only stealing and eating it. He would lose every crop he planted.

"I won't be the prince's maid," snarled Lynn. Owen flashed her a fierce smile of approval.

"Nor would I ask you to be," said Master Tyson. "Each of you has certain skills that I appreciate. Miss Lynn, you have a talent at reading people and gathering information from them. There are many pretty faces, but those with something behind the face are rarer than I'd like. Young Randall. You and your partner also have good minds. Planning robberies, executing them, and keeping your people alive? All based upon your own ingenuity and skill? Impressive at any age, but quite remarkable from a pair so young."

"And me?" asked Owen. "What do I bring to the table? A washed up watchman who could not catch a thief?"

Tyson snorted. "Please. No need to run yourself down," he said. "You're a trained investigator. From what I gather, one does not last as long in the Loach City Watch as you did without having considerable skills. Surely you must have solved a few crimes in your time."

"A few," Owen admitted. "But that was years ago. Mainly, I arrest drunkards that brawl in alleyways."

"Don't sell yourself short," said Tyson. "That's more than most can say."

"And what if we don't want to work for you?" asked Lynn. "In case you haven't noticed, Owen has a wife and child, and Randall and Tigun have many children that they are responsible for."

"All will be accommodated," said Tyson. "We'll find jobs and homes for all of you. And if you don't like working for me..." he shrugged. "I'm sure the princes will be more than happy to reward you for your service."

"What's a wraith and what would we be doing for you?" Randall asked skeptically. He was not going to sit behind a desk reading all day. By the gods, he did not even know how to read.

"Oh we do a little bit of this and a little bit of that," said Tyson. "Some of us attend balls, others steal things, others kill people, and still others catch enemy wraiths."

Randall leaned forward, a sense of excitement growing within him. What Tyson offered sounded much more exciting than robbing simple merchants. Judging from the expression on Tigun's face, Randall knew his friend was thinking the same thing. Temples, mansions, and the like provided such a challenge that it made life worth living.

"Balls?" Lynn mused. "You mean, people would think I was a lady?"

"You already are miss," said Tyson. "The trick is allowing others to see it."

Owen hesitated before answering. "I do not know if I can accept your offer," he said. "I quit the City Watch because I feared for my family's life. Your job sounds a sight more dangerous than what I was doing." His wife and daughter each looked scared as he spoke. Randall could not blame them. After Tiona died, he felt the same way each time one of the children went out to steal.

"Now now, Owen," said Tyson as he tried to placate the man. "I am not asking for an answer right now. Feel free to talk it over with your family. All of you are free to talk it over. Come to me with any concerns. I am sure we can reach an understanding."

Owen sighed as he looked wearily at the man. The bullish man flourished his bow one last time before slipping out the back of the wagon.

Randall lay back on the wagon bed. He did not need to speak it over with Tigun. New adventures and new cities sounded simply grand.

CHAPTER FORTY-NINE

B yron rummaged through the trunks of clothes in his room for the fifth
time. The Irving disguise was gone. The likely culprits were either his
brother or Master Tyson.

It was the pair of them that had convinced him not to travel in the garments.
Being seen entering the capital dressed as the known tormentor of Loach was
a poor idea. That gave the duo plenty of opportunities to have the clothes
removed from his possession. Force him to dress as befits a prince.

The door to his chambers slammed open as a parade of people entered his
room. Jeron, Dalton, and Cole were to be expected, but Olivia, Atrisha, Jayna,
and Nelson were not. With the exception of Cole, they all stopped and gawked
at his chest.

The scars left behind by the arrows were large wrinkled pink gashes. They
were bunched in the middle and left portion of his chest, near his heart. Byron
scowled at them. He was not some sideshow that belonged within a menagerie.

"They stole your clothes too?" Cole asked as he pushed his way through the
throng. He wore black leather armor over an outfit that resembled the style of
clothing Master Tyson usually wore about. "Mine too. It appears that I have a
wardrobe full of these."

Byron grunted in acknowledgment. "No such luck for me," he said. "Not
even a military uniform." He picked out one of their bravo uniforms. Matching
brown clothing, studded leather armor, and a garish and ostentatious scarlet
cape. He strapped on six blades to the ensemble. Two swords on his back, two
swords at his hips, and two dirks just inside the swords at his hips.

"How do I look?" he asked the gathered crowd.

"Like a scoundrel," said Atrisha disapprovingly.

"Like a land dweller who could not make it with a Nuquanian crew," said Nelson.

"Like a man bereft of all sense of fashion," chimed in Dalton.

"I like it," said Jayna as she slipped her arm within Jeron's. "The color reminds me of some of the things people used to wear back home."

"Fitting that he would dress like a dead man," mused Jeron oblivious to the look Jayna shot at him.

Byron ignored the comments, if only because he could not think of a clever retort. "Prince Nelson. To what do I owe the pleasure?" he asked. "Shouldn't you be at Biona's embassy?"

Nelson glanced over at Byron's other uninvited guests with irritation on his face. "I came to speak with you and your brother regarding the selection of the next king. The Loachians are maybe a day away from the capital. Clearly, they value the crown if they abandoned their smoldering city for it. But I will speak later when your brother and father are present. They're words that should be said in private, not in the presence of those without the title of prince."

"What about princess?" chimed in Jayna with an impish smile on her face.

Nelson paled. "Forgive me, my lady. I completely forgot."

Jayna rolled her eyes. "Forgiven."

Nelson twisted the sash around his waist. "I also ahh wanted to know why you intervened along the King's Road," he asked, his face blushing in embarrassment.

Byron shrugged nonchalantly. "You were beset by bandits. Intervening seemed like the right thing to do."

"And then staying all the way through Talendor?"

"Travelling by yourself gets boring," answered Byron as he tried to shoo everyone out of his room. "Despite my current predicament. And besides, I needed to get close to Duke Havram. Granted my plan did not precisely play out the way that I thought it would, but I did get to kill one of the twins out of the deal. So there is that."

Byron sighed as his friends refused to move out of the room. He brushed by them without a word of apology. He had things to do besides being cooped up within his room all day.

"So where are we going?" asked Jeron as he fingered his axe handle and looked around the hallways suspiciously. "Is there going to be trouble."

"I am going to see my father and brother," said Byron placing emphasis on the words.

"That sounds simply grand," said Dalton armed with his spear and mace. "I'm sure your father will have a fantastic spread ready for us."

"Is food all you ever think of?" Olivia wondered aloud with equal parts fascination and contempt.

"It's not the *only* thing," Dalton said as he waggled his eyebrows at her.

"Yes. Sometimes he sleeps," said Byron.

"And sometimes he tries to eat while he sleeps," confirmed Jeron with faux solemnity. "That never ends well."

Dalton mumbled under his breath while Nelson shook his head sadly. The banter felt unfamiliar to Byron. After months of essentially only having Cole for company, he just was not used to the conversation. Cole, while livelier than he was when they first met, was still by nature a quiet man.

Thankfully, the conference room was not far from his quarters. It would save Byron from further banter. His heart just was not in the conversation. How was he supposed to explain to his friends that he was no longer the same man from before?

You could always try talking to them. Byron pushed the voice aside. He did not have the time or inclination to argue with himself either.

Byron pushed the doors of the conference room open before the guards could announce him. Darik was already present, flanked by Renaldo, Emkario, and Vincent, his usual cadre of friends and bodyguards.

Darik frowned at him as he entered. "You're finally here," he said sternly. "And for once you aren't the last one to arrive."

Byron furrowed his brow as he surveyed the room. "I beat father?"

Darik frowned back at him. "Yes. You did. Strange."

"But father is never late," said Byron. "He hates tardiness. More than any-thing. Says it's an immense sign of disrespect."

"And yet you still show up late," said Darik, his voice dripping with disap-pointment.

Byron ignored his brother's barb and shoved his way past his friends and back into the hallway. Something was wrong. With Loach's forces so close to the city he suspected trouble was brewing.

Byron sprinted through the hallways drawing strange stares from the few guardsmen and servants he passed. He swore at himself for dressing like a bravo and not a prince. He did not need any delays.

A reedy bald man was shouting at him to stop. Byron ignored him, bowling him over and tossing the man into the wall. People were shouting but he ignored them as well. The guardsmen standing outside his parents' rooms lowered their spears to bar his way while shouting something that sounded like "halt."

Diamond seeped from Byron's pores coating his skin. He felt it thicken and harden. The guardsmen flinched at the sight before he plowed into their spears. *It's probably the skull.*

The door splintered as he burst through it. Byron's mind raced to process the scene. Two bodies, a man and a woman. His parents. *Mom and dad*, he thought sadly.

A hooded man in black stood over them, startled at the noise. *He must have expected the door to be opened as if civilized people lived here.* He had not even had time to stash or hide the bloody dagger in his hand. *Kill him!*

Byron obliged the voice in his head. Anger pounded with every step he took. He did not slow down as he hit the man with the full force of his body. They went tumbling through the large glass windows in a tangle of limbs.

The wind rushed past Byron as he plummeted in a freefall. He snarled as he tried to strike the assassin as they fell. A lower section of the roof thwarted his vengeance as it broke his fall in a hail of tiles. Byron skidded across the roof continuing to dislodge tiles with his passing.

The tiles vanished beneath him and his arm darted out clawing for the edge of the roof. His right hand closed around the edge and with one quick jerk he swung himself like a pendulum, catapulting himself back onto the roof.

The assassin was already running across the roof in an uncertain off-balanced gait. Byron felt the smile stretch across his face. His time in Loach had given him plenty of experience running across rooftops and uneven surfaces.

Byron sped across the roof gaining ground on the assassin. He supposed he could have grown his wings, but he just did not have that much experience using them. The first time he used them he accidentally set an entire city on fire. *Not exactly a good idea when surrounded by our own people.*

The intruder glanced back over his shoulder and apparently reached the same conclusion as Byron. He was not going to escape without a fight. The assassin spun around, flinging a dagger at Byron with one hand as he drew a shortsword with the other.

Byron dodged without thinking. He had not yet grown fully accustomed to his diamond skin and did not know its limitations. Could he be poisoned through it? Were thrusts more effective? Too many questions. His gamble had only worked on Duke Camen as he had somehow consciously thickened and strengthened his diamond skin and dictated the duke's attack land at that specific location.

I guess I'll just have to try to win this fight the old way.

Byron drew the two swords on his back as he charged the assassin. It felt good to have two blades in his hands again. During his time as Irving, he had limited himself to only the one sword. Prince Byron dies, and his body is not recovered, but a dual wielding swordsman arrives from the same area where Byron's corpse vanished? *Yeah. Someone would have put two and two together rather quickly.*

The assassin sprinted at Byron, his sword weaving in an effort to keep Byron guessing. One blade against two. On paper it would appear that Byron had an advantage. But he could only lunge with one arm at a time. If the assassin knew what he was doing, and it was safer to assume that he did, he would try to keep Byron on the defensive. Otherwise, sooner or later one of Byron's blades would find its target.

Byron parried the first few strikes with ease. They were well practiced, but slightly off. The assassin was well trained, but not heavily experienced? *Interesting.*

The assassin attacked with reckless abandon trying to finish things quickly. *Time is on our side.* Byron crossed his blades, catching the assailant's blade. He gritted his teeth and struck out with his own counterattack. *Sure. Don't listen to me. I'm only the part of us that thinks up the good ideas.*

Byron ignored the pesky part of his brain. It was a losing argument. The assailant was out of practice and Byron was not. He needed to press the advantage while he could.

His flurry of slashes placed the assassin on the defensive. His blade and body contorted as he avoided Byron's strikes. The assassin backed up, retreating as best as he could. But he could not anticipate every move in Byron's arsenal.

Byron focused and grabbed hold of the world, namely the assassin's cloak. It only took a little exertion of willpower to ignite the cloth. The cloak burst into flame and the man promptly panicked. Byron did not blame him. Fire would bother most people. But not Byron. Not a man whose totem was a literal flaming bird.

As the flames consumed the clothing, the assassin hurriedly tried to disrobe. As he yanked the cloak off Byron calmly stepped forward and rammed his sword through the assassin's intestines. The man shrieked as he collapsed to the tile roof, finally tearing himself free from the smoldering garment. Byron willed the fires to extinguish. It would not do to have the building catch on fire.

He placed his boot on the assassin's stomach and pushed, yanking his blade free of the man. The howls intensified as blood and guts followed the sword out. Sweat plastered the man's dark brown hair to his head. Finally chiseled features twisted into fear and pain.

Byron smiled an exaggerated smile at the man. He had to exaggerate the smile; it was the only way he could cause the diamond skull to show any emotion. For now. Everything he did with the diamond skin and bones felt like training his muscles. He just needed to practice and grow stronger.

He leaned over the assailant. "Hello, Prince Setlin," he chortled. "How nice to make your acquaintance."

The Loachian prince opened his mouth, trying to speak. Blood and spittle dripped out the side. Eventually, he squeaked out a few words. "Go to hell," he gasped.

"How droll," said Byron. "Banter just does not run in your family. You realize you make four deaths for me? I suppose I could have ended Fotlin had I wanted to. A vicious boy, but not yet deserving of death."

"A duke for a duke," coughed Setlin. "Justice has returned and the down-trodden shall rejoice."

Guilt. It was a terrible feeling. It settled on Byron, weighing him down like a second heavier skin. His actions had led to his parents' deaths. *Don't be an idiot. They would have killed them anyway. They already tried to kill you and your brother.*

Byron remained silent for a few heartbeats. He allowed his brain to go back and forth, arguing each position out. He supposed that he could trace the killing back for generations. All that mattered now was that his parents were dead. *Move forward.*

A fluttering of wings briefly drew his attention. It was Atrisha in that all white angel of war getup she insisted on wearing. *Maybe others find it intimidating. A little too theatrical for my tastes.*

"Byron! Are you okay?" she shouted as she slowly descended.

"I'm fine," Byron said before pointing his sword downward. "He's not."

She alighted next to him on the rooftop. "Loachian?" she asked uneasily, her eyes flickering back and forth towards Byron's diamond skull.

Prince Setlin laughed harshly. "I am no mere Loachian," he said while succumbing to a fit of coughing. Atrisha looked at him appraisingly as if she were trying to ascertain his sanity through a quick glimpse.

"Atrisha, allow me to introduce you to the soon to be departed Prince Setlin of Loach," said Byron with his most courtly manners laced with only a hint of sarcasm.

"What? No priest?" said Setlin, his face contorting in pain.

Atrisha frowned thoughtfully. "Well we do have—"

"None that would reach you in time," interrupted Byron stone faced. "I can guarantee you that."

"I'm not...going to tell you..." Setlin doubled in on himself, curling into a ball without finishing.

Byron smiled coldly down at Setlin. "Well then. There's no reason to keep you alive is there?"

"Byron," began Atrisha with a slight warning in her voice. He waved her off.

"Tell me, Setlin, how would you prefer to die?" he asked. "Your options are bleeding to death of a stomach wound, or burning to death. Your choice."

"Not slitting my throat?" Setlin asked with a rueful laugh.

"And risk you having a holdout dagger somewhere on you?" chided Byron. "I think not. Choose."

"I'll bleed to death, thank you very much," said Setlin with a grimace.

"Burning to death it is!" declared Byron cheerfully.

Setlin's eyes widened in fear as flames danced between Byron's fingertips. Slowly the flames trickled down from his hands, coating and consuming the Loachian's princes' boots. The smell of burning meat and leather filled the air as Setlin weakly tried to swat the flames out. Byron continued to pour the fire on until the flames had spread across the prince's entire upper body and were licking at his face.

Byron stretched his hands out and willed water into existence, dousing the man in a painful hiss. *Good.*

"You know, I should respect your wishes," said Byron as he looked down at the prince. "Bleeding to death is the way to go. I mean we wouldn't want anything to happen to that face of yours. That might spark outrage at your funeral. And as you well know, we don't need to add fuel to the animosity burning between our two duchies."

Setlin did not reply. He merely gasped, his remaining skin stretched tight across his face. His breathing slowly faded until it came to a complete stop.

"Byron...that was not necessary," Atrisha said softly. "You went too far."

"I don't care," said Byron through a clenched jaw. "He killed my parents. Would you have done any differently if it was someone you loved?"

Atrisha paled, a feat that Byron was surprised she could manage. She shook her head in the negative until she barely whispered, "No."

The windows to the embassy swung open as Jeron and Dalton tried to push by each other to exit onto the roof. While they struggled, Cole and Nelson opened an adjacent pair of windows and slipped out onto the ledge.

"Prince Byron, have you detained the assailant?" asked Nelson as he drew his cutlass warily.

"No, he killed him," remarked Cole. "Or does your nose not work." Cole knelt down beside the body and began searching it. The man was certainly thorough. "Did he say why?"

Byron winced. "A duke for a duke, and because justice has returned and the downtrodden shall rejoice."

Cole turned his face up in disgust. "Seriously?" he asked. "How dumb did he have to be to think that Loach was the downtrodden? I thought we made it painfully obvious who we were referring to."

"He wasn't a very bright guy," agreed Byron.

"Sweety," said Atrisha in as warm a voice as Byron had ever heard from her. "Can you please explain what you two are talking about?"

Byron rubbed at his face. The idiot was misquoting a fake prophecy. Fantastic. "When we get back to everyone. Jeron, Dalton, if you would be so kind as to bring Prince Setlin to my brother? I'm feeling a little burnt out."

CHAPTER FIFTY

D arik rubbed at his burgeoning migraine. Things never seemed to get any easier when he was in charge.

"Let me get this straight," Darik said to Byron and Cole as the rest of the gathered friends, nobles, and advisors looked on. "You stole a tome from a temple-"

"Several in fact," quipped Byron.

"—and Cole forged a prophecy in the stolen tome," continued Darik. "Which you then left at the scene of another crime, where you then burned the same prophecy into the temple's stone?"

"Right so far," said Byron with a happy smile. Darik ignored his brother's apparent mirth. It was all a false front. Byron always dealt with unpleasant situations by using humor as a defense mechanism. No matter how annoying or inappropriate.

"And the Loachians misinterpreted this prophecy, believing that they are the deliverers of justice and the downtrodden?" asked Darik wearily.

"No one ever said they were smart."

"So what you are saying is that thanks to you, Prince Matlin will be arriving to the Conclave of Nobles feeling self-righteous and believing his cause to be a holy duty ordained upon him by the heavens?" asked Darik in a deadpan. "Not to mention that he will be furious over the murders of his father and brothers."

"Killings," corrected Byron. "Not murder."

Darik scowled as he waved his hand, dismissing the comment. He most certainly was not going to argue semantics with his brother in front of their company. Even if Prince Nelson was nodding in agreement with his younger brother. A stickler for manners was that one. But apparently, also a man fond of holding grudges.

"What's done is done," said Darik grimly. He did not feel like dealing with this garbage. His parents were barely an hour dead and he was having to discuss the future of the kingdom without even having time to breathe, much less grieve. And unlike his little brother he could not flee and disappear into humor.

"Nelson, how does your father stand on the succession issue?" Darik asked.

"He stands with you, Your Grace," said Nelson. The title made Darik flinch. He never expected to be Duke of Antier. Some part knew it was inevitable, but he never could bring himself to conceptualize his own father's death. "Some of the other noble families of Biona may not though. Their trade ties with Loach are strong." Nelson hesitated for an instant. "Although the destruction of Loach's economy may give them pause."

Byron flashed an annoying little half smirk in Darik's direction causing his migraine to spike. Darik was not wholly convinced that Byron and Cole's crime wave had been a well-intentioned plot to destabilize Loach's economy. Things probably happened to break in their favor and they took credit for it.

Irvin cleared his throat. "And what little remains of Kelon stands with you as well," he said. Try as he might, Darik just could not think of him as Vernon after learning the truth.

"Thank you," said Darik graciously. "But even if the combined nobles of the kingdom name me king, that still leaves Matlin. I doubt he's gone through all of this to just meekly back down."

"So it'll be a fight?" asked Renaldo. "Good. I could use a good fight."

Byron yawned, feigning boredom. It would be a believable act except for the tightness around his eyes. "I vote I fight him," he said lazily. "I've already killed most of the family. One more won't hurt."

"Hey. I killed one too," protested Jeron.

"Yes. You both are so proud to be killers," said Darik with a glare. "Priestess Jayna. Could you please talk some sense into the young man? I am afraid my brother is a lost cause. He apparently thinks he is invincible despite having only recently acquired his totem."

"I can handle Matlin," insisted Byron.

"Oh really?" said Darik. "Do you know what his totem is? Do you know if you die again if you'll stay dead? Do you need all of your limbs to come back? What can your diamond skin not stop? Well?"

"I'll figure it out," his brother grumbled.

"No, you won't," said Darik sternly. "You're to stay away from Matlin if it comes to a fight. I'll handle him."

"I'm not particularly comfortable with that idea either," said Emkario. "Why can't we all fight together instead of everyone wanting to do lone wolf style combat?" The man sighed. "We have a razor thin margin as it is. No offense, Byron, but Darik, if you fall, we don't have a backup plan."

"That would be chaos," agreed Nelson. "I bet Nuqua would love to have the crown."

"I'm confused. What's our plan and who is on our side?" asked Renaldo as he scratched at his head.

Darik sighed. "Nelson, Irvin, and I are going to play nice with the rest of Ochandor's nobility," explained Darik. "Some of you will go with us. Our side right now consists of Antier, Biona, Kelon, and Talendor. Every other duchy is up in the air."

"Ehh. I don't know about that," said Irvin.

Darik swiveled his head to the older man. "What do you mean?" he demanded. If Byron had done something to piss off Duke Havram, Darik might actually blow up.

Elfred leaned in to say something to Irvin, but the prince brushed his hand away. "No. It's time," he said. "Your Grace, what I mean to say is do not be surprised if Talendor sides with Loach."

"Because Duke Havram is a scorpion? I have heard the warnings before," said Darik. "But Duke Havram has a strong relationship with my father."

"He *had* a strong relationship with your father," corrected Irvin. "He also had a strong relationship with Loach." Suspicion gnawed at Darik while recognition bloomed on Byron's face. The boy had an irritating habit of putting connections together quickly. "What do you mean?" snapped Darik. "Stop dancing around the issue and tell me."

Irvin sighed and took a deep breath, reluctant to speak. "By now you probably assumed that our willingness to fight Loach was because they destroyed Kelon," said Irvin. "That is true. But they didn't do it alone. Talendor and Duke Havram helped them. Because he was greedy and it made him more money."

Horror gripped Darik. "But you all defended the city of Talendor countless times!" he protested.

Irvin shrugged. "We were scouting for weaknesses," he said nonchalantly. "We know that city's defenses very well now. And well, if an opportunity for revenge presented itself, we were in the right place to take advantage of the moment."

"I bet letting me go after Matlin is sounding like a better idea now," said Byron.

Darik glared at him as he strongly considered seeing what his dragon breath could do to his little brother. "Right. Because assassinating a duke worked out so well for the last assassin," said Darik sarcastically as he jerked his thumb towards Prince Setlin's still steaming corpse.

Nelson stared on in shock during the interchange, his fingers moving back in forth as if he were moving ideas around within his head. "So Loach and Talendor worked together to destroy Kelon?" he asked absently. "Fascinating."

"Not how I would describe it," grumbled Elfred.

Nelson looked up with a mortified expression on his face. "Oh, I am terribly sorry," he apologized. "I did not realize I was speaking aloud. Please forgive me. What I meant was it is fascinating that they worked together, but one of the twins from Loach still tried to murder Prince Bondoril. Why do that if they are allies?"

The question troubled Darik as well as the others. Silence greeted the question and Nelson continued on. "What if the destruction of Kelon was merely a business venture? A one time partnership between the two? And Duke Camen and Duke Havram never bothered to tell any of their children. No reason to admit to guilt in the murder of thousands, after all."

"That would make sense," said Byron. "The twins were vicious and cruel twits, but stupid? No. Not stupid. If there was an ongoing alliance, they would not have risked killing Duke Havram's son out of jealousy over his daughter. No offense Nelson, but I doubt your well-being concerned them."

"None taken."

"Was it all out of jealousy?" asked Jeron. "I mean don't princes and princesses routinely have their marriages arranged?"

Darik tapped his finger thoughtfully on the side of his chin. "An interesting question. Perhaps Duke Havram turned down such an overture," he mused. "It's pure speculation at this point though. Nelson, you and I need to meet with Duke Havram as soon as possible. Irvin, you'll understand if I don't ask you to go."

Irvin smiled sadly. "A pity."

Byron opened his mouth to make what Darik assumed would be a wisecrack, but wisely shut it before saying anything. Darik breathed a quick prayer in his mind for small blessings.

"Alright everyone," he said. "We have little time before the Steward of Ochandor begins the Conclave. Those of you who need to meet with other nobles, do it quickly. The rest of you, hang tight, and would someone please figure out how Prince Setlin snuck into the embassy?"

"Chimneys," said Cole simply. Everyone in the room turned and looked at him in shock. "What? He left behind soot in the bedroom."

Darik closed his eyes as the image of his parents' bodies, their throats slashed, rose to the forefront of his mind. "Thank you, Cole. Now if everyone wouldn't mind, I do have work to do."

CHAPTER FIFTY-ONE

Matlin tore up the missive and threw it across the room. Duke Seamus claimed that he did not know if he could support Matlin's claim to the throne at this point in time? Horseshit! Matlin overturned a table and smashed a wooden chair into kindling.

It was the third such missive he had received that morning. The duchies of Nuqua, Erlon, and Rondmon all answering his letters with the same response. Duke Havram from Talendor had not even acknowledged receiving Matlin's communique. Not that Matlin expected a response from him. His brothers attempted to murder the duke's son. Idiots. Their recklessness might ruin everything he fought and clawed for his entire life. And with the state that Loach was in, he could not afford to threaten and bully his way to the crown.

And the other dukes knew it.

They would keep him churning in the wind while they waited to see which way it blew. Matlin grabbed the table and jerked it upright, his claws scoring the wood. He knew which way events would turn. Against him. Luck had abandoned him.

Clara entered his room looking stately in her flowing red robes. Matlin nodded in appreciation at her outfit. Now was exactly the time to be wearing house colors.

"Cousin," she said in greeting. "There has been no news of your brother. Prince Setlin is still missing."

"And Duke Cedric?" he asked.

"Deceased. Along with his wife," answered Clara.

"Then Setlin is dead too," said Matlin grimly. At least he managed to do his job. Except now the family was down its wraith too. Pity. "Are my sisters on their way?"

"Yes, Your Grace. They should arrive momentarily."

Clara was true to her word. Within moments, Catalina and Olina walked into the room with the type of arrogant elegance all noble girls perfected at a young age. They were in their late teens, only separated by a year. Tall and willowy, their faces were stuck in what seemed like perpetual frowns. The effect made everyone assume that they were constantly irritated and annoyed.

"Brother, where is Setlin?" asked Catalina, the elder sister. "You said we would meet him here, but he is nowhere to be found."

"He promised he would explain the Conclave to me," said Olina. "It still doesn't make any sense."

Matlin debated telling them a comforting lie. They had already lost so many people and been through so much. But that was exactly why they deserved the truth. They were strong, like all members of House Loach. They could handle the truth.

And he was running out of family. He needed those that he could trust.

"Setlin is most likely dead," Matlin said grimly as his sisters' countenances took the ever so slight detour to crestfallen. "The duke and duchess of Antier are dead. We can only assume that he perished in his escape."

"Of course, those monsters would kill him," seethed Catalina.

"What do we do now?" asked Olina.

Matlin's heart ached for his sisters. After all their loss, they barely registered grief over their brother's death. They deserved better than that.

"We carry on," said Matlin. "We have no choice but to win the throne. Anything short will result in a death sentence for us. Our enemies are simply too strong after our city burned. I want you two wearing your swords at all times."

"Yes, brother," said Catalina. "Wearing the swords is the easy enough. But how do we win the throne?"

Matlin nodded grimly at his sister. "We do to our enemies what we should have done ages ago."

CHAPTER FIFTY-TWO

"What's the plan here?" Telwin asked again.

Tyson sighed as he shook his head sadly. The young warrior was a good lad, but not the sharpest instrument available.

"It's simple," said Tyson in exasperation. "The nobles of the kingdom gather in the Conclave. The dukes all have the opportunity to nominate someone to take the throne. The nobles that have gathered at the Conclave confer amongst their duchy. Each duchy casts a vote. The winner becomes king."

"That's dumb," remarked Lentil. A boy of remarkable intelligence. Lentil made Telwin look like a luminary. "Why don't they all just vote for their own nominee?"

"Because that would result in a tie," said Tyson as he covered the ground that their parents should have years earlier. Even nobles could fail at educating their own children on important matters. "And ties are settled by a melee to the death between the nominees. To the victor goes the crown. Most nobles really don't want to die. They're usually willing to make a deal."

"That's great," said Telwin thoroughly unimpressed. "But I meant what is the plan *here*?" He asked as he gestured vaguely at the surrounding area.

Tyson bared his teeth before answering. "Why, we're protection my boys."

"Protection for every noble in the kingdom?" asked Lentil confused. "Shouldn't Telwin and I be in the palace then?"

"No. You're the children of nobles, not the actual title holders," said Tyson dismissively. "You don't get votes. But think about it. If you want to be king and you don't have the votes, what do you do?"

"You attack the Conclave," whispered Telwin as recognition dawned on him. Maybe he was not hopeless after all. "But isn't that incredibly risky? All of the most powerful nobles are within the palace."

"It sure would be," answered Tyson. "But if someone was on the lookout and spotted the double cross, the nobles would be able to defend themselves from the treachery."

"But what are the chances that anyone actually attacks the palace?" asked Lentil.

"You're asking that after fighting at Fort No Hope?" asked Telwin incredulously.

Tyson ignored the soldier's derogatory name for Fort Hope. He had been there as well, and the appellation had merit. What he needed to do was focus on his surroundings. Loach would have to try something. They really did not any other option with the way the war transpired.

"Okay. I get it," said Lentil as he held up his hands in surrender. "Loach is capable of doing terrible things. But why are we in the Antierian segment of the capital and not near the palace?"

"That's simple," said Telwin with full confidence. "We're here because...err...umm...you know I don't really know why we're here. Master Tyson?"

Tyson ignored the question for a moment as he continued to survey the marketplace. Something there was bothering his instincts, but he could not put his finger on it. "We're here because this is what I would do," he answered. "The palace is going to be filled with nobles and the Royal Guard. Launching an attack there would be suicidal. Your forces would never make it. But at the embassies? That is a different story. Many of the nobles came with their families, retinues, et cetera. And their guards will be lax while everyone is within the palace. Making them the perfect sort of targets for either quick killing or hostage taking."

Telwin closed one eye and bunched up a cheek as he thought. "But wouldn't the king already be chosen by them."

"Maybe," said Tyson. "But maybe you acquire leverage before the vote. Or, if you're planning on fighting the other nobles within the palace, you force other duchies to not participate for fear of losing their loved ones."

Lentil clenched his jaw in anger as he stared at the crowd. "That does sound very familiar. Sucker punch when they aren't looking."

Tyson nodded absently as he scanned the crowd. It was not a particular subtle strategy. It merely required that your enemy not be looking your way before you hit them with everything you had.

He frowned at the marketplace. That strategy required might, not deception. Loach would need weapons and armor for any assault. And there was certainly not enough of that in the marketplace.

They needed armed men and they needed them to remain inconspicuous. The answer was obvious. Tyson suppressed a curse. It would not do to swear before these two particular lads. They were nervous enough as things were without him adding to their worries.

"Who wants a drink?" Tyson asked cheerily. The boys looked at him befuddled as he led them into the nearest tavern.

The tavern was nothing special. Dark, slightly dirty without being filthy, and populated by dim bleary eyed individuals. And too many mercenaries. Not abnormally so, but more than Tyson would expect to find in such an establishment at this time of day.

"Hmm. Not this place," he said to the boys. "The atmosphere just isn't right."

He dragged them to another tavern. Same story. "Sorry boys, the lighting just doesn't favor my mood here."

Four more taverns and his excuses began getting weaker than the ale served in these parts. But each tavern told the same story. Too many solemn, grim-faced mercenaries drinking during the middle of the day.

"Well boys, that is it for our tavern crawl," Tyson declared.

Telwin glared at him. "Master Tyson, I wasn't thirsty when we went to the first tavern, but I am now."

"Too bad," said Tyson as he began leading them back to the palace. "I've seen what I needed to see, and we need to get word to our embassy as well as the others."

"Huh?" said Lentil. "You saw something in the taverns? Is Loach going to try to get the guards drunk?"

Tyson sighed as he ignored the boy. There just was not any time to waste educating the boy when there was so much work to be done. He knew where the attacks were coming from, he just did not know how much time they had before the Loachian strike arrived. Minutes? Hours?

The door to a nearby tavern opened and a group of mercenaries walked out. Their motions were smooth and steady. Each of their faces looked like death masks.

Tyson burst into a sprint, urging his legs to carry him faster. Time was all but up.

CHAPTER FIFTY-THREE

Jeron twitched anxiously as they walked past the Royal Guardsmen in their resplendent purple tabards worn over chainmail, and gleaming halberds. You could not walk ten feet in the palace without bumping into one of the guardsmen. Their eyes were focused and faces stoic. They were sworn to protect the crown, whoever wore it.

Everyone was bedecked in their house colors. Although almost every noble chose to bedeck themselves in their duke's colors with only accents and jewelry for their own house. The nobles took great stock in pledges of loyalty, and the opportunity to demonstrate to each other how loyal they actually were.

Jeron thought the real reason was a lack of color combinations. No one wanted their house to be confused for another. Or associated with being on the losing side.

Which led to Jeron finding himself garbed in what Master Maxus referred to as an Antierian paladin's formal dress uniform. Full platemail with exaggerated pauldrons, a blue cape with orange embroidery, and a blue and orange tabard draped over the ensemble. Jeron had his axe looped onto his belt, a shield on his arm, and a pair of short swords strapped to his back with the hilts poking out from beneath the cape.

"Easy man. Just relax," advised Dalton in a matching outfit with the only difference being the spear in his hand and the mace on his belt. "Jayna is a grown woman who can take care of herself."

"I know that," growled Jeron. "I just don't like there being so many potentially hostile nobles between me and her if fighting breaks out."

"And you having to stick by Byron's side," chimed in Cole from Jeron's other side.

"I don't need bodyguards," insisted Byron for the twentieth time that morning. "I can look after myself just fine."

"The last time we let you look out after yourself you managed to get yourself shot in the chest with four arrows," Jeron observed.

"And look how great that turned out!" said Byron. "See? No need to look after me. Take care of Jayna if there is a problem."

"Would you all shut up?" asked Atrisha. "Byron you'll accept the bodyguards otherwise the rest of us cannot go in as we are not the heads of our houses."

Olivia smiled a tight smile at Jeron from beyond Atrisha. "And I'm quite certain that Jayna can manage without you running to the rescue."

Jeron fought the urge to sigh in frustration. Olivia had acted prickly towards him since his return. He tried ignoring the barbs and allowing her what time and space she needed to accept his being with Jayna. But his patience was wearing thin. Olivia was the one who ended things between them. Why should he keep acting like everything was fine to protect her feelings? After all, she always insisted that she did not need protection from anyone.

Emkario glanced back over his shoulder. "If you all don't be quiet, I'll see to it that all of you sit outside the throne room."

Byron smirked at him. "I have to be there. I'm a prince."

Emkario smiled coldly at him. "And not the head of your house. You'd be there only for tradition's sake. If you're not there, no one will be able to nominate you."

"That seems like a strange rule," said Dalton.

Emkario shrugged. "It's supposed to prevent situations like those between King Delmon and his brother Saimon. The latter was late to the Conclave and led a rebellion when he found out his cousin had been crowned king."

"What happened?" asked Dalton.

"It's a fascinating bit of history really," said Emkario as they walked along the marble tiles of the palace. "Delmon and Saimon fought. Delmon defeated his brother and banished him from Ochandor."

"Please don't get him started on history," griped Byron. "I'm really not in the mood for a lecture."

Emkario glowered at Byron. "Just be quiet," he admonished. "If you don't want to learn about history, that's your prerogative."

"Doomed to repeat history's failures?" asked Byron with a grin.

"Right now, I think you're destined to be a first of a kind," muttered Emkario.

Dalton placed a restraining, calming hand on Byron's shoulder. He whispered something in Byron's ear, causing the prince to snort.

They walked in relative silence until reaching the throne room. Jeron had seen a few grand and wonderous things in his lifetime, but the throne room, the center of the Kingdom of Ochandor, was something else entirely.

Marble tile and pillars decorated the circular room. Along the circumference of the room were alcoves carved into the wall. Statues of kings and religious icons filled those alcoves. The room was simply beautiful, while lacking all the glitter and ostentatiousness of its counterpart in Talendor.

Seating was broken up into segments. Rows of benches cordoned off for each duchy in a semi-circle around the throne. Someone had wisely split Antier and Loach up, forcing them to opposite sides of the room.

Jayna, Vernon, and the rest of the Kelonian survivors were already in the throne room. Someone in the palace must have heard of their survival and arranged a section for them. Kelon's section was next to Antier, wedged in against the wall. Almost as if they were trying to be shoved away, out of sight and out of memory.

"Huh. Looks like someone wanted to keep Vernon and the others away from any duchies that might want to harm them," remarked Dalton.

Jeron supposed Dalton may have a point. Even if he was wrong, the seating placed Jayna close by, and that was all that mattered. She was garbed in a robe bearing the pink and green of House Kelon.

"Let's see, the yellow of Talendor, the green and blue of Biona," mused Byron as the crowds worked their way to their seats. "Ahh and there they are. The red, silver and black of Loach. The only house boorish enough to have three colors."

"Sit down and be quiet," ordered Darik with a scowl on his face. "You are years too old to be acting like a child. If you aren't careful, you'll start a fight in here."

"You know that I'd win," retorted Byron.

"Your record on that front is not exactly pristine."

Jeron ignored the sibling bickering and studied the layout of the room. If any trouble broke out, he would have to cross three, maybe four duchies full of nobles whose intentions were unknown before he could reach the Loachian delegation. If only he knew how Talendor would play this.

"Why are the temples and Church here?" whispered Atrisha.

Darik turned around from the bench in front of Jeron and smiled at the blonde girl. "Good question, captain," he said. "When you develop and have a stranglehold on the glyphs that keep the dead inside their resting place, you tend to develop quite a bit of influence."

"So they get a vote too?" asked Atrisha.

Darik chuckled lightly. "No. They do not," he said as he schooled his features back into a serious expression. "But by being here they get to claim the king is blessed by God or the gods. It all depends on your point of view."

"Handy for them," remarked Olivia. "And fortuitous for the king."

Darik arched an eyebrow at her. "Indeed," he said before turning back around and scanning the crowd.

Dalton nudged Jeron's arm. "Hey man. See that lady over in the Loachian section?" asked Dalton in a low voice. "The one in the red robes next to the big guy?"

"I see her," said Jeron as he narrowed his eyes. "You think she's the Loachian wizard throwing around lightning on the battlefield, don't you?"

"Yeah," said Dalton as determination steeled his voice. "And if a fight breaks out, we need to go for her right away."

Jeron stiffened. "And leave everyone else unprotected?" he asked incredulously.

"Man, everyone is unprotected against her." Dalton shook his head in frustration. "Look, this isn't the same thing as Fort Hope. We're not getting caught up in the battle and doing our own thing. This is different. We're the only ones here that we know can take her."

"Maybe take her," said Jeron. "She has more training than we do."

"Dammit Jeron," whispered Dalton. "You didn't see Calabella's body. Or any of the others. If we don't beat her a lot of people are going to die very painful and horrible deaths."

"Okay," whispered Jeron in resigned capitulation. "But we inform our people of our plan beforehand. So this time they can prepare."

"Sounds good. But you may want to do it quickly. Things look like they're about ready to get started here."

CHAPTER FIFTY-FOUR

Vernon stared out over the gathering masses. It took an extreme amount of effort not to turn that gaze into a terrible glare. He knew that the vast majority of them did not have anything to do with the destruction of Kelon. But that did not mean they were innocent.

Survivors of the destruction, like young Toran, had a rough time getting by after losing everything. In nearly every duchy the refugees were preyed upon. And those in attendance did little or nothing to stop it.

Vernon tried to do what he could over the years to help those he came across. But they were few and far between. Kelon's destruction had been thorough.

"They're looking at us like we're some sort of freak show found at a menagerie," grumbled Aron sourly.

"Aye. Let them," said Brukel. "Maybe the shame will help them make up their minds."

"Why should they start feeling shame now?" Toran asked bitterly as he glared daggers across the chamber at Prince Matlin and the robed woman, Clara.

Marcela ruffled Toran's hair, then remembering where they were, pulled back her hand. "Easy there," she said. "If there is to be any trouble, let them be the ones to start it. Unprovoked."

"Why?" asked Toran, his voice raw.

"Because it will remind everyone how our people died," said Elfred in clipped precise tones. "Unprovoked. It will remind them we did not deserve to die then, and we don't deserve to die now."

"You all put a lot of stock in people who have done nothing for years," said Toran.

"It's because we've been all over this kingdom," answered Jayna. "We've seen the good and the bad it has to offer. And there is a lot of good if you only take the time to look."

"Quiet," ordered Vernon. "It's starting."

A middle-aged man with graying curly brown hair marched into the room. He was garbed from head to toe in purple clothing and a cape. All of which was trimmed with gold. He carried a golden staff and walked with the kind of self-importance known only to those who elevated their institutions above everything else.

He was the king's steward. A trusted advisor, and the man designated to oversee the Conclave and the transition of power. Judging by the smug expression on his face, the steward was probably the only person in the room thankful that there was not an heir.

"My lords and ladies, welcome to the Conclave of Nobles," he began in a voice just beneath shrill. "Our duty is clear. To select the next king of Ochandor. Each duchy will have the opportunity to nominate one of their own for the position. The Duchy of Ochandor will abstain as it lacks a duke following the king's death."

The man lowered his head in sympathy for the dead. After a brief moment of silence, he continued. "As is tradition, the nominees for king shall not be permitted to speak to the assembly. If one is to lead the Kingdom of Ochandor, that man's deeds should speak for themselves. Now then, shall we get on with it?"

Vernon arched an eyebrow in surprise. Was that truly how the grand ceremony of the Conclave was supposed to go? Or had the traditions been lost to time since a Conclave had not been necessary for generations?

Kelon was not going to nominate anyone for the position. Vernon had determined that. If a melee became necessary, he was not prepared to lose any of his people. They were just too few.

Prince Matlin began the ceremony by nominating himself, to the shock of absolutely no one in attendance. Nuqua was next, and to the surprise of everyone, Duke Seamus Nuqua nominated himself. Perhaps the old buccaneer thought he would have a chance to steal the crown following the discord and turmoil that Matlin and Darik were expected to leave in their wake.

Duke Havram hesitated when it was Talendor's turn. He took quick glances at his frail son, still struggling to recover from his wounds, and a sidelong twitch in Vernon's direction. He stood there for a moment, motionless, his giant scorpion's tail swaying gently back and forth. Finally, he shook his head in the negative and sat down without uttering a word.

Lastly, Prince Darik nominated himself. He stared defiantly across the chamber at Matlin as if daring the man to speak. The Loachian prince smiled contemptuously at Antier causing a hushed murmur to run through the crowd. Vernon felt his own hand start drifting slowly towards his sword. It never hurt to take precautions.

The steward cleared his throat in an effort to gain everyone's attention. "My lords. Your nominees are Dukes Matlin Loach, Darik Villa, and Seamus Nuqua. Please discuss the matter amongst yourselves and decide your votes."

"Well this just got interesting," murmured Vernon.

"How so?" asked Brukel as he looked suspiciously at the gathering of nobles.

"Duke Seamus nominating himself," said Vernon as his mind raced. "Do the math. He'll vote for himself. Darik has at least three votes in hand with us, his own, and Biona's. If Matlin votes for himself that leaves three votes remaining."

"And he'll need all of them to win," chuckled Elfred bitterly. "Including Talendor."

"The irony is overwhelming," said Vernon drily. "If the situation weren't so dire I would be holding my sides laughing."

Jayna rolled her eyes. "Right. Mister dour and serious laughing at a formal event," she said. "If you don't mind, I'll do the laughing for us."

Her lilting laugh sang out over the crowd drawing the attention of a few nobles. "Shh," admonished Vernon. "You know that it wouldn't be unheard of for Talendor to betray our side."

"And show their true colors to the rest of the kingdom?" said Elfred skeptically. "Not a great look for merchants."

"And then there is young Nelson to think about," said Brukel. "The duke's daughter is engaged to him."

"Hush," said Vernon. "It looks like everyone has made their decision."

"Well that was quick," remarked Brukel.

"The dukes have had years to contemplate this decision," said Jayna. "And unlike us, they weren't bouncing around from town to town."

Vernon did not answer. He was fixated upon the steward. Everything his entire life had built up to hinged upon this moment.

The steward gazed out over the assembled nobles with a small frown on his face. Clearly, he expected his time as the center of attention to last longer. "Very well then. Let us begin," he said without his previous enthusiasm. "All those in favor of Duke Seamus Nuqua please step forward."

Duke Seamus stepped forward, a jovial smile on his bearded face. The man looked positively amused at the entire situation. Like he was not entirely taking it seriously. Duke Seamus gazed out over the throne room and burst out laughing when none of the other dukes stood up. He sat down chuckling all the while.

"All in favor of Duke Matlin Loach?"

Dukes Erlon and Rondmon stood up along with Matlin. Every eye in the room focused on Duke Havram. He closed his eyes and took a few calming breaths that Vernon swore he could hear in the silence of the throne room. His own heart sounded like a war drum beating in his chest. He was surprised that Jayna did not tease him and tell him to be quiet.

Duke Havram's oversized scorpion's tail swayed back in forth while he sat there. He opened his eyes and looked in Darik's direction. He held the prince's gaze for a solid ten seconds before turning his head and glancing over at Matlin.

The duke shrugged at the prince and sat back in his bench, a vicious look of self-satisfaction upon his face. Vernon exhaled as did most of the nobles in the throne room. Judging by the looks on their faces they were as surprised as Vernon to discover that they had been holding their breath.

Matlin stared at Duke Havram, his face impassive, betraying no emotion. His wings spread and flexed, scarlet scales glistening beneath the sunlight streaming in through the skylights.

"All in favor of Duke Darik Villa of Antier?"

Vernon rose along with Darik, Duke Havram, and the man that Vernon assumed was Nelson's father. Hands began to shift slowly towards their weapons. Antier and Loach were at war, and everyone felt like it was moments away from being settled and one side considered the victor.

The atmosphere was not lost upon the steward. His mirth at being the centerpiece of this spectacle vanished. The man did not even try hide his unease. Sweat beaded on the ends of his nose and he kept glancing around searching for the quickest exit out of the throne room.

"Ahem. Four votes," said the steward in a squeaky voice. "That makes Duke Darik the winner. Long live the king!"

"I don't think so!" hollered Matlin. "His vote does not count!" His finger trembled as he pointed directly at Vernon. "Kelon is gone! They no longer have a vote! Three to three! It is a tie!"

Rage boiled within Vernon. It was a familiar feeling. As a boy it comforted him at night. Planning his vengeance, envisioning the death of his enemies. It kept him going in those first few years. Eventually, he bottled those feelings up and locked the bottle away. A desire for revenge led to recklessness, and that led to death for himself or his people.

But that was then, when he had nothing. Here, standing in the center of the kingdom with a chance to give his people their lives and land back? And the son of the man responsible for the death of his people stood against him. A man who had profited off of their suffering. That man was trying to deny him the opportunity to protect his own. That was quite another story.

Vernon let the years of anguish and rage out of the bottle. It coursed through his body, his chest heaved as his breathing increased. He stood, strong confident. His voice thundered through the throne room, infused with his anger.

"You dare? You the duke who rules the duchy that oversaw the plot to slay Kelon and all its people. You dare try to deny us our place after all the crimes your family has committed?" He felt his hands clenched the hilt of his sword. "No. Your brow does not deserve the opportunity to befoul the crown."

Matlin drew his claymore. It was a giant hideous weapon. He smiled wickedly across the room at Vernon. "Well then. It looks like I'll have to correct father's mistake. A tie is a tie. And the tradition says there is a melee." Red scales covered his skin until his human frame was covered by the overlapping material. "I guess we'll just have to expand the entry field."

Matlin roared and charged across the throne room, his allies surging a step behind him as pandemonium gripped the kingdom.

CHAPTER FIFTY-FIVE

J eron reached out trying to snag any part of Byron's body. He grabbed only air as the prince vaulted over the bench, his skin already beginning to gleam and sparkle. Jeron swore as he followed over the bench, his mane sprouting from his face. Dalton landed next him, a long-suffering expression on his face. "He always has to rush in, doesn't he?"

"Just once I would like him to warn us," shouted Jeron as he drew his axe while running.

The throne room had devolved into madness. Every nobleman pitched in to the melee, but not always on their duchy's side. Men were taking the opportunity to settle scores with neighbors and competitors. Jeron saw at least two men stabbed in the back by people wearing the same colors.

Byron had his two swords drawn and his skull was already fully diamond. Matlin's face registered shock, fear, and anger at the sight. Jeron could not blame him. He felt the same feelings toward the Loachians.

The orange and white of Erlon flashed out of the corner of Jeron's eye. The Erlonian nobleman bellowed as he whipped a flail in Jeron's direction. Before the man's blow could land, Dalton's spear whirled and darted in, jabbing the nobleman through the throat.

"We lost track of Cole again," said Dalton, unconcerned with the fate of the dead nobleman.

"This is not going to be a repeat of Fort Hope," growled Jeron.

"Damn right," said Dalton as he felled a bandana wearing Nuquanian nobleman clothed in bright shades of crimson and yellow. His saber fell harmlessly to the ground as surprise registered on the nobleman's face. "Now where is that damn wizard?"

Matlin and Byron were seconds away from colliding when Jeron saw her. The red robed woman was running in Matlin's wake. She slid off to Matlin's dominant hand placing as much space between herself and the battle raging throughout the throne room and began to raise her hands.

"Dalton!" screamed Jeron in warning.

"I see her!" hollered Dalton in reply.

Lightning sprang from her fingers and coursed through Byron. His swords slipped from his twitching hands as a steady stream of energy entered his body. Byron collapsed to the floor, and still a constant stream of lightning hit his body.

Matlin roared as he raised his claymore, hilt to his ear, blade pointed down as he intended to skewer Byron. Time froze as a sense of helplessness consumed Jeron. There was no way that he could close the ground and reach his friend in time.

A slight tremor shook the throne room. Matlin pitched forward, unable to gather his footing. He was not the only one. Panicked cries rang out in fear and confusion as noblemen fell. Jeron looked over at Dalton in shock. The tall man was kneeling on the ground, snarling in rage, while his fingers dug into the tile floor. Was he insane conjuring up an earthquake inside the palace? He could have brought the entire structure down.

Jeron was not the only one in shock. The red robed woman stared at Dalton as comprehension crawled across her face. In her surprise she ceased shooting lightning into Byron. She raised her arms again; hands extended towards Dalton. It seemed to take minutes to Jeron.

He did the only thing he could think off.

He thrust his axe forward as a he ran, forcing a column of water to erupt out of the air before his hand. The water blasted the wizard, dousing and drenching her robes. But failing to knock her off her feet.

Her eyes widened at the sudden attack, but the surprise was short lived. She sneered at them both as sparks sprang from her fingertips. The sparks shot every which way and fizzled out. Her eyes widened as the sparks grew at a frenzied pace. But no lightning blasts came forth.

Dalton's spear found her heart before she even had a chance to attempt any nonmagical forms of defense. Jeron tore his eyes from her as she fell. He had seen enough people die; he did want or care to have the death of a pretty woman playing through his memories.

With the immediate threat dealt with, Jeron altered his course away from the woman and slightly back towards Byron. Matlin had regained his footing and was standing over the fallen prince, claymore raised high in the air. A deathblow for certain; if he could cleave through the diamond exterior.

Jeron tried to aim his hand to fire off another blast of something. But he knew he would be too late. Why could Byron not wait for him? Just once. Matlin's sword began its descent as flames began to wreath his body. Matlin howled in surprise, but the claymore did not stop.

Steel rang out against steel as Darik plowed into Matlin with a shoulder charge. The rivals hit the ground, flipped over, and rolled a few times before springing back to their feet, weapons at the ready.

Jeron slid on his knees across the floor, stopping at Byron's head. His chest was still moving albeit in a staggered pace. Jeron returned his axe to his belt and tossed his shield aside as he scooped his friend into his arms. Of course, the man had to be heavier than he had ever been before. How inconsiderate.

A Loachian charged them, a wild look in his eyes as he screamed something about fire, demons, and bastards. A brown blur streaked past Jeron, striking the man in the throat, and by the sounds of it, crushing his windpipe.

Jayna smiled warmly down at Jeron. "Do be careful sweety. I can't always be there to protect you."

Jeron stared at her in disbelief before barking out a laugh. Renaldo, Emkario, Vincent, and the other Antierian noblemen rushed past him in a swarm, determined to reach Darik. Vernon and the other survivors of Kelon fanned out around Jeron.

"Alright lad, slowly retreat," said Vernon. "We'll help defend Byron."

Jeron glanced around. "Umm, retreat where exactly?" he asked. "The palace kind of has turned into a war zone here."

"To the throne then," said Vernon. "It's elevated and no one is there at the moment."

"Is that wise?" asked Elfred cautiously.

"No, but we're out of good options," answered Vernon.

Jeron stood with aid from Atrisha and Olivia. "Huh. You two are helping?"

Olivia rolled her eyes. "Of course we are genius. You did hear the part that we are helping to protect Byron."

"It's not our fault you all charged in without formulating a plan," said Atrisha.

"I said what we were going to do," protested Dalton, his eyes never leaving the melee, his body positioned between Jeron and harm.

Olivia rolled her eyes. "Saying something seconds before the action starts isn't a plan."

Jeron mumbled under his breath as he lugged Byron's unconscious body towards the throne. He never used to suffer from headaches.

A thousand clever and not so clever responses to the girls belatedly played their way through his mind. Instead of utilizing them he decided to change the subject. "Where's Cole?"

Atrisha's face tightened as worry crept into her eyes. "I don't know. One moment, he was beside us, and the next he was gone.

A gout of flame burst forth from the rear of the Loachian nobles. More and more small flames exploded amongst the ranks of Matlin's allies. The fires were small due to all the nobles being intertwined amongst each other.

"I think I know where Cole is," said Dalton sarcastically.

"We have to help him," declared Atrisha.

"We can't," said Elfred. "And even if we could, we have no idea where he is."

"And it would ruin his distraction," said Olivia.

Atrisha looked at the other girl aghast. "So we should just leave him all by himself?" she demanded.

"Use your brain," scolded Olivia. "Cole is distracting them so they can't organize and charge our position."

"She's right," said Jeron as he laid Byron down on the ground. Jayna immediately knelt next to him and placed a hand to his diamond head. "Sometimes the smartest strategy is not fighting. Dalton and I learned that when we fled Fort Hope. But just because it's right doesn't make it any easier."

"Talk later," said Brukel as he twirled his mace. "It looks like we're about to be extremely busy."

Jeron drew his axe and one of his swords as he faced a pair of buccaneers. And to think that he thought the ceremony was boring.

CHAPTER FIFTY-SIX

Thiago loosed another arrow down the hall. The arrow found its mark, burying itself in the chest of the ersatz Loachian mercenaries. The soldier stumbled and fell into the fountain leaving a slowly spreading cloud of blood to mark his resting place.

It was a pity really. Biona's embassy truly was a lovely structure. Even with all of the bodies.

Antier's embassy was not any less bloody. Master Tyson, Telwin, and Lentil had arrived at the embassy mere minutes ahead of Loach's assault. Their warning saved untold countless lives. Instead of catching the residents and guards unaware, the Loachian soldiers mounted an assault on a fully armed and prepared embassy.

Master Tyson had assigned a squad of five soldiers to accompany Thiago, Telwin, Lentil, and Atticus to Biona's embassy. Nine was not an overwhelming or sufficient force by any stretch of the imagination. But their mission was not intended to be a direct assault.

Their orders were simple. Reconnoiter the embassy and determine whether Loach had attacked. If they had not, warn the inhabitants. If they had, gauge the situation. If combat was still ongoing, pitch in. If it was not, use stealth to infiltrate the embassy and free the inhabitants.

Thankfully, the battle was already underway when they arrived. Thiago shuddered to picture Lentil and Telwin sneaking through an embassy. A stampede would be more effective, and less quiet.

Thiago loosed another arrow down the hallway, killing another Loachian soldier. Fortunately, the invading force was unfamiliar with the layout of the embassy. Otherwise, they would not keep charging down hallways, making themselves easy targets for his bow. If they began to use their minds, he would have to abandon that strategy and draw his sword.

He disliked using his sword. Lately every time he held it in his hands his mind would wander back to the siege of Talendor. Standing on the city walls, out of arrows, as the vampires tried climbing over.

Thiago had killed what felt like more than his fair share of the creatures. They did not fight like normal humans. Those too white fangs stretching towards his neck. Almost as if they could sense the blood pumping through his veins.

He shuddered at the thought and let loose another arrow. Sooner or later, he would get past the feeling. But that would take time. Creeping through the brush and ruins of the outskirts of Kelon had not done his nerves any favor. He had traded vampires for the threat of ghosts and werewolves lurking behind every tree and wall. It was a wonder he ever slept at all.

Between the war and this mission, it was pleasant to not be fighting against nightmare inducing creatures. Instead, he battled treacherous soldiers from a duchy that wanted to seize control of the kingdom by any means necessary, and grind his people into dust. A nice, normal, and entirely human threat.

Silence fell upon the hallway as his last target lay dying on the ground. The sounds of fighting and men dying violently still echoed throughout the embassy. Thiago quickly surveyed his men. Two were dead, rendering their already small force even tinier. They would need to be even more careful.

"Alright everyone," whispered Thiago. "We move quickly. Take the Loachians from behind when we can. And above all else find us some living allies."

"How do we know if there are any allies here?" asked Lentil as he rubbed at one of his bull horns.

Telwin smacked the large man upside the back of his head. "They're not fighting themselves, man. Think."

Thiago shot the pair his best withering glare and held a finger up for silence. That pair of men were never going to be geniuses, but Thiago thought by now that they would have learned the value of silence.

The embassy was beautiful if one enjoyed the water. The tiling was all shades of blue and white with pictures and sculptures all relating to the sea or the swamplands. Judging from the paintings, the swamps were a source of great fear and respect amongst the people of Biona.

All that water was deeply unsettling. Thiago preferred his forests large, and his rivers small and manageable. At least these corridors had more in common with his forests and not the sea.

Thiago peeked his head around the next corner. The hallway spilled out into a large room, more of an atrium, but with a narrow fountain in the middle instead of trees. Multiple corridors and rooms branched out from the non-atrium. Which was a good thing as it accommodated all of the soldiers trying to fight within them.

"Well we found the party," remarked Atticus. "Where to now?"

Thiago chewed his lower lip. He could not sneak his way around this. It just was not possible. They would be seen. A direct confrontation was inevitable, and he did not have the first clue where to start with one of those.

"What do you think boss?" asked Telwin as he wiggled his shoulders loose. "Skim the outside edges, stabbing Loachians in the back until we reach the end of the room or find someone in charge of Biona's defenses?"

Thiago could have hugged the man. Maybe he misjudged him. "Yes. Telwin, you and Lentil take the lead. Atticus, you and I follow after with our swords out. But be ready to switch to your bow at a moment's notice." Atticus heaved a sigh of disappointment. He disliked being without his bow as well. "You three," said Thiago as he gestured to the soldiers Tyson had assigned him. "You bring up the rear and keep your eyes out for any Loachians trying to stab us in the back."

Lentil raised his left hand in triumph, nearly slicing Telwin in his exuberance. "Yes!" he exclaimed. "Finally, a plan I can get behind."

A long-suffering expression crossed Telwin's face as he sighed in exasperation before charging off after his friend. Thiago tried to calm his racing heart and did the same.

They darted through the room, the wall to their right, the fountain to their left. Lentil took the lefthand side and Telwin the right. They did it without talking. The two were accustomed to fighting alongside each other and knew not to run with their sword arms next to each other. And then there was Thiago and Atticus, both busy trying not to cut themselves or each other with their own swords.

Telwin bypassed the first group of fighters down a corridor branching off of the atrium. It was a mess and a large corridor to boot. Too easy for their forces to be ground up between the two forces, or confused for the enemy. Thiago understood that much. Counting enemies quickly was becoming a specialty of his.

They killed a few Loachians as they crossed the room, skirting combat whenever possible. Telwin made a beeline for the door along the far wall. Right where the fighting was the loudest. Thiago gulped. Sneaking up on an enemy force was one thing. Charging it was something else entirely.

"How do you stay so calm?" asked Atticus in a hushed voice. "Man nothing bothers you."

Thiago ignored the man. Calm? Laughable. He was dying over here. Why could Atticus not see that?

Lentil lowered his head and charged at the door. Thiago winced in anticipation. Just because he had horns did not mean it would not hurt. Bulls were not precisely battering rams.

The door cracked as it flew off of its hinges from the strain of the force generated by the young warrior. The room beyond was pure madness. Once it may have been a quasi-throne room or audience chamber. Maybe a ballroom for dignitary functions.

Now it was a warzone. Rubble was strewn about the room. Bodies both alive and wounded lay scattered, as men fought and died. Thiago felt his eyes widen. This was where Telwin led them? Straight to the fiercest part of the fighting?

Telwin lay into the Loachins from the rear with Lentil a half step behind him. Thiago hesitated for a heartbeat and was nearly trampled by the Antierian soldiers behind him as they skirted around the two scouts. The Loachians fell quickly, caught between two forces.

"Umm, Thiago, are we heading in there?" asked Atticus hesitantly, holding his sword in both hands.

Thiago jerked his head back and forth. The battle was fierce and he was most likely to get in the way. A loud crunching sound drew Thiago's attention. A tall, green scaled alligator-man was tearing into the Loachian forces with a cutlass.

"There," said Thiago as he pointed at Prince Nelson. "We go there."

Atticus flashed him a nervous grin. "Why not?" he tittered. "There's only a decent chance either side will hack us to bits."

"That's why we need to reach Nelson," said Thiago. "Either he's in charge, or he knows who is. If we get his attention, we'll be safe."

"Great plan. If only we had the men used to using their swords still with us," said Atticus devoid of his usual blissful cheer.

"Exactly. That's why we're not charging straight ahead," said Thiago. "We'll use our brains. Hug the wall. Keep your sword out and cover me. I'm going to feather a few Loachians and get Nelson's attention without being within reach of his arms."

"Why do you get to shoot?" grumbled Atticus petulantly.

Thiago tossed him a rare smile. "Because I'm in charge."

He concentrated, trying to calm his nerves and stop his hand from shaking. He loosed arrow after arrow, striking the Loachian soldiers in the back. The men tumbled forward, either dead or dying. It hardly mattered as Nelson's forces hacked the men to pieces as they tumbled forward.

"Allies on deck!" shouted Nelson. "Careful of the men from Antier!"

Sometimes the best intentions go to waste. This was one of those times. Nelson's warning did more than alert his forces to the presence of Thiago and his companions. It alerted the Loachians to their presence as well.

Some of the ersatz mercenaries broke off from their Bionan counterparts and tried to counteract the assault on their rear. One of the Antierian soldiers was quickly disemboweled by a sword thrust. Atticus yelped at the sight of three burly Loachians charging in their direction.

Thiago fired off another arrow, puncturing the throat of one of the Loachians. The bow was already falling from Thiago's hands the instant the arrow left his fingers. He did not have time to draw and aim another shot, and the bow would be a liability against armed men. Not to mention that he did not want the wood being damaged from blocking steel. He was fond of that bow. They had been through a lot together.

He drew his sword again and tried to rely on Captain Levren's training. He was a competent swordsman, but not a professional. His only advantage was that these men were already exhausted from the battle.

Thiago crossed swords with the Loachian and felt his eyes widen in surprise. This man was not a professional killer. He was younger than Thiago, barely more than a boy if one could judge from the lack of lines on his face, and the absence of pain in his eyes. This very well might be his first battle.

The Loachian youth was young, wild, and a little bit reckless. He was trying to win the fight with one swing. Thiago could handle one swing. Maybe more.

There was no pattern, no elegance to the blows. Only sheer desperation. Thiago blocked the first two before lashing out himself. His sword tugged slightly as he scored a hit on the Loachian. He swung another at the stunned youth, terror in his eyes. The boy screamed as the blade tore through his stomach.

Thiago did not have any time in which to celebrate his victory, not that he would. Death was not something he found worthy of celebration. Death was merely one person surviving at the expense of another.

Which must have been what the other Loachian was thinking as his sword sliced through Thiago's cheek. Thiago howled in pain as he fell to the ground next to Atticus's corpse. Cold, unblinking, uncaring eyes stared back at him.

Thiago tried to crawl backwards, the palms of his hands scraping against the floor. He tried desperately to get away from Atticus's body, and the Loachian advancing upon him. It was a small mercy that his left eye was only covered in blood, obscuring his vision.

Green scales blurred from his right side. Nelson carved straight through Thiago's adversary and on through the rest of the Loachian lines. His cutlass was a blur, and he did not seem to pause for rest. Nelson had found his opening in the enemy, courtesy of Thiago, and he latched onto it.

Thiago slid down onto the floor. He was trembling. Worse than when that vampire almost killed him in the sand dunes of Talendor. Maybe it was the wound. Maybe it was killing the young Loachian. Or maybe it was seeing Atticus die as a result of his own orders. He closed his one good eye and let himself slip into the waiting nightmares.

CHAPTER FIFTY-SEVEN

D arik shook the marble powder coating his body and armor out of his eyes. He had tackled Matlin straight through the wall and out of the throne room. He should not have been so soft with Matlin. The treacherous winged rat deserved much worse, but he was not going to risk harming his little brother to reach Matlin. That would qualify as the dumbest rescue attempt in the history of mankind.

He spun, swinging his greatsword in a smooth arc towards Matlin. The other man's claymore parried the blow, but not without considerable effort. Whether from being pushed through a wall seconds earlier, or from a discrepancy in their talents, Darik did not know, nor care. Matlin tried to kill his little brother twice. He failed both times, but that did not absolve him from the attempts or from the countless other Antierian lives lost as a result of his actions.

Everything stemmed from Matlin's betrayal at Fort Hope. For the first time in his life Darik had known despair, and understood why his soldiers referred to the place as Fort No Hope. It burned him up inside. The rage, the hatred, the guilt. All of it.

Darik opened his dragon's mouth and spewed flames at Matlin. The Loachian jerked his head away, dodging the majority of the blast, but not before it scorched the skin on his right shoulder and jaw.

Darik glared down the length of his blade as Matlin squared off to face him. "Ahh Prince Matlin," said Darik, his voice simmering with poorly contained disgust. "I thought I recognized you by your crusty disposition. Soon everyone else will as well." And people had the audacity to suggest that he did not have a sense of humor.

Matlin snarled, a thin trickle of blood dripping from his mouth and onto the marble dust covering his face. "What are you talking about?"

Darik sighed in exasperation. For once, he tried to make a joke, and of course the intended target of the joke was too stupid to thoroughly understand it. Just his luck.

Matlin lunged at Darik and the two entered a deadly dance. Each combatant favored a large two-handed weapon prone to large sweeping strikes by most men. However, Matlin and Darik were not most men. They were two of the most physically strong men in the kingdom. Their giant weapons might as well have been rapiers the way that they handled them. Light quick thrusts were interspersed with quicker cuts, slashes, and great cleaving attacks.

In Darik's experience, most fights with death on the line were brief affairs. Someone was either too cautious or too reckless, and paid the price for it. The problem was in their training. Everyone was taught a similar style. When someone slashed one way, you had to parry in exactly this way and so forth. Most combatants learned the same combinations and attacked in the same beats and patterns. Few strayed from what they learned. Fear of failing when the stakes were the highest were too great of a risk for most people.

But life was risk, and the greatest rewards always required daring. And doing what was unexpected was certainly a risk. Creativity in high leverage situations was more than most people could stomach.

Matlin apparently subscribed to the same philosophy at Darik. He slashed when he should have thrust, parried when he should dodge, and retreated when he should press the advantage. It was beautiful and terrifying at the same time.

Darik's brain strained with the effort involved to keep up. Inventing on the fly was always difficult. He was creating combinations and maneuvers that he had never practiced before. His muscles protested at the foreign movements. His only consolation was that Matlin's body must be dissenting in a similar manner.

Part of him ached to take to the sky and transform fully into a dragon. The hallways were too constrained for that sort of transformation. The original architects must have planned for someone like him. Not that he needed to be inside the palace to level it. In fact, he was trying to prevent it from being destroyed. It was a tricky balance, trying to destroy and save at the same time.

Matlin grinned a red smile as the fought. "Clever move with the fire," he said. "But even if you win, what is your move? My move is simple. I've made it so that history will always doubt you. Half the kingdom will resist your rule."

Darik snorted sending a puff of smoke into the room. "And you're going to what? Fly off and start a rebellion? With the capital of your duchy destroyed and your armies in tatters? Not a great plan."

Matlin laughed manically as he swung his sword. "Well that was never my original plan," he said as Darik glided away from the blow. "But life intervenes and one makes do with what is in his possession. And what I have is the opportunity to tear you down bit by bit. And then, I will tear down Antier, absorb it into Loach. Destroy every one of those gods' forsaken churches that you have littered the towns with. And then. Then after I have removed every vestige of you and your family from our lands, will I rule and lead the people of this kingdom to greatness."

Darik glared at the man. Most people could not drive him to anger. But most people had not murdered his parents. "There is one flaw in your plan you son of a bitch," said Darik in an even voice. If he was going to lose his temper, he was going to do it in a controlled fashion. "You assume that I am going to let you leave here alive. That I won't hunt you to the ends of the earth to see you burn."

His muscles began to bulge as he spoke. The cerulean scales began to cover his skin as his wings sprouted from his back. Matlin's eyes widened as he stumbled backwards. Matlin flapped his wings and shot up through one of the skylights, transforming further as he gained altitude.

Darik roared as he took off after him, his shoulders scraping against the walls, knocking stones loose. His eyes focused on the red scales above him. Matlin was not a dragon like Darik. Not exactly.

Matlin had a barbed tail and was smaller than Darik. A wyvern then. Darik had never encountered one of those before. His mind raced trying to recollect every story he had ever heard about wyverns. He did not have Byron's innate memory, especially as it related to stories. Instead, he had numbers and iron will. Practical skills. But that did not mean that he lacked a memory. Wyverns were supposed to have some type of breath. Fire, ice, poison, or something of the like.

Darik smiled a toothy smile as he felt the wind blast against his face. He had a plan of his own for the future of the kingdom. Its elegancy was in its simplicity. He would grasp Matlin in his claws and roast the treacherous man within his own scales.

Chapter Fifty-Eight

Olivia stalked back and forth across the dais the throne sat upon. Atrisha had seen feral cats that looked more serene than Olivia. All the dark-skinned woman needed to do to complete painting the picture of an unhinged woman was to gnash her teeth.

Atrisha sympathized with her. They had invested so much of their selves to gain the ability to fight in the army. They put everything they had into it, and they had succeeded. There were casualties, and friends were lost, but all they wanted was the choice to be able to live their lives the way they saw fit.

But Olivia did not experience war in the same way as Atrisha. Most of her time was spent on tactics and overseeing Antier's army. She had led a beautifully efficient war, but there were not that many battles that allowed her to swing her saber.

The battle raged around them and it felt as if time had been turned backwards within the throne room. They were forbidden from fully engaging in the fight because a reckless young prince nearly got himself killed through his own stupidity. And so other more seasoned fighters, such as themselves, were forced to babysit him so as to prevent the kingdom from descending into another war. All because of who his father was, and not due to any accomplishments of his own.

Atrisha's mind hesitated as she watched Jayna work with whatever priestly magic was available to her. Byron's skin still glittered, a testament to the fact that despite her misgivings he had accomplished something with his life. Judging by the look in the eyes of the Kelonian refugees, few of his actions should be considered a worthy accomplishment.

"We should be out there fighting," complained Olivia as she continued her circuit.

"We have to protect Byron," said Jeron, his head turning back and forth as he scanned the crowd looking for someone to fight.

"I know that," snapped Olivia. "And I don't need you to explain it to me. But all of us sitting here is a waste."

"I agree," moaned Byron softly. "Go kill a few for me."

Jeron hesitated, clearly eager to join the fracas but also torn in leaving the prince behind.

"We cannot," said Prince Irvin emphatically. "We need to pull back out of this madness. None of us gain anything by joining the fray. This matter will be settled in the sky between Darik and Matlin. However, if we die, all is lost."

A small burst of flame flashed brightly across the room. It was accompanied by shrieks whose higher pitches were distinct over the sounds of men shouting and dying.

The fire meant Cole was still in the throne room. Still fighting. If he was still fighting, then Atrisha would be fighting as well. It was that simple.

"Everything that means anything to me is here," said Atrisha, her face locked in determination. "I'm fighting."

"As am I," said Olivia as she leapt off the dais and onto the floor of the throne room without bothering to check if Atrisha was alongside her.

Atrisha charged after her, careful not to take flight. She had not seen any nobles carrying bows into the throne room, but that did not mean they were not there. And daggers could reach her if she chose to fly low enough to actually be of use in a fight.

"Don't think we'll be charging out there to save you from yourselves," hollered Dalton, his voice barely audible.

Atrisha paid him no mind as she glided through the lines. To her surprise, men and women fought for the future of the kingdom with different degrees of effectiveness. Most of the people battling appeared to have some, if not a lot, of training with their weapons. However, many, especially the women, did not appear to be particularly experienced in utilizing those weapons in a fight.

A grim expression crossed Atrisha's face as she sliced through a contingent of uncertain Loachian noblewomen. Swords and maces streaked towards her, but always a hair too slow or too wide as their owners needed to think on what to do next instead of simply doing it.

That particular problem did not burden Atrisha as she dispatched them one by one in a cold fury. These women were part of Loach as much as their husbands were. They caused so much pain and suffering. She was merely the instrument of God's justice upon them.

Five bodies and a few broken chain links on her left arm later, and Atrisha was through them. Olivia was having a little more difficulty with the noblemen she was engaged with. Two men with bloody gashes in their fancy clothing squared off against her. Hate and anger shone in their eyes. A third roared as he charged Olivia from the right, her shield side.

Atrisha lunged, her sword biting into the third man's side. She ripped her blade viciously out of his body, hopefully rupturing the man's kidney.

The leftmost man struck nearly simultaneously at Olivia's flank. She brought her sword up effortlessly in a parry, a calm expression on her face. A scorpion's tail swung out from behind her and drove into the man's thigh. He howled in agony as he fell, his doom mere minutes away.

The remaining Loachian nobleman backed up hesitantly, suddenly unsure about fighting Olivia alone. The calm expression vaporized from Olivia's face in a wordless snarl. She advanced on the man, beating his useless blade out of his hands. He died moments later, his corpse a monument to Loach's heartless actions.

"A scorpion?" Atrisha asked with a raised eyebrow.

Olivia shrugged. "My grandparents are originally from Talendor."

"It's just that I expected some kind of cat."

Olivia glowered at her. "Well I'm just thankful it wasn't a frog. They have those in Talendor too you know."

"Do they now?" asked a tall willowy teenage woman with scorn in her voice. "And here I thought you rabble playing at being soldiers were from Antier." She was joined by another woman, who shared similar features. They both were clad in the red, black, and silver of Loach.

"I am from Antier," hissed Olivia as she leveled her saber at the girl.

"Oh she's a feisty one," said the younger of the pair as she drew circles with her rapier. "Sis, I think she would do quite well as a courtesan. After she's broken of that sharp tongue of hers."

The taller one clucked her tongue. "Perhaps. That might teach her to address her betters in such a manner. We should have her work double—"

Atrisha did not wait for her to finish the sentence. She closed the distance between them quickly and slashed at the older of the pair. The girl leapt backwards in an attempt to dodge the strike, but not before it grazed her chin and tore a rent in her red gown.

The girl's face flushed red in shock and anger. Atrisha doubted anyone ever confronted the girl in her life. Atrisha did not wait for the spoiled girl to recover. She pressed the attack, as did Olivia.

The sisters retreated unsteadily. Their blades sweeping up in elegant fencer's parries. Atrisha continued to rain down blows with her heavier sword, hacking her way through the girl's defenses.

Desperation entered her opponent's eyes as her breathing began to labor. Fencing was nothing like a real battle. There were rules and your opponent was supposed to abide by them. Atrisha had no intention of following the Loachian girl's script.

Atrisha pushed her blade against the girl's, forcing her opponent into a defensive position from which she could not easily counter. Atrisha leaned her weight into the girl, momentarily causing the girl to stumble backwards in her fancy slippers.

And then she punched the girl. A solid left hook straight to her already bloodied jaw. The girl's body went wooden as she raised her arms up in defense as she fell. Atrisha's sword darted out, removing the girl's throat.

Atrisha panted and looked up. Olivia was standing next to her with a red saber, her opponent already dispatched. "They never fought for anything in their lives," she said disgustedly.

"But they have," said Atrisha as she pointed at the four noblemen advancing upon them with murder and lust in their eyes.

Olivia glanced around, looking for allies. "I have a bad feeling about this," she muttered, her breathing labored.

Atrisha did not answer. She needed to conserve her breath and strength. All the running and fighting in armor was draining.

The men roared as they charged the duo. Atrisha raised her sword, bracing herself while also trying to keep her legs light and limber.

The first man swung his sword in a two-handed arc towards her. She danced back out of the way, Olivia keeping pace with her. The men continued to advance, their weapons moving back and forth as if to frighten the two of them. Atrisha wished she could spare the time to roll her eyes at the effort.

The men screamed and Atrisha raised her sword. But they did not charge. The screams quickly transformed into shrieks as the smell of burning flesh filled the air.

They fell to the ground, rolling and trying to slap the flames out. Rolling was a mistake. It merely brought the unburned side of the men into the path of the flames. They voluntarily turned themselves into human spits, rolling back and forth as they roasted themselves to death.

Cole stepped over the smoldering bodies, ash and blood decorating his black garb. "Ladies. Don't draw attention to yourselves. Just keeping moving and get your business done quickly."

"Don't draw attention to ourselves?" asked Olivia incredulously. "You've been setting people on fire left and right."

Cole walked past them and motioned them to follow. "Yes. I have," he answered. "But that's the thing with fire. The crowd stares at the flames, not at the person who lit the fire."

Atrisha quickened her steps to catch up to Cole. "Wait. Where are we going?" she asked. "The thick of the battle is back behind us."

"Indeed it is," Cole answered. "And I'm putting as much distance between the three of us and it as I can."

"How chivalrous of you," said Olivia drily. "But what if we don't want your protection?"

Her words did not seem to bother Cole one bit. "Doesn't matter what you want," he said. "You two can't stay there. Not after what you did."

"What we did?" asked Atrisha, her voice rising as she became more offended with every word. "What we did was our job. We killed a bunch of Loachians. That's what we do."

"Your job was to protect Byron," replied Cole, anger rising on his face. That effect disturbed Atrisha. He was usually so calm and nonconfrontational. "What you did," said Cole in a slightly condescending voice. "Was kill Matlin's two remaining sisters. That isn't something he or his followers will let go."

"Then we fight," said Olivia. "Which is what we should be doing."

Cole ignored her. "If you two stay there, more lives are going to be lost," he said. "Trust me. I've been around these people. This battle here? It solves nothing. They have an army outside and long memories. Keeping you two around the battle will cause problems. His sisters dying in battle? That's one thing. Them being killed by Byron's personal guards? After what he and I did? And believe me that will get out. That is an entirely different story. Now move."

Atrisha and Olivia gaped at him. He truly had changed from the shy awkward boy. What he was now, Atrisha did not know. Nor did she know if she particularly cared for the change.

Cole navigated throughout the battle with ease. He barely lifted his sword. He walked through the thick of combat passing by men and women from every duchy without a shred of concern. Atrisha and Olivia followed in his wake, their heads jerking back and forth, certain that enemy forces would stab them when they were not looking.

But they never did. When they reached the throne, Dalton leapt off the dais to rush towards them. Apparently, he had resumed Olivia's constant vigil.

"There you all are," he shouted. "What were you thinking? Were any of you?"

"Doing my job," said Cole as he brushed past him without another word.

Dalton gaped at the man in shock. Atrisha empathized with him. It was one thing to know that Cole had gone through a lot in a relatively short period of time. It was quite another to see the impacts that it left on his personality.

Cole walked up to Byron without another word to the rest of the group. The prince was standing with Jeron and Jayna as they surveyed the battle. He nodded silently to Cole as if his return was expected.

"Anything out of the ordinary?" he asked the red haired man.

"Not on my end," replied Cole. "But the girls killed Matlin's sisters."

Byron looked amused, a single syllabic chuckle emitting from behind his closed lips. "I thought killing Loach's ruling family was my job," he said drily.

"Hey, I killed one," said Jeron indignantly.

"Apparently everyone has," said Byron. "But this changes our plans. Prince Irvin, are you alright watching over things here? Holding the throne and making sure our people don't get slaughtered."

The older man narrowed his eyes suspiciously and silently appraised Byron before answering. "I'm not going to like what happens next am I?"

"Doubtful," said Byron. "But can you do it?"

"I can," said Prince Irvin with a sigh of resignation.

"Very good," said Byron as he clapped the man on the shoulder. "Cole, you and the others are to watch over Irvin here as if he were me."

Cole scowled at him. "Don't do it," he said. "It's crazy and you have no idea what you're doing. You'll be an ant caught between two giants."

Byron grinned at him as diamondine wings began to sprout from his back. "Well then, I'll just have to dodge their feet."

Atrisha glanced over at Olivia to see if the other woman had any clue as to what they were talking about, but her face was burrowed in a frown. She glanced around at Jayna and the other Kelonians, but their faces reflected similar reactions. Only Cole, Jeron, and Dalton showed any emotion other than puzzlement. Varying degrees of anger, amusement, exasperation, and resignation flickered back and forth between their faces.

Byron's body continued to change. In a few more seconds the diamond skull stretched and transformed into a beaked birds face. He kept growing, his body transforming into a large diamond bird. His skin and feathers were comprised of varying colors of the diamond material. He sparkled as he moved and stretched before the throne.

Atrisha stared at him in surprise. He was strangely beautiful. It took a few moments for her to realize that the throne room had fallen silent. The nobles ceased fighting and were openly gawking at what Byron transformed into.

The prince shrieked out a cry as flames coursed through his diamond feathers and exploded outward, his body wreathed in an inferno. He flapped his wings as he took off through a skylight, showering the crowd below in glass.

"Where is he going?" Atrisha whispered in awe.

"To Matlin and Darik," answered Cole with a scowl on his face.

"And why are you so upset about that?" asked Olivia with wonder etched on her face.

"Because he has no idea how to fly," grumbled Cole. "And the last time he transformed into the phoenix he nearly burned down all of the city of Loach."

CHAPTER FIFTY-NINE

F lying was a strange sensation. Byron's mind screamed constantly that he was falling. But instead of plummeting to the earth, he inexplicably kept rising into the sky. Each flap of his wings felt like a struggle against gravity. Maybe one day he would become used to it like the others were. Until then he would manage it to the best of his abilities.

It was not like flying was his biggest problem. Landing still posed a serious issue. Setting the capital on fire would likely be frowned upon by high society.

He would worry about that later. There was still a dragon and wyvern clashing in the sky. His brother looked like he was holding his own, if not outright winning the fight.

But why take chances? Especially, when it would be so easy to tilt the balance in this fight.

Byron wished he could smile, maybe just a cocky grin. But beaks were not designed for human expression. One more thing he needed to adapt to.

That and all the flames.

Flames wreathed his body. Flickering in and out between what passed as feathers. The color of the flames was not constant. While primarily shades of red and orange, each heartbeat brought change. Every color of the diamonds incorporated into his body were reflected within the flames.

And then there is that? How does that work? Are we invincible? Why am I saying "we"? I'm only one person talking to himself. Get back to the topic at hand. Right. Invincibility. No, I'm susceptible to harm. Right, the wizard lady's lightning. Interesting. So only physical weapons? Maybe? Oh God. One more thing that I'll need to be careful over. Yup. Overconfidence will be the death of us.

Byron shook his head trying to silence his internal monologue. It was a bad habit. It made him lose his focus at all the worst possible times. Less thinking and more action.

In this case, action was what he needed. But he needed a plan. For instance, how was he supposed to fight in this form?

He flapped his wings with more strength and speed as he tried to gain altitude and a vantage point. The solution to his problem seemed obvious. He had talons and a beak. Close quarters weapons. A simple dive onto Matlin's back should provide him with ample opportunity to inflict damage.

Every instinct in his body screamed that he should shriek out a battle cry as he dove. Establish his supremacy. Byron fought that urge with everything in his body. Stealth and silence served him well. And he had no intention of signaling his attack to Matlin. The odds were good that the Loachian had already glimpsed him. A fiery bird was a hard object to miss. *But why take any chances?*

The sky seemed to shake as he picked up speed. The wind buffeted his body causing the flames to dance and writhe. The colors flickered, the brightness and clarity of the flames intensifying and changing rapidly as he gained speed. His bones and skin strained as power surged and raged within him. A scream tore from his throat as he strained against the energy building within him.

Darik's cerulean scaled head jerked up at the sound. Those big dragon eyes widened as the thickened eye ridges rose in surprise. His brother rolled to the side and dove, trying to place as much distance between himself and the imminent impact.

The red scales on Matlin's back grew larger as the distance between them shrank. Matlin's head jerked around as he became aware of Byron's presence. *Too late.*

Byron screamed in pain as he collided with the Loachian prince. Shades of purple and violet filled his eyes as the flames within him exploded outward, enveloping Matlin.

A sense of relief and immense relaxation consumed Byron as he plummeted towards the earth. He had no recollection of what happened at Fort Hope. He remembered being shot with arrows and falling off the cliff towards the river below. He woke up days later with Cole's anxious face hovering over him. Talendor? He barely lost consciousness and did not let loose nearly as much power when he plunged into the subterranean lake. Loach was a combination of the two prior experiences. He lost consciousness for a few moments when he impacted with the ground. He had no memory of the fires erupting from his body. He thought it would be a small localized flame. Instead, he opened his eyes to find most of the city engulfed in a terrible blaze.

Consciousness did not abandon him this time. He remained awake and saw everything as his body fell limply towards the earth. The flames were gone from his body. Crystalline limbs hung loosely, his body lacking the strength to lift them.

He did not feel terror. He had died before, and made peace with the fact that he would perish again. It was a serene experience as he watched the palace grow in his vision. Pity washed over him. There was no way for him to change his trajectory. His friends would witness him crashing back through the ceiling into the throne room, and there was nothing he could do about it.

Hopefully ,they don't see me die. Hopefully, I don't die.

The skylights of the throne room filled his vision. He could see the nobles beneath him staring up in awed wonder. And fear.

They can't comprehend what they just saw. They have no idea what happened and it frightens them. Glad I'm not the only one.

His body jerked with the force of the impact, but he did not feel any pain. Shards of glass bounced harmlessly off of his diamond feathers. The world spun and colors blurred as he lost his equilibrium and perspective.

Mercifully, he blacked out.

Chapter Sixty

D alton was quicker than everyone else. The advantages of having a cheetah totem. He shoved nobles out of the way when he could not speed between them. Most of the nobles were doing one of two things. Some stood around gawking, while others ran around in a mindless panic, demanding that someone answer their inquiries as to what was going on.

It was an understandable reaction. It was not every day that a dragon crashed through the ceiling. When that dragon happened to be your duly appointed king of less than an hour? Well, that was the stuff found in stories and legends.

Part of Dalton was vaguely aware that the nobles would begin plotting as soon as they regained their senses. That was not his problem. He left that sort of big picture thinking to the people around him. They were devious and well equipped for that sort of thing. In this moment, his only focus was on Darik.

Dalton did not fight three wars only to see everything he fought for demolished at the very end. And where were Byron and Matlin? Three had flown into the skies, but only one had returned. What happened up there?

Dalton vaulted over Darik's tail as he rushed towards the king's head. His body was curled up in a ball, his head drawn down to his stomach with his tail wrapped protectively across his stomach and head.

Dalton turned around and pushed against the tail trying to create some space. It moved, but only slightly. He grunted as he threw his body weight against the tail over and over again. It moved, slowly at first, before sliding haltingly across the ground.

The scales of Darik's stomach moved. Slow and steady. In and out. Relief washed over Dalton. Darik was alive.

Dalton dashed towards the king's head. His eyes were closed, almost as if he were asleep. Dalton's eyes nearly spun out of his head as he searched the body for wounds. There was nothing. No scales were smashed or burned. There were a few scratches, probably from Matlin's claws, but nothing serious. No blood. No wounds.

Darik's hands were clutched to his chest. One overlapped the other. Almost as if he were holding something.

Dalton's brow furrowed as a frown crossed his face. Why would Darik be holding something? That did not make any sense. What was there to grab in the sky? A cloud maybe?

He pulled against Darik's hands. He expected a dragon's claws to be less pliable than steel. However, the fingers moved easily, the greatest challenge being that he could only move one finger at a time due to their size.

Dalton pried the giant fingers loose and felt his heart sink. Darik was clutching Byron's body in his hands. The diamond skin was gone, replaced with pink human flesh. It looked fresh, as if newly grown. He pressed his fingers against that flesh. It was soft and tender, but beneath it all he could feel a pulse thrumming through Byron's body.

Relief was a feeling that Dalton found in short supply recently. Every body he came across always seemed to be that of a dead friend. One of them actually being alive was a pleasant surprise.

"Is he okay?" demanded Renaldo as he vaulted over Darik's tail. "Dammit Dalton, is Darik okay?"

"I'm okay," whispered Darik. The deep power in his dragon's voice vibrated through every bone in Dalton's body at this distance. "How is Byron? Did I catch him in time?"

"He's fine. Um. Your Majesty," said Dalton as he struggled to wrap his mind around the situation. "He's breathing. His skin doesn't even appear damaged. It looks brand new."

"Good," said Darik. "I was certain that fireball killed him. He fell out of it looking like deadweight. I had to let Matlin go. It looked like he fled west."

"To Antier?" asked Renaldo worriedly.

"I don't know," whispered Darik. "I only had a glimpse."

The conversation was cut short as others climbed tentatively over Darik's tail. Jeron led the way with Cole, Jayna, and Vernon close behind him. Jeron's eyes widened as he saw Byron's body. Jayna pushed past him and knelt beside Byron's unconscious form.

Dalton let his tired head droop towards his chest as he took a moment to catch his breath. The war was over. There was no longer a need to run, a need to fight. With Darik in charge of Ochandor, perhaps they would have a chance to move forward and cease fighting.

Darik gently set Byron down as he began to transform back into his human form. The nobles looked at him warily, unsure of what just transpired. Matlin's supporters kept glancing towards the exits, uncertain if they should stay or flee.

The king knelt beside his brother and exchanged a few words with Jayna regarding Byron's health. His body language appeared tired and worn out. His eyes however sparkled with intensity as he gazed out over the assembled nobles. He held their stares for a silent minute before ascending onto the dais and sitting upon the throne.

Darik gestured for the steward to step forward. The man was drenched in sweat. Clearly, he spent the battle in a frightful panic. Dalton had to give the man some credit though. He assumed the steward would have fled the palace at the first sign of fighting. He had no clue where the steward found shelter, but it was a brave man who would stay for the duration of a battle while unarmed.

"My crown?" was all Darik said to the steward. The steward paled noticeably. The man mumbled something softly before executing a hasty bow and darting out of the room.

Darik did not wait for the steward to return before addressing the crowd. "My lords and ladies," he began, his voice carrying easily throughout the throne room. "The traitor and usurper Matlin Loach has fled the capital in disgrace."

Murmurs swept through the crowd as everyone tried to process the information. Darik let the talk spread for a few moments while he glared at those in attendance. "As my first act of king, I am stripping Matlin of all of his lands and titles. For his treacherous actions, both here today and in the face of a monstrous invasion force in western Antier, Matlin is hereby exiled from Ochandor. May no man or woman in the kingdom grant him succor or aid."

More whispers spread throughout the crowd. The Loachians in attendance were silent, staring daggers at their new king. "It is my understanding that Matlin has one brother remaining," continued Matlin. "Let it not be said that I started my reign with cruelty. Prince Fotlin shall receive his brother's titles and henceforth be known as Duke Fotlin Loach." Sounds of approval echoed throughout all of the duchies represented in the throne room. Even the Loachian nobles nodded approval while remaining less than enthused about the situation.

"My lords and ladies, let there be no mistake," intoned Dark. "There will be peace. We have a kingdom that has been ravaged by war and destruction these past decades because of pettiness and greed. Kelon and Loach will be rebuilt. We will need to remain vigilant on our borders. The monsters to the west and vampires to the east are growing bolder. I wish I could claim that it was simply a coincidence, but I doubt any of us believe in that."

The room sobered at the king's words. Dalton could not blame the nobles of being scared at talk of the monsters. He had fought both groups and only a fool would not be frightened of them.

"Duke Havram Talendor, please step forward," said Darik sternly.

The duke looked at the young king apprehensively and stepped before the throne. "Your Majesty," he said as he flourished a fancy bow.

"Thank you, Your Grace," said Darik with a blank calm face. "I appreciate your support in obtaining the throne and value your counsel."

"You have it, Your Majesty," said the desert duke. "Talendor long remembers those that fight for it."

"As do I, Your Grace," said Darik. "Which does beg the question. When do we let past wrongs lie? When do we stop seeking vengeance for those wrongs and let there be peace?"

Duke Havram nodded as if in deep contemplation. "An interesting conundrum, Your Majesty. I must say that I agree with your actions. Matlin should be punished for his actions, but there is no need to inflict further suffering upon his family or his duchy."

Darik tapped his fingers against the arm rest of his throne as the steward returned. A thin band of gold was in his hands. Dalton squinted and saw an array of eight gems arrayed around a large diamond. Doubtless each stone's color would correspond to one of the eight duchies surrounding the diamond of the duchy of Ochandor.

The steward placed the crown upon Darik's head and opened his mouth to proclaim Darik ruler of the Kingdom of Ochandor. Darik shot a stern look at the steward causing the man's mouth to snap shut. Instead of speaking, the man waved his hands grandly at Darik and beat a hasty retreat from the dais. Apparently, even the steward had a limit to his courage.

"An interesting choice of words and wise counsel, Your Grace," said Darik after the steward exited the dais. "You see I have a problem. And that problem is what to do with Kelon and those who destroyed it."

Duke Havram paled at the words as his eyes darted towards Vernon and back to the king. He glanced dubiously at the survivors of Kelon and forced a smile back on his face as he addressed the king. "Ahh, Your Majesty, it was my understanding that the late Duke Camen was responsible for the destruction of Kelon."

"In part," confirmed Darik. "As you are aware, Prince Irvin and his people were present for the treachery that destroyed their own. You are familiar with Prince Irvin, yes? As I understand things, he and his people helped defend your home from vampires many times over the past few years."

"That is correct," said Duke Havram hesitantly.

"A good man, Prince Irvin," said Darik absently. "You have to imagine my surprise when he informed me that Talendor conspired with Loach to destroy Kelon." Anger crept into Darik's features as he glared at Duke Havram.

The throne room buzzed like an agitated hornet's nest. Every noble had a theory as to the destruction of Kelon. And in his first minutes on the throne, Darik was solving that mystery while accusing one of his most powerful allies of the crime.

Duke Havram did not respond to the king. He stood there silently under Darik's gaze, bearing the brunt of the king's rage.

Vernon also did not say a word. He merely looked on at the duke with those sad brown eyes of his. There were not any smiles from the other Kelonians. Merely grim sad faces. None of this was a surprise for them.

"And so you place me in a difficult situation," said Darik. "One that I believe I have an answer to." The duke's eyes narrowed suspiciously as the crowd's noise grew louder, more anxious. "Prince Irvin, it is your goal to rebuild Kelon, is it not?"

"It is, Your Majesty," said Vernon.

Darik nodded, expecting the answer. "An expensive proposition," he said. "It appears that Talendor is in your debt, not only for your defense of their home, but for their wrongs against your own. Duke Havram, Talendor with its sizeable merchant wealth will bear the brunt of rebuilding Kelon. The Crown will help, lending soldiers and priests for recapturing the land from ghosts."

Duke Havram swallowed at the proclamation, his jaw tightening as he waited anxiously for news of his own fate. Hands had returned to weapon handles as the tension mounted.

"That leaves me with your fate," said Darik. "Under different circumstances, I would order your death for your crimes. But the realm has seen enough killing. I have no desire to orphan your children. The kingdom needs Talendor to help rebuild Kelon. A grueling task, and one that would interfere with your son's recovery. And Duke Havram, believe me, I will be watching events in Kelon closely. Be a better neighbor this time around."

Duke Havram exhaled in relief. Dalton suspected that the man believed his death to be imminent after his involvement in the destruction of Kelon became public.

"Prince Irvin. I trust this is acceptable to you?" asked Darik. His tone of voice clearly conveying the answer he expected to hear.

"Yes, Your Majesty," said Vernon with a bow of his head. "There has been enough blood shed. We merely want our home restored to us and our people."

"Excellent. Now if each duke and their retainers will step forward and swear fealty, we can all go about setting things right throughout Ochandor," said Darik. "I suggest we do so with some alacrity. I think some of you may find your embassies have some uninvited guests that you'll want to evict."

Dalton blinked in surprise. Had Master Tyson uncover some sort of plot, or was the king just guessing?

Byron groaned as he sat up. "What did I miss?" he asked groggily.

Jeron knelt next to Byron. "Your brother is king. Fotlin is duke of Loach. Talendor is rebuilding Kelon. And you're the new Duke of Antier."

Byron looked at Jeron, his face aghast. "But I don't want to be a duke," he protested as he glanced around at the faces surrounding him desperately seeking aid.

"Too bad," grumbled Olivia. "Some of us would love to rule a duchy."

"Byron, you should probably be the first to swear fealty to your brother," whispered Dalton.

Byron grimaced at the words. "The first?" he asked skeptically. "This may be the most painful thing that I have ever done in my entire life."

Chapter Sixty-One

J eron peeked around the corner before dashing across the courtyard to the stables. The fighting had wrapped up shortly after Darik's coronation. Loach's forces had remained within the embassy of Erlon. The Erlonian nobles took their embassy back with extreme prejudice, and from what Jeron heard, the Loachian forces did not put up much of a fight.

Word had yet to be received from the new Duke of Loach. Jeron assumed he would bend the knee and swear fealty. His forces were devastated as was the capital city of his duchy. Loach was bereft of allies, having betrayed and backstabbed most of the realm. Resisting Darik's rule would be foolhardy at this point.

Peace should tentatively reign over the kingdom even with Matlin's disappearance. And Jeron intended to take advantage of that peace. The duchy of Kelon needed rebuilding and he always dreamed of constructing buildings.

The only roadblock in that dream was Byron. How was he supposed to tell his best friend, now a duke, that he was leaving his service to build structures in a foreign duchy with the woman he loved? Byron most likely would not take it well. He blamed Jeron and Dalton for his being named duke. He claimed he never would have accepted the position if he were clear headed, and that everyone hoodwinked him into becoming a duke.

Jeron did not want to be there when Byron was informed that he would need to become married for the good of the duchy. Or that a duke could not drink in a tavern. Or buck all authority and do whatever it was he did while gallivanting about in Loach.

The stable was dark and Jeron held his breath as he squeezed through the ajar door. It was the middle of the morning and he was reduced to sneaking around. So be it.

His horse was in one of the backmost stalls. Technically it was not his horse but Antier's. But with all of his service to the duchy it was a fair trade. He slipped the stall door open and gently closed it behind him. Jeron turned around and yelped as he jumped backward tumbling over the stall door.

Cole, Dalton, and Byron's heads appeared over him. Different stages of amusement registered on their faces.

"Well, well, what do we have here?" asked Byron as he exited the stall with a self-satisfied grin on his face.

"I believe Jeron was deserting," said Cole solemnly.

"Oh goody," exclaimed Dalton. "We hang deserters, right? I was hoping to see a good hanging."

Something sad flashed over Byron and Cole's faces. Byron extended his hand downward and pulled Jeron to his feet. "You didn't think you could sneak off and leave without saying goodbye, did you?" he asked.

Jeron glowered at them in mock rage. "Actually, I did," he said. "How did you know I was going to leave?"

Byron shrugged. "Jayna mentioned that you were going to be leaving with her. After that it didn't take much effort for the three of us to figure out what you were going to do."

Jeron closed his eyes and sighed heavenward. Jayna. Of course. And he believed he had thought of everything.

"Sorry," said Jeron. "I didn't know how to say goodbye."

"You could try by saying 'goodbye'," quipped Dalton. "I hear it isn't that difficult."

Cole nodded sagely. "Leaving your liege lord's service without a word is frowned upon by paladins is it not?"

Jeron rolled his eyes. "Technically, I was never in his service," he said. At Byron's frown, Jeron shrugged. "I never swore an oath."

"Ahh, true," agreed Byron. "You didn't. Just like I didn't order Olivia to accompany you and Jayna."

Cold fear gripped Jeron. He did not want his former love interest to accompany him to Kelon. "You did not," he whispered in disbelief.

Byron laughed as he punched Jeron's shoulder. "Of course not. Didn't you hear me say that I didn't order her to accompany you? Besides, she is apparently too good of a military commander. A few more years of seasoning and I'll have her commanding the duchy's armies."

Jeron breathed a sigh of relief. "I knew it," he said as he shook his head ruefully. "Well. I mostly knew it. You're too good at lying. Cole, Dalton, try not to let that habit rub off on you."

"I'm a spy and an assassin," said Cole drily. "Lying goes hand in hand with being the duke's Shadow."

Jeron grinned at him. "Like Atrisha is going to let you go out on long missions ever again. I'd be surprised if she ever lets you out of her sight."

Cole hesitated for a moment before grinning like a little kid. "I can live with that."

"Well I cannot," declared Dalton. "And don't ask me what I am going to do. I don't make my orders," He jerked his thumb at Byron. "This guy, and the Church will dictate where I go."

Jeron winced. "The Church. Right. Forgot about that part. Byron, do you think you can...?" His voice trailed off as he grasped for the words.

"Diplomatic mission to Kelon on behalf of the duchy?" Byron asked quizzically. "I could do that." Jeron breathed a sigh of relief. "For someone who was sworn into my service." He added belatedly with a mocking grin.

Jeron ignored the quip and drew his friend into a giant bear hug. "I am going to miss you guys," he said. "I have no idea why, but I'll miss you guys."

"Open a nice inn in Kelon, stock it with good food and wine and I'll be there," said Dalton.

"I'll do that," said Jeron as he leapt onto his horse. His friends had been kind enough to saddle it for him. He waved goodbye one last time and rode towards the exit.

"Umm, guys," he called back over his shoulder. "Can you open the stable door for me?"

"Idiot," muttered Byron and Dalton in unison.

EPILOGUE

M atlin could not recall flying so far in his lifetime. He fled Ochandor in a panic, flying in whatever direction he was facing at the time of the explosion. For the first time in his recent memory, he feared for his life. Not from Darik, but from that fire.

It was not orange like normal. It was violet. And it burned something fierce. He had screamed and screeched as it engulfed him. His whole world felt like it was burning. He flew as fast as he could, certain that the flames were still burning through his entire body.

Once he was hours away from the capital, and certain that Darik was not following him, he had taken stock of his injuries.

His scales were unblemished. No sign of charring existed upon them. He was not bleeding, nor did he show any other sign of wounds.

Strangely, he felt fine. Better than he ever had. His body did not have any new aches or pains to it. He did not feel tired. Nor did he feel worry or any sort of fear. Matlin's mind was clear. Maybe for the first time in his life.

That moment of clarity was days ago. He had continued flying into the sunset, pausing only to hunt. Game was abundant in Antier and the lands beyond. He flew over Fort Hope with nary a tug of regret. That was the past. He could not go back to it, nor could he go back to Loach. Not with the way things currently stood.

So he continued to fly west. Away from pursuit or from anyone who knew who he was. There were bound to be other lands and people beyond the Kingdom of Ochandor. People that he could conquer and rule. People that word serve him and help him extract his revenge upon Darik and his murderous brood of heathens.

The land west of Antier was rural and peaceful. Soft rolling plains and lakes dotted the landscape. He spied numerous herds of animals running free through the tall grasses. It was a beautiful land full of life and color. Completely unlike the dreary landscape of Loach.

Eventually, a city arose on the horizon. The first thing Matlin noticed was the lack of walls on the city. It was a sprawling collection of buildings that appeared to spread outward without any rhyme or reason.

Buildings were constructed from a hodgepodge of materials. He saw wood, stone, clay, grass, and other substances that he did not recognize. It was not just the materials that varied. Even the style of construction used on the structures varied from structure to structure.

Matlin could not believe his luck. He wanted people to rule, and he found a disorganized mass of people just dying for proper leadership.

Near the center of the city was a larger structure. It was built from stone and appeared finely crafted. A predatory smile spread across Matlin's face. The building had to be his competition's abode.

The center of the building lacked a roof. It was a strange architectural feature, but one that suited Matlin's purposes just fine. Matlin banked around the structure, slowly spiraling downward towards the opening in the roof.

His landing was sudden, with a buffet of wind that sent the building's occupants scampering for cover. Matlin focused his mind as he transformed his body. His full wyvern shape would be too constricting inside the building.

Matlin was surprised to find that he did not transform back into his usual body. Instead, his mind shaped his body into a human shaped form with a wyvern's head, wings, and tail. Scales covered his body, including his humanoid shaped arms and legs. He flexed his muscles in appreciation. Everything worked and moved just like his normal human body, but it looked so much more fierce and powerful.

"Alright, listen up people," he bellowed as wisps of smoke curled up from his mouth. "I am Matlin Loach. Duke of the Duchy of Loach, and rightful king to the Kingdom of Ochandor. I am your king and ruler now. Order will come to this land."

Silence greeted his proclamation for a few heartbeats. Laughter rang out throughout the chamber. "I am afraid you are wrong on all counts, Your Majesty," sneered a clear baritone. "You are in my kingdom now."

Matlin sought out the voice. A group of shadowy figures emerged from the ends of the room. The leader looked similar to Matlin. Black scales covered a humanoid shaped body with a dragon's head and wings. The creature was taller and more powerful in appearance than Matlin.

The sight of the being made Matlin's heart sink as his head swiveled around the room, his eyes scanning his surroundings in a panic. A minotaur and centaur flanked the dragonman. More of their kind, including satyrs and harpies occupied the room.

Matlin had not found a city beyond the monsters. He had found a city of the monsters.

The black dragonman smiled a toothy predatory smile at Matlin. "Welcome to my kingdom Matlin Loach. But, as I said, I am afraid you are wrong about more than that," he intoned as a puff of smoke left his nostrils. "Allow me to introduce myself. I am Saimon Ochandor. And I have long been the rightful King of Ochandor."

Fear gripped Matlin for the second time. It was an unpleasant feeling.

Saimon continued to grin malevolently at him. "Ahh. I sense you have undergone some changes recently young Matlin. Your first experience with soulfire?" The grin seemed to stretch wider upon his face. "Allow me to be the first to welcome you home, boy."

FOR THE READER

I would like to acknowledge you the reader, and thank you for reading. I hope you enjoyed the story. Please consider leaving a rating and review for the book. Both help the book achieve visibility for other readers.

This book is part of a trilogy. All three books are finished and slated to be released within months of each other. If you're interested in these books, or in other future projects, please consider signing up for the Author Newsletter here: https://calixtowayne.com/newsletter/.

ABOUT THE AUTHOR

Calixto Wayne is a fantasy author who enjoys telling fast-paced stories. The goal of every story should be to create characters with whom the reader enjoys spending their time. Calixto builds worlds where the reader can daydream about inserting themselves into the action.

He currently resides in Florida. You can find more about the author and his works at https://calixtowayne.com/

www.ingramcontent.com/pod-product-compliance
Lightning Source LLC
Chambersburg PA
CBHW030926260626
47169CB00002B/389